Golden Bloodline

Golden Bloodline, Volume 1

Richard Moorman

Published by Old Fella Writes, 2023.

GOLDEN BLOODLINE

First edition. November 30, 2023.

ISBN: 979-8223001751

Written by Richard Moorman.

To my wife Leonie - an author's widow.

PROLOGUE

A figure emerges from the sombre depths of a dimly lit cell within the aged confines of the Russell Street Gaol. Dan Farley, a convicted murderer aged twenty-five, wields a quill tipped with a feathered nib. With a sense of purpose, he sets the point to parchment. Each stroke of his pen is a careful deliberation, etching words onto the worn surface of a manuscript page. Thus, the narrative unfolds: *"This manuscript stands as a testament to the last remnants of my cursed life, a chronicle destined for the eyes of others. The world may label me mad for recent deeds, but some moments transcend the realm of mortal comprehension."*

Undeterred, he continues, the quill flowing like a river of ink across the page: *"I embark on this written journey not in search of redemption – my soul surely descends into damnation – but to find solace in the looming shadow of my impending demise. It is also a legacy for my descendants, a vessel through which truth may be unveiled when time's shroud unravels."*

As the inked narrative progresses, the contours of Dan's world unfurl – a voyage into realms of uncertainty populated by a cast of captivating characters. The tapestry of intersecting fates, unexpected allies, and the uncharted territories of his quest for salvation shall guide our voyage. From the bustling thoroughfares of the Port Phillip Bay Settlement on the banks of the Yarra River to the untamed expanses of Australia's unforgiving frontier, Dan's journey spans the crucible of adversity, testing his mettle and shaking his beliefs.

Each word on the parchment is a thread woven into the fabric of the Riley legacy. This saga, an echoing resonance from history's archives, captures a tumultuous era while embodying the indomitable spirit of a man grappling with his search for solace.

As the narrative unfolds, Dan's personal recollections intertwine with poignant accounts drawn from the histories of family and kindred spirits, forming a tapestry of historical intrigue. It exposes the concealed underbelly underpinning their age – a journey into hidden truths, their echoes still reverberating through the corridors of our present existence.

Dan's odyssey becomes a luminous testimony guided by the author's craft. As ink mingles with parchment, a door opens – a portal leading to revelations and epiphanies to unravelling human intricacies that transcend time.

Chapter One

PORT PHILLIP BAY 1837

Dan, a youth still in the blush of his twenties, disembarks from the sailing vessel "Enterprize," which rests at anchor in the Yarra River Settlement of Port Phillip Bay. A carpenter's tool bag hangs from his shoulder, and a carpet bag dangles at his side. His countenance mirrors a blend of uncertainty and wonderment as he steps onto the bustling shore. The cacophony of activity engulfs him, a sensory onslaught that threatens to overwhelm him.

Amidst the whirlwind of sights and sounds, a group of Aboriginal warriors, accompanied by their families, stands apart. Their eyes fix curiously upon the newcomer, watching with interest and caution.

Dan's legs waver beneath him, and he stumbles to his knees, grappling for balance. A fellow passenger from the ship, witnessing his vulnerability, steps forward and extends a steadying hand. "Allow me, friend. Are you injured?"

Grateful for the assistance, Dan accepts the gesture and rises, his equilibrium restored. "Thank you... I... I'm not certain what came over me. This place is unlike anything I've experienced."

The stranger's features soften with understanding. "You're not alone in feeling disoriented by the transition to Port Phillip. It has that effect on many. Come, let's find solace in a nearby inn. A moment to gather your thoughts."

Together, they make their way to a local inn, the clamour of the settlement receding behind them. Inside, Dan finds refuge at a worn table, a glass tumbler of rum before him.

The sympathetic stranger stands by his side, concern etched on his face. "Are you feeling better now, sir? You still appear troubled. Should I fetch help?"

Dan takes a deep breath, his gaze drawn to the amber liquid in his glass. He offers a faint, appreciative smile. "No need. Your kindness is more than enough. I'm Dan Farley from Hobart Town. Your help has been a true comfort in this moment of vulnerability. There's something about this place, like an unseen force casting a shadow over me."

The stranger nods, empathizing with the overwhelming nature of the unfamiliar. "It's not uncommon, especially here. Port Phillip has a way of humbling even the strongest of individuals."

As Dan's fingers trace the rim of his glass, his thoughts drift to more profound reflections. "The wilderness and the sight of the indigenous people... they bring back memories of Van Diemen's Land. I was a bounty hunter there, chasing escaped convicts and troublesome indigenous groups."

The stranger meets Dan's gaze, acknowledging the weight of his words. "Fear not, for here the indigenous community has found a treaty with John Batman of the 'Port Phillip Association.' Their land is leased, a truce established."

With these words, Dan's tense shoulders ease, his fears abating. "The 'Black War' memories back home have haunted me. But I never expected to be so profoundly affected here. Thank you for shedding light on this. Your kindness will stay with me as I find my bearings."

The stranger's understanding look speaks volumes. "The indigenous people have their place within the peace accord. Their allowances are granted annually under its terms."

Dan musters a faint smile, his resolve rekindling. "I've always prided myself on my resilience, my unwavering spirit. A man of modest beginnings, resolute in the face of adversity. Yet, this place has humbled me in ways I never imagined. Still, I'll find my way. I'm grateful for your compassion."

The stranger's nod conveys respect for Dan's determination. "If ever you need assistance, remember that kindness is never distant. Farewell, Mister Farley."

With newfound assurance, Dan rises from the table, revitalized by his purpose. He steps forward, ready to confront the challenges and revelations that await in the vibrant tumult of Port Phillip Bay's settlement.

Unbeknownst to him, these initial encounters mark the start of a transformative journey that will shape his destiny and the fates of those he encounters. With renewed determination, Dan steps forward, prepared to face the trials and triumphs that lie ahead. This, dear reader, is the beginning of the saga of Dan Farley, a man whose past shadows him and whose future offers no redemption, only the possibility of forging a legacy for his descendants.

Chapter Two

Dan strolls down the vibrant village street, his toolbag a steadfast companion in his hand. The rhythmic clanging of a blacksmith's forge captures his attention, a siren call of craftsmanship that beckons him closer. Curiosity guiding his steps, Dan approaches the skilled blacksmith and offers a friendly greeting. "Good day, sir. Might you know of anyone needing a skilled carpenter from Hobart Town?"

The blacksmith pauses, his response measured and tinged with caution. "Aye, there might be a chance with Jack Riley. He's been lamenting the state of his shattered tables. But be warned, his words can cut as keen as the blades I fashion. If you're considering working there, brace yourself for his curt manner."

Dan takes the lead with gratitude. "Thank you for the information. I'll keep that in mind."

As Dan is about to continue his journey, a peculiar sight arrests his attention. An Aboriginal attendant propels a man in a three-wheeled perambulator along the gravel road. The man, John Batman, conceals the lower part of his face with a bandage. Intrigued, Dan inquires, "And who might that unfortunate gentleman be?"

The blacksmith leans on his hammer; sympathy is evident in his gaze. "That there is John Batman, the founder of our modest village. He arrived from Launceston two years ago and has seen better days. Some say it's the liquor and women that brought him low. Others claim it's the nasal syphilis, linked to his wife who was once a Hobart Town 'Ticket of Leave convict'."

Dan's curiosity deepens, his gaze fixed on the bandaged figure. "Has the ailment marred his whole face?"

"It's eaten away at his nose, hence the bandage. Rumour has it he's estranged from his wife, left with seven children to tend."

Dan averts his gaze from the unfortunate sight and remarks solemnly. "A tragic fate. Thank you for the information. Good day to you."

Continuing his stroll, Dan directs his steps toward an established hotel. The establishment, nestled by the picturesque Yarra River, radiates a welcoming aura. The sign above the entrance proudly bears the establishment's name – "FAWKNERS HOTEL."

Stepping into the inviting interior, Dan is embraced by the familiar scent of wood and the lively hum of conversations. The bar, a focal point at the rear, exudes rustic charm. Patrons lean casually against it, their feet resting on the well-worn footrail. Spitoons dot the wooden floor, capturing intermittent tobacco remnants.

Dan confidently positions himself at the bar, resting his foot on the rail. Holding his Fedora hat, he engages in lively banter with the seasoned Barman, who leans against the counter, engrossed in the exchange.

"Looking quite dapper today, Farley. Has a certain lady caught your eye? Or are you planning another daring escapade at Jack Riley's? Watch out for his gut-rot whiskey – known to corrode metal!"

Dan playfully smirks. "Not much different from the 'gut rot' here, I'd wager. I'm taking refuge in Fawkner's upper room until better lodgings come by this village. Though 'elsewhere' seems to translate to 'nowhere' for now."

The Barman's laughter resonates with a sense of camaraderie. "At least you get a hearty meal in exchange."

Dan raises an eyebrow, a hint of rebellion in his tone. "True enough, but you have to stomach whatever Fawkner dishes out. Overcooked or undercooked, it's all to his taste."

The Barman's laughter blends camaraderie with caution. "Mind your words, Farley! Criticise Fawkner too openly, and you might find yourself on the street before you finish your sentence!"

Unfazed, Dan adjusts his Fedora hat with a touch of defiance. With a nod of respect, he bids the Barman farewell. "I'm off now. Not for gambling or wooing ladies. Riley's got gambling tables in need of mending. Seems they're breaking more often – either due to his abominable spirits or people catching onto his rigged games." With a wink and a tilt of his hat, Dan strides away, poised to face the challenges and escapades ahead.

Chapter Three

Dan navigates along the cobblestone lane adjacent to the Highlander Hotel, his tool bag slung casually. He reaches the "Curiosity Shop," an emporium that teases his curiosity with its eclectic display of handed-me-down items in the front window and on outside racks. Despite the allure, Dan resists temptation and steps into the shop. He traverses its aisles until he reaches a rear door. The door opens to a bustling, boisterous gaming room and concealed sly grog shop, a realm hidden behind a veil of secrets.

Dan's gaze falls upon the room's muscle, a formidable figure overseeing the lively scene. Dan raises his voice above the clamour, addressing the guardian in charge. **"Is Jack Riley present?"**

The minder nods. **"Riley's in his office. What brings you here?"**

In response, Dan lifts his tool bag and the muscle gestures toward the rear. With a word of thanks, Dan advances toward the broken tables, eager to gauge the extent of repairs required. The air is charged with the intensity of gambling, tinged with the lingering scent of grog, adding an unexpected layer to his inspection.

Meanwhile, a front office door opens, revealing Jack Riley, a stout figure in his late fifties. His barrelled belly and stern expression speak of a life of success and trials. A young woman beside Riley adjusts her attire and walks briskly away. Riley approaches Dan, extending a handshake and offering a smile that belies his rugged appearance. "Jack Riley, at your service. A pleasure to meet you."

Dan shakes Riley's hand, a momentary connection transpiring between their eyes. Riley swiftly assesses the repaired gaming tables. "Your work seems commendable. What do you think, Norm?"

Riley turns to the muscle named Norm for a second opinion. Norm, a discerning figure, scrutinizes the tables closely. "First-rate work, Mr Riley."

Riley chuckles warmly, and Dan senses a camaraderie in his demeanour. "Seems you have talent, Dan. Care to earn a silver florin or two by offering additional services?"

Intrigued by the proposition that suggests more than carpentry, Dan contemplates the offer. Mindful of its implications, he responds thoughtfully. "I might consider it, Mr Riley. Could you shed light on the nature of these 'additional services'?"

A wry smile tugs at Riley's lips as he explains. "I need someone firm to help settle debts and disputes. Do you catch my Drift?"

The subtext is clear. Dan's face reflects understanding and contemplation, weighing the potential risks and rewards. His response conveys his readiness to explore uncharted territories. "Indeed, Mr Riley. I find the prospect intriguing. One never knows when their next opportunity might arise."

Riley's grin widens, and he adjusts Dan's neckerchief before patting him on the shoulder. "Norm here will brief you on your role and responsibilities. You seem to have a certain flair, Dan. You'll be a fitting aide as I conduct business around the village."

Norm nods in agreement, poised to guide Dan. "Absolutely, Mr Riley. I'll show him the ropes."

As Riley strides away, Dan and Norm are left to chart their course within the enigmatic world of Jack Riley's operations. The door closes behind Riley, leaving Dan with anticipation and apprehension. He senses that his journey has taken an unexpected twist, unveiling a future fraught with challenges and hidden prospects in the shadows of Riley's realm.

Chapter Four

Jack Riley's colonial mansion is a testament to local craftsmanship, its grandeur proudly showcased across sprawling acres. The imposing structure is further elevated by a sweeping gravel driveway that stretches from Swanston Street, offering the estate a commanding view. Besides a sleek one-horse gig carriage, Dan Farley awaits patiently, ready to embark on their journey. Before long, Jack Riley, the estate's master, and his spirited daughter, Alice, emerge through the wide-fronted portico of the manor.

"Good morning, Mr Riley. A splendid day to you, Miss Alice," Dan's greeting carries genuine warmth. Turning to Riley, he inquires with respect, "Where do our ventures beckon us today, sir?"

Riley's response is succinct, his tone decisive. "To the curiosity shop, Farley. Let's not squander time."

With a subtle tilt of his hat and a discreet bow, Dan pays his respects, his courteous gesture unnoticed by Riley. Yet, his playful wink doesn't elude Alice's notice. A soft blush graced her cheeks as she responded with an infectious smile. As Alice steps toward the carriage, Dan extends his hand, offering the grace of assistance. In that fleeting moment, his eyes glimpse her stocking-clad ankles beneath the gentle sway of her bell skirt.

> "Very well then, off we venture, Mr Riley," Dan's address to his employer conveys irreverence."Shall we allow the horses their liberty, sir? - Aye!"

Maintaining his stoic demeanour, Riley doesn't engage with Dan's light-hearted remark. However, Alice's mischievous smile betrays her appreciation for his wit. Taking his place on the front box seat of the carriage, reins held with practised ease, Dan readies himself. He sets the horses in a skilled motion, guiding the carriage away from the estate in a brisk, purposeful trot. The promise of the day's adventure and the secrets it may unveil beckon as the estate's grandeur fades in the distance.

Later that day, the entrance to the gaming room yawns wide, spilling forth the chaos and cacophony hidden within. Outside the dimly lit chamber, tension hangs heavy like a storm ready to break. Dan Farley, a man of imposing stature, has Lofty, a slender figure, cornered against the back wall. Dan's grip is unyielding, his powerful punches driving into Lofty's gut, while Lofty's shirt front is bunched in Dan's fist. The alley's atmosphere is pregnant with the anticipation of inevitable consequences.

"Listen well," Dan's voice is firm, the weight of responsibility evident. "These debts can't be ignored any longer. Mr Riley expects me to settle these matters, and when polite requests fail, I must make sure you idiots start paying attention. Even if it means reshaping your ears into something resembling cauliflowers. Do You Comprehend?"

Lofty's plea is desperate, his words rushing forth. "Dan, me wives due to give birth any day now. Fawkner never pays us on time. I'll get you the money; just give me another week!"

But Dan's resolve remains unshaken. He starkly warns Lofty, "Failure carries a hefty price, my friend. You know what follows, don't you? Bruiser, Riley's enforcer. The most feared man in his employ. When I can't finish the job, he steps in. And let me tell you, his reputation... well, it's something else. He wields a Bowie knife and performs a procedure normally reserved for stallions, only he applies it to your manhood. Now, Leave... Go!"

With a release of his grip, Dan watches Lofty retreat down the alley, leaving him alone with the weight of his duties. As he returns to the gaming room's entrance, his expression becomes a canvas of determination tinged with exhaustion. It's a fleeting glimpse into the toll this life of enforcing debts and confronting desperate souls extracts from him.

Dread lingers like a haunting echo inside the dim-lit gaming room early the following day. Dan finds himself in the company of Bruiser Conroy, a man marked by a tragic fire in his youth, his face forever deformed, and another unfortunate victim. The figure, held firmly in Dan's grasp, stares into the abyss of Bruiser's malevolent eyes, their terror palpable.

Bruiser's voice carries a chilling edge as he addresses the victim, "Our Dan here tells me you've been given ample chances to clear your debt with Mr Riley. Yet, you persist in your defiance. A man like you is either a fool or lacks the spine to face your obligations."

Fear courses through the victim's trembling frame, the severity of the situation crashing down. Bruiser's knuckles rap against the victim's skull with each emphasised word, punctuating his message with menace. The victim reveals a desperate predicament, forced into criminality under Riley's yoke.

"Bruiser, Riley stripped me of everything. He's stoked my gambling, and now he wants me to rob the bank I manage, the 'Port Phillip Saving Bank.' I can't... I won't do it! Trapped whichever way I turn. But Riley won't escape unscathed; Mark My Words!"

Bruiser's reply is a frigid whisper, "You don't fathom the weight of your words, do you? Initially, I planned a simple incapacitation. But with your threats to Mr Riley... well, now I'll be taking more!"

The room's tension crescendos as the victim and enforcer stand on opposing precipices. The victim pleads for another path, for justice to prevail. But it's a plea in vain. Dan's grip tightens, and a cruel fate looms. Bruiser's action is swift and ruthless. He wrenches the victim's head forward, the Bowie knife flashing deadly in his grip. A scream pierces the room as blood spills, the blade twisting before withdrawing, leaving the victim to crumple, gasping their last.

Dan and Bruiser dispose of the lifeless form, slipping it through the back door into the alley. On an unhitched wagon, they lay the body, shrouding it with a tarp. The lane bears silent witness to the village's sinister underbelly, where debts are settled in fear, violence, and tragic ends.

Chapter Five

The village streets pulse with vitality as Dan Farley sits with confidence upon the seat of the gig carriage, reins in hand, his grasp relaxed. Beside him, Alice Riley embodies elegance and lightheartedness, and their journey through the bustling streets is imbued with an enchanting quality. Amid their shared laughter, Dan playfully assures Alice. "Oh, Alice! You know I'm always punctual. Your father won't have Bruiser taking me to task. We'll reach the 'Curiosity Shop' before you can utter 'trinkets and treasures.'"

Alice can't resist teasing. "I do have my doubts, Mr Farley. You might need to coax some extra speed from our horse to avoid mishaps."

Undaunted, Dan leans closer, a playful glint in his eyes. "If you promise a reward, I might make this horse sprout wings."

Her smile deepens, and Alice responds. "Your charm truly knows no bounds. But let's focus on the matter at hand, shall we? I'd rather not disappoint Father."

With a melodramatic sigh, Dan concedes. "Ah, Father Riley and his formidable enforcer, Bruiser. I've had my share of dealings with that brute. But don't worry, Alice, I won't burden you with those tales."

"Thank you, Dan. I'd rather not delve into the darker aspects of my father's affairs. Let's keep our conversations delightful."

A mischievous grin graces Dan's lips as their playful exchange continues. "You've got it, Miss Smarty Pants! So, tell me, where have you been hiding all these years? Your return feels like uncovering a hidden treasure."

With a playful sparkle in her eyes, Alice responds, "I wasn't hiding, Mr Farley. I spent the past few years in Sydney Town, attending a Finishing School to refine my manners and etiquette."

Dan raises an amused eyebrow, "A refined lady, eh? Well, you've certainly won a place in my heart. But fear not; I won't let it go to my head. I'm quite adept at keeping things uncomplicated."

Their laughter dances on the air as Alice clarifies, "Uncomplicated it is, Mr Farley. Just so you know, I am not engaged to anyone. However, I must clarify that orchestrating 'sweet moments' is not my immediate agenda."

Dan concurs, leaning back with a smile, "Agreed, my dear Alice. Friendship it is, then. But I won't deny that your beauty has captured my attention. I'll content myself with admiring from a distance."

Blushing, Alice playfully scolds him, "You certainly have a way with words, Dan. But let's not get carried away. We must stick to friendship, especially considering my father's views."

With a touch of admiration, Dan responds, "Friends, it is. But I won't promise to suppress my admiration entirely. Your beauty demands attention, even drawing the eyes of the reverend himself. Why, even Reverend Matthew Williams proclaimed you celestial. He believes that after God fashioned your form, He shattered the mould to prevent overwhelming our senses."

Alice rolls her eyes, laughing. "Please, Dan. I highly doubt the reverend said anything of the sort. You're incorrigible."

Winking, Dan counters, "You might be surprised, Alice. The reverend and the other gentlemen in town can't help but be captivated by you. You're a sight to behold."

Playfully punching his arm, Alice revels in their jovial banter. Their laughter lingers as the gig carriage approaches a lane near the Highlander Hotel. A veil of intrigue and enchantment surrounds them, poised to unravel the mysteries that lie ahead on their unforeseen journey together.

That evening, the sun's descent below the horizon gifts the village street with a captivating orange hue. Amid this twilight transformation, Dan Farley strides purposefully, his Fedora hat slightly tilted, hands nestled in his pockets. The vivacious pulse of the bustling village embraces him as he navigates past shops and vibrant establishments, each radiating its unique allure.

Within this animated tableau, Dan's gaze alights upon Alice Riley, gracefully traversing the street. She wears an elegant dress that accentuates her beauty, captivating attention wherever she treads. Their eyes converge, igniting a fleeting connection that elicits a warm smile from Dan.

"Dapper Dan, it seems you're drawn to the heart of the village once more," Alice remarks playfully, dissolving the silence between them.

A chuckle escapes Dan as he replies, "Well, how could I resist your captivating presence, Miss Riley? After all, wherever you are, that's where the heart of the village resides."

Alice's cheeks carry a delicate flush, her smile radiant. "Flattery might open doors for you, but don't think I'll be swayed easily."

With a touch of admiration gleaming, Dan responds, "I wouldn't expect anything less, Alice. You possess substance, impervious to hollow words."

Reciprocating the sentiment, Alice's smile deepens as she remarks, "I'm relieved you recognize that. Tell me, what mischief have you found yourself in today?"

"Mischief, you say?" Dan feigns innocence. "I assure you, Alice, I'm a model citizen. Just attending to my affairs, mending tables, and ensuring the gaming room runs smoothly."

Alice arches an eyebrow playfully. "Is that right? And have you managed to evade Bruiser's watchful eye?"

A hearty laugh spills from Dan's lips. "I have my methods for sidestepping trouble, don't you worry. Bruiser may be Riley's muscle, but I've become adept at navigating his surveillance."

Alice's expression turns earnest as she cautions, "Be cautious, Dan. Bruiser's actions can be unpredictable."

Nodding appreciatively, Dan acknowledges her concern. "I won't underestimate him, Alice. I've witnessed the aftermath of crossing his path. But let's not dwell on shadows. Let's revel in the village's vitality and the music and perhaps even share a dance."

Alice contemplates his proposal, her smile softening. "I'll consider it, Mr Farley. On one condition: you must promise to behave yourself."

Hand over his heart in mock solemnity, Dan pledges, "I vow to behave, Alice. Tonight is about embracing joy and leaving worries behind."

As the evening unfolded, they continued their stroll, laughter blending harmoniously with the village's soundscape. With every stride, the twilight's embers weave a magical aura around them, drawing them closer on a path of camaraderie and, perhaps, the emergence of something more profound.

Chapter Six

In the concealed recesses of the gaming room's obscure alley, a dense cloud of tobacco smoke lends an air of enigma and allure. Against the dimly lit backdrop, two silhouettes find respite against the wall, seizing a fleeting moment of tranquillity from the bustling cacophony. Norm, an imposing figure radiating rugged authority, engages in dialogue with Dan, the quick-witted and self-assured employee, as they relish an unusual interlude.

"I've heard whispers that you've been spending time with the boss's daughter, Dan," Norm muses, a knowing curve on his lips.

Dan's grin is a blend of cunning and authenticity. "True enough, Norm. But always with the utmost respect. She's an extraordinary woman."

A chuckle escapes Norm, acknowledging the fortune that accompanies such a connection. "Luck's on your side, Dan. Keep vigilant, though. Bruiser keeps his sights locked on her."

Dan's demeanor assumes gravity as he responds, "I've no intent to cross boundaries, Norm. While I may not belong to her world, I won't make a fool of myself."

Norm nods in tacit agreement. "Most folks around here are too wary of riling Riley to make any advances. It requires a hearty dose of courage."

Dan interjects with a hint of irony. "Or a wardrobe filled with ostentatious coats and a chest puffed up as they strut down Bourke Street. More show than substance, if you ask me."

Their conversation meanders toward the challenges Alice confronts in her social spheres, as Norm keenly observes. "Even the supposed highborn ladies are wary of her. Alice attributes it to her father's reputation. Yet you and I discern that envy and awe render them speechless."

Dan concedes the accuracy of Norm's insight. "You're right, Norm. To win her affection would necessitate a man as spirited as she is, if not someone who garners her father's blessing."

Their discourse veers toward Bruiser, the enigmatic sentinel shielding Alice. Norm offers glimpses into his character. "And then there's Bruiser, Riley's watchdog over her. His coarse exterior is a remnant of a traumatic fire from his youth. Now he despises any man more handsome than he is... which, according to his measure, encompasses most."

Dan recollects with a shudder the brutality he's witnessed at Bruiser's hands. "I've seen the aftermath of his savagery, Norm. It's an image one wishes to erase from memory."

Norm's visage darkens, the looming threat resonating within him. "He wields that Bowie knife like a harbinger of death. A single stroke and destinies are forever altered."

Dan concurs with a sombre nod. "He's even taken to discussing me with another of Riley's henchmen, branding me a 'Pretty Boy' who warrants close surveillance. But I won't bow to his words. I've confronted graver perils."

In unison, they extinguish their briar pipes, a shared symbol of their resolve. They adjust their attire, preparing to rejoin the pandemonium of the gaming room. Amidst the uncertainties and threats that encompass them, Dan stands unwavering. He recognizes that the allure of the gaming realm and the enchantment of Alice's presence is worth the stakes.

The night remains youthful, and the games of chance have just resumed. Amidst the chaos, Dan stands tall, his wit and perseverance rendering him a compelling contender within this high-stakes arena.

Transitioning seamlessly from the alleyway into the vibrant nucleus of the gaming room, Dan melds into the dynamic atmosphere. Anticipation electrifies the air, saturated with the shuffle of cards, clattering dice, and clinking glasses. The room pulsates with various hues and personalities, each bearing its narrative.

With effortless navigation, Dan's charisma is a magnet, drawing people toward him with an irresistible allure. He shares hearty exchanges, swapping laughter and tales with fellow gamblers. Despite his history, he commands respect and admiration, his presence an embrace amid the fervour of gaming. Players briefly suspend their games for camaraderie, clinking glasses and sharing jests with Dan, fostering a sense of kinship.

Here, fortunes ascend and plummet, risks are embraced, and alliances are forged amid shared ardour for the game. As Dan immerses himself in the pulsating milieu, he embraces the euphoria and vibrancy that saturate the room. He leaves an indelible imprint with each interaction, his confidence and charm forging enduring connections.

Chapter Seven

With a poised descent, Dan alights from the gig carriage, his gaze turning to Alice, offering his hand in a gesture of chivalry. Amidst the symphony of village sounds, their laughter harmonizes, infusing the surroundings with an otherworldly enchantment. It's as if the air has absorbed their joy, radiating ethereal magic as Alice's delicate hand graces his arm; a subtle touch, an electric warmth, courses through Dan's veins.

A playful glint sparkles in Dan's eyes as he teases, "Alice, your touch holds a captivating spell. Your laughter, akin to enchanting incantations, bewitches our world. In this dance of the moment, it's just you and me, caught in the embrace of sheer delight."

Alice's response is an effervescent giggle, her eyes alight with merriment. "Oh, Dan, you're incorrigible! Take heed, or our whimsical banter might reach unintended ears and draw Father's ire."

He nods in agreement, a lighthearted grin lingering. "You're absolutely right, Alice. Prudence is key. We mustn't invite your father's scrutiny through any imprudent escapades."

A softening of his expression reveals his sincerity. "However, Alice, my affection for you knows no confines. Our bond is a radiant star in my sky."

Alice's reply holds contemplation, her voice a hushed caress. "We must tread carefully, Dan. Our path is fraught with challenges and uncertainties."

Dan's tone lifts once more, teasing defiance in his words. "Understood, Alice. Our love, a fragile flame, deserves shielding from the gusts of our world."

"Indeed. Society may not comprehend, but it won't diminish the depth of our sentiments."

Dan absorbs her words, then speaks, his tone tender. "Alice, I'll honour your wishes. We'll continue as colleagues, though know this—my heart beats solely for you."

Alice's voice carries a gentle caress, nearly a whisper. "And mine for you, Dan. Patience must be our companion. A time will come when our love can thrive openly."

As Alice glides towards the Curiosity Shop, Dan watches her, a fusion of yearning and resolve in his gaze. His heart swells with love and purpose, aware that their connection is extraordinary, a passion worth pursuing.

Taking a deep breath, Dan readies himself for the trials that await. Filled with purpose, he guides the horse down the alley leading to the rear entrance of the gaming establishment. Amidst the bustling world, his focus remains singular: Alice, the woman he adores, and the promise of a future where their love reigns unbridled.

Unbeknownst to them, their journey will test their mettle, challenge their hearts, and reshape their fates. In a realm shrouded by peril and secrecy, where Jack Riley's machinations cast ominous shadows, Dan and Alice must navigate treacherous waters. Yet their love shall emerge as a guiding beacon, illuminating the path through the darkness. Together, they'll unearth that certain secrets are destined for revelation, regardless of the cost.

As the day progresses, Alice emerges from the shop, a spring in her step, her gaze scanning the alley in both directions. Her elation propels her towards the open barn doors across the way. Within the stables, Dan's embrace awaits, brimming with enthusiasm. Settling on a straw bale within a stall, they share an intimate moment.

Peering into Dan's eyes, Alice speaks with fervent emotion. "Oh, Dan, your words fill me with hope and courage. Defying my father, forging our happiness—it's a dream I've held dear. I believe in us, in our love. I'm ready to brave any trials."

Dan smiles warmly, his affection unwavering. "That's my Alice, a beacon of courage. We'll carve a life uniquely ours, unburdened by shadows of fear. Our love shall fortify us."

Alice confides in him about her family's struggles. "Mother's shackled by what father's dictates, her freedom curtailed. But my love for you is mightier. I love you, Dan, with heart and soul. Let's cherish each instant."

With a reassuring touch, Dan responds. "Alice, there's no cause for fear. United, we can defy your father's will. We'll find happiness, emancipated from his grip."

Alice's heart flares with Dan's words. "Yes, Dan! Let's seize it!"

Their embrace deepens, and passion intensifies. In this charged moment, they relinquish restraint, succumbing to a fervent desire only lovers share. Love takes centre stage as they yield to reckless, passionate longing. Within that stall, their hearts beat as one. The world fades, leaving them in a dance of love and yearning. This stolen moment offers solace and strength, their love a beacon guiding them through trials. With hearts heavy with emotion and passion ablaze, Dan and Alice begin crafting their own narrative that transcends convention and embraces love in its purest form.

Chapter Eight

Mounted gracefully upon a saddled horse, With a display of poise and fluidity that mirrors his every move, Dan arrives and dismounts at the expanse of the grand Riley estate. Gathering a stack of mail, he executes it with practised ease, his arms cradling the letters with purpose as he moves toward the imposing house. His intent is unmistakable as he firmly raps on the sturdy door. It yields willingly to his touch, swinging open to reveal a maid standing within. She accepted the bundle of mail from Dan's outstretched hands, her demeanour gracious, and a genteel smile graced her lips.

Dan's smile remains as he speaks, "Greetings to you, miss. It seems we have not yet had the pleasure of an introduction. Might I have the honour of knowing your name?"

The maid curtsies, her movement fluid and practised. "Cloherty, sir, is the name I bear."

Dan's smile widens as he replies, "A pleasure to make your acquaintance, Miss Cloherty. I am Dan, in the service of Mr Riley. Would it be a burden for you to inform me of the current whereabouts of the Master and Mistress? Moreover, may I inquire – might Miss Alice be found nearby?"

The maid, measured and polite, responds, "The Master and Mistress still repose, sir. Yet, Miss Alice has chosen the rear veranda as her present location. Would you permit me to convey your arrival to Mr Riley?"

Dan's quick and decisive response: "That would not be necessary, Miss Cloherty. I would rather not disturb their rest. Instead, I shall proceed to the back and deliver my message directly to Miss Alice."

A glance of anticipation accompanies Dan's words as he commences his journey down the corridor, the passage leading to the back of the house, where Alice's presence beckons like a guiding light.

The maid offers a final gracious smile, "Very well, sir. May your news bring about joy!"

Acknowledging her sentiment with a nod, Dan presses on, his steps marked by determination and eagerness, his heart buoyed by the promise of seeing Alice.

And so, as the day unfurls its possibilities, Dan finds himself stepping onto the back veranda. There, Alice is seated gracefully upon a loveseat, her form enveloped by the gentle caress of the morning breeze. Seeing her brings a smile to Dan's lips, a gesture mirrored in her own as their eyes meet, a blend of warmth and deep affection passing between them.

Alice's words carry a teasing note, "Mr Farley, what prompts your early appearance? Might it be my allure that has summoned you so promptly?"

Dan's grin is infectious, "You've unearthed my secret, Miss Riley. Your presence alone can illuminate even the earliest hours of my day. I've brought a small surprise for you."

Alice leans forward, curiosity evident in her expression, her eyes alight with anticipation. Alice's voice is a playful melody, "Pray, share your secret, Mr Farley. I'm all ears."

From within his pocket, Dan produces a delicate bouquet of wildflowers, their arrangement artful, held together by a simple ribbon. He extends it toward Alice, who accepts it with a sparkle in her eyes that matches the morning sun.

Dan's words are infused with a sincere charm, "While these blossoms might pale next to your radiance, I thought they could introduce a touch of nature's enchantment to your day."

Alice's response is genuine, her smile radiant, "Oh, Dan, they are utterly charming! Thank you. You truly possess the art of making my heart dance with delight."

In the following silence, their fingertips brush lightly, a connection sparking between them. Yet, even amidst the enchantment, Alice's eyes wander discreetly, a fleeting assessment of their surroundings.

In the whirlwind of emotions that engulf them, Dan and Alice find themselves enveloped in an embrace that speaks volumes of their affection for each other. Yet, as the tendrils of their bliss extend, a cruel interruption shatters the moment. Two formidable hands grasp Dan's shirt from behind like a tempest, yanking him forcefully away from the loveseat. Bruiser, the enigmatic enforcer with an iron grip, has laid his formidable clutches upon Dan.

A sinister laugh escapes Bruiser's lips as he taunts, "Gotcha, you slippery snake! Your games end Now! Mr Riley wants a word with you in the basement, and you're coming with me."

Gasping for air, Dan fights against the vice-like chokehold, his struggles futile against the immense strength of Bruiser. The brute drags him backward, his feet scrabbling to maintain purchase against the relentless force.

Stunned by the abrupt upheaval, Alice springs to her feet, her heart thundering with alarm. Without a second thought, she propels herself toward Bruiser, her fists pounding with unrelenting fury against his back.

"No, Bruiser! Cease this! Dan is my friend. He poses no threat. I implore you, release him," Alice's voice resonates with courage and determination.

Bruiser pauses for a fraction of a moment, pivoting slightly to face Alice while still maintaining his unyielding grip on Dan's throat. The tension is palpable, a confrontation between Alice's unwavering resolve and the enforcer's brute force, all for safeguarding her friend.

In that critical instant, Jack Riley, the imposing figure of Alice's father, makes his appearance. His very presence casts a shadow of intimidation, commanding the scene. "Alice, desist this instant! I shall take control. You retreat into the house, IMMEDIATELY!"

His words blend stern authority and concern, and his intentions are crystal clear.

Tears brimming in her eyes, Alice implores her father, her voice a mix of desperation and defiance. "Father, I beg you to spare Dan from Bruiser's wrath. I shall never forgive you if harm befalls him! He has been my sole friend since my return from Sydney."

Riley moves closer to Alice, his hands gentle as he places them on her shoulders. Urging her to turn away and seek refuge inside the house, his voice carries a mixture of apprehension and protection. Alice complied, her steps heavy with worry as she vanished through a backdoor, leaving behind a trail of anxious thoughts about Dan's fate.

"Basement!" Riley commands Bruiser, his gaze firmly set upon Dan, a hint of unease colouring his expression. "Hold him tight, but ensure no permanent harm. I intend to converse with him in the basement."

Bruiser obeys without question, the relentless pressure on Dan's neck unwavering as they proceed along the verandah's length. Their footsteps resound with tension, the aura fraught with impending conflict and revelations. As they approach the entry to the basement, the weight of confrontation and the unknown looms heavily. The fate of Dan Farley hangs precariously in the balance, at the mercy of the formidable Mr Riley and his unyielding enforcer, Bruiser.

Chapter Nine

Beneath the welcoming façade of the Riley homestead, a stark contrast awaits in the form of the basement, a space akin to a grim dungeon. A wooden ramp descends from a door leading off the verandah, revealing a chilling expanse beneath the home's timber flooring. The bluestone walls, coated in layers of dust and draped with cobwebs, emit an unsettling aura, creating an atmosphere of eerie desolation.

Bruiser's forceful determination propels Dan downward, his journey ending at a solitary chair, which becomes both his seat and prison. Bruiser secures Dan's wrists and feet with calculated efficiency, cinching them tightly with ropes that bind him to the chair. The cold, unyielding metal presses into Dan's skin, eliciting a grimace of discomfort. Bruiser's grip then migrates to Dan's shoulder-length hair, yanking his head backward in an act of dominance.

"You're walking a dangerous line, lad. Mr Riley doesn't tolerate vermin lurking around his daughter, and you've flagrantly broken his cardinal rule. Expect fireworks!" Bruiser's taunt drips with venom, his words a manifestation of his malevolence.

Yet, before Bruiser's cruelty can escalate, Jack Riley intervenes, stepping forward to wrest command from his enforcer's grasp. "Bruiser, step back... I'll handle this!" Riley's visage contorts with wrath as he regards Dan, who now finds himself ensnared within the grip of a furious father's ire.

"How dare you entangle yourself with my daughter beyond your duties? Who granted you the audacity to lay your hands on her? You vile wretch, a disgrace of the lowest order! I could have you castrated for this transgression!" Riley seethes, his fury threatening to boil over.

Riley seizes Dan's collar, shaking him with unchecked ferocity. His clenched fists hammer down Dan's jaw, a relentless barrage of blows sending Dan's head into a whirlwind of agony. Dan's gaze shifts toward Bruiser, who looms menacingly, a formidable knife glinting ominously in his grasp.

In a relentless exhibition of aggression, Riley delivers a series of stinging slaps to Dan's head.

"The audacity — you ruffian! What am I to make of you?" Riley's voice drips with scorn and rage.

Dan endeavours to speak amid the pain, his words a plea for clemency amidst the onslaught. "I beg your pardon, sir! My intentions were never untoward... Alice and I are only friends."

Yet Riley remains unmoved, his rage unabated. "Friendship, a mere excuse! Your flesh and blood are forfeit! I've heard of your indecent advances toward my Alice, devoid of honour. You're a conniving scoundrel!"

Still, Dan presses on, attempting to articulate his side of the story, knowing his fate hangs in a precarious balance. "Sir, inquire of Alice. Since she arrived from Sydney, she's been adrift in loneliness and desolation. My sole intent was to lift her spirits. No harm intended. Any punishment you exact upon me will only turn her against you... I'm certain!"

Riley's heart remains unyielding, his disdain for Dan palpable. "Curse your impertinence! Your insolence exacerbates your plight. I'll not have a roguelike you counsel me! Bruiser! He's yours to handle. Spare his manhood for some wench's pleasure, but brand him with my mark. My Alice is sacrosanct, accessible only to the chosen man."

With that final edict, Riley departs the basement, leaving Dan in the clutches of Bruiser's menacing presence. An ominous weight hangs heavy in the air, the basement a canvas of uncertainty, as Dan confronts an indeterminate and treacherous destiny under the oppressive rule of the brutal enforcer.

Within the murky depths of the basement's feeble illumination, Dan finds himself ensnared, bound to a chair that cements his fate within the clutches of the sadistic Bruiser. The enforcer's demeanour reeks of perverse delight as he savours the sickly sweet sensation of power. A malicious sneer stretches across Bruiser's face, a twisted grin that bares the malevolence that courses through his veins. "Count yourself lucky, Farley. Were it not for Miss Alice, you'd be a lifeless husk within my grasp."

Bruiser's fingers curl around Dan's throat, tightening like a vice, a visceral display of dominion over the defenceless man. His voice drips with cruelty, a chilling symphony of torment. "Today, Farley, I'll ensure you receive an education that teaches every miserable wretch in this village the cost of laying hands on anything linked to Mr Riley. Tell me, what can you do without, eh, Farley? A man must find a way to earn his keep!"

Struggling for breath, Dan's pleas reverberate, a desperate symphony that seeks to chip away at Bruiser's malevolent resolve. His voice trembles with fear and desperation. "Bruiser... You can have the money I've banked. Please... I meant no harm to Miss Alice. I'm not a threat. Just release me, and I'll disappear from this town. I'll go upcountry or to Sydney—whatever you want!"

Yet Bruiser stands unmoved, deriving a perverse satisfaction from the terror he instils. His taunt is delivered with an unmistakable tone of sadistic glee. "What's that, Farley? Your screams will serenade my ears. Did you forget? I'll miss the sight of you writhing like a decapitated serpent."

Bruiser drags Dan's chair across the dirt floor, maneuvering him toward a solid-topped table in a corner. With calculated malevolence, he forces Dan's arms to extend flat across the table's surface, hands still tightly secured. Bruiser positions Dan's palms and releases the chair's long-restraining rope.

A cruel glint gleams in Bruiser's eye as he taunts, revelling in the impending act of brutality. "Let's see... Ten dainty fingers all lined up. One for Bruiser – that is one for his Master, meaning one less for... You!"

Before Dan can react, the heavy thud of Bruiser's substantial Bowie knife strikes the table. Time seems to slow as Dan watches in sickening horror, realizing the impending catastrophe. In a gruesome instant, his right thumb is severed from his hand. Blood spurts, and Dan's face contorts in a silent symphony of agony. Pain radiates through his body, but his spirit remains unyielding as he gasps for air, determined to endure.

Bruiser jeers and basks in Dan's torment, subjecting him to slaps. "Don't fade on me, Farley! Savour this exquisite moment, the pain etching into your memory!"

Dan's bloodied stump is wrapped with a crude strip of cloth, the tightness meant to quell the bleeding. With chilling finality, Bruiser delivers the crushing blow to Dan's already-shattered psyche.

"I detest a messy scene down here, Farley. I'm the one who has to clean it up. You'll need to seek out Doc Evans in town and show him the remnants of my handiwork. Ensure the entire village knows the fate awaiting anyone who dares to cast eyes upon Miss Alice. Consider your tenure here null and void."

As Bruiser unshackles Dan's hands and feet, a surge of determination propels Dan to his feet, the urge to escape overpowering the agony. Yet Bruiser thwarts his attempts, delivering a punishing kick to Dan's back that sends him sprawling, face-first, onto the earthen floor.

Despite the searing pain, Dan claws his way back to his feet, propelled by a storm of rage and an oath of retribution. "Remember my words, Bruiser! Mark them well... Regret shall be your constant companion!" Dan's declaration reverberates through the basement, an ominous prophecy of vengeance awaiting his tormentor.

Chapter Ten

Amid the opulent splendour of their grand residence, Jack Riley confronts his daughter, Alice, in the lavish living room. The room drips with luxury, adorned with antique furnishings that exude an air of refinement. Despite the extravagant surroundings, Alice appears dwarfed by her father's imposing presence, a delicate figure cowed by the weight of his anger.

"What possessed you to involve yourself with that ruffian, Farley?" Riley's voice reverberates, a cacophony of disappointment and fury that fills the entire room. "I sent you to Sydney to be educated by the finest governess, to cultivate relationships with respectable suitors. Yet you've surrendered to the advances of a worthless vagrant, a man with nothing to offer but fleeting pleasures."

Alice's voice trembles with fear and defiance as she attempts to explain herself. "No, Father! You misunderstand. My intentions were innocent. I sought friendship, not pleasure. In this town, I am isolated. You've discouraged gentlemen from approaching us, and the ladies here shun me without reason. Your reputation precedes you as anything but honourable, and I bear the consequences of your actions."

Riley dismisses Alice's words with a dismissive wave. "Nonsense, girl! My standing in this colony is impeccable. I command respect from the highest echelons of society. I sent you to Sydney for your own betterment, not mine. I wish for you to secure a title and ensure your future happiness. I will not have you tied to a man seeking marriage only to secure my interests!"

Alice's frustration spills forth, her voice ringing with the bitterness of pent-up emotion. "And what interests and future do you speak of, Father? The money earned from debts squeezed out of those ensnared in your gambling dens? The funds obtained from those who can't repay, the misery you've inflicted on the cheated and injured? My dear mother, refined as she was, has been cast aside, rejected, locked away while you continue to revel in your debauchery."

Riley's rage ignites in response to Alice's defiance. "YOU INSOLENT WRETCH!" His hand rises with brutal force, delivering a blow that propels Alice backward, her fragile form colliding with the floor.

At that moment, Riley's anger wanes, giving way to guilt and regret as he beholds the consequences of his actions upon his own flesh and blood. An unsettling silence envelops the room, pregnant with raw emotion and tense stillness.

In the doorway, Elizabeth Riley, a woman marked by her forties, stands stricken and pale, witnessing the turmoil unfolding within the room. Her presence is a plea for sanity and compassion. She steps forward, her voice trembling with concern and care. "Jack... Stop this madness. You've caused enough harm."

Elizabeth's words pierce the stormy atmosphere as she stands protectively beside her bruised daughter, extending a sheltering arm around Alice. The young girl's whimpering form is guided away from the scene of turmoil, creating a safe haven within her mother's embrace.

Haunted by the consequences of his actions, Jack Riley stands amidst the wreckage of his temper. Struggling to regain his composure, he watches Alice leave the room, allowing his anger to fully descend. *"She knows full well the implications of her actions,"* he roars to an empty space. *"I won't tolerate insubordination from anyone. She's no daughter of my making!"*

Riley storms out of the house, his fury unabated. Accompanied by Bruiser, the enforcer, they traverse the path to the Royal Highlander Hotel. The hotel, for Riley, is a temporary escape from his torments, where he can lose himself in its fleeting distractions.

Within the hotel's opulent room, Riley finds solace in the company of Charlotte, a woman of captivating allure. While lacking the conventional beauty of Riley's wife, Charlotte possesses an enchanting magnetism that draws him in. She understands Riley's needs, providing the comfort and flattery he craves. Their connection finds a passionate culmination at the end of the bed, where they seek refuge from their troubles.

Meanwhile, Bruiser enters the lively bar, a contrasting figure amidst the merriment. Despite his intimidating exterior, he engages in jovial conversations, ordering the finest ales and blending into the animated camaraderie that fills the space.

In the hotel's diverse corners, people gather to seek solace, finding momentary respite from their personal burdens. Laughter fills the air, strangers uniting in a shared experience. The hotel transforms into a sanctuary where concerns can be briefly set aside and where the pursuit of solace joins a diverse tapestry of lives.

Chapter Eleven

Elizabeth Riley tenderly consoles her daughter, Alice, whose tear-streaked face bears witness to the recent storm that swept through the household. The livid bruise on her cheek tells a silent tale of the conflict and her fears for Dan Farley's safety.

"I'm here for you, my dear. We'll uncover the truth about Mr Farley's fate. Do not fret," Elizabeth soothes Alice, enfolding her in a nurturing embrace.

A sudden spark ignites in Alice's eyes, a mixture of determination and realization. She springs up from her mother's comforting hold, propelled by an irresistible urge to unravel the mystery surrounding Dan Farley's predicament. Swift and purposeful, she departs from the sitting room, her steps echoing with purpose along the passageway.

In her haste, Alice spots the maid-servant, Cloherty, striding briskly. Without hesitation, she calls out, her voice laden with urgency and concern. "Cloherty! Did you chance upon Mr Farley upon his return from the basement?" Alice's words pierce the air, carrying the weight of her worry.

Taken aback by the urgency in Alice's tone, Cloherty responds with haste, her words tumbling forth. "Yes, ma'am! I did. I saw Mr Farley emerging from the basement, his right hand wrapped in a bloodied bandage."

A knot of anxiety tightens in Alice's chest, her apprehension deepening as she realizes she cannot rest until she unravels the enigma that shrouds Dan Farley's fate. Driven by a sense of purpose, she beseeches Cloherty to act with haste. "Please, take the spare gig carriage and make your way to Dr Evans's residence at allotment one, situated at the crossroads of Queen and Collins Street," Alice's words are charged with urgency. "Inquire about Mr Farley's condition... and hasten!"

Cloherty absorbs the gravity of the situation with complete comprehension. She hurries down the passageway, her footsteps resolute as she advances toward the back door. Alice's urgent plea has set a mission in motion, and Cloherty is determined to carry it out without delay.

In the waiting chamber of Dr Evans' clinic, Cloherty is perched on the edge of her seat, every fibre consumed by apprehension. Each passing moment seemed to stretch into eternity as she anxiously awaited Mr Farley's fate tidings. As the door to the surgery room finally creaks open, Dr Evans emerges, casting a grave and concerned gaze upon her. With a beckoning gesture, he invites her to step inside.

"Good day, Doctor Evans," Cloherty greets him, her voice laced with respect and trepidation. "Might I inquire if a young man with an injured hand has been under your care today, sir? My Mistress Alice Riley holds great concern for Mr Farley's well-being."

A sigh escapes Dr Evans, his features reflecting a mixture of weariness and disappointment. "Indeed, I have attended to him," he responds, his tone heavy. "Yet, it is with little thanks to your master's actions. The lad, though battered, refuses to divulge the identity of his assailant. The assault upon him was brutal, leaving him without his right thumb. The risk of infection looms, and the possibility of losing his hand is distressingly real. Kindly relay to Mistress Elizabeth that I've exerted my utmost efforts. I've strongly advised Mr Farley to remain in Melbourne for a full day, for his recovery is threatened by significant blood loss. He intends to depart for Geelong tomorrow, driven by fear for his life."

Cloherty's heart plummets at the weight of Dr Evans' words. She nods, her gaze a mixture of sorrow and gratitude for the physician's diligence in caring for Mr Farley. Stepping out of the surgery room, she carries the weighty news like a solemn duty, steadfast in her resolve to deliver it to Mistress Alice Riley without delay and, therefore, returns to the homestead.

Amid the confines of the stables, Alice's restless steps echo a cadence of worry and anxiety. Her eyes alighted with concern, tracking Cloherty's departing figure until it dwindled inside the confines of the homestead. In this moment of distress, Elizabeth, her mother, approaches with a knowing apprehension etched across her features.

"Alice, my dear," Elizabeth's voice is imbued with a mixture of trepidation and empathy, "What did Cloherty convey? Have we received any word about Mr Farley?"

Alice's eyes shimmered with unshed tears as she prepared to share the unsettling news. "Mother, it's dire. Dr Evans attended to him, and the extent of his injuries grievous. His right thumb was severed, and the spectre of infection and further harm to his hand looms ominously. He's to remain in Melbourne throughout the night, and tomorrow, he plans to journey to Geelong, fearing for his own safety."

A gasp escapes Elizabeth, her hand instinctively covering her mouth in a mixture of shock and sorrow. The weight of the situation hangs heavy, bonding mother and daughter in shared distress.

"Oh, my dear child," Elizabeth's voice trembles with compassion, her heart aching for the suffering that has befallen Dan Farley. "We must act. We cannot let him bear this burden alone."

Alice, fueled by unwavering determination, speaks her resolve with steadfast conviction. "Mother, I care not for what Father's dictates. I refuse to forsake Dan in his hour of need. I am going to town to stand by his side."

Elizabeth regards her daughter with a blend of concern and pride, her voice tinged with unwavering support. "So be it, my love. You will find a way to offer him solace and ensure his safety."

With their decision cemented, mother and daughter exchange resolute glances, their bond fortified by the trials they face together. Alice moves purposefully toward the waiting gig carriage, claiming the reins. As the carriage sets forth, it carries her down the estate's winding drive, disappearing into the distance en route to the heart of the town where Dan Farley resides.

The story of a young woman's courage unfurls within the whirlwind of a household gripped by secrets and tensions. Defying conventions and social norms, she strides forth for the sake of love. In this momentous journey, Alice acknowledges the repercussions her actions might entail, yet her heart beats as a testament to the risks taken in the name of love's enduring power.

Chapter Twelve

In her search for stables, Alice is unaware of their proximity. She secures the horse's reins to a signpost outside a two-story weatherboard building, where a sign reads: "MISS M. HODSON'S LODGING HOUSE - BOARD FIVE SHILLINGS PER WEEK." Anxiety courses through her as she descends from the carriage, her heart a persistent drumbeat of worry. Aware of the townspeople's afternoon rest, she knocks on the narrow blue door with a fervent urgency.

A voice calls out from within, slightly annoyed, "Hold yer horses... I'm coming. No need to wake the dead with your announcement!" The door creaks open, revealing Miss Hodson, a woman in her fifties with a plain appearance and an elongated nose. Seeing a refined lady with a bruised face leaves her momentarily taken aback.

"Yes, mistress... How can I help you?" she inquires, a mixture of curiosity and hesitation.

"I need to find Dan Farley. He's injured, and he may need my assistance. Does he reside here, Miss Hodson?" Alice's voice conveys both urgency and concern.

"Please, call me Mary, dear. And who might you be, seeking information about Mr Farley's condition?"

Mary responds, her tone softened by familiarity. "Alice Riley. I'm a friend, and I've come to offer my help."

"Ah, come in. I must say, your family has already been quite involved. I'll ask Mr Farley if he's willing to be seen by you."

As Alice enters the lodging house, a small sitting room adorned with a floral couch and matching armchairs greets her. A fireplace stands ready for cooler weather, and the dark, polished floorboards lend the room an inviting ambience. A lace curtain graces a bay window, veiling the view outside.

After a brief absence, Mary Hobson returns with a sombre expression etched on her face. "Mr Farley says you're foolish to be here and that your presence might cause him and yourself more harm than good. He will let you attend to him, but you assume the risks. He's in the room behind the second door off the landing."

Alice wastes no time, ascending the staircase and cautiously opening the door to Dan's room. The dimly lit space is sombre, containing a single bed, a small bedside table, and a tall, narrow wardrobe. Dan lies beneath a thin blanket, his trembling form immediately catching her attention. Alice hurries to his side, her concern evident in her gaze. As their eyes met, tears glistened in Dan's bloodshot eyes.

"Dan! What have Father and Bruiser done?" Alice's voice trembled as she fell to her knees beside him, her emotions overtaking her. She lays her head on his shoulder, finding solace in his presence.

"Alice, I'm so sorry for the turmoil I've brought into your life. Enduring this ordeal feels insurmountable. You should leave. My situation is dire, and you shouldn't be further ensnared. Bruiser took my thumb, and tomorrow I must leave."

Alice's determination remains unwavering. "I don't care, Dan. I can't bear the thought of your suffering. If I stay the night, I can help with your fever."

Through the long night, Alice tends to Dan's fever, offering comfort and relief as he wrestles with delirium. Amidst the darkness, Dan's fever-laden mind leads him into a vivid and haunting dream.

In this dream, he battles Bruiser Conroy, defending himself against the enforcer's relentless pursuit with a Bowie Knife. Amidst fear and desperation, Alice emerges in the dream, embodying hope and trepidation. As Bruiser's blade threatens Dan's life, Alice intervenes bravely, shielding him from the blow. The dream shatters, and Dan awakens with a scream, his body thrashing in his bed.

A familiar voice reaches him, its soothing tones grounding him. "It's okay, Dan. I've got you. Everything will be alright." Alice's voice pierces the tumult, dispelling the nightmare's grip.

Gradually, Dan's frantic breathing subsides as he recognizes his reality. He meets Alice's gaze, reassurance and calm mingling in the room's soft illumination.

Alice quells Dan's fever by morning, but the circumstances remain dire. Dan speaks with a mix of resignation and concern, urging her to leave. "Alice, you must go. If your father or Bruiser learn of your involvement, they'll inflict even more pain. My hand is inflamed, and I feel unwell. Leaving for Geelong is my only option."

Alice's response carries a mixture of sadness and resolve. "I understand, Dan. Though I cannot heal your hand, I'll support you from a distance. I'll send money for your sustenance until you find your footing and regain freedom. Then, we'll be reunited, and we will marry."

Dan's voice holds unwavering determination as he makes a promise. "Alice... I promise you. Despite the challenges ahead, we'll face them together as one."

With their commitment solidified, they share one final act of intimacy to cement their love. Afterwards, Alice slips away from Dan's room, determined to fulfil her role in their plan.

Chapter Thirteen

Dan disembarks from the boat, his boots landing on the bustling shore of Geelong. The vivacity of the scene engulfs him as he takes in the spirited activity surrounding him. The village seems alive, with people bustling about, carts unloading cargo, and boats docking at the harbour. Struggling to manage his luggage—a small wooden trunk containing his modest belongings—Dan's gaze lands on a porter nearby. He approaches the stout man and makes a polite request. "Excuse me, sir. Could you lend me a hand with my trunk? I'd gladly offer you three pence for your assistance."

The porter nods, his face a portrait of grizzled experience, and takes the wooden chest in his capable hands. Guided by the porter, Dan navigates the vibrant streets, the rhythm of his steps aligning with the pulse of the village. Their journey leads them to a rustic, two-story establishment constructed from weathered split boards. Above the entrance, a sign swings, bearing the worn inscription: "THE BLACK BOAR," its image of the animal's grotesque visage painted with rustic charm. Dan follows the porter inside.

As they enter, Dan's footing adjusts to the uneven stone-paved floor. The interior exudes an inviting colonial character—four bench tables scattered across the space, each a potential gathering point. The barkeeper, a figure reminiscent of a storybook buccaneer with a sweeping black beard and a glinting gold earring, extends a hearty greeting. "Come, lad, take a load off and claim a seat. I'll fetch something to quench that weary thirst of yours. A few nips of rum will work wonders for your constitution."

Dan offers his gratitude, though his needs lean towards practicality. "Thank you, but at the moment, I require a room. Please inform me of your weekly lodging rates and the cost of the midday meal."

The barkeeper, grinning with welcoming warmth, conveys the offerings. "Well now, young man, you're in luck. We boast the finest fare on this side of Fine's Creek. You'll savour two tender mutton chops, a boiled potato, and a steamed carrot for a mere sixpence. And if you're feeling peckish, add a penny for a spread of mutton lard on bread. As for lodging, it's a reasonable one shilling and sixpence per week. A steal indeed, considering the shearing season has the village bustling with more hands than ever."

Dan weighs the options, his thoughts a whirlwind of considerations. Despite some disappointment, he ultimately accepts the barkeeper's offer. "Very well, I'll take a room. Thank you."

With a nod, the barkeeper guides Dan upstairs, trunk in tow, his steps steady and sure.

Weeks roll by, and Alice finds herself seated in her bedroom. A lavish kerosene lantern casts a warm glow on her face, accentuating her features. Holding a letter delicately in her hands, she studies it intently. The sender's name—"**Dan Farley - Geelong Town**"—adorns the envelope. Alice takes a deep breath, her heart a flutter of anticipation, and unfolds the letter to reveal its contents. Her eyes trace the words, absorbing their essence:

"*My Dearest Alice,*

Time has flown swiftly during my stay at the Black Boar Hotel in Geelong. Thanks to your generous monthly cheques, totalling one crown (five shillings), I've managed to sustain myself even without work. Your sacrifices for my well-being resonate deeply, and I'm genuinely grateful.

My hand has healed, albeit leaving a mark in the absence of my thumb. While most tasks remain manageable, specific nuances require adjustment.

Recently, I've learned that the Learmonth Brothers, proprietors of a splendid sheep station near Buninyong Village, are searching for a shepherd. Their need has surpassed their discernment, and I've decided to embark on the next supply run with a Bullocky journeying to Buninyong. Once I arrive, I'll write again to share news of my progress.

All my love to you, my dearest Alice - ***Dan.***"

Alice's emotions sway between relief and affection as she absorbs Dan's words. Her expression softens, reflecting her care for him. *"Despite his challenges, he remains steadfast and determined,"* she muses.

With renewed hope, she folds the letter gently, returning it to its envelope. Cradling it close to her heart, Alice savours the love and pride that warms her chest. Their connection endures despite the distance, and she is resolute in supporting him from afar. The letter serves as a beacon, guiding her towards a future where their dreams will converge, and love will flourish amidst life's challenges.

Chapter Thirteen

Dan is struck with awe upon his arrival at "Ercildoune," the vast sheep station owned by the Learmonth Brothers. The sweeping expanse of open grasslands stretches before him, a serene panorama framed by the grandeur of a two-story homestead at the heart of the property. The gentle bleating of sheep fills the air as they graze peacefully, lending tranquillity to the Australian countryside.

Walking alongside Burt, the seasoned bullocky, who expertly guides his bullock dray drawn by a team of eight oxen, Dan approaches the station. Waiting there to welcome them is Thomas Learmonth, a distinguished gentleman with an air of authority that commands respect. Thomas's voice rings out in warm greeting to Burt. "Gid'day, Burt! Been a while, hasn't it? There's a load of wool bales at the shearing sheds for you. Once you're loaded up, go to the manager's house and catch up with Bill Brody. And who do you have with you today?"

As he introduces Dan, Burt doffs his hat, his brow glistening with sweat and dust. "A traveller from Geelong, Mr Learmonth. This is Dan Farley. He's a carpenter who's hit a rough patch and is seeking employment."

Dan steps forward, bearing confidence and respect as he confirms his identity. "Indeed, Mr Learmonth, my name is Dan Farley. While I did suffer an injury to my hand, it's healed well. I've heard that you might need shepherds in these parts."

Thomas nods, his countenance affable as he responds. "Follow Burt and speak with Bill Brody, our Station Manager. We're always looking for skilled workers like yourself, especially with the shortage of labour we've been facing."

Dan expresses his gratitude with a nod, acknowledging the opportunity bestowed upon him. He trails after Burt, the promise of potential employment adding a spring to his step as they make their way towards the manager's house, where discussions about his future role await.

The station's buildings, standing as a testament to the industriousness of the Learmonth Brothers, exude an atmosphere of enterprise and determination. As Dan stands before the gothic-style manager's house, the setting sun casts long shadows, creating an ambience of solemnity as he converses with Bill Brody, the station manager.

Bill's demeanour is self-assured, his presence commanding respect. He extends a warm welcome to Dan. "We're pleased to have you join the station, Farley. The Learmonth Brothers are known for their fairness in all matters. If you can demonstrate your skills and abilities, they'll be more than willing to provide long-term employment as a shepherd. You'll be working alongside our current shepherd, King Billy. Should things go well, you might earn your own flock to shepherd and a basic hut in a different section of the Brothers' unfenced territory."

Intrigued, Dan inquires about the station's vastness. "Could you share the size of the station's run?"

Bill's response underscores the expansive nature of the property. "The station's run stretches for miles in every direction, encompassing vast stretches of grassland country. It's one of this region's oldest and most established properties."

Noting the unique name of the current shepherd, King Billy, Dan raises a question. "I couldn't help but notice the name of the current shepherd, King Billy. I assume he's an Indigenous Australian."

Bill's response is measured and understanding. "That's correct. Is that something that concerns you?"

Dan's reply is prompt, reflecting his open-minded outlook. "No, Sir."

Bill acknowledges Dan's response, offering insights into King Billy's role. "Indeed, he is. King Billy is a respected leader among his people. The Learmonth Brothers have trained him as a shepherd; in turn, he assists in teaching others from his community. Many Indigenous workers here trade labour for food and occasional clothing, often going on Walkabouts with the change of seasons. You, however, will receive the same monthly supplies as Billy, along with an eventual twenty-pound cheque at the end of six months."

Dan expresses his agreement, appreciating the transparency of the arrangement. "That sounds more than reasonable, Sir."

With a friendly and inviting demeanour, Bill extends familiarity. "Just call me Bill, and I'll call you Dan. I'll have one of the young lads help load you up and show you the way."

Dan responds with a nod, a sense of gratitude and anticipation accompanying him as he embraces this fresh start at Ercildoune Station.

Chapter Fourteen

Under the relentless sun, Dan traverses a parched and dusty trail, his swag slung diagonally across his back. His destination is a primitive timbered hut nestled in a clearing. Observing him from outside the humble dwelling is King Billy, a young Aboriginal leader of the Wadawurrung tribe. Tall and sinewy, his robust physique bears the marks of tribal initiation through scars on his chest and neck. Clothed only in weathered cream-coloured moleskin trousers cut short below the knees, his ebony skin shimmers under the blazing sun.

In his native tongue, Billy greets Dan. "Kaya gubbafella, Bungi. Cooee, Geelong Mob... Aye? Allawa Biloela, fella... Jim'boomba!" He pauses and provides an English translation. "Gid'day, Whitefella - you come here from Geelong... Aye? You'll live with me, a Blackfella... in Paradise on Earth."

Dan responds with a touch of amusement. "Gid'day, Billy! Aye! While it might be paradise on Earth for you, it looks more like Hell to me." Fanning himself with his hat to combat the heat, Dan swats at black flies buzzing around him before replacing the hat on his head.

Billy reassures Dan with a grin. "Soon enough, you'll be accustomed to me "Country," fella. I'm a good teacher. Let's rustle up a hot cuppa. Toss yuh swag inside."

Entering the hut, they find Billy's sleeping swag on the earthen floor, his makeshift bed. The modest interior features a tree stump repurposed as a table and wooden tea chests repurposed as seats. A rudimentary wooden shelf holds tinned provisions, while cotton flour bags containing essential supplies hang from hooks on the rough-hewn walls. A fireplace with a locally crafted stone chimney is set into one wall, and a billy can of water hangs from an iron rod over a bed of glowing embers.

The atmosphere within the hut is unpretentious yet inviting, embodying the simplicity of bush life. Billy's smile radiates warmth. "Make yerself comfortable, mate. We'll have a cuppa brewin' in no time."

With a nod of gratitude, Dan embraces the sense of camaraderie that emanates from Billy. He settles into his new environment, ready to embrace the challenges and adventures in this unfamiliar territory.

At the end of the day following, Billy leads a procession of sheep while Dan walks closely behind, both wielding walking sticks. The obedient sheep follow Billy's direction, moving into a pen for the night. As the sheep settle in, Dan and Billy return to the hut. Billy pauses at a skinned mutton carcass hanging from a tree branch on their path. Shooing away the flies, he drew a sheathed knife and cut off a sheep's leg for their evening meal.

Inside the hut, they set about preparing their meal. Billy stirs the glowing embers in the fireplace, places the meat on a metal grate above the coals, and lets it sizzle and cook. Meanwhile, Dan retrieves a small flour bag from a hook and deftly fashions a flour ring on the table. Pouring water from a canteen into the centre of the ring and adding a pinch of salt, he kneads the dough with his hands, expertly forming it into damper bread ready for the fireplace embers.

As they work together, Dan is startled by an unexpected visitor. A blackhead suddenly appears beside the hessian covering the doorway, causing him to jump back in surprise.

Billy reassures Dan with a wave and a grin. "It's me, cousin! From the Wadawurrung tribe. What brings you here, Nulla?"

Observing Nulla, who appears wary and anxious, Billy introduces them. "Nulla's all right, Dan. Dan, meet Nulla, me cousin. He's a friendly blackfella, like me. No need'em worry."

Nulla urgently conveys news to Billy. "Your lubra, Billy... she's made a heap of trouble! An angry fella from another tribe takes her. You need'em sort it out, Billy... Hurry!"

Dan grows concerned as he sees Billy preparing to leave. "How long do you think you'll be gone, Billy?"

Billy shakes his head. "No tellin', mate. Me wife she stirrin' up a heap. I'll have to settle it. It might be a long while. You tell'em, Brody, I won't be back soon... maybe never."

Billy packs up his swag and quickly gathers a few essential supplies, preparing to leave with Nulla. They are seen running up the track, silhouetted against the quarter-moon darkness.

Left alone in the hut, Dan contemplates the unexpected twist of events. Gazing into the night, uncertainty looms ahead, but he is resolved to face whatever challenges come his way with determination and courage.

Chapter Fifteen

Months have passed since Dan embraced life in the bush, and now every rustle, creak, and shuffle in his surroundings carries meaning—the swaying of tree branches, the distant echoes of tin-roofed lean-tos, and the subtle scampering of rodents. As he cooks two mutton chops over the fire and boils potatoes in a billy can, he catches a faint sound, nearly imperceptible to urban ears. Dan recognizes these subtle signals and understands that the sheep's bleats carry a tale of trouble.

With swift precision, Dan retrieves the double-barreled flintlock shotgun hanging on the wall. He carefully cocks the hammer over one barrel, then cautiously cracks the door open, just a fraction. He mutters under his breath. *"Bloody dingoes having a go at the sheep again... DAMN!"*

Through the narrow opening, Dan's eyes pierce the quarter moon's darkness, catching sight of a person's shadow clutching a motionless sheep. Without hesitation, he wrenches the door open. "STOP! Drop that carcass and step away—or I'll Blast You To Pieces!"

Caught red-handed, the thief hesitates, torn between complying and escaping with his plunder. He faces Dan, teetering on the edge of the action. From in front of Dan comes the whizzing flight of a long spear, barely missing his ear as it slams into the hut's wall with a resonant *Thud* before skittering away. Acting swiftly, Dan dives, bracing himself for more incoming projectiles.

In the blink of an eye, Dan could have been impaled. Stunned but quick to react, he rises to one knee, his breath held, and pulls the trigger with a single resounding shot. A shriek of agony pierces the air as the thief drops the lifeless sheep and clutches his face. Spinning around, he staggers and collapses, the sheep's limp form beside him.

With the second barrel ready, Dan keeps his senses sharp, surveying the surroundings. Two shadowy figures vault over the sheep pen's hurdles and vanish into the concealing embrace of the bush.

Emerging from behind a gum tree near the pen, a tall and lean Blackfella steps forward. He hesitates momentarily, brandishing his empty woomera (spear-thrower) menacingly over his head as if testing whether Dan would follow through on his threat. Eventually, he approaches the fallen thief, discarding the sheep's body. Kneeling beside the figure, he hoists the limp body onto his shoulder, glancing back at Dan one last time before disappearing into the enigmatic depths of the wilderness.

Dan remains standing, heart pounding and adrenaline coursing through his veins, grateful for his quick reflexes protecting the sheep and himself. The night reclaims its silence, yet Dan is acutely aware that danger might still lurk beyond the shadows in the unforgiving Australian outback.

Seated at her writing desk, bathed in the gentle glow of a kerosene lantern, Alice pens a letter to Dan, pouring her emotions onto the parchment.

Dearest Dan,

I have forgiven Father for how he treated me on the day of your injury. I realize I provoked him with my defiance and insolence. However, I will never absolve him for what he allowed to happen to you through Bruiser Conroy.

I am relieved to hear about your employment as a shepherd near Buninyong Village. Knowing that my financial assistance is no longer necessary brings me solace.

I am resolved to join you soon and be wed as planned. Though I respect your wish to wait until the following year, allowing you time to save for our cottage, I am eager to begin our life together.

I have diligently saved my weekly allowance and deposited it in my "Port Phillip Savings Bank" account. This fund will aid me in reuniting with you next year. I eagerly await the day when we will be together again. Stay steadfast, my love.

Yours most affectionately, ***Alice****.*

With the heartfelt letter complete, Alice makes her way down the homestead's corridor, clutching the paper tightly in her hand, her heart brimming with hope and longing. As she approaches the front door, ready to post the letter to Dan, her mother calls out from the living room. Alice pauses at the threshold, turning to face her mother, Elizabeth.

Concern laces Elizabeth's words. "Alice, my dear, please visit Dr Evans when you're out posting your letter. Your health worries me; you look pale and fatigued. It's concerning, given your previous robustness. I believe the good doctor can provide a remedy to alleviate your condition."

Alice responds with gentleness and understanding. "Of course, Mother. I'll consult Dr Evans to allay your concerns. I believe my discomfort stems from the new cook and the changes in our diet. Her culinary offerings have hardly been nutritious."

With her mother's concern acknowledged, Alice continues her mission, stepping through the doorway, heading to the post office with her letter, and seeking the doctor's counsel. Her determination to be with Dan and her unwavering love for him remains unshaken as she confronts the challenges ahead.

Chapter Sixteen

Within the confines of Dr Evens' meticulously organized surgery room, Alice sits, her gaze fixed on a distant point as the doctor listens attentively to her chest through the stethoscope. The room is tidy, with an array of medical instruments and bottles of medications neatly arranged on shelves. Sunlight streams in through the curtains, enveloping the space in a warm embrace.

With a gentle touch, Dr Evens removes the stethoscope from Alice's chest. "Well, Alice, physically, there seems to be no evident cause for your fatigue. I'm inclined to prepare a remedy—a tincture with a touch of Cocaine, to restore your vitality and address your ailment. Your anxiety over the Dan Farley situation might be playing a role."

Alice takes a deep breath, her emotions a blend of relief and apprehension at the doctor's assessment. "Dr Evens, I appreciate your attention. My mother is deeply concerned. As for my symptoms, I've been experiencing mild nausea in the mornings and afternoon lethargy. Additionally, my monthly flow has ceased recently."

A hint of surprise flickers in Dr Evens' eyes before his professional demeanour reassumes control.

"How long has it been since your last cycle?"

"Over two months, Doctor."

A contemplative pause ensues as Dr Evens processes the information. "I must say, Alice, I didn't expect this. You, a young lady of your upbringing. Have you been intimate with a man before your cycles stopped? Do you grasp the implications?"

Alice's response is a mixture of embarrassment and candidness. "Yes, Doctor."

"Was it that rascal, Dan Farley?"

Alice admits with a soft voice. "Yes."

A momentary silence follows, then Alice adds, exposing her naivety on such matters. "I believed it would take multiple encounters for such a thing to occur." Her vulnerability becomes evident as she raises a lace handkerchief to her eyes. "I'm quite ignorant in these matters, Doctor. I never suspected a connection to my monthly flows. I'm frightened now and uncertain about what to do."

Alice's admission seeks both reassurance and guidance from the experienced physician. Dr Evens looks at her with sympathy, well aware of the gravity of the situation. He speaks gently, blending urgency with compassion. "I need to conduct an examination using 'Chadwick's Sign' to confirm matters. The sooner, the better."

Alice nods, her face mirroring anxiety and hope as she prepares for the examination, placing her trust in the doctor's expertise to guide her through this uncertain journey.

Lying on the examination table, covered by a pristine white sheet, Alice waits. Dr Evens stands nearby, expressing concern and empathy, poised to deliver the examination's outcome with care. "Alice, there's no denying it—you're pregnant."

The weight of the revelation settles over her, and Alice sits up, tears brimming in her eyes. She reaches for the edge of the sheet, using it to wipe away her tears.

"You should have considered this before giving in to your desires, Alice," Dr Evens continues, his tone a delicate balance of advice and understanding. "Your choices now include carrying the child to term or terminating the pregnancy before the quickening—before sixteen weeks. There are legal options for termination with parental consent."

Emotions surge within Alice, and she shakes her head, her voice trembling. "No, Doctor... I could never contemplate that. Please, don't reveal this to Father or Mother. I'll tell them when the time is right."

Understanding the gravity of Alice's decision and the delicate nature of her predicament, Dr Evens nods. "I'll keep your secret safe, Alice. But I must stress the importance of taking good care of yourself. The months ahead will require special attention and care."

Alice nods, her heart heavy with the weight of her choices. The realization of her situation, combined with the responsibilities it entails, fills her with a mix of fear and determination.

With resolve, she responds, gathering the strength to confront the challenges. "I will, Doctor. Thank you for your understanding."

Dr Evens places a reassuring hand on her shoulder. "I'll stand by you, offering support in any way I can. Remember, you can always seek my help or advice."

Armed with newfound support, Alice departs from Dr Evens' surgery, her mind a whirlwind of thoughts about her future and the decisions she must make. While she acknowledges the road ahead will be arduous, she is determined to face it with bravery and resilience.

Chapter Seventeen

Alice is seated inside the grand sitting room of the homestead, her gaze fixed on her crochet work, her mind undoubtedly lost in thoughts that weigh heavily upon her. On the other side of the room, Elizabeth, her mother, occupies a plush armchair, her hands deftly knitting, her eyes periodically lifting to watch Alice with a mixture of concern and suspicion. The tension within Alice becomes too much to bear, her emotions rising like a tidal wave.

Trembling hands lead Alice to drop her crochet onto her lap as she stands, driven by a force she cannot restrain. She crosses the room with hesitant steps, tears welling in her eyes. Her heart feels like a lead weight as she kneels before her mother, wrapping her arms around her mother's legs and resting her head on her mother's knees.

Tears stream down Alice's face as Elizabeth gently strokes her hair, aching to soothe her daughter's pain. "Stop, dear! What has provoked such tears? You've been engulfed in melancholy for weeks now. Surely, the matter with Dan Farley is behind you?"

Amidst tears, Alice confesses her truth, her voice cracking with raw emotion. "No, Mother... It's only just beginning. Dr Evens confirmed that I am carrying Dan's child!"

Elizabeth gasped, her hands flying to her mouth in shock. Rising from her chair, she pushes Alice aside as she paces the room, her mind racing with a torrent of thoughts. Her words escape in a murmur, the distress evident in her tone. "Good heavens... My Lord! What will become of Alice? What fate awaits, my dear girl?"

Alice gazes at her mother in fear, her heart breaking at the pain she's caused. Elizabeth begins to swoon and sinks back into her armchair. Desperate for help, Alice rushes to the doorway, calling for Cloherty, the trusted housekeeper, "Cloherty! Help me, please... Mother has taken ill!"

Cloherty hurries into the room, instantly attending to Elizabeth. She tries to revive her, gently patting her face to no avail. Quick-witted, Cloherty leaves the room and swiftly returns with a bottle of ammonia from the laundry. She holds it beneath Elizabeth's nose, and though she stirs, coughing and choking, she regains consciousness.

Alice, in her own distress, tries to comfort her mother. Her voice quivers yet holds determination as she turns to their servant. "Thank you, Cloherty. I can manage from here. I'll give Mother a tincture of laudanum to calm her nerves."

Cloherty exits, leaving Alice by her mother's side. With a heavy heart, Alice continues to provide care and support.

Elizabeth remains seated, holding Alice's hand while Alice sits beside her, seeking solace and reassurance. Elizabeth speaks, her voice laden with concern and empathy. "My poor girl, what a tangled web you've found yourself in. The scandal could tarnish your father's reputation within high society, jeopardizing his business endeavours."

Alice's voice trembles with regret as she responds. "I am truly sorry, Mother. My lapse in judgment was never intended."

Elizabeth acknowledges their roles as pillars of her husband's business and reveals the stakes of their positions in upholding his reputation. "We are the ones who lend an air of legitimacy to your father's endeavours. What is to be done now?"

Alice grasps the gravity of their situation and offers a suggestion. "We must keep it secret, Mother, sharing only with Dr Evens, who is bound by confidentiality."

Elizabeth recognizes their danger and the fallout if her husband were to uncover the truth. "We cannot tell your father. He would disown you, cast you out into the street."

Alice breaks down, tears flowing as she envisions losing her family. "I cannot bear the thought of losing my family, Mother."

Elizabeth attempts to console her daughter, a glimmer of hope in her voice. "There, there, my dear. We shall find a way. My distant cousin, Miss Creswick, resides in the Dandenong District. She visited you in Sydney once. She will surely offer shelter until after the child arrives. Then we shall determine our next steps."

Alice wipes her tears, finding comfort in her mother's words. She inquires of Elizabeth about what to tell her father, fearing his reaction. Elizabeth replies, "I will inform him that you will visit Miss Creswick for an extended respite to recover from your recent ailment. Father has distanced himself from you since the Dan Farley incident, and your absence will likely relieve him."

Taking a deep breath, Alice embraces her mother's plan, feeling secure in the way forward. "Thank you, Mother. Miss Creswick's home might be the sanctuary I need."

In this moment of shared understanding and unwavering determination, mother and daughter forge a bond of mutual support, facing an uncertain future with strength and resilience.

Chapter Eighteen

Beside Mr Rushton, Alice sits on a two-horse cart, the supplies they carry securely covered by a tarp. They journey through rolling green hills, the landscape painted with picturesque beauty. As they drew closer to a charming yellow wooden cottage, Alice's eyes widened with awe. The house stands proud and tall, its second story beneath an arched roof, adorned with a small balcony that overlooks the lush fields. Brick chimneys peek from behind the rooftop. A colonial English garden bursting with vibrant perennials embraces the cottage's front. A narrow gravel path guides the way to the front door.

Waiting before the cottage is Miss Creswick, a petite and radiant woman in her middle years. She waves enthusiastically as the cart nears, dressed in a pink Dowager dress and a lacey Poke bonnet. Alice and Mr Rushton disembark from the cart, and Alice finds herself momentarily stunned by the enchanting setting. They approach Miss Creswick, who welcomes them warmly with a radiant smile.

"Good day, Mr Rushton. Thank you for bringing my niece. Alice, my dear! It's delightful to see you. After your long journey, would you care for some refreshments, Mr Rushton?"

"Thank you kindly, Miss Creswick. I'm much obliged, but I have a quarter-mile drive to Dunn's Inn and another three-quarter of a mile to pioneer Joseph Hawdon's homestead to deliver their supplies. I'll find refreshments there."

"Always a pleasure to have you, Mr Rushton. I assure you that living in such an isolated place brings me joy. But I always relish a visitor or two. Thank you again."

Miss Creswick leads Alice inside, carrying her bags through the front door. Inside the cottage, Alice is charmed and slightly overwhelmed by her new surroundings. She smiled as she looked around, the house's beauty captivating her senses. Miss Creswick shows her to her room, and Alice takes in the cozy sanctuary that will be her refuge.

Colonial-style antique furniture, accompanied by delicate crystal glassware, elegant clocks, and porcelain figurines, graces the cottage. The walls are adorned with pink floral-patterned wallpaper, and sizable paintings depicting scenes from the English countryside and ships on tumultuous seas add sophistication.

"Thank you, Miss Creswick, for welcoming me into your cottage during this challenging period."

Miss Creswick smiles warmly and corrects her. "Call me 'Aunty,' dear. Since I last saw you as a young girl in Sydney Town, you've blossomed into a stunning young woman. It's truly wonderful to see you, such a vision of loveliness."

Alice blushes slightly, her response tinged with modesty. "Thank you, Aunty."

With an exuberant expression, Miss Creswick continues. "What a joy! I'm soon to become a great aunt, and you, my dear, are about to be a mother to a beautiful baby boy, judging by the shape of your bump. Your mother shared the circumstances of your situation. A new life is on the horizon... how splendid indeed!"

Miss Creswick gives Alice's arm a gentle squeeze, her smile brimming with warmth and excitement for the forthcoming arrival of the baby.

In a cozy parlour, Miss Creswick, a woman of elegant grace in her fifties, sits at a quaint wooden table, attentively caring for Alice, who sits across from her. The room emanates comfort, dressed in floral curtains and furnished with antique pieces. A pot of tea releases a gentle wisp of steam on the table, accompanied by a plate of biscuits. Miss Creswick pours a cup of tea for Alice, extending a biscuit with a warm smile.

Miss Creswick addresses Alice in a soothing tone filled with genuine concern. "Please, my dear Alice, allow me to care for all your needs. There's no need for you to worry about a thing. Simply relax and enjoy your tea."

Alice, ever considerate and eager to contribute, later attempts to rise and assist with household tasks. However, Miss Creswick motions for her to stay seated, a gentle admonition in her gesture. "No, no, my dear. You mustn't exert yourself. Let me tend to the chores. You now must rest and nurture the precious life growing within you."

With a hint of reluctance, Alice eases back into her seat, understanding that her well-being and the health of her unborn child must take precedence. She offers Miss Creswick a thankful smile, relieved to have found such a caring and empathetic refuge.

Miss Creswick takes up a broom, moving gracefully towards the entryway, sweeping away errant leaves and dirt. Alice watches her with admiration and gratitude, appreciating the reassuring presence of her newfound "Aunty" during this demanding juncture.

Chapter Nineteen

Alice and Miss Creswick embark on a leisurely stroll along the banks of the crystal-clear Dandenong Creek. The morning sun casts a glistening spell upon the water's surface, enveloping the surroundings in a tranquil and almost mystical aura. Miss Creswick's eyes gleam with enthusiasm as she directs Alice's attention toward the creek banks, her voice brimming with childlike excitement.

"Look, Alice! Those are the water burrows of the charming platypus. Watch how they dive and play in such a carefree manner. These creatures are truly remarkable."

Alice's gaze widens with wonder as she observes the playful platypus in its natural habitat. The enchanting sight infuses her heart with joy and awe, and a shared sense of wonderment sweeps over them. Their laughter harmoniously melds with the gentle melodies of nature.

Continuing their leisurely stroll, Alice and Miss Creswick meander through the expansive grounds surrounding the delightful cottage. The landscape unfolds like a haven for naturalists, bustling with vibrant and abundant birdlife. The air reverberates with the melodious songs of various birds, creating a symphony that wraps around them like a warm embrace.

In the distance, a graceful dingo slinks away, a kangaroo with a Joey on board observes them curiously, and a koala high in a tree indulges in its beloved eucalyptus leaves. As they pause to take in the awe-inspiring beauty surrounding them, Alice and Miss Creswick's faces light up with awe and admiration. The breathtaking scenery evokes a deep connection to the raw splendour of the Australian wilderness.

After their picturesque escapade, Alice and Miss Creswick return to the cottage and settle into the inviting sitting room. Bathed in the gentle sunlight that filters through delicate lace curtains, they engage in a heartfelt conversation, their voices carrying the weight of their emotions.

Alice confides in Miss Creswick, her eyes welling up with tears. "Aunt, I believe it's time to confront the truth and inform Dan that he's about to become a father."

Miss Creswick gently pats Alice's hand, offering a comforting touch. "My dear, men can be quite unpredictable in such situations. We must proceed cautiously. Dan's presence could complicate matters, especially as the delivery time draws near."

Alice nods, her voice tinged with longing. "But I miss him terribly and yearn for him to be by my side during this challenging period."

Miss Creswick imparts her wisdom. "Sometimes, distance can provide the necessary perspective for clarity and reflection. We must consider what is best for you and the baby."

Tears glisten in Alice's eyes, her determination unwavering. "You're right, Aunt. I'll embrace the waiting and postpone sharing the news until after the baby is born."

Miss Creswick smiles knowingly, acknowledging Alice's strength. "You're showing remarkable resilience and wisdom, my dear. Together, we will navigate this path."

"I am deeply grateful for your support, Aunt. It means the world to me."

Miss Creswick nods, her caring nature evident. "I've arranged for Mrs Hawdon's trustworthy and experienced maid to be present during the birth. You will be in capable hands, my dear."

"Thank you, Aunt. Your thoughtfulness knows no bounds."

Miss Creswick tenderly holds Alice's hand, their connection growing more robust in the face of adversity. "Our focus must be on your well-being and the baby's. Our love and support will guide us through these trying times."

In that tender moment, the bond between Miss Creswick and Alice deepens, offering solace and strength as they navigate the uncertain journey ahead.

The cottage's front door suddenly swings open, revealing Rosie, a cheerful and rosy-cheeked maid-servant in her forties. Donning a black dress and a pristine white pinafore, Rosie enters with a warm greeting.

"Good day to you, Miss Creswick, ma'am. Is this the expectant mother before me?" Curiosity fills Rosie's eyes with her gaze towards Alice.

"Yes, Rosie. Allow me to introduce you to Alice, my lovely niece." Miss Creswick gestures towards Alice, who offers a friendly smile, finding comfort in Rosie's presence.

"I'm pleased to meet you, Miss Alice. How far along are you, dear?"

Alice responds, a hint of nervousness in her voice but grateful for Rosie's attention. "Thirty-seven weeks, more or less."

"Well, well, Miss Alice! You should have called me out sooner. I'll need to examine you before the birth to ensure everything is well for the big day."

Miss Creswick reassures Rosie. "Fret not, Rosie. We would have summoned you earlier had there been any concerns. By the way, this little one is kicking; I suspect it will be a boy."

Amused by Miss Creswick's prediction, Rosie chuckles. "We'll see about that, won't we? Since I'm a fair distance away, I'll make it a point to visit every few days leading up to the delivery, just in case the little one decides to arrive ahead of schedule."

With a caring touch and experienced expertise, Rosie places her ear on Alice's stomach, gently massaging it and listening attentively for any signs of the baby's movements. Excitement fills the room as they prepare for the arrival of the new life that will soon grace the cottage with joy.

Chapter Twenty

Alice's anxious pacing persists within the confines of the cottage's parlour, her breaths emerging in strained gasps, clearly indicating her distress. Every movement she makes is tinged with a sense of urgency. Standing by, Miss Creswick's eyes widen with deep concern, meticulously observing every nuance of Alice's demeanour. A suggestion escapes Miss Creswick's lips, her voice a mixture of worry and the situation's urgency.

"Rosie mentioned that the baby's due early next week, my dear. We should monitor the contractions closely, shouldn't we?"

Alice struggles to form coherent sentences, the contractions taking a more forceful hold over her body. Words emerge in fragments amidst the waves of discomfort. "The contractions... closer... every five minutes... lasting over a minute. We might have to handle the delivery ourselves, Aunt. The thought... overwhelming."

Miss Creswick's anxiety escalates, and she bursts out with heightened alarm. "We need help! I must fetch Rosie. I have no experience in such matters. I'll ride to Hawdon Station immediately!"

Driven by panic, Miss Creswick rushes toward the front door, which abruptly slams shut behind her. Desperation colours Alice's voice as she cries out, a blend of fear and urgency underlining her words.

"Aunt, no! I can't handle the delivery alone. You don't have transportation! Please, come back!"

Through the parlour window, Alice witnesses the sight of Miss Creswick pedalling relentlessly on a hobby horse (a two-wheeler bike), the moonlight casting an ethereal glow upon her figure as she speeds toward Hawdon Station.

A mixture of fear and resolve envelops Alice as she begins to whimper, her pacing morphing into a frantic dance of self-soothing. "It will be alright... Everything will work out fine!"

In a sudden surge of intensity, Alice's water breaks, prompting her to waddle away, leaving a messy trail on the floor. Clutching her abdomen and lower back in agonizing pain, she collapses onto the rugged parlour floor, her strength ebbing away. Rapid pants and shallow breaths mirror her escalating distress.

Then, the distant rumble of a buggy draws closer, Rosie and Miss Creswick rapidly approaching. Bursting into the cottage, their arrival infuses the room with much-needed relief. Though weakened, Alice raises her arm weakly in acknowledgment of their presence.

Witnessing Alice's prone form on the floor, Rosie and Miss Creswick are taken aback, their worry growing palpable. Rosie, her experience lending her a sense of purpose, urgently exclaims, "Miss Creswick, quickly! We need hot water and plenty of clean towels!"

With swift determination, Miss Creswick springs into action, hurrying to retrieve the necessary supplies. In the meantime, Rosie attends to Alice with a blend of authority and empathy.

"Push, my dear... like a bowel movement. Tuck your chin down. Give it everything you have. Stay focused. You're doing wonderfully. Rest between contractions. It won't be long now. Trust your instincts; the progress is as it should be."

In a race against time, Miss Creswick returns with the hot water and towels, her eyes a mixture of relief and lingering anxiety. On Alice's final push, Rosie catches the baby, and amidst a symphony of emotions, the room reverberates with the infant's first cries.

Overwhelmed and near-exhaustion, Miss Creswick collapses into an armchair, fanning herself with breathless fatigue and relief as if she had undergone the labour herself.

With tender care, Rosie lays the baby—a boy adorned with a crown of hair—upon Alice's chest, swathed in a snug, warm blanket. Looking at her child, Alice's eyes reflect a blend of exhaustion and an overwhelming surge of love. A sense of profound significance colours the atmosphere as Alice articulates her sentiments.

"Aunt! In Dan's absence, I shall name him Levi. I believe Dan would approve. The name signifies 'Joined in Harmony,' a reflection of my feelings toward Dan, our child, and the unity of our future."

An unspoken understanding passes between Rosie and Miss Creswick as they exchange a warm, knowing smile, comprehending the depth of meaning encapsulated within the chosen name and the beauty of the transformative moment they have just borne witness to.

Chapter Twenty-one

The bunkhouse at Ercildoune Station stands as a vast tin shed, its interior lined with orderly rows of beds along the walls. Within this humble abode, Dan now occupies one of these beds, a smile of elation dancing upon his lips as he pores over a letter. Nearby, a seasoned station hand sits engrossed in whittling a piece of wood, his pocket knife moving with the finesse of a practised hand.

A surge of excitement propels Dan's words, carrying his jubilant news to the attentive air. "Can you fathom it? I'm a father now! Alice has brought our child into the world—a son named Levi—a name that encapsulates the harmony of our shared history and the life we're destined to forge together."

The whittling hand stills in response to Dan's announcement, replaced by a nod of congratulations. "Well done, Farley! Seems like your carpentry skills have also extended into the realm of plumbing."

The weight of Dan's news settles within his chest, bringing forth a sigh of contentment. "I'm relieved to hear that Alice and Levi are healthy. Levi is a name of profound beauty and significance. I intend to pen a heartfelt letter to Alice, expressing my overwhelming joy at embracing fatherhood. She has found sanctuary under the wing of her aunt, Miss Creswick, safeguarded from her father's control."

Practical wisdom filters into the conversation, imparted by the seasoned hand. "You'll want to consider announcing your marriage sooner rather than later. Levi shouldn't carry the stigma of being labelled a child born out of wedlock."

Dan's affirmation is tinged with a resolve rooted in foresight. "You're right, of course. Yet, I can't hastily depart for Melbourne. My commitments here at Ercildoune Station and the Learmonth Brothers' contract are threads that weave my future. Especially now, in these uncertain times, maintaining my standing is paramount."

The station hand's faith in Dan's prospects gleams in his eyes. "Brody holds you in high regard. Keep your partnership strong, and you'll find consistent work from here to Geelong."

Dan's conviction echoes through his words, deeply rooted in the foundation of his newfound family. "Alice and Levi shall relocate to Geelong—a realm far from her father's reach. Although Buninyong Village is nearer to my place of work, it's not an ideal environment in which to raise a child. Alice's return to Melbourne would risk Jack Riley's discovery of our situation."

The utterance of Jack Riley's name injects a palpable weight of caution into the air. "This Jack Riley fella sounds treacherous enough. Considering what he did to your thumb, I'd prefer not to cross paths with him, especially in the shadows."

A solemn expression darkens Dan's features, acknowledging the lurking dangers. "He's not one to hesitate in disowning Alice or seeking retribution against both of us. Only time will reveal the bounds of his vendetta."

Within the rustic bunkhouse walls, their dialogue resonates with significance, mirroring personal stakes and the broader challenges that life in an unforgiving world imposes.

Dressed in sturdy moleskin attire, Dan stands in the company of a six-man workforce at the station. Despite the absence of his right thumb, his countenance radiates determination and resilience. Dan actively assists the shearers during the shearing time, his movements precise and graceful. He maneuvers sheep into position with a fluidity that eases the process, his ambidextrous finesse proving invaluable as he orchestrates their wool removal. His fellow workers regard him with nods of admiration, acknowledging his prowess.

Dan's profound affinity with the animals is fully displayed in tending to the horses. He grooms and feeds them with adept hands, his mastery evident as he manages their reins and saddles. The horses respond to his gentle touch, underscoring the bond he has nurtured despite his physical impediment.

Undaunted, Dan scales ladders and scaffolding, fearlessly embracing building maintenance tasks. His grip is sure, his balance unshaken. Faced with a missing thumb, he devises innovative solutions, adapting seamlessly to overcome any obstacle. His peers witness his resourcefulness and stand inspired by his unwavering dedication.

The montage artfully captures Dan's resilience and tenacity, showcasing his ability to shine across diverse tasks despite his physical setback. Each scene paints a vivid picture of his unyielding spirit, proving that even in the face of adversity, a missing thumb cannot deter him from contributing and achieving.

At night, the bunkhouse pulses with vibrant energy, its walls echoing with the jubilant mirth of the hired hands. Laughter dances through the air, intertwined with animated conversations and the lilting melodies of lively Irish jigs. An adept station hand adds to the song, his skilful violin weaving a musical tapestry enveloping the room. Amid this jovial symphony, the station manager, Bill Brody, relishes a tin mug filled with the warmth of rum.

In a pause within the revelry, Brody and Dan slip away from the heart of the festivity, seeking the solace of the outdoors. The exterior wall becomes their refuge as they lean against it, tendrils of smoke curling into the air as they indulge in their cherished vice. Their unburdened and sincere conversation flows like a river that knows no constraint.

Dan takes a contemplative drag on his clay pipe, his eyes momentarily lost in thought. "Bill, all these years living alone in your Manager's house... Did you ever have a marriage of your own?"

Brody's features soften into a wistful smile, his gaze distant yet tender. "Yes, Dan. Once upon a time, I did. My wife was a vision, a beauty that could rival the stars. But the cruel grip of tuberculosis claimed her life within a year of our arrival here. We clung to dreams, only for life to carve its own path."

A profound understanding graces Dan's expression as he listens to Brody's tale. "Your companionship, Bill, has been more than just camaraderie. Between your irreverent antics and the depths of our late-night conversations, I've felt a resurgence of the old 'Dapper Dan'. Our bond, it's like that of mates—forged in the crucible of the bush, cemented by shared moments and confidences."

Brody's nod is accompanied by a knowing smile. "More than mates, Dan. We've peeled away the layers that often guard us, discovering that our backgrounds fit together like puzzle pieces. True mates, like brothers."

Dan's grin mirrors Brody's sentiment. "Alice and I are arranging our wedding. Given the circumstances, it'll be a modest affair, a civil union."

A surge of warmth lights up Brody's expression. "A civil wedding, officiated by a Justice of the Peace. And if you're asking, Dan, I'd be honoured to stand beside you as your best man." The flicker in Bill's eyes is a dance of eagerness, mingling with a trace of playful anticipation.

Dan's affirmation carries an infectious enthusiasm. "Absolutely, Mate!"

Brody's laughter rings out, a testament to his joy in their camaraderie. "Then it's settled! Your wedding is an event I wouldn't miss, not for all the liquor in Jamaica. And that's saying something, given my soft spot for rum."

With a camaraderie that transcends words, Brody playfully delivers a couple of affectionate jabs to Dan's midsection. These light punches are not just physical gestures but symbols of the profound bond that holds them together, weaving their shared history into the fabric of their interactions.

Chapter Twenty-Two

Within the intimate haven of their home's cozy sitting room, Alice and her mother, Elizabeth, find themselves enshrouded in an air of secrecy and watchfulness. Nestled in Elizabeth's arms rests her infant grandson, Levi, whose cherubic features testify to new life and boundless possibilities. Elizabeth's gaze, aglow with radiant adoration, is fixed on the tiny wonder before her.

Clad in a cloak of modesty, Alice wears a simple dress, her attire completed by a dowdy Poke Bonnet perched atop her head—a veiled guardian of her identity when she ventured into Melbourne Town.

A teardrop glistens like a dew-kissed petal in Elizabeth's eye, a crystalline reflection of emotions too profound for words. Her voice, laden with years of experience and a mother's depth of feeling, resonates with gentle gravity. "To see you here, my dear, and to hold my first grandchild—a boy, no less—fills my heart with joy beyond measure."

Alice's reply bears a hint of vulnerability, a shadow amidst the glow. "Father would hardly share the same sentiment if he were to uncover the truth. As I journeyed into town with Hawdon's manservant, this unassuming attire was my guise."

Tender and steady, Elizabeth's voice seeks to quell the ripples of concern that lap at the shore of their conversation. "You need not carry the weight of your father's presence on your shoulders. His time is more often spent at the Highlander Hotel, ensnared in the arms of his paramour, Charlotte, than within the walls of our home."

A sombre note colours Alice's tone as she unburdens herself. "I bear a burden of blame, Mother. It seems that everything has unravelled due to my choices."

Elizabeth's voice carries a sage assurance, her words from the tapestry of life's inevitabilities. "My dear, the currents would flow this way regardless of your actions. It was a path we were inexorably set upon."

Amid the quiet communion, Alice's voice takes on a contemplative cadence as she shares her concerns. "How shall you explain my absence to Father now that I embark for Geelong, where I must await the six months until Dan and I can be wed?"

Elizabeth unveils a strategy that melds necessity with compassion. "I shall inform him that you have undertaken the role of devoted nurse to my cousin, Miss Creswick. She has fallen ill, and your care is indispensable until a professional nurse can relieve you."

Alice's gaze, brimming with gratitude, reflects the depth of her appreciation. "Mother, your ingenuity knows no bounds. Mary Hobson has extended her kindness, offering overnight accommodations for Levi and me. She has also equipped me with a letter of reference and an introduction to a lodgings provider upon my arrival in Geelong."

The narrow gravelled street of High Street in Geelong Township reverberates with the soft clip-clop of hooves, marking the arrival of a lone horse-drawn cab. Stepping out from its snug embrace, Alice's eyes sparkle with curiosity and anticipation as they take in the scene before her. An enchanting two-story building stands before her, its rustic charm emanating from every nook and cranny. Unpainted timber palings lend the facade a quaint appeal, while flower boxes brimming with vibrant perennial blooms adorn the windows, a riot of colours against the day's backdrop. The air carries the delicate fragrance of flowers, a welcoming embrace.

Alice's gaze is drawn upward, where a notice board proclaims its message in bold lettering: "MR AND MRS CRANBERRY'S LODGING HOUSE - LODGERS TWO SHILLINGS PER WEEK - MEALS FROM SIXPENCE." The words are a beckoning call, an invitation to a new chapter, a place of refuge and new beginnings. Alice stands on the cobbled path, her heart a blend of nervous excitement and eager anticipation—this, she knows, is where her journey truly begins.

With a composed breath, she approaches the lodging house's entrance, knuckles rapping gently on the wooden door. It swings open, revealing a figure that radiates warmth and hospitality. Mrs Cranberry, a woman of petite stature, stands before her with rosy cheeks and a perpetual smile that lends a glow to her features. Her mousy brown hair is neatly secured in a bun, while a colourful apron, a testament to her domestic competence, almost sweeps the floor in graceful folds.

Mrs Cranberry's smile widens, lit by a delighted spark. "Well, hello there, dear! And what a sweet little one you have. Such a precious angel, indeed. I'm guessing you're in search of lodgings, my dear. Leave your trunk right there; Mr Cranberry will consider bringing it up for you."

Alice's heart skips a beat as she hands over the letter provided by Mary Hobson, which holds the promise of welcome and acceptance. The letter is accepted with curiosity and eagerness, Mrs Cranberry's fingertips gently tracing the inked lines. "Alice, allow me to introduce you to Mr Cranberry."

From the street behind her, Mr Cranberry emerges, a figure whose tall and lean presence casts a gentle shadow over the scene. "George... say hello to Alice and Levi here, and lend a hand with their trunk to room number three."

As Mrs Cranberry's attention returns to the letter, George steps forward, a silent pillar of strength and a reassuring presence. He extends his greetings, his eyes warm as they rest on Levi. "Hello there... and you, little one."

Levi's laughter tinkles like a chime; his delight is infectious as George playfully tickles him under the chin. Alice joins in, her voice blending with the exchange—a simple act, yet it bridges the gap, connecting them in this moment. Her amazement lingers, observing the stark contrast in size between the petite Mrs Cranberry and the towering George. It's a visual representation of the diverse paths that have converged at this juncture, a reminder that every journey has a unique trajectory.

As the door closed behind them, sealing the moment in memory, Alice's journey has led her to this very doorstep, and with George's assistance, her belongings cross the threshold, a symbolic initiation into a new chapter that awaits within the walls of Mr and Mrs Cranberry's lodging house.

Chapter Twenty-Three

Within the heart of Mr and Mrs Cranberry's welcoming lodging house, a haven of serenity unfolds, eagerly awaiting the arrival of Alice and her precious charge, Levi. The space exudes coziness, with its whitewashed walls basking in the gentle touch of sunlight filtering through a modest window.

Standing alongside Alice are Mr and Mrs Cranberry, a pair whose warmth and compassion envelop them like a comforting embrace. Their presence serves as a soothing reminder of the comfort this sanctuary offers.

A tall boy cabinet stands in one corner, a sentinel of storage gleaming under daylight's affection. Nearby, a small yet inviting bed adorned with linens that whisper of comfort and rest beckons. A table and chair beneath a delicate floral curtain invite quiet reflection.

Mrs Cranberry's heart is as golden as her demeanour shares in Alice's joy as they survey the room, her husband Mr Cranberry's tall and reassuring presence complementing her grace. Mrs Cranberry inquires about the room's suitability, her voice a caring melody. "I hope the room suits you, dear. While we lack a cot, I believe the baby's size will allow him to slumber comfortably at your side."

Alice's eyes sparkle with gratitude, her heart touched by the thoughtful preparations. "Everything is simply perfect, Mrs Cranberry. My heartfelt thanks."

Mrs Cranberry's response carries the weight of her genuine kindness, reflecting her deep understanding. In this room, walls bear witness to past and present narratives, becoming a canvas for the tapestry of life itself. "Will you be dining with us or seeking your meals elsewhere?"

Alice briefly contemplates the question, her thoughts fluttering to the community that has extended its arms to her and Levi. "We would be most pleased to join you for meals, Mrs Cranberry."

A nod from George—a figure of strength and courtesy—signals his departure from the room. Mrs Cranberry's smile is a pledge of shared moments and nourishment—both for the body and the soul. The room seems to exhale contentedly, welcoming its new inhabitants into its embrace.

Alice and Levi are left alone in this newfound sanctuary as the door softly closes. The room enfolds them with each passing second, its walls whispering stories of lives in its haven. As they settle into their temporary abode, the spirit of the lodging house wraps around them, a gentle embrace murmuring tales of comfort, connection, and the promise of brighter tomorrows.

Later that afternoon, Alice walks with purpose along High Street in Geelong Village, her steps measured and steady, Levi cradled in her arms. The bustling street paints a lively tapestry—merchants peddling their wares, townsfolk engaged in their daily routines. Alice's vibrant eyes capture the kaleidoscope of sights and sounds that dance through the air.

She pauses at a market stall, her fingers lightly brushing against the fresh produce. She selects the finest fruits and vegetables, promising nourishing meals during their stay at the lodging house.

Carrying Levi, she continues her stroll along the waterfront. The sea breeze has the tang of salt and adventure, ships gliding in and out of the harbour. Their unfurled sails against the cerulean sky embody freedom and exploration.

Alice's fingers graze over fabrics and materials in a local shop, each touching a silent conversation. She envisions the garments she will craft with care for Levi—a testament to her determination to provide him with a future of love and security.

Within the snug embrace of a small bookstore, her gaze sweeps over the shelves, each book a portal to another world. With carefully chosen selections cradled to her chest, she anticipates the solace and escapes these pages will offer in the coming days and nights.

These scenes paint Alice as a woman of resolve and resourcefulness. Geelong is more than a village—it is a canvas for her dreams, a terrain she navigates with unwavering strength. Each vignette captures her determination to create a haven for herself and Levi, a sanctuary built upon her courage and the promise of better days.

In the afternoon's later hours, Levi cradled in her arms, Alice follows the welcoming lead of Mrs Cranberry into a small yet inviting room. Soft sunlight streams through delicate lace curtains, caressing the modest furnishings that grace the space.

Mrs Cranberry's voice, warm as a hearth, fills the room with a sense of homecoming. "Allow me to introduce you to our cherished house guests."

Alice, composed and poised, offers a gracious curtsy, acknowledging those gathered.

Mrs Cranberry's words weave introductions like an artist with a brush. "May I present to you, Mr Jasper, a dedicated dockworker of Corio Bay?"

The scene unfolds like an elegant dance, exchanging courtesies in the afternoon's glow. "And here we have the esteemed Miss Staples, whose talents are interwoven into James Ford Strachan's merchant empire."

Each introduction adds another layer to Alice's emerging world. "Mr Wardle, a clerk at Harwood Andrews, a renowned law firm."

Their names become threads in Alice's narrative, connections forming like fate's brushstrokes. "Lastly, Mr Rubbles, a sage presence among us, a widower whose wisdom enriches our tapestry."

The circle is complete; Alice's presence is acknowledged, her trepidation melting into a warm embrace of welcoming voices.

Alice responds with grace. "I am humbled to stand among you. This is Levi, a blessing in my arms. May his presence bring joy to our shared abode?"

The affirmation flows like a gentle river; murmured assurances envelop Levi like a comforting cocoon. Mrs Cranberry's face blooms with a joyful smile. "Alice has shared with me her musical talent. She studied music as part of her training in Sydney. She has offered to grace us with her piano playing, performing recitals from memory."

Mr Wardle's excitement is palpable. "Excellent! Bravo, Alice!"

With seamless grace, Mr Cranberry takes Levi into his arms. Alice, guided by purpose, approaches the piano. Her fingers, both gentle and determined, alight upon the keys, evoking the hauntingly beautiful strains of Beethoven's "Moonlight Sonata."

In that suspended moment, the room transcends time—a tapestry of notes and emotions woven into a melody that touches hearts and captivates souls. Joy, as radiant as the sun's rays, bathes each face, casting aside cares in favour of shared enchantment. It's a tapestry woven from the threads of chance and choice, each strand interlacing with another to craft a narrative that will shape the days ahead.

Chapter Twenty-Four

A timeless allure breathes life into the dining room in the heart of Mr and Mrs Cranberry's resplendent lodging house. Vintage treasures grace its walls, and scarlet floral-designed wallpaper wraps the space in a vivid tapestry of colours. A grand vintage dining table, polished to a reflective sheen, takes pride of place, illuminated by the soft glow of a central kerosene lamp. Around it, eight elegant chairs stand as witnesses to countless shared moments. Cabinets along the walls hold treasures—plates, dishes, cups, and saucers—each with its own story.

Amid this scene, Alice, adorned in a modest apron, moves with a natural grace, falling into a familiar rhythm. By her side, Mrs Cranberry orchestrates a table-setting ballet, their movements a testament to a bond that transcends words.

"Your care, Mrs Cranberry, knows no bounds," Alice's words are imbued with gratitude, reverberating throughout the room.

Mrs Cranberry's smile radiates warmth, a confirmation of their unspoken connection. "Alice, dear, you're like family. The bonds of the heart require no shared blood to be strong."

Alice's gaze softened as the room seemed to hold its breath, and her voice took on a sincere tone. "There is a truth I must reveal, Mrs Cranberry. The narrative I've spun about widowhood and a second marriage—it's woven with half-truths."

A moment of stillness hangs in the air as Mrs Cranberry places a gentle hand on Alice's arm—a gesture of silent understanding. "My dear, you needn't expose your soul unless ready. Within these walls, you are embraced for who you are."

Alice's eyes shimmer with unshed tears, her vulnerability laid bare. "I feel compelled to unburden my heart. My path has been stumbling, and I carry the weight of my past. I await the day when the father of my child can be my husband—a chance at redemption."

The words tremble on her lips, the room enveloped in hushed anticipation.

"Dear Alice," Mrs Cranberry's voice is a wellspring of compassion, "judgment finds no refuge within these walls. We offer refuge and acceptance, and your love for your child radiates strength."

Alice's voice wavers, the air heavy with uncertainty. "Thank you, Mrs Cranberry, for your kindness."

"In this home," Mrs Cranberry's gaze is unwavering, "Mr Cranberry and I find solace in our faith and shared convictions. Your worth remains untarnished by circumstance."

A different truth awaits its revelation, and Alice summons the courage to lay it bare. "There is more, Mrs Cranberry. My savings dwindle, and my mother's modest allowance hardly sustains us. I intend to teach piano to students within these walls. Would such an endeavour be met with approval?"

Mrs Cranberry's response is swift and encouraging. "Absolutely, dear. James Harrison, whose voice resonates through The 'Geelong Advertiser,' will undoubtedly announce your venture to the village. Our home will soon reverberate with the notes of culture."

The room, steeped in a tapestry of shared stories, becomes a witness to moments spun with care. Here, acceptance and support create a symphony, and Alice's journey is at the centre of a community built on empathy.

In the cocoon of night's quietude, a dream unfurls, painting the canvas of Alice's mind with vibrant shades of another reality. The Cranberry's sitting room transforms into a wedding haven, transcending its everyday purpose. *Elegance permeates the air, and the space seems to hold its breath in anticipation: Dan and Bill Brody stand at the front, immaculately attired, embodying the moment's gravity.*

Before them, Mr Bigot, a 'Justice of The Peace', assumes the role of officiant, an authoritative figure in this transformative scene. Miss Staples' nimble fingers dance across piano keys, coaxing the "Bridal March" into life—a melody that weaves through the air like a thread of destiny. Mr Jasper and Mr Rubbles, united by pride, bear witness to the union with knowing smiles.

Then, as if crescendoing in a symphony, the door opens, and Alice steps forward. She glides along, linked arm-in-arm with Mr Wardle, a paternal presence that offers solace. Cloaked in ethereal beauty, Alice wears a white wedding gown inspired by the iconic style of Queen Victoria.

As Dan and Brody behold her, their expressions reflect the moment's awe. Brody's smile radiates like sunlight, a beacon of joy, while Dan's eyes widen in silent reverence. The scene fades, leaving a trace of magic—a dream that transcends slumber, settling into the chambers of Alice's heart.

But even as her dream embraces her, the reality remains steadfast. Alice's sleep is restless, her movements agitated as she navigates the landscape of her subconscious. In the night's quiet cocoon, her mind grapples with the weight of the dream, dissecting its significance thread by thread.

The room, veiled in shadows, bathes in the pale moonlight, casting delicate patterns upon the walls. Across Alice's features play a symphony of emotions—longing and uncertainty waltz upon her visage. Her fingers trace the contours of her own heart, torn between the allure of her dream and the tensions of wakefulness.

As the scene fades, like a curtain drawing to a close, Alice remains suspended between two worlds—dream and reality. Her heart, a vessel for hope and trepidation, beats in rhythm with the infinite possibilities that stretch before her.

Chapter Twenty-Five

Dan and Brody executed their dismount with the practised grace of those accustomed to equestrian pursuits, drawing their horses to a halt before the bustling 'Fyans Street Inn'. The lively pulse of Geelong's central artery permeates the air, infusing it with the very essence of vitality. Standing resolute in its architectural splendour, the inn is a gem of English Tudor design—a façade that speaks eloquently of the craftsman's art.

Their steeds are secured to a robust hitching post, the leather reins looped securely. A moment's pause—a heartbeat's breath—allows them to absorb the unfolding panorama. In Dan's expression, there's a dance of eagerness and the thrill of anticipation, a boyish excitement that radiates from his eyes. In contrast, Brody exudes a measured practicality, a cautiousness that informs his demeanour.

Dan's lips curl into a mischievous grin as he quips, "Bill, my friend, our journey has reached its destination. Behold Fyans Inn, or as the locals affectionately dub it, the 'Adam and Eve.' This shall serve as our sanctuary as the overture to the wedding celebrations is played."

His gaze sweeps across the bustling thoroughfare, drawn inexorably toward the Cranberry's Boarding House—an establishment that shelters Alice and Levi.

" And there, Bill stands the Cranberry's Boarding House—a haven that cradles Alice before we venture beyond the wedding into the heart of Buninyong Village."

Their exchange is steeped in the lighthearted camaraderie of faithful companions. "Steady on, Dan. Recall your self-imposed vow—no glimpse of Alice until tomorrow's nuptials."

Dan responds with a smirking nod, acknowledging the challenge he's set for himself. "True, but a fleeting, stolen glance from a distance—what harm could that do? My yearning for Alice's presence is undeniable. To capture even a fragment of her silhouette would ground me, a reminder of the impending reality."

A thread of jest weaves into their rapport, a testament to their shared history. With a tone of sympathy, Brody adds, "Perhaps a stolen glimpse can be excused. After all, as your unwavering Best Man, it's my solemn duty to provide my seal of approval. We can't have you, dear friend, marrying the first lass who caught your eye without my esteemed endorsement."

A chuckle escapes Dan's lips, acknowledging the unique bond they share. "Your friendship, Bill, is my compass. And what better vantage point than this inn's haven? A calculated perch, with the boarding house a mere stone's throw away—almost as if the fates required a gentle reminder."

They attend to their saddlebags, relieving their steeds of their burden, before making their way toward the entrance of Fyans Inn.

Dan hesitates momentarily as they stand before the inn's inviting entrance. "Shall we step inside and uncover the mysteries this establishment holds? But, Bill, a word to the wise—subtlety is key. We wouldn't want to raise Alice's suspicions."

Brody's nod is solemn and steadfast. "Indeed, Dan. Subtlety shall guide our way."

Determinedly, they cross the threshold, poised to embark on a clandestine expedition—a journey fueled by the crescendo of anticipation heralding the imminent wedding day.

The following day dawns, and Alice emerges from the embrace of the boarding house. She exudes grace, a pram with three wheels gliding smoothly before her. An umbrella holder adds a touch of sophistication to the scene. Her parasol, an emblem of poise, shelters her delicate complexion from the sun's embrace. Each step she takes is a symphony of confidence and refinement, a testament to her innate elegance.

Dan and Brody stand inside the inn as sentinels, gazes riveted to Alice's presence beyond the window pane. For Dan, surprise mingles with a poignant ache of yearning—a potent concoction that flushes his features. His heart gallops like an unbridled steed, urging him to charge forth and confront the vision that captivates him. Beside him, Brody is an anchor, his grip on Dan's arm a steadfast barrier against impulsive action.

"Easy there, old friend. Keep your wits about you. If that fair maiden is your intended, consider yourself touched by fortune. How you managed to secure her heart remains a mystery. And remember, when you marry a woman, it's not only her affection you secure... her dowry also finds its place in the union."

Dan inhales deeply, a deliberate effort to rein in his unbridled emotions. "Can you believe it, Bill? Back in Melbourne Town, they christened me 'Dapper Dan,' the charmer, the suave one. Would you believe I was a man of swagger before Bruiser Conroy's knife had its way? Once upon a time, I was complete." His hand lifts, the absence of his thumb a sombre relic of past struggles.

"Dear Dan, before you assume the mantle of fatherhood and bid farewell to bachelorhood, a proper celebration is in order. We must raise our glasses to your impending vows and young Levi's arrival."

With a camaraderie that only comes from months of shared experience, Brody raises his glass, inviting Dan to join in the time-honoured ritual. "To the days ahead, Dan—to the journey that awaits!"

Dan's glass lifts in unison, the tinkling of crystal against crystal marking a moment of shared celebration. "Indeed, Bill... Here's to that! Cheers!"

As their glasses clink, the harmonious chime encapsulates a moment of kinship, an ode to their enduring friendship, and a promise of the joyful days ahead.

Chapter Twenty-Six

That night, amidst the bustling domain of the Fyans Street Inn, Dan and Brody's exuberance ignites into a crescendo of rowdy revelry. A bottle of rum, their jovial accomplice, passes between them as they engage in a spirited Irish jig. Laughter erupts like effervescent bubbles, merging with the cheers of fellow patrons to create a cacophonous symphony of merriment. Yet, as the line of decorum blurs, the revelry escalates beyond bounds. Two vigilant barmen, appointed custodians of order, step forward to intervene. With a blend of firmness and exasperation, they guide the overzealous celebrants toward the exit, the culmination of their journey marked by an insistent expulsion onto the street.

In the shadowy embrace of a dimly lit alley adjacent to the inn, Dan finds himself kneeling, besieged by a torrent of nausea that escapes with unrestrained fervour. Leaning against the inn's brick wall for support, Brody balances his form with both forearms, his uproarious laughter punctuating the chaotic aftermath.

“Hey, Dan! Quite the send-off, wouldn't you say? Tomorrow's dawn will find you nursing a throbbing head, my friend!"

However, Dan's expression remains devoid of mirth, a testament to his disarray. Despite his efforts, composure seems beyond his grasp. Amid this tableau of chaos, a dull thud resonates, capturing Dan's attention. Through blurred vision, he perceives Brody's arms surrendering to gravity, his body collapsing against the ground, and unconsciousness claiming him.

In the obscurity of the alley, a silhouette materializes near Brody, its presence a harbinger of apprehension. As the figure speaks, Dan's bewilderment morphs into dread.

"Greetings, old mate. It's been a while, hasn't it? Jack Riley thought he'd send his regards through me concerning your state of health. Judging by appearances, your prospects aren't promising, with a wedding on the horizon. Riley's dispatched me to carry out a task I would have gladly undertaken if circumstances had permitted. It's time to end your line, lest you release more delinquents into the world."

Dan's voice trembles, his plea infused with desperation. "No, Bruiser... This is beyond the pale! Riley won't find redemption... Alice won't forgive him. Show some shred of mercy, man!"

The word "mercy" seems out of place in the presence of the figure before him, Bruiser's sneer a clear testament to his disdain. He reaches for a formidable Bowie knife, its presence accentuating the menace of his advance. Chill proximity stirs desperation within Dan, his hands raised instinctively in defence.

Yet, an unexpected twist unfolds with Brody's resurgence. Rising to his knees behind Bruiser, Brody propels himself toward the hulking figure. His arms encircle Bruiser's legs, resulting in the brute's collapse—face-first into the earthen ground.

Seizing this advantage, Brody applies a stranglehold, his grip resolute and unyielding. Gurgling sounds erupt from Bruiser's throat. His frantic attempts to disentangle himself prove futile, his desperate struggles mirrored by his futile clawing at Brody's unyielding grip.

Amidst this life-and-death struggle, Brody's voice reaches out. "Dan! Lend me your aid! Seize the knife... Quickly!"

The gravity of the situation renders Dan sluggish, his reactions dulled in the face of the unfolding tragedy. Striving to reach the knife, his movements embody an uncertain hesitance.

In a swift and merciless maneuver, Bruiser's arm ascends, the blade plunging into Brody's right thigh. With a piercing scream, Brody relinquishes his grip. His form recoils in agony as Bruiser withdraws the blade. Crimson rivulets weave through Brody's trembling fingers, a macabre tapestry of pain and torment, as he whimpers in anguish.

With Brody incapacitated, Dan propels himself toward Bruiser, his limbs carrying him with a mixture of urgency and fear. His focus narrows upon the knife, and with a vehement kick, he sends the blade soaring through the air, away from immediate reach.

Struggling for balance, Dan's efforts prove futile, his body yielding to the relentless pull of gravity. He falls, the alley's unforgiving surface a fitting resting place for his dishevelled state.

Bruiser lies nearby, an outstretched hand reaching menacingly toward Dan. A ferocious kick repels Bruiser's approach, Dan's boot connecting solidly with his adversary's visage. A calculated retreat follows, Dan keeping his distance and evading the looming peril that Bruiser presents.

As he regains his footing, Dan propels himself toward the discarded knife. Dan's desperation becomes palpable in the direct line of Bruiser's menacing proximity. His fingers close around the blade's hilt with a determination born of necessity.

Bruiser, however, remains on bended knee, his advance halted by the unexpected turn of events. His uncertainty hangs heavy in the air. Dan's actions, unbidden by rationale, demand his attention, and the knife transforms into an instrument of fate.

With measured precision, the blade descends, its trajectory swift and unwavering. Bruiser's moment of respite is short-lived as the knife finds its mark—the side of his neck—a fateful juncture where destiny converges with judgment.

A blood-curdling scream escapes Bruiser's lips. The blade finds purchase with chilling ease, its lethal journey unimpeded. A stunned hush envelops the scene, a moment of suspended time where reality defies comprehension. Then, a hand—clenched and bloodied—finds its place upon the wound, the crimson tide flowing between Bruiser's fingers—a grotesque baptism of gore. His posture wilts, his visage pressed into the earthen floor, a tableau of agony and mortality.

Chapter Twenty-Seven

Alice sits in the elegantly furnished parlour of the Cranberry's lodging house, her fingers moving with a practised grace as she sews, her concentration unwavering. Sunlight filters through the windows, lighting the room's refined decor warmly. In a corner, Mr Wardle is engrossed in the morning newspaper, his brows furrowed in deep concentration as he absorbs the printed words. The room is steeped in tranquillity, each inhabitant absorbed in their pursuits.

Abruptly, Mr Wardle's attention shifts from the newspaper, his expression morphing into one of gravity. His gaze lifts from the pages, meeting Alice's eyes with a weighty solemnity. The atmosphere in the room shifts, a tangible tension settling like a heavy curtain.

"Alice," he begins, his voice carrying a sombre undertone, "there was a violent altercation last night in the alley adjacent to Fyans Inn. A man named Bruiser Conroy lost his life."

Alice's sewing needle slips from her trembling fingers, clattering softly onto the table before her. Her gaze, comprehensive with a mixture of fear and recognition, lifts to meet Mr Wardle's solemn gaze. Her usually rosy complexion has drained of colour, replaced by a pallor that highlights the gravity of the news.

"I... I know a Bruiser Conroy," she stammers, her voice quivering with shock and trepidation. She swallows hard, her throat suddenly dry, before continuing, "What else does the newspaper say, Mr Wardle?"

Mr Wardle's gaze remains fixed on her, his expression reflecting the heavy burden he carries in delivering this news. He clears his throat; his tone is measured and compassionate. "You won't believe it, Alice," he responds, "It's about your Dan. The newspaper alleges that Dan Farley is the accused murderer. According to their account, he fatally struck Bruiser Conroy with a knife. Currently, Dan is being held in custody at the Moorabool Street Gaol."

The room seems to close around Alice, her breath catching in her throat as the news settles over her like a suffocating shroud. Now trembling uncontrollably, her hands reach out to grasp the table's edge for support.

"No," she whispers, her voice barely audible, "it can't be true, Mr Wardle. There must be more to the story. It has to be a case of self-defence. Bruiser had attacked Dan upon my father's orders before. My father must have sent him, knowing about our upcoming wedding. It was an act of my father's revenge! I need to go to Dan immediately."

Empathy and concern soften Mr Wardle's features, observing the turmoil in Alice's eyes. With a solemn nod, he responds with understanding. "Yes, Alice. Go to him. We will take care of Levi while you're away."

Alice rises from her seat, her movements swift and purposeful. She drapes a shawl around her shoulders, her eyes reflecting a determination that could not be quelled. The urgency of the situation ignites a fire within her, propelling her forward with unwavering resolve. As she leaves the parlour, her footsteps echo with a sense of purpose, each step a testament to her fierce determination to uncover the truth and fight for Dan's innocence.

The imposing walls of the Moorabool Street Police Station loom before Alice, a formidable facade that holds both answers and uncertainty. The air is thick with tension and unease, yet Alice's determination radiates through the shadows. With a deep breath steadying her resolve, she steps forward, her footfalls echoing in the quiet anticipation of the unknown.

Guided by a Constable, Alice navigates the gaol's dimly lit and sombre corridors. Their steps reverberate against the stone walls, each echo a reminder of the heavy truth that hung in the air. Eventually, they reach a cell, the iron door, a barrier between Alice and the one she seeks. The Constable unlocks the door, revealing Dan within.

Dan sits on the side of the bed, his gaze lifting as Alice enters the cell. Disbelief mingles with a raw longing in his eyes, his pale features a canvas of conflicting emotions. He starts to rise, but the Constable's firm hand on his shoulder keeps him in place. "Easy now, mate! No sudden moves. You have a visitor, but remember, no touching." Dan nods his expression, a mixture of gratitude and restrained longing. He eases back onto the bed, his trembling hands reaching out toward Alice, yearning for the closeness denied by the Constable's watchful presence.

The Constable steps aside, granting Alice a fleeting moment to bridge the distance between them. Tears welled in her eyes, and her emotions threatened to spill over, fighting to maintain her composure. The desire to hold him, to offer comfort, is almost overwhelming, yet the Constable's presence remains a steadfast barrier.

"Dan," Alice's voice trembles, her eyes locked onto his, "why must fate deal us such a cruel hand? I blame myself for not foreseeing the depths of my father's malevolence. He must have orchestrated this, knowing that we were on the cusp of happiness." Alice's voice quivers with sorrow; her heartache is laid bare. She longs to bridge the gap between them, to hold him close and erase the turmoil etched on his features.

"Dan, I will engage 'Harwood Andrews' Law Firm. They will represent you at the Melbourne Courthouse. We will fight for your innocence, for justice. Bruiser's death is an unfortunate accident, a necessary act of self-defence. You are not a murderer, Dan. You are a victim of circumstance."

Dan's gaze remains locked with hers, his eyes reflecting pain and gratitude. His voice, a fragile thread of hope, holds the weight of their shared commitment. "And Bill? How is he? Is he recovering?"

As Alice's eyes soften, her voice becomes reassuring and speaks of another they are concerned for. "Bill is recovering under a doctor's care at a lodging house. His leg was gravely injured during the altercation, but he will come to Melbourne to testify on your behalf once he's well enough. We can rely on his support to counteract my father's manipulations."

Dan's gaze holds a fierce determination, his resolve unshaken in the face of adversity. "Alice... Soon, I will be transferred to Russell Street Gaol in Melbourne for the trial. When you visit Bill, please inform him of all this. We must remain united and confront this darkness together. I believe in our strength."

Alice, tears glistening in her eyes, meets Dan's gaze with unwavering determination. "I promise you, Dan. I will leave no stone unturned. Justice will prevail, and our love will endure."

As the Constable leads Alice away from the cell, she turns for a final glance at Dan. Their eyes lock in a silent exchange of love and resilience, a testament to the bond that transcends the barriers of their current circumstances. "I love you, Dan," she whispers, her words carrying a promise that echoes in the air, lingering long after the cell door closes, leaving Dan alone.

With her heart heavy yet determined, Alice walks away, her steps a testament to the unyielding strength of their love and her commitment to uncovering the truth. The journey ahead is fraught with challenges, but Alice is propelled forward by the unshakable belief that their love will triumph over the darkness that has befallen them.

Chapter Twenty-Eight

The reverberating clang of metal echoes as a prison van grinds to a halt outside the foreboding walls of the historic Russell Street Gaol. Two mounted constables carefully guide the van, their stern countenances mirroring the moment's gravity. Emerging from the van's rear, Dan steps down, his hands shackled, a stark reminder of his loss of freedom. Flanked by the vigilant constables, he begins the solemn march toward the imposing entrance of the prison, a reluctant journey into the heart of his confinement.

In a seamless transition, the scene dissolves, and the narrative shifts. Within the depths of the prison, Dan finds himself ensconced in a dimly lit solitary cell. The heavy, impenetrable walls shut out the world beyond, cocooning him in isolation. The wooden door slams shut with a resounding thud, sealing him from any semblance of sound beyond the cell.

The cell's furnishings are stark and utilitarian—a narrow bed, a small table, and a lone chair. A small bell dangles within arm's reach, a lifeline for emergencies that may arise in the desolation. The only trace of illumination filters through a small barred window near the ceiling, casting meagre light that barely penetrates the dimness.

Seated on the edge of the bed, Dan faces his lawyer, the distinguished James Hunter Ross. Mr Ross occupies a chair placed before Dan, commanding attention and respect.

"Drawing from the evidence presented during the court proceedings," Mr Ross begins in a measured tone, "there's potential for your charge to be reduced from murder to manslaughter. This shift could result in a sentence ranging from five to ten years without the additional burden of hard labour. Alternatively, if we can effectively convey to a sympathetic jury that your actions were rooted in self-defence, the possibility of acquittal exists."

Dan's gaze is steady and intent, his eyes locked onto Mr Ross as he absorbs the intricacies of the legal strategy before him. "In light of this," Dan inquires, his voice carrying both anxiety and resolve, "what are my odds of receiving a fair trial, Mr Ross? I've encountered rumours about Jack Riley's pervasive influence—how he seems to hold sway over law enforcement and, perhaps even more disconcertingly, the judiciary itself."

With an air of assurance, Mr Ross responds, his tone measured and confident. "You can rest assured, Mr Farley, that Judge Beckett is a man of integrity. I firmly believe he will preside over your trial with impartiality. However, I do share your apprehensions about Jack Riley's influence."

Dan's expression reflects concern and wariness as he contemplates the implications of the power dynamics. "Jack Riley wields influence with a heavy hand," Dan asserts, his voice tinged with frustration and apprehension. "He lacks ethics, yet his wealth empowers him to instil fear even in those who hold esteemed positions."

Mr Ross acknowledges Dan's concerns with a nod, his understanding evident. "He paid me a visit, Mr Farley. Riley stormed into my office, demanding to know why I took on your case despite being aware that the deceased was one of his associates and that you had a history of conflict involving his daughter."

Dan's eyes gleam with defiance and resignation as he contemplates the implications. "To receive such a visit from a man of his stature is troubling. Riley's grip on the upper echelons of society is a stranglehold fueled by their insatiable greed. He's nothing more than a scheming ruffian."

Dan's hands clench involuntarily, his frustration palpable. "But what of the jury's perspective, Mr Ross?" Dan's gaze remains unwavering, seeking insight amidst the complexity. "How might they interpret the situation, especially in the shadow of Riley's influence?"

Mr Ross adopts a contemplative posture; his response is candid yet cautious. "The perspective of the jury is variable, Mr Farley. Some jurors may be swayed by personal biases and susceptible to manipulation. Nevertheless, we must maintain trust in their commitment to honouring their oath and delivering a verdict free from preconceived notions. The judge must interpret the law and pronounce the sentence. While he might face scrutiny, his obligation to fulfil his role typically shields him from reprimand."

The historic stone-built courthouse at the intersection of Russell and La Trobe streets stands as the backdrop for the trial of Dan, the accused facing the grave charge of murder. The courtroom emanates a sombre aura, heavy with the weight of the impending proceedings. Wooden fixtures and tall windows punctuate the dimness, permitting rays of sunlight to pierce the dense atmosphere, casting a muted, reverent luminance.

Positioned before the elevated judicial bench, the Court Officer commands the room's attention. In the felon dock, Dan takes his seat, his countenance a canvas of mixed emotions—anticipation tangled with anxiety, the gravity of the trial etched onto his features.

At a table nearby, the distinguished barrister, the Honourable James Ross, arranges his materials with focused diligence, preparing to navigate the intricacies of the trial.

In a resounding voice, the Court Officer announces, "This court's trial will be presided over by Judge William Beckett, the esteemed resident judge of the Supreme Court of New South Wales for the district of Port Phillip. All rise!"

The room stirs as attendees stand, an outward display of deference to Judge Beckett. He strides into the courtroom with an aura of authority, taking his place behind the bench.

Judge Beckett epitomizes wisdom and gravity. Clad in full judicial regalia, a cascade of silver hair flows from beneath his wig, a testament to his years of experience. His presence commands respect, his sharp features—noble nose and a hint of bushy sideburns—bestowing upon him a venerable air.

"All Sit!" Judge Beckett's command resonates, and the room complies, individuals retaking their seats while keeping their gazes fixed on the judge. The weight of the trial hangs as a palpable spectre, a collective acknowledgement of the gravity of the proceedings.

"The prisoner stands accused of the heinous crime of first-degree murder. If the jury finds him guilty, the penalty shall be the most severe—death by hanging," Judge Beckett intones solemnly.

An air of sobriety envelopes the space, the weight of these words pressing upon everyone present. Judge Beckett's gaze shifts to rest upon Dan, awaiting his plea.

"How does the prisoner plead?" Judge Beckett's voice carries a blend of authority and curiosity.

"Not Guilty of murder, your honour!" responds Mr Ross, his voice resonating with conviction.

Judge Beckett's gaze transitions to the jury, twelve men assembled to undertake their solemn duty.

"I trust that each jury member understands the importance of their duty," Judge Beckett asserts, his gaze sweeping the faces before him. "Our justice system hinges upon the willingness of honourable individuals, like yourselves, to render a verdict that is both equitable and just. Remember, your grave duty lies in deciding the punishment for crimes committed."

A weighty silence follows, the room steeped in reflection. Judge Beckett's attention shifts back to Dan. "If any person abandons this solemn responsibility when their fellow man suffers, they may someday find themselves bereft of the support of a diligent jury when they seek their own justice. Let this stand as a sobering reminder to all."

His words hang in the air, a solemn refrain that resonates within the hearts of those present. Judge Beckett then turns his gaze towards Mr Ross, an unspoken signal that the defence may commence deliberations.

"Your Honour and esteemed jury members," Mr Ross begins, his tone measured yet compelling, "I shall present evidence that elucidates Mr Farley and Mr Brody's unfortunate predicament. Seeking refuge in the alley adjacent to Fyans Inn due to ailments that befell them during the revelries leading to Mr Farley's wedding, they encountered an unforeseen assault by the late Bruiser Conroy. In the ensuing life-or-death struggle, Mr Farley, driven by self-preservation, wielded a knife wrested from Conroy, inadvertently inflicting a fatal blow. Our defence asserts that Mr Farley's actions were borne out of a need for self-defence, a response to dire circumstances threatening his life."

Tensions heighten within the room as Mr Ross concludes his opening statement. The air is charged with anticipation, the narrative poised on the precipice of revelation.

Chapter Twenty-Nine

The courtroom hums with a charged energy as the Prosecutor positions himself, ready to delve into the forthcoming examination of the next prosecution witness. He stands tall, a pillar of confidence before the witness box, emanating an air of poise that hints at the imminent initiation of his line of questioning.

"I call Mr Jack Riley to the stand," the Prosecutor's declaration cuts through the ambient tension, his voice unwavering and authoritative. With a stride marked by self-assuredness, Jack Riley strides towards the witness box, a commanding presence that demands attention. Upon reaching the box, he places his hand upon the Bible, a prelude to the solemn oath about to be taken.

"State your full name," the command from the Court Officer echoes in the space.

With an aura of gravitas, he responds, his voice infused with authority, "Jack Riley."

"Do you swear upon the Bible to tell the truth, the whole truth, and nothing but the truth, so help you, God?" The words of the Court Officer resonate with the solemnity befitting the occasion.

"I most certainly do," Riley's declaration carries the weight of unwavering conviction, a statement of allegiance to the truth. The Court Officer acknowledges the response, accepting the Bible from Riley's grasp. The air becomes heavy with anticipation, the courtroom collectively holding its breath as the Prosecutor steps forward, poised to engage with Mr Riley.

"Mr Riley, please elucidate for the court your knowledge concerning this case," the Prosecutor addresses Mr Riley directly, his gaze a testament to his unwavering focus.

The complex amalgamation of emotions surges through Riley as he begins, "I am both astounded and humiliated by my daughter Alice's accusations against me and my employee, Mr Conroy." His voice is laden with emotions, blending disbelief and sorrow. "Farley and my daughter have conspired to tarnish the Riley family name, which has stood for honour across generations."

"Elaborate on that statement, Mr Riley," the Prosecutor prompts, his tone unyielding, demanding clarity.

Riley's gesture directs the gaze of the courtroom towards Alice, seated in the second row of the gallery. "My daughter, right there," his words contain a tinge of sombre disappointment, "has cast a shadow upon our family legacy, bearing a child out of wedlock with the accused. And now she stands before us, driven by some misguided sense of loyalty, adding yet another layer of disgrace to the Riley name."

A ripple of hushed murmurs briefly disrupts the solemn proceedings, a tempest quickly quelled by Judge Beckett's authoritative gavel.

"Order! Any further disturbances will not be tolerated. Continue, Mr Riley," Judge Beckett's words are unyielding, carrying the weight of his authority. Riley regains his composure, a renewed resolve defining his posture.

"Believe me when I say that my actions were motivated by a father's concern for his daughter's well-being," he states resolutely. "When Alice left our household, and I later learned of her pregnancy, my paternal instincts were ignited."

Pointing towards Dan Farley in the dock, Riley's voice takes a sharper edge, "That man there," his words resonate with firmness, "was the catalyst for my daughter's predicament."

A nod from the Prosecutor signals Riley to continue, giving momentum to his narrative.

"In Conroy's quest to find my daughter, their paths must have converged with Mr Farley in an alleyway. Their animosity was palpable, given Farley's prior threats to Conroy during their shared time in my employment," Riley's words are both declarative and explanatory.

"Conroy had confided in me about Farley's unwanted advances towards my daughter, which ultimately culminated in a confrontation. During this confrontation, Farley warned, 'You will regret this, Bruiser... Mark my words... YOU WILL REGRET THIS!'"

Urged on by the Prosecutor's unspoken cues, Riley's narrative flows on, " The convergence of these two inebriated men in the alley provided an opportunity for aggression on seeing Conroy. A violent altercation ensued, resulting in Conroy being grievously injured. Brody, another party involved, sustained an injury due to Conroy's resistance. Fueled by a vengeful spirit, Farley seized upon Conroy's holstered hunting knife and, in a fateful moment, delivered the blow that proved to be fatal."

A point of contention surfaces as Mr Ross interjects, "Speculation, Your Honour!"

Riley's narrative finds resonance among his henchmen in the courtroom, igniting a swell of fervent support. An air of escalating tension saturates the atmosphere as Riley's advocates, situated at the rear of the gallery, amplify the chaos with their boisterous endorsement. The courtroom resonates with amplified cries and clamour, a tempest threatening to spiral out of control.

Amidst the tumult, the scene captures the fervour and turbulence stirred by these agitators. Judge Beckett's patience wears thin, and he employs his gavel with a firm **thud**, a declaration of his resolve to restore order.

"Order! Order! Any further disruptions will result in your removal from this courtroom! Maintain decorum or face the consequences!" Judge Beckett's expression conveys an unwavering determination, an insistence on reclaiming authority over the proceedings.

The reverberations of the gavel resonate, acting as a temporary salve to the mounting disarray. The spectators, understanding the gravity of Judge Beckett's stance, begin to subdue their fervent reactions. While still tense, the room succumbs to a subdued quiet, occasionally punctuated by hushed murmurs.

"The court will not countenance such disruptions," Judge Beckett asserts, his voice an embodiment of sternness and command. "Our pursuit is one of justice, a pursuit that demands an environment of composure and respect. Let us proceed without further interruptions."

The room settles, and the lingering tension is temporarily quelled. With unwavering determination, the Prosecutor positions himself to continue his inquiry. "No further questions for this witness, Your Honour," The prosecutor's declaration carries a finality, a precursor to the next phase of the proceedings.

Judge Beckett's gaze shifts towards Mr Ross, an expectant pause anticipating his response. Confidently, Mr Ross responds, "No questions for the witness, Your Honour."

The exchange acknowledged Judge Beckett turned his attention back to Riley, delivering a directive. "You may step down, Mr Riley."

Riley, embodying a composed self-assurance, vacates the witness box and resumes his seat at the forefront of the gallery. The room reverberates with the lingering echoes of his testimony, a testament to the complexity and depth of the unfolding trial. The proceedings press onward, each side prepared to present their interpretation of events before the impartial gaze of justice.

Chapter Thirty

The Prosecutor, his examination of Riley concluded, takes a measured step back. Positioned now before another witness within the witness box, he gathers his focus, preparing to extract the pivotal details required.

"Mr Blight," the Prosecutor's voice resonates with the gravity of the trial, "as someone close acquainted with Jack Riley and his inner circle, could you illuminate the true character of the victim, Mr Bruiser Conroy?"

The figure of Mr Blight, characterized by his composed demeanour and impeccably groomed appearance, inhales deeply, collecting his thoughts before addressing the court. With unwavering conviction, he begins, "Bruiser Conroy embodied a gentleness and kindness that belied his formidable stature. His presence exuded a quiet strength, his interactions marked by a tenderness akin to a kitten's. He was a man who wouldn't raise a hand to harm even the most insignificant of creatures, let alone harm a mosquito resting on the back of his hand."

A hush settles over the courtroom, and Mr Blight's words cast a complex light upon the victim, starkly contrasting the prevailing narrative of those who know Conroy.

"No further questions or witnesses, Your Honour," the Prosecutor's statement marks a transition, signifying the conclusion of his line of inquiry.

Judge Beckett, his demeanour composed yet resolute, acknowledges this shift. "Mr Ross, in the absence of further witnesses for the defence, you may proceed with your closing statement."

Mr Ross, the defence attorney, rises from his seat, a subtle adjustment of his robes denoting his preparedness to address the court. "Thank you, Your Honour," his voice a blend of gratitude and purpose.

His gaze turns to the jury, his words directed at them with a sincerity that resonates. "Ladies and gentlemen of the jury, if there existed an individual within this community with the fortitude to challenge the assertions made by Jack Riley and the prosecution's witnesses, then the only recourse would be to declare the accused innocent," Mr Ross commences, his voice carrying the weight of unwavering belief. "The defence has incontrovertibly established that Mr Farley acted in self-defence against a proven aggressor."

A strategic pause follows, allowing his words to linger, their significance sinking with the jury. "Should you be convinced that Mr Farley harboured no premeditated intent to inflict harm upon Mr Conroy, as the defence has compellingly demonstrated, and should you be inclined to believe that this tragic incident transpired without premeditation, devoid of any malice—merely a fight for survival in the face of the victim's aggression—then you are left with no alternative but to pronounce the accused—Not Guilty of Murder." His words hang in the air, their resonance encouraging the jury members to delve into the intricacies of the evidence before them.

In the final scene, the twelve jury members re-enter the courtroom, their expressions composed yet betraying the internal battles they have waged. As they take their places, a weighted hush descends, an anticipatory silence enveloping the room. The courtroom's palpable tension escalates, an impending sense of resolution hanging heavy.

"Has the jury reached a verdict?" Judge Beckett's voice, a blend of gravitas and solemnity, marks the moment's significance.

With a resolute demeanour, the Jury Foreperson, a middle-aged figure, rises, delivering his words with unswerving clarity. "Your Honour, indeed we have." A hush deepens, a collective breath held, the moment fraught with implication.

"Kindly state the verdict," Judge Beckett's instruction reverberates.

Unperturbed by the moment's weight, the Jury Foreperson speaks with a conviction befitting the moment, his words a verdict that will reshape destinies.

"We find the accused, Dan Farley, guilty of first-degree murder—as charged."

A gasp ripples through the courtroom, followed by a chorus of murmurs—shock, disbelief, and perhaps, for some, an exhalation of tension. Amid this tumult, Alice clings to the rail before her seat, her heart pounding in her chest, her emotions bare.

Judge Beckett's gavel strikes, sharp and authoritative, cutting through the room's cacophony. "Order! Order in the court!" His potent and commanding command gradually stills the room, quelling the rising tide of unrest.

In addition to his judicial attire, Judge Beckett dons the sombre black cap—a symbol of solemnity. With gloved hands, he turns his focus to Dan, his voice measured yet laden with significance.

"Dan Farley, the court's judgment pronounces you guilty of murder. Your sentence is that you be held in confinement until the week's end, at which point you shall be led to the place of execution. There, you shall hang from the noose until life departs from you. May God, in His benevolence, grant favour to your soul."

As Judge Beckett's words descend like a gavel, Dan's world fractures beneath their weight. The culmination of the trial's ordeal crashes upon him, his composure faltering in the face of the crushing verdict. In a fleeting yet intense exchange of gazes, Dan and Alice lock eyes—a shared testament of unyielding love, standing defiant against the nightmarish reality thrust upon them.

Chapter Thirty-One

In the heart of Melbourne Town, Alice finds solace within the welcoming walls of Mary Hobson's lodging house. Nestled in the inviting parlour, the weight of their personal trials is etched across their countenances. Soft rays of sunlight cascade through the intricate lace curtains, enveloping the room in a gentle, golden glow.

"Mary," Alice's voice resonates with a blend of gratitude and emotional depth, "I want you to know how truly appreciative I am of your unwavering support during these tumultuous times. Your kindness has been an unbreakable lifeline for me, especially in light of Father's abandonment of Mother and me. His bitter words aimed at Mother—sometimes, it feels like he's cast aside every sacrifice she made to bolster him and help establish his business in this fledgling Colony."

Mary Hobson, a rock of constancy in Alice's world, responds with a voice suffused with compassion and empathy. "Alice, you are kin to me in every sense. It wounds my heart to witness the injustice your father inflicts upon you and your mother. This world, as we know, can be harsh and unrelenting. Yet, within these very connections, these bonds of friendship, we find solace and strength to endure."

Agreeing with a solemn nod, Alice's features mirror a blend of unwavering conviction and profound gratitude. "Mary, your words resonate deeply. These trials I face illuminate the genuine value of steadfast friendships. But I cannot help but feel a heaviness, a realization that I must shoulder the weight of nurturing my child independently. The dreams I once shared for my future now seem distant and defeated."

Mary's gaze softens, offering insights forged through empathy. "News has reached me regarding Mr Brody's condition. It appears he is on a path toward recovery, though his wound runs deep. The doctor predicts an extensive healing process, and regrettably, it's anticipated that he will bear a permanent limp due to nerve damage."

Alice processes the information with concern and resolves that flicker within her eyes. "This very afternoon, I must seek out Dan. That's news he must hear—about Mr Brody's recovery. We must join our efforts to craft a plan for Levi's future and mine."

Alice and Mary exchange a resolute look in a moment of shared understanding. Their spirits merge, an unspoken vow of unyielding support and indomitable resilience binding them. Empowered by this connection, Alice rises from her seat, a newfound determination propelling her forward. As she steps towards the unknown challenges that await, the unwavering strength of their unbreakable bond fuels her resolve. Together, Dan and Alice must brace themselves to navigate the uncertain path ahead, fortified by the enduring power they draw from one another.

A tangible sense of desperation permeates the air in the dimly lit prison cell. Alice is seated on a worn chair, her fingers intertwined with Dan's. Their eyes meet, and in that unspoken gaze, a profound connection blooms—a language of love and understanding that transcends their circumstances.

"Do I dare ask this of you, Alice?" Dan's voice blends vulnerability and sincerity, underscoring the gravity of his plea. "Will you go to Bill on my behalf and make an extraordinary request? Ask him to bestow upon you his name through marriage."

Alice's brows furrow as she contemplates, her voice echoing a mix of incredulity and a yearning for clarity. "Dan, I struggle to grasp the enormity of your appeal. Is it conceivable that you truly wish for me to enter a marriage devoid of affection with a man I scarcely know, all in pursuit of his name?"

Dan responds, his tone brimming with unwavering conviction. "Alice, try to fathom that Bill intimately understands the pain of orphanhood, having suffered it himself and the unyielding judgments society casts upon us. He comprehends the adversities Levi would confront without the protection of a father's name—a burden he'd carry for a lifetime."

Alice's gaze searches as if seeking solace within her own uncertainty. "Yet, Dan, will Bill even entertain this extraordinary proposition? Will he even contemplate such a profound sacrifice?"

Dan's determination remains steadfast, his reassurance offered with sincerity. "Alice, you must understand that Bill is a man of honour. He perceives you not as a burden but as a person unbound by the constraints of a dowry. He has tasted the bitterness of loss and heartache firsthand. His cherished wife, the love of his life, was snatched away by illness. Since then, he has vowed never to love again."

Emotions play across Alice's face, a complex dance between resolve and inner conflict. "For your sake, Dan, I shall approach Bill as you've asked... if only you can trust him as you would a brother."

A beat of time hangs suspended, Dan's gaze delving into the depths of Alice's eyes. "My dearest Alice," he murmurs, his words a gentle affirmation of unyielding faith, "believe in Bill's sanctity to me, akin to a brother. Dispel your apprehensions, for he will shelter and provide for you both, just as I would."

In the confines of their shadowed cell, their clasped hands stand as a testament to their shared bond—a bond that carries the weight of their predicament. Amidst the silence, their connection remains unshaken, a symbol of unity in the face of adversity.

Chapter Thirty-Two

Within the confining walls of his cramped cell, Dan resides amidst the stark austerity of stone, a reflection of the emotions that weigh heavily upon him. His countenance bears the imprints of profound sadness mingled with a sombre acceptance. With quill poised in his hand, he continues to transcribe his innermost thoughts onto parchment, the amassed pages a testament to the gravity of his endeavour. His voice, soft and laden with emotion, is a murmur that seems to converse with the shadows enveloping him.

"From the wellspring of this ink, I inscribe my words to eternity's end," Dan's utterance is gentle, as if he speaks to an unseen audience, to the very essence of his emotions. The dawn approaches, heralding the imminent arrival of the hangman's noose, yet he persists in his cathartic endeavour. The quill dips into the inkwell, each stroke a deliberate articulation of his heart's most profound lament.

"Dearest Alice, with the last letter I pen, I offer my final gift to you," his voice is a mixture 0f sorrow and longing, as if he believes that his words possess the power to transcend the confines of his cell and traverse the distance to her heart. The quill wavers in his hand, each stroke a testament to the sincerity of his emotions.

"Amidst the looming oblivion, I implore you, Alice, to find within your heart the grace to pardon my ignominious departure." His gaze shifts to the stack of pages, a collection of his thoughts solidified on parchment—a tangible embodiment of the depth of his feelings.

"In the fleeting span of our shared existence, love found solace in our hearts. Amidst moments that gleamed like stars in a velvety night sky, we experienced the enchantment of a bond that defied our adversities." His eyes alight upon a photograph of Alice and Levi, positioned as if they were peering through the very walls of the cell.

"Alice, my gaze rests upon our cherished Levi, a living testament to the purest essence of my being. Shower him with the love that you so

generously lavished upon me. And when the circumstances permit, share the story of a father who held you in the highest regard along with him."

A deep inhalation steadies his resolve, his thoughts coalescing into coherent expressions. *"Within this abyss that engulfs me, I find a sliver of tranquillity, knowing that our love was real, even though its flame was prematurely extinguished by the hand of destiny. As I tread the uncharted path that beckons, the memories of our shared moments shall be my constant companions."*

A profound sense of finality takes root with each word scripted onto the parchment. As the quill is laid to rest, Dan surveys the culmination of his labour, a mosaic of emotions etched into the paper. A bittersweet smile graces his lips, a testament to the complex interplay of sorrow and acceptance.

"These words may never reach the eyes they were meant for," he concedes, his voice imbued with a deep-seated ache, *"yet they stand as an enduring testament to the love that blossomed between us, Alice. Farewell, my beloved."*

In the solace of that solitary moment, the scene transitions, leaving Dan alone in the embrace of his final words—a poignant reminder of a love that transcends all barriers, even those as unyielding as the walls of his prison cell.

In that dimly lit Holding Cell, a solemn aura envelops Dan and the Priest, who reverently clutches a Bible. The echoes of sacred recitations fade, the Priest's voice marked by reverence as he bestows the final blessings. "In the name of the Father, the Son, and the Holy Spirit. Amen."

The Priest's words resonate in the confined space, carrying the weight of benediction. Completing the ritual, he traces the cross sign and rests a consoling hand upon Dan's shoulder, a gesture that acknowledges the moment's gravity. The approach of heavy footsteps signals the arrival of the Turnkey.

Guided by the Turnkey, Dan emerges from the cell, his hands cuffed behind his back. The Gaol Warden awaits their emergence, a figure of authority on the threshold of the gallows. Together, they traverse the gate, crossing onto the chilling expanse of the execution platform.

The Warden's gaze turns to Dan, his words a sombre inquiry. "Daniel Farley, do you wish to convey any final words?"

With his gaze fixed ahead, Dan embodies a fusion of strength and compassion, qualities shimmering in his eyes. Below, the witnesses stand in solemn silence, their attention lowered to the ground. Dan's voice emerges with a resonance that resounds.

"May God forgive you all, for you hang an innocent man!"

Simultaneously, the Hooded Hangman steps forward, his actions measured and purposeful. With a swift adjustment, the noose is positioned; the hangman then places a hood upon Dan's head, a shroud that veils his visage in darkness.

Across the platform, the hangman positions himself by the release lever, its significance tangible in the air. The Warden retreats, affording the moment its solemn space. The hangman pulls the lever swiftly and resolutely, initiating a descent that thrusts Dan into a sudden void. The prison bell's mournful toll resounds in the stillness.

Dan's body sways violently, a silent struggle against the implacable grip of the noose. It becomes evident that death does not claim him swiftly; instead, torturous suffocation takes hold.

The witnesses below react with visceral horror, gazing at the haunting spectacle. Amidst the gurgling noises emanating from Dan's lips, the sound of his struggle reverberates—a poignant embodiment of the unbearable tension.

Amidst the assembled onlookers, the Prison Doctor rushes forward, his stethoscope swaying about his neck as he races toward the dangling figure. Summoning every reserve of strength, the Doctor intervenes, exerting downward pressure on Dan's legs until the motion subsides. Moments stretch, as agonizing as they are eternal, the Doctor's efforts ceasing as Dan's body settles into stillness.

"I... I pronounce the prisoner deceased," The prison Doctor's voice trembles as he conveys the inevitable truth. His declaration hangs heavy in the air, mingling with the collective sorrow and shock that envelop the witnesses looking on.

Chapter Thirty-Three

Alice is seated within the comforting embrace of Miss Hodson's parlour, her demeanour a tapestry woven with threads of grief, tear-stained trails on her handkerchief a testament to her sorrow. Her voice quivers as she speaks, bearing the weight of the sombre execution the day before.

"The aftermath of Dan's execution only strengthens my conviction regarding Jack Riley's sinister manipulations during the trial," Alice's voice trembles, a symphony of sorrow and determination resonating within her words. "I cannot, under any circumstances, acknowledge that brute as my father any longer. Not for as long as I draw breath."

Miss Hodson's presence is a testament to empathy, an unspoken pillar of support. "Your resolve is firmly grounded, my dear," Miss Hodson's voice is a gentle river of solace, acknowledging Alice's pain with a shared understanding. "Considering the circumstances, your stance is entirely justifiable."

The cloak of sorrow that envelops Alice gradually gives way to a sense of urgency as she confides in Miss Hodson. "I feel a compelling need to share with you the response I received from Bill Brody. His words arrived just before the tragic turn of events leading to Dan's execution," Alice's voice gains a note of determination, her words imbued with a purpose that pierces through the emotional haze.

"With Mother no longer here to guide me, the burden of uncertainty has grown weighty within my heart. I yearn for clarity, to discern whether my decision is sound."

Miss Hodson nods in steadfast understanding, extending a gentle encouragement. "Please, Alice, share Mr Brody's words with me. I am here to stand by your side and offer support in every way you may require."

With a steadying breath, Alice gathers her composure before recounting Bill Brody's message. "Mr Brody's words are as follows: *'If circumstances conspire to lead to the gravest outcome—may Heaven forbid it—I would be honoured to take you as my wife, Alice. In doing so, I will willingly bestow upon you and Levi my name, guaranteeing financial security and societal acceptance. However, our lives will remain separate, just as they are now. My singular wish is to have the privilege of visiting Levi during my leaves and to partake in moments as a paternal figure.'"*

Alice's voice wavers momentarily, a few tears wiped away with a delicate touch. "I believe this declaration illustrates Mr Brody's honourable intentions, Mary," Alice continues, her voice an exquisite blend of vulnerability and conviction. "And, as you know, Dan held him in high esteem."

Miss Hodson's response encapsulates wisdom and insight. "It appears that Mr Brody possesses a character of true nobility, my dear. The fact that Dan held him in such high regard is of immense significance."

Alice, though her emotions are raw, composes herself, seamlessly transitioning to discussing her immediate plans. "I must expedite my return to Mrs Cranberry's establishment, Mary. Mr Brody has outlined our intention to be wed in Geelong upon his return to Ercildoune Station, contingent upon receiving medical clearance for work."

In the reassuring presence of Miss Hodson, Alice catches a fleeting glimpse of hope. "Count your blessings for the opportunities that await you, dear," Miss Hodson's voice is an anchor amidst the tumultuous sea of emotions. "Bid farewell to the trials of the past and embrace the boundless potential the future holds."

With a nod, Alice's face becomes a mosaic of emotions, reflecting her attempts to discover solace amidst the uncharted path ahead. The scene remains anchored within Miss Hodson's parlour as Alice and Miss Hodson continue their conversation, the weight of shared grief weaving their words together.

"No one can fully comprehend the depths of anguish and torment that the manner of Dan's passing has etched into my soul unless they too have walked a similar path," Alice's voice becomes a vessel for her experience, carrying the weight of her grief and the gravity of her words. "And, honestly, I fear that those who truly understood such trials are few and far between. He was a young man filled with goodness and love, only twenty-five, unjustly cut down by the fabrication of a murder charge."

Miss Hodson's response is a symphony of unspoken empathy. "It was a grievous miscarriage of justice, my dear," Miss Hodson's voice resonates with the understanding only true companionship can bring.

Alice's voice trembles as she vocalizes the turmoil that grips her heart. "How am I supposed to come to terms with this reality? Where will I find the strength to forge ahead? Even though it's rooted in the past, I fear I may never truly overcome it."

Miss Hodson's reassuring words offer a salve for Alice's wounded spirit. "No one expects you to erase these memories, my dear. It is a burden that no individual should bear in isolation."

Emotion swells within Alice's voice as she continues to share her heart. "The tolling of the bell within Melbourne Gaol, that haunting sound as the prison's trapdoor opened and Dan descended into the abyss of death—I can still hear it."

"It is an indescribable tragedy," Miss Hodson's words echo with a poignant ache.

Alice's voice carries the weight of her sorrow as she speaks further. "And, as if to add to the burden, The Herald Newspaper reports this day that the executioner made an error, misplacing the knot of the noose. Dan's fall did not grant him swift release from life."

"It is a burden that no soul should carry as their own private torment, day and night," Miss Hodson's voice encapsulates the shared sentiment of anguish.

The moment's tranquillity is disrupted by a knock at the front door, prompting Miss Hodson to rise and welcome Reverend Geoghegan, a Roman Catholic priest who has travelled to Alice's side.

"Please, Reverend Geoghegan, come in," Miss Hodson's words are a warm invitation.

Reverend Geoghegan enters the room, radiating compassion as he approaches Alice, extending his condolences.

"Thank you, Mary. I have come as requested by Dan Farley to speak with his betrothed," Reverend Geoghegan's voice is a gentle embrace as he offers his support to Alice. "And, Alice, please accept my deepest condolences. How are you holding up, my dear?"

Alice, her eyes reflecting both tears and resolve, responds somberly. "I am doing my best, Reverend. There are moments when tears are my sole companions."

Reverend Geoghegan's expression is empathetic as he addresses the depth of Alice's grief. "Alice, Dan summoned me yesterday to administer the Last Rites before he departed from this earthly existence. I want you to know that he faced the gallows with unwavering strength and dignity."

As she responded, tears shimmered in Alice's eyes, gratitude mingling with sorrow in her voice. "Thank you, Father."

"Take comfort in the knowledge that Dan sought absolution, his heart set on departing this world untainted by sin," Reverend Geoghegan's words are a soothing balm.

"He stood before the Divine, proclaiming his innocence, declaring that he never intended to take another's life and acted in self-defence. His prayers will now guide him on his journey to Eternity."

Alice finds a measure of solace in the Reverend's words, a healing touch as she navigates the depths of her grief, seeking refuge in the final moments of her beloved Dan.

Chapter Thirty-Four

Alice stands poised at the threshold of Cranberry's Lodging House, the grand entrance before her. Her eyes, though clear, still bear the glimmer of recent tears, a testament to the emotions that have defined her journey. As if in response to her arrival, Mrs and Mr Cranberry approach, arms open wide, their expressions radiant with warmth and affection. Levi, held within their embrace, is enveloped in joyful hugs—a tangible manifestation of the sense of family that awaits.

Together, they step over the threshold, crossing into the heart of the house. The sitting room welcomes them, vibrant with the presence of fellow lodgers who have gathered, a gathering of empathetic souls. These familiar faces, turned towards Alice and Levi, hold gazes filled with understanding and solidarity. Unspoken words of condolence ripple through the air, woven with a network of unyielding support.

"Welcome back, dear Alice!" Mrs Cranberry's voice resonates with genuine comfort, a voice that seeks to soothe. "Both you and Levi have been greatly missed. Please know that our hearts are with you, sharing in the weight of your loss. With your return to our midst, we can shoulder your grief together and offer strength through unity."

Alice's response, tinged with gratitude, carries a quiet yet undeniable strength. "Thank you, Mrs Cranberry. Your kindness, and that of everyone here, has meant the world to me. As I mentioned in my recent letter, I have decided to marry Mr Brody. I hope this choice does not impose upon you or disrupt the harmony of this house."

Mrs Cranberry's dismissal of any inconvenience comes wrapped in a genuine and warm smile. "Oh, my dear, do not worry. Your decision brings no inconvenience at all. All arrangements have been attended to, and we stand ready to support you every step of the way. Your piano students are well aware of your return, and they eagerly await the resumption of their lessons."

Alice's eyes brightened; gratitude and anticipation mingled in her gaze. Music—her eternal solace and expression—beckons her back.

"That news fills me with such joy," Alice responds, her voice a melodic embrace of hope. "Music has always been a sanctuary for me, a language transcending words. I am eager to reconnect with my students and dive into the beauty of their progress."

Around her, the lodgers converge, their presence a living testament to camaraderie and shared compassion. "We are truly elated to have you back, Alice," Mr Wardle's voice holds the sincerity of a friend's welcome. "Your absence left a void that resonated with us all."

"Your fortitude and resilience inspire us," adds Mr Jasper, his words woven with admiration.

Miss Staples' concern is genuine and heartfelt. "Should you ever require any assistance, know that we are here to lend a hand without hesitation."

Alice's eyes shimmer with emotions, gratitude mingling with the wellspring of feelings within her.

"Thank you, every one of you," Alice's voice is a vessel of authenticity. "Your kindness touches the very depths of my heart. To be surrounded by such remarkable individuals during this challenging chapter is a blessing beyond words."

In unison, the lodgers nod, their presence a silent affirmation of the strength that blossoms within a community bound by shared experiences and the empathetic thread of humanity. Within this house, this gathering, and this moment, Alice finds herself embraced by more than just walls and roofs. She is enfolded in a web of empathy, a tapestry woven by hands and hearts that understand—proof that even in the face of adversity, the human spirit is a force that can bridge the spaces between individuals and bind them in an unbreakable union.

The dining room has been transformed into a realm of festivity, with decorations adorning every corner. The attendees of the boarding house wedding are now gathered around the table, each person decked in their finest attire for the occasion. The air crackles with anticipation and excitement as the guests hold glass tumblers, poised for a moment of significance.

At the head of the table stands Bill Brody, an embodiment of responsibility and unwavering devotion. His presence radiates a sense of purpose as he raises his glass, a silent cue for all to rise from their seats.

"May I ask everyone to stand?" Brody's voice resonates with authority and warmth. The attendees comply, their gazes fixed on Brody, their collective attention directed toward the momentous toast about to unfold.

"I propose a toast," Brody's voice carries the weight of his words, "to Dan Farley — a man who held a special place in the hearts of Alice and Levi. And here's to us, forging a new beginning as a united entity — a family that emerges from unique circumstances. I invite you all to raise your glasses."

In response to Brody's words, the glasses are elevated, and the room is filled with a tangible atmosphere of respect and gratitude.

Brody's gaze remains steady as he continues to speak, his words infused with sincerity and unwavering commitment. "Among this esteemed gathering of Alice's friends, I wish to convey the depth of my pride. It is my honour to extend my family name to Alice and Levi. The privilege of witnessing Levi's growth into the man that Dan would have been proud to call his son is a responsibility I embrace."

Brody's voice is a testament to his dedication, the words flowing forth with conviction and a sense of purpose. "I reaffirm my vow, my unwavering commitment to Dan," Brody's declaration resounds in the room, "to safeguard the well-being and happiness of Alice and Levi, even if it demands my very existence."

As the echoes of his proclamation reverberate through the air, glasses clink together in unison. The room becomes a symphony of celebration, a chorus of support and camaraderie that fills the space with a warmth that transcends the tangible. Amidst this collective embrace, the room pulses with friendship and the promise of a brighter chapter. Alice and Levi embark on their journey, guided by the memory of Dan's enduring love.

Chapter Thirty-Five

Alice's heart finds solace within the cozy confines of the quaint lodging house. Her slender fingers move with practised ease, weaving threads into intricate patterns as she engages in the soothing dance of crocheting.

By her side sits Levi, a cherubic young boy of six, his auburn hair cascading like a waterfall of molten copper down his shoulders. His attire, a pair of knickerbockers and an air of innocent curiosity add to the enchantment of the scene. The room is steeped in tranquillity, accompanied by the gentle rustling of a slate board bearing evidence of Levi's chalked triumphs. Nearby, Miss Staples is engrossed in her own world, the rustling of her newspaper a reassuring constant in the background.

Amid this domestic symphony, Alice's voice emerges like a summer breeze, carrying words of encouragement. "Levi, your printing is a masterpiece in itself. I'm brimming with pride for you. My next piano student will be arriving shortly. As for you, my dear, you're welcome to venture outdoors and enjoy some playtime. Just remember to stay within close proximity to the house. We'll delve into your arithmetic studies later this afternoon."

Miss Staples, the embodiment of pragmatism, interjects with a voice infused with wisdom. "Levi, mark my words. Steer clear of the dock area, lad. It's not unheard of for boys your age to vanish without a trace, spirited away by ship captains with motives as murky as the horizon. They often seek young cabin boys for voyages that stretch beyond the horizon. Or, worse yet, you could find yourself tending to sheep for a rogue squatter in the unforgiving outback."

Levi's response is a blend of youthful conviction and self-assuredness. "Rest assured, Miss Staples. I possess the ability to take care of myself."

With that declaration, the room transforms into a theatre of energy as Levi springs into action, propelled by the anticipation of the world beyond these walls. Lighter than air, his feet carry him toward the docks and the enigmatic warehouse district. However, before he fully embarks on his adventure, he comes to an abrupt halt, ensnared by the enchantment of the shoreline. Corio Bay stretches before him, an expanse of azure kissed by the benevolent rays of the sun. His gaze follows the graceful dance of Barques and Clippers upon the water, their billowing sails a ballet against the canvas of the endless sky.

The scene shifts to the rustic charm of a wayside inn, a haven of warmth and camaraderie. The stone floors and meticulously crafted wooden furnishings are witnesses to many a story. Behind the worn bar stands Carl Meyer, the guardian of this establishment, his white apron a badge of his dedication. Levi finds his familiar place at a worn table, a sense of belonging evident in the ease with which he settles into the space. Carl Meyer's acknowledging nod is a silent testament to the unspoken bonds between old souls.

From the tapestry of the inn's charm emerges Mary, a barmaid whose presence is like a spark igniting the room. She enters the light, her attire a harmonious blend of black and white—a bodice dress adorned with an apron. In her hands, she cradles a glass tumbler, a vessel of refreshment to quench the thirst of a summer day. Her smile, warm as the sun's embrace, welcomes Levi into her realm.

Her voice, a serenade of tenderness, floats through the air as she addresses the young adventurer. "How fares my handsome companion on this fervent day? I thought a cooling offering might provide solace."

Levi's gratitude takes form in words, a glimmering pearl of appreciation. "Thank you, Mary. You look adorable today."

She echoes his sentiment with a twinkle like stars in the night sky. "Ah, that's because I knew my dear boy would grace my realm.

And what of your stepfather, young sir? Surely, the season of shearing signals his return."

Levi's words dance excitedly, like fireflies on a summer's eve. "Indeed, Ma expects him to arrive next week."

Curiosity dances in Mary's eyes as she delves deeper. "Well, when he does make his entrance, ensure he pays me a visit promptly. I eagerly anticipate that reunion. And what grand plans does he have for your adventures this time?"

Levi's response is as natural as the ebb and flow of the tides. "The usual adventures—horseback riding, casting lines along the river's edge, and nights spent under the stars, with stories kindled by campfires."

Approval colours Mary's voice like a gentle breeze. "A fatherly figure he seems to be, even if circumstances allow for mere weeks of togetherness."

With a wistful sigh, Levi's voice carries a hint of longing. "My mother often dreams of more than just his seasonal cheques after the shearing. A more generous purse would grant me the privilege of attending Mr Sharp's School instead of the confines of home."

Mary's response is a playful yet profound dance of light and shadow. "Your mother is blessed to have his support in her orbit, even if conventional labels elude their connection. He's a welcome presence under my roof—though the depths of that sentiment might be beyond your grasp."

Levi's laughter chimes like bells in the breeze, his innocence a joyful melody. "You, Mary, are truly amusing. You always manage to make me laugh."

Mary's affectionate response is a cherished melody in itself. "And you, Levi, are my favourite young man."

The camaraderie between the barmaid, Mary, and Levi is abruptly shattered by the jarring intrusion of a figure that exudes an unmistakable air of menace. This newcomer appears as a Sulky

Ruffian and strides into the inn with an aura of roughness that chills the air around him.

Despite his relatively short stature, standing at about five feet, his presence carries a scruffy and rugged appearance. His face bears the rough resemblance of a bulldog, and his eyes gleam with a vulture's predatory intensity. Five other men follow in his wake, each exuding an equally rugged demeanour of a 'Vandemonian'. They are armed with revolvers hanging prominently from their belts, and intimidating Bowie Knives are sheathed at their sides.

The Sulky Ruffian's voice booms through the room, a demand that brooks no disobedience. "Where's the owner of this fine establishment?"

Carl Meyer, the inn's proprietor, stands his ground. Known for his composed German demeanour and staunch aversion to troublemakers, he faces the intruder with calm authority. His voice carries a measured strength as he addresses the man before him. "You're looking at him, mate. What business brings you here?"

The Sulky Ruffian's tone remains brazen as he states his intent. "We've come for drinks, mate. Nobblers all around!"

Carl Meyer's response is marked by his trademark poise, undaunted by the challenge before him. "If that's your desire, then so be it. But make no mistake: no payment will be required. Each of you will receive a single drink... No More! Afterwards, you'll leave. Do we understand each other?"

The Sulky Ruffian's agreement is a begrudging acceptance of the terms. "Yeah... Yeah! We'll go along with that. Get on with it, then."

By the inn's established custom, a subtle smile tugs at Meyer's lips as he places two brandy decanters and an array of tumblers on the bar. With a gesture of invitation, Meyer addresses the group. "Help yourselves, gentlemen."

The six ruffians eagerly pour generous brandy into their glasses, yet their greed is thinly veiled as they attempt to shield their intentions beneath their hands.

The Sulky Ruffian's voice rings out once more. "Well, landlord, your brandy is indeed a fine choice! Truly a delight, I must say. Now, how about topping up our bottles, mate? Let's have another round. After all, you extended the courtesy of those nobblers, didn't you? It's only fair we return the favour!"

Meyer's demeanour remains composed, his hidden plan unfurling in the shadows. As one of the ruffians starts to edge toward the bar, assuming the role of a bartender, Meyer intervenes, urging restraint and promising a unique offering from the inn's backroom.

Meyer's voice carries a measured warning. "Hold on a moment, friend. I have something even more exceptional for you—some top-notch Champagne and Cognac."

Meyer withdraws to the back with deliberate steps, yet it is not the anticipated drinks he brings upon his return. Instead, he reemerges with two pistols drawn, ready for action. Simultaneously, his business partner steps forward, a stout and determined figure of German origin armed with a double-barreled shotgun. This Partner embodies an unwavering determination, a presence capable of instilling fear in even the most brazen of hearts.

Unfazed by the barman's bluster, the Vandemonians continue their raucous behaviour, seemingly unfazed by their inability to pay for the drinks they await. Meyer, faithful to his manners and resolute character, takes command of the escalating situation.

He places a decanter of Cognac on the bar, his steady pistols aimed at the unruly group. Meyer's words resonate with commanding authority. "Lay a finger on it... if you dare! It will be your last action if you attempt to pour even a drop from that decanter."

The Partner's voice adds a chilling note of finality. "I'd put a bullet through that man before he could blink."

Suddenly confronted with the dire consequences of their actions, the ruffians shrink back in fear and haste. Driven by self-preservation, they hurriedly vacate the inn, leaving behind their bravado in favour of a desperate scramble for safety. As the scene unfolds, Levi and Mary remain hidden beneath a barroom table, silent witnesses to the swift and unexpected turn of events.

Chapter Thirty-Six

Nestled alongside the gentle curves of Cowie Creek in Geelong, an aged cottage stands as a stoic witness to the ebb and flow of time. Its weathered countenance wears the marks of countless seasons, its dry-stone walls etched with the stories of a grander past. A poignant sense of neglect hangs in the air, a testament to the relentless passage of years that have weathered its once-stalwart facade. The compacted earth that forms its floor bears the imprints of countless footsteps, a silent reminder of lives once lived. Void of glass, two windows are swathed in curtains of humble calico, their gentle dance a whispered tribute to the stories sheltered within.

Within the embrace of this weathered sanctuary, a hearth and chimney rise like ancient sentinels, fashioned from stones that have witnessed the march of time and above a modest kitchen bench, a solitary window frames a patch of sky, while a table of roughly hewn wood and chairs handcrafted by a skilled bush carpenter stand as relics of rustic artistry. The interior, partitioned by calico panels, weaves together two distinct sleeping spaces, each with its own whispered dreams.

Alice and Levi stand before this tapestry of history, their carpetbags clutched tightly as if seeking an anchor in the uncertainty ahead. Their eyes, fixed upon the timeworn dwelling, hold a dance of emotions—resilience twined with hesitation, determination entwined with the unknown.

Alice's voice, a soft cadence in the air, breaks the silence. "It might not possess grandeur, Levi, but Bill insists that we claim it today before his arrival tomorrow."

Levi's voice carries a note of uncertainty, a hesitant melody. "I don't find myself taken by it, Ma. Staying closer to the docks, at Mrs Cranberry's place, seems more appealing."

Alice's resolve shines through, her words carrying a quiet strength. "Bill has assured me that repairs will be made upon his arrival. I'll continue teaching piano at Mrs Cranberry's, and your education will remain undisturbed. You'll have ample time to explore and play, just as you have in the past."

Alice and Levi cross the cottage's threshold with a shared breath, stepping into a realm where past and future converge. The elegance of their attire casts a stark contrast against the aged backdrop, a reminder of the chasm between the lives they've known and the uncharted territory that stretches before them.

Their footsteps echo through the chambers, a duet of footsteps intertwined with the whispers of the past and the secrets this cottage holds within its walls. As they wander deeper into the heart of this timeworn dwelling, the emotions etched upon their faces form a bittersweet mosaic.

Brody's entrance fractures the silence, a stark contrast against the weathered threshold. His towering presence, six-foot-three of dishevelled chaos, bends to accommodate the humble doorway. Once held with purpose, Saddlebags fall to the dirt floor in a sombre thud, an echo reverberating through the confined space.

The tale of indulgence is etched upon him—clothes awry, hair in disarray, a clouded mood borne of potent spirits. The room breathes the scent of his indulgence, and his every step betrays unsteady resolve. His gaze sweeps across the room, capturing the figures of

Alice and Levi, both seemingly overawed in the shadow of this imposing, dishevelled figure.

The exchange of glances between mother and son speaks a silent dialect—a shared understanding laced with trepidation. They stand united, side by side, a wall of solidarity awaiting the first tremor of Brody's words.

In a voice that reverberates with authority, Brody addresses the room. "Well, Levi, you've been stretching skyward since my last visit. Gonna have to keep an eagle eye, or you'll cast shadows over me soon enough."

Alice responds with a measured warmth, a salve to quell the tension. "Hello, Bill. How was your ride into Geelong?"

His speech slightly slurred, Brody recounts, "Bloody good, I'll admit. Rode on a reliable trail horse with no breaks needed. Mares in fine fettle. Can't vouch for this place, though. Aye! Bought it sight unseen from a bloke heading Blackwood's way. Clearly, it yearns for some dire fixing."

Curiosity flavours Alice's sincerity. "What prompted this choice, Bill? It might've been simpler to persist with the Cranberry's arrangement."

Leaning in, Brody's intentions loom larger. "Here's the gist, Alice. The Cranberry's arrangement don't offer us solitude. My thoughts have taken a turn about how we ought to be living. Now that we're wed by law, should we not share the same roof like any other married souls when I'm around?"

Defiance bristles in Alice's tone. "Are you suggesting, Bill, that this was our understanding?"

Slightly slurred, Brody insists, "Times have swayed, Alice. You're a woman of grace and shouldn't wither away alone. I've provided, haven't I? Those bonus cheques, year by year. It's high time I earn something in return."

Indignation flares within Alice, her words sharper now. "You're intoxicated, Bill. These words hold no weight of sincerity. Where are your values now? What of your oath and respect to Dan concerning Levi and me?"

The mere mention of Dan is like striking a hidden nerve within Brody. His visage twists, a tempestuous clash of fury and inner conflict. Fists hammer the rough-hewn table, the wood trembling under the onslaught. Raw emotions spill from his lips, a tumultuous mixture of resentment and anguish. An accusing scowl is directed at Alice before Brody unsteadily departs the cabin, his footsteps mingling with the distant rhythm of his horse's retreat. The quiet shack is left to bear the aftermath of this tempestuous encounter.

Brody bursts into the dim-lit cottage with a frenzied fervour as the evening casts its shroud. The wooden door slams open with a forceful thud, proclaiming his stormy arrival. His presence is amplified by a deeper layer of intoxication, an unsettling aura that envelops him like a thundercloud.

In the cramped confines of his bed, Levi's heart gallops with fear. He becomes a small, trembling creature, curling into himself and clutching the threadbare blanket as a feeble barrier against the chaos around him.

Alice steps forth from her room in a delicate nightdress like a guardian of the night. The calico curtain flutters gently as her eyes take in the turmoil that now envelopes their refuge. Shadows dance upon the walls, a dance that mirrors the chaotic tempest within.

Brody's gaze, marred by a haze of inebriation, locks onto Alice—a predator's fixation. The glint in his eyes is predatory, an unsettling fire stoked by unchecked impulses. With a determined stride, he steps into her personal space, his intentions evident.

Alice's voice reverberates with anger, fear, and unwavering defiance. "NO, BILL!" Her words are a fierce proclamation, a plea for sanity amid chaos. Her eyes blaze with determination as she asserts her boundaries.

"Control yourself. This behaviour is not acceptable. Think of Levi in the next room."

The words hang in the air, a plea for reason, for humanity. But Brody's retort is a venomous command, a sharp retort that cuts through the air like a blade.

"Shut UP, Woman!" The words are a lash, a stark reminder of the power dynamics that underlie their relationship.

Yet, Alice's courage does not waver, her resolve resolute. Her stance remains unwavering even as Brody advances. His fist swings with the force of anger and entitlement, landing upon Alice's cheek with a sickening thud.

Staggering back from the impact, Alice finds herself sprawled on the bed. The room feels like a suffocating trap, its walls closing around her as Brody's presence looms like a malevolent storm. The tempest of his presence is overwhelming, a storm that refuses to be quelled.

"I've been too lenient, Alice," Brody's slurred words hold a venomous edge. The veil of intoxication has stripped away restraint, leaving behind raw desire. "It's time I considered my wishes—right now... that means you!

Alice's heart races within her chest, her mind a whirlwind of conflicting emotions. Her body becomes a battleground, where her spirit fiercely fights to maintain its dignity.

In the neighbouring room, Levi trembles beneath his blanket. The world outside is a discordant symphony, a nightmarish melody threatening to shatter his innocence. He squeezes his eyes shut, tears trickling from beneath the fragile shield that offers scant protection from the horrors he can sense but not fully comprehend.

In this realm of shadows and suffering, the limits of humanity are tested, and the very essence of hope is pushed to its breaking point.

The first tendrils of dawn stretch through the cabin's windows, casting a gentle glow over the timeworn interior. Brody moves regretfully, gathering his belongings as if each item carries the burden of his choices. His gaze sweeps the room, laden with the gravity of his actions. Sighing, he shoulders his saddlebags and steps out into the nascent day.

Alice, her cheeks stained by the trails of tears, hears the sound of Brody's departure. She hurries to the front window, her eyes fixed on the figure fading into the distance atop his horse. A whirlpool of emotions churns within her—pain, anger, and a tinge of relief.

Alice's countenance mirrors a tapestry of emotions too intricate to untangle. She inhales deeply, her chest expanding as she braces to weather the storm. Sensing his mother's anguish, Levi emerges from his room and rushes to her side. They embrace each other, and their tears mingle as they find solace in shared sorrow. Alice hugs Levi, "We'll find our way, my dear. We'll ascend beyond this turmoil and forge a path toward healing. A life free from the anguish we've endured is within our grasp."

Levi holds Alice close, "I believe it, Ma. Together, we possess the strength to shape a future that gives us hope."

In their embrace, they discover a haven—a place of solace and strength nestled within the cocoon of their love. As they stand united, confronting an uncertain horizon, a glimmer of hope kindles within their eyes.

Chapter Thirty-Seven

Alice sits at the weathered kitchen table within the cabin's worn embrace. The letter lies before her, a veil of mystery waiting to be lifted. Her fingers traced the edges of the envelope as her mind wanders to the sender's address. The envelope yields to her touch, and she extracts the letter, the timbre of Brody's voice echoing in her thoughts as she reads:

Dear Alice,

I commit these words to paper with a heart heavy with remorse, hoping that someday, grace might find its way into your heart. My actions, laden with cruelty, have inflicted pain upon you and Levi that cannot be undone. This remorse courses through me as a current of shame and self-reproach.

Fueled by my inner demons and unbridled drinking, I was propelled down a path of unforgivable actions. No explanations can absolve me—only a forthright admission of guilt and an embrace of the consequences.

Reverend Hastie in Buninyong Village has become a source of guidance for me. Through confession and a pledge to change, I'm on a path toward sobriety and self-improvement.

The hurt I've inflicted upon you and Levi is a wound that cuts deep. My words can never fully mend the damage, but I solemnly swear to strive for redemption and ensure your safety and well-being.

A builder has been engaged to restore the cottage by Cowie Creek. Its transformation will render it a haven of comfort and renewal for you and Levi. This endeavour is an earnest testament to my commitment to making amends.

Alice, the pain I've caused and the trust I've shattered gnaw at me. In time, I hope that forgiveness might bloom within your heart. While my deeds will forever haunt me, I am resolute in my quest to change and become a better man.

I beseech you to grant me the chance to visit Levi as the shearing season draws near. The yearning to rebuild our connection is a fervent ache within me. I understand if space and time are required, yet I long for the possibility of reconciliation.

With the sincerest remorse,

Bill Brody.

Alice lowers the letter, her cheeks dampened by the tracks of tears. A whirlwind of emotions courses through her—a maelstrom of anger, pain, and an enigmatic inkling of something yet to be unveiled. Levi stands by her side, attuned to her distress. He enfolds her in his tiny arms, offering solace in his embrace. Alice's voice quivers with emotion, "Levi, my heart, it's a challenge to make sense of it all. But we must uncover our strength to mend and stride toward the light. For you—for us."

Levi clings to his mother, a silent testament to the weight of their shared burden. United, they stand as two souls navigating the shadows, driven by the glimmer of hope that promises a future illuminated by the warmth of the sun's embrace.

The Cowie Creek cottage has undergone a remarkable transformation. No longer a humble dwelling, it has become a haven of comfort and elegance. Once marked by modest thatch and weathered mortar, its exterior now exuded refinement—white walls adorned with intricate mortar work and a slate roof replacing the rustic thatch. Inside, the rooms bear an air of sophistication, with English wallpaper gracing the walls. The cottage boasts a cozy kitchen/diner and two inviting bedrooms. A low veranda crowned with a galvanized metal roof adorns the front, embraced by a colonial English garden that paints the scene with picturesque grace.

Amid this transformation, Alice stands by an open window, her gaze fixed on the horizon. A contemplative air surrounds her as if she is attuned to the secrets whispered by the expanse before her. In hushed tones, she murmurs, *"Bill Brody has remained steadfast in his promises, his unwavering devotion evident over these past two years. Each visit is a testament to his commitment, a pledge fulfilled with genuine intent. As I await his arrival this day, each encounter has evolved into a beacon of anticipation."*

A rider approaches the cottage, and Alice's heart quickens. She hastens to greet the newcomer, her white dress adorned with a graceful, dark-hued muslin shawl—emanating an aura of poise and elegance. In her presence, inner beauty blends seamlessly with outward grace.

"Hello, Bill," she greets with a warmth that radiates from within. "It's a pleasure to see you once again. How was your journey from Buninyong?"

A smile tugs at Bill's lips as he responds, his eyes reflecting the sun's radiance. "The journey was scorching, but the sight of you makes it all worthwhile, Alice."

Alice's cheeks flush with a delicate blush, manifesting the joy accompanying his arrival. "Please, step inside," she invites her voice to a gentle melody. "Levi is just finishing up his studies. Where do you plan to take him for the upcoming holiday?"

Brody's enthusiasm is palpable. "No camping adventures this time. I have a novel proposition in mind. I'll reveal the details after we catch up."

Guiding him indoors, Alice introduces him to the transformed cottage. As he approaches Levi, his demeanour takes on a light-hearted tone. However, Levi's response is curt, an air of indifference enveloping him.

"How's our young scholar?" Brody's voice holds a teasing note. "Seems like you've grown another inch since I last saw you."

Levi's response is concise and uninterested. "Doing fine."

With a moment of suspended excitement hanging in the air, Alice's anticipation is evident across her features.

"Alice," Bill's gaze holds a depth of emotion, "our connection has flourished over these years. We've bridged the gap that once separated us, and I've upheld my promise of sobriety. Our correspondence has deepened, revealing our mutual yearning for a closer bond. The legal tie that binds us has awakened dormant desires within me—a call to bridge the distance, to establish permanence. If we don't seize this opportunity, we risk losing the potential for a brighter future—for Levi, for ourselves."

Alice's nod holds a resolute conviction, her eyes mirroring the connection that unites them. "Bill, I agree. The legal marriage has intensified my longing for you, igniting a desire for a deeper connection. I'm still young, and the prospect of a better life beckons. I won't let it slip away."

Bill's words hold a tender sincerity. "My proposal involves you and Levi travelling to Buninyong Village. The village has thrived, and I've arranged accommodations for both of you at the Buninyong Hotel under the care of Mother Jamieson—a woman known for her Scottish hospitality. This arrangement would enable more frequent visits from Ercildoune Station, allowing us to spend more time together."

Alice's enthusiasm is infectious. "That sounds wonderful, Bill. Your letters have kept me informed, and I understand the complexities of a potential move to Ercildoune Station."

Bill's explanation carries thoughtfulness. "Indeed. A swift transition could disrupt the station's harmony, causing worker friction. My transformation from a solitary man to one with family ties might unsettle the station's operation—Victoria's best-run station. It could lead to temporary turbulence until the workers adjust."

Alice grasped the situation. "I understand, Bill. Levi and I welcome this change. For Levi, you've been the cherished uncle who brings joy each year. With more frequent visits, I hope he'll come to see you as his true father."

A look of conflict flickers across Levi's face as his gaze settles on his mother. The stage is set for a tumultuous journey—a tale of family, love, secrets, and transformation against the backdrop of a nation's birth and rebellion.

Chapter Thirty-Eight

The village of Buninyong has evolved over the eight years, shedding its previous status as a minor settlement. It thrives with a vibrant pulse, exuding life and vitality at every turn. Nestled at its core is a jovial wayside hotel presided over by a beloved figure known to all. The village boasts a hotel, school, a bustling general store, and a blacksmith's shop and stables that have witnessed a change of guard.

Amid this transformed landscape, a mother and her young child wander along the main dirt road of Buninyong Village. Their conveyance from Geelong was upon a cart pulled by a team of sturdy bullocks, their handler orchestrating a scene with energy and a touch of chaos. This handler is a vivid character, celebrated for his spirited language and distinctive attire of a flannel shirt and moleskin trousers tucked into high boots.

As the trio traverses the village, their passage stirs up clouds of dust that shroud the surroundings. The handler's whip cracks through the air, a bawdy command that urges the bullocks onward, each addressed by its name.

From a distance, the local reverend Hastie observes this spectacle with disapproval. His discomfort becomes evident as he tugs at his round collar, increasingly agitated. He retreats into the haven of the church, seeking solace from the discordant scene.

Within the confines of the two-storey, wood-panelled Buninyong Hotel, an atmosphere of liveliness prevails. Laughter intermingles with animated conversations, creating an ambience that brims with joy. At the epicentre of this merry space stands a meticulously carved front bar, a hub around which patrons gather on barrel seats and at round tables.

Amid this bustling scene, Alice and young Levi enter the hotel. Each carries their belongings, their presence adding to the excitement. The hotel's gracious host approaches them, a warm smile gracing her features. "Greetings," she offers warmly. "We've prepared a snug room upstairs for the both of you."

Alice responds with gratitude, expressing appreciation, "Thank you kindly, ma'am.

"You can call me Mother," the host continues, inviting a sense of familiarity. "You and your young one are welcome here – Bill has confided in me. Let the lad join the camaraderie with the other children."

Alice's gratitude is palpable, mirrored in the eager agreement of the young boy as Levi heads for the front door and outside.

In the heart of the blacksmith's shop, flames dance within the forge, casting a warm glow over the surroundings. The blacksmith, a robust figure with a thick beard and formidable strength, wields his tools with practised precision. The rhythmic sound of a hammer striking an anvil reverberates through the air.

Levi's eyes widen with fascination as he watches this mesmerizing display. Levi approaches the blacksmith with an amiable smile, who concludes his task.

"Well, who do we have here?" he inquires genially.

"I'm new to the village," Levi responds, a mixture of excitement and nervousness colouring his voice.

A hearty chuckle escapes the blacksmith's lips. "You must be connected to that lovely lady I saw at the inn. There's been talk about you."

Levi affirms this with a nod.

"Call me Tommy," the blacksmith offers, extending a hand in friendship. "No need for formalities around here."

The boy's gratitude is evident as he offers his thanks, and the echo of Tommy's laughter fills the air. The evolution of Buninyong, the warmth of the inn's embrace, and the forging of unexpected connections intertwine to create an inviting tapestry. As bonds form in unlikely places, the stage is set for new relationships to blossom in the heart of this thriving village.

Chapter Thirty- Nine

As evening descends upon the village, the Buninyong Hotel springs to life with an atmosphere of liveliness and mirth. Patrons from various corners of the hamlet gather, drawn by the promise of new acquaintances. Mother Jamieson, the heart of the establishment, takes on the role of the introducer, connecting the newcomers with the faces of their burgeoning community.

The first introduction is to the Presbyterian Reverend Thomas Hastie. He is a community pillar with an imposing stature and an air of distinction. His appearance is marked by a tall, slender frame, his clean-shaven face exuding handsomeness. Curly black hair crowns his head, a natural halo accentuating his perpetual smile, revealing teeth as white and prominent as pearls.

"Allow me to present Alice and Levi," Mother Jamieson declares, her voice warm and inviting. "This is the Presbyterian Reverend Thomas Hastie."

Alice and Levi extend their greetings, their expressions a mirror of politeness and genuine pleasure. "We are delighted to make your acquaintance, Reverend."

Reverend Hastie's response is gracious, his tone a blend of warmth and hospitality. "The pleasure is mine, Alice, and yours too, young Levi. Our Sunday morning services are open to all denominations, the sole church on this side of Geelong. What faith do you uphold, Alice?"

With candour, Alice reveals her spiritual background. "I was christened Catholic, Reverend, but I'm more than willing to join your congregation on Sunday mornings."

Amidst the lively exchanges, Mr Bedwell steps forward, a stout figure with a commanding presence. His bald head is adorned with a winged moustache, and he wears a black suit that strains to contain his ample frame. He greets Alice and Levi with a genial smile, revealing his role in the community.

"Allow me to extend my greetings, Mrs Brody and Levi," he proclaims. "I am the principal of our village school, an initiative supported by Reverend Hastie."

Alice responds with gratitude, reflecting her appreciation for the educational opportunity offered. "Thank you, Mr Bedwell. We are truly grateful for the chance for Levi to attend your school."

Mr Bedwell's enthusiasm is palpable as he continues. "We are thrilled to have him as a student. The Learmonth Brothers have generously covered his day pupil fee, invested in fostering the growth of our educational institution."

Alice's gratitude shines through as she responds. "Their kindness is deeply appreciated, as is your dedication to nurturing education within our community."

The evening unfolds as Alice and Levi mingle, their interactions spanning a tapestry of personalities and backgrounds. They encounter individuals of diverse walks of life—labourers in their work attire, the blacksmith Thomas Hiscock, and well-dressed gentlemen accompanied by elegantly attired wives.

Whispering to Levi, Alice observes the mosaic of characters before them. "Look, Levi, this village is a mosaic of intriguing stories, each from a different corner of the world. It's a remarkable place we're privileged to call home."

Levi's eyes shine with excitement, his voice brimming with anticipation. "I'm eager to start school, Ma. And everyone is so friendly here."

With each introduction, Alice and Levi find themselves entwined more deeply within the vibrant tapestry of Buninyong's heart. The Buninyong Hotel, once a simple inn, has now become a bustling crossroads of relationships, where laughter harmonizes with camaraderie, weaving bonds that tie the village together.

As the evening unfolds, Alice and Levi engage in conversations that span the spectrum of human experience. Labourers share tales of triumphs earned through hard work and the resilience to endure struggles. Thomas Hiscock imparts stories of the blacksmith's craft, the very pulse of the forge brought to life through his words. Distinguished couples exude grace and resilience, their life stories etched into the lines of their faces.

Levi's gaze dances from one face to another, his curiosity lighting up his eyes. The diversity of stories he encounters only amplifies his anticipation for the days ahead. "Ma," he wonders, hope and eagerness blending in his voice, "do you think I'll make friends at the school?"

Alice responds with the gentle assurance of a mother who knows the world's mysteries. "Certainly, Levi. Like the mosaic of people gathered here, friendships are woven from shared moments. And this village, our new home, is an inviting tapestry, ready to embrace you."

With each exchange, Alice and Levi contribute their threads to Buninyong's rich mosaic. The Buninyong Hotel becomes a symbol of unity, where the differences among the villagers become threads that shape the vibrant community fabric.

As the night deepens, Buninyong is shrouded in a curtain of darkness. Inside the Buninyong Hotel, laughter and camaraderie continue to echo through its walls. The hotel's interior pulses with life as the lively violin tune "Van Diemen's Land" strains mingle with the patrons' hearty voices. They sing a bawdy ballad, the lyrics a testament to their shared spirit of merriment and carefree abandon: *"Young men all, do beware, Unless you get caught into a snare... come all you gallant poachers that ramble void of care, that walk out on a moonlight night with your dog and gun and snare...*

Joined by all in the room, an Irish jig takes hold, the wooden floor reverberating beneath the rhythm of dancing feet. From Levi's vantage point atop the landing, Levi can't help but burst into laughter, captivated by the intoxicating atmosphere of exuberance and cheer that fills the space below.

Levi's laughter weaves into the chorus of the night, his enjoyment and elation a testament to the uncontainable energy enveloping the hotel. As the music sweeps through the air and bodies sway to its lively cadence, he is swept up in the current of jubilation, embracing the night's carefree spirit.

Amidst the jubilant revelry, Alice's ears catch the familiar sound of Levi's laughter drifting down from the landing. Her lips curve to a gentle smile, her heart warming to the reassurance that her son has found his place of contentment and connection. The mirthful echoes of his joy convey the assurance that they have become part of Buninyong's welcoming embrace.

Alice's gaze turns introspective as she reflects on their journey. Their trials and uncertainties have led them to a moment of laughter and companionship. As the joyful sounds persist, Alice allows herself a moment of gratitude. Their new life in Buninyong has brought them a sense of belonging and kindled the anticipation of future possibilities. The path ahead, filled with Levi's education and the companionship of newfound friends, shimmers with hope and promise.

The Buninyong Hotel, pulsating with laughter and camaraderie, has become more than just a place to rest—it's a sanctuary of shared moments and shared lives, a testament to the resilience of the human spirit in the face of challenges.

As she gazes out the front window, the village's twinkling lights forming constellations of promise, Alice is filled with the certainty that this chapter in their lives is merely the beginning—one of growth, connection, and the enduring power of community.

Chapter Thirty-Nine

Nestled in a gully a mile east of Buninyong Village, a prospecting tale unfolds. Thomas Hiscock and young Levi, aged thirteen, step into this landscape of possibility. Their attire, a blend of twill shirts and mud-dappled moleskin trousers tugged into sturdy boots, and the iconic cabbage tree hats paint them as seekers of dreams. The wheelbarrow, shovel, and gold prospecting pan stand ready, emblematic of their quest for the elusive glint of fortune.

With Levi's shovel sinking into gravel and Hiscock watching intently, an unspoken understanding between them deepens. Hiscock's voice carries a blend of mentorship and camaraderie. "Levi, lad, you're shaping up nicely. I see the sinews growing in those arms of yours. Before you know it, you'll be as solid as a gorilla."

Levi's brow furrows in amusement, his youthful scepticism peeking through. "Why would I want to resemble a gorilla, Tommy?"

Hiscock's laughter dances in his eyes. "Because, young one, those girls are taken by the robust ones. And with your age, changes are on the horizon. The harder you toil, the more they'll compete for your attention."

Levi's amusement mingles with a dash of exasperation. "I've had enough of girls acting oddly around me, Tommy. They try to assist me with tasks I can handle myself."

Hiscock's laughter is a hearty echo. "Ha! You're a true character, lad. Just wait a bit, and you'll be singing a different tune. You'll pursue those same girls like a hound chasing a scent. Now, keep shovelling. I've got a feeling our work's about to pay off."

Levi's shovel works diligently, curiosity alight in his eyes. "How can you be so sure there's gold here, Tommy? This doesn't look any different from your backyard. We could save a long walk by digging there."

Hiscock's assurance gleams like the sun on the water. "Gold's been discovered not too far off in Clunes. Gold accompanies white quartz rock, something absent in my backyard. But look around, lad. The earth here—it's as if it's snowing, like the scenes from Christmases back in old England."

The wheelbarrow filling, Levi inquires, "What's the next step, Tommy?"

Hiscock's tone holds a blend of instruction and anticipation. "Now, young one, we wash this earth well. Among these grains, we might just find those glimmers of gold gazing back from the pan's depths."

Together, they amble to the creek that weaves through the gully. Their knees kiss the water's edge as Hiscock tends to the prospecting pan. Levi watches, captivated, as dirt dances and dissipates, leaving behind the hint of treasure. As the final swirl is executed, both lean in, eager for discovery. Hiscock's reaction is one of awe—wide eyes and a hint of a grin.

Hiscock's triumphant shout rings out, a melody of triumph. "**Brilliant, lad! Eureka!** We've hit gold, and there's a bounty of it! Look here! A nugget, sizable. Must weigh more than half a troy ounce."

This discovery ignites a dance of elation, their cabbage-tree hats soaring as if lifted by the currents of their jubilation. In this gully, the promise of prosperity surrounds them as Hiscock and Levi stand united in laughter and exhilaration, a shared song echoing across the vast expanse of the land.

The gully's heart hosts an unwavering endeavour as Levi and Hiscock's endeavours persist. Their resolve is a beacon, a testament to their shared purpose. Side by side, shovels cleave into the earth, hands sifting through the gravel's hidden potential. The sun reigns supreme, a relentless companion, yet its fervent rays dissolve into the background of their newfound mission.

Hiscock's voice, a steady undercurrent of determination, punctuates the rhythm of their labour. "We'll keep digging, lad. The deeper we delve, the grander the treasures that await."

Levi's rejoinder resonates with a fierce determination, an ember sparked by boundless possibility. "Count me in, Tommy. We'll press forward until every last glint of gold sees the light."

Hiscock's laughter dances in the air, an enchanting symphony of camaraderie. "Indeed, my lad. But only for another hour. Soon, I'll chart a course to Geelong, staking my claim before another snatches the prize. There's a reward for uncovering a promising goldfield that will be mine to seize."

Amidst the embrace of earth and sunlight, two figures toil ceaselessly, embodying a spirit that refuses to relent. Their partnership is the linchpin, shovels and hands moving harmoniously, weaving dreams from the soil below. The gully, a silent witness, bears testimony to their unyielding perseverance. Their labour extends beyond personal ambition; it's a pact for a future where the glint of gold materializes as a vow fulfilled.

Chapter Forty

Upon the expansive front verandah of the Buninyong hotel, Mother Jamieson and Alice position themselves as contemplative witnesses. Before them unfolds a tableau of unwavering determination—the Diggers embarking on a fresh day of prospecting. Each figure is cloaked by the cool grip of winter, a season that holds no power over their resolute spirits. The air carries not just the bite of the cold but also an intangible undercurrent of potential, mingling with the very essence of the season itself.

Mother Jamieson's voice, a blend of exasperation and empathetic knowing, threads through the air. "Alice, there they go. Off in pursuit of that elusive metal as if their souls hinge upon its discovery. Borrowing my pots and pans for the sake of sifting through the earth! If I catch even one of them in the act, they'll taste the sting of a proper scolding, make no mistake."

Alice's response resonates with the gravity of the situation. "Mother, the fever has taken hold of them. Bill has mused about joining their ranks should this goldfield continue to bestow its riches."

Mother Jamieson's laughter dances upon the breeze, a harmonious blend of understanding and the wisdom of age. "No need to be overly concerned, my dear. A couple of our own, John Dunlop and James Regan, have abandoned the prospects of Hiscock's Gully. Their gaze now rests upon Ballaarat, a mere six miles from here. It's hard to fault them for seeking their fortune in fresh soil. The initial promises of Hiscock's Gully have yet to fully bloom."

Alice imparts her own insights, weaving a tapestry of vivid imagery. "Bill and I journeyed to Ballaarat. It's a sight to behold, a place where a meandering creek carves through the embrace of a lush valley. Above, on the plateau, wattle forests and expansive grasslands create a breathtaking tableau. William Yuille established his claim there in 1838, naming it 'The Black Swamp.' A sheep station now represents his vision, a place Bill and I had the privilege to visit not long ago."

In Mother Jamieson's tone, a trace of hope glimmers. "Perhaps those two Diggers will uncover their fortune somewhere in Ballaarat. Their discoveries may well usher a touch of serenity to our midst."

As the shared moment between Alice and Mother Jamieson deepens, their gazes extend toward the distance where the Diggers have vanished. The air seems to bear the weight of aspirations and dreams yet unfulfilled, interwoven with the allure of uncharted territory. Amidst the tranquillity of this exchange, they stand as silent witnesses to a pursuit that transcends the quest for mere gold—a journey into destiny itself.

Amidst the vibrant symphony of the hotel's bar room, Mother Jamieson and Alice are drawn together by the currents of concern. Their faces mirror a tableau of unease and anticipation, capturing the weight of the impending revelation.

Mother Jamieson's voice, tinged with a gravity that matches the weight of her words, reaches out to Alice. "Alice, our most sombre apprehensions have materialized. The latest revelation of gold has ignited a wildfire of excitement in Ballaarat. A deluge of men, driven by the insatiable pursuit of gold, have cast aside their lives in Geelong and Melbourne. Chaos and tumult follow in their wake—this is the embodiment of sheer madness!"

Alice's rejoinder carries her own reservations, a reflection of her inner turmoil. "Mother, I fear that even Bill has fallen under the intoxicating spell of gold's allure. He teeters on the brink of relinquishing his responsibilities at Ercildoune Station, swayed by the frenetic frenzy sweeping toward the goldfields. He regales us with tales of nuggets akin to hen's eggs and each pan of soil yielding two ounces of gold, commanding three pounds per ounce in Geelong."

Mother Jamieson's reply bears the weight of experience, mingled with exasperation and sagacity. "A game for the reckless, my dear! But what then? When will the ceaseless flood of wealth run dry? We shall be left bereft of sustenance, and the entire nation will descend into economic despair."

Within this fleeting instant, ensconced in the rich tapestry of time, Mother Jamieson and Alice witness the tempestuous trajectory fueled by insatiable greed. The bar room reverberates not merely with the chatter of patrons and the clink of glasses but with the unspoken anxieties that resonate within the hearts of those who perceive the ephemeral shimmer of gold as a harbinger of profound unrest.

Chapter Forty-One

The colonial Ballaarat goldfield of 1852 comes alive before our very eyes, a vivid tapestry woven with hues of unyielding ambition and the glimmer of hope along the sinuous banks of Yarrowee Creek, Diggers labour with a fervency known to the chosen few, their every motion orchestrated in the pursuit of coaxing the elusive precious metal from the depths of water and earth.

The sprawling tent city stands as a testament to dreams etched in the very fabric of the land, its backdrop a pulsating theatre of ceaseless activity. The air seems to hum with the sounds of scraping cradles, the barking of dogs, and a symphony of triumphant cheers and muttered frustrations. Above, black ravens weave their flight into an eerie symphony, their cries a haunting melody that merges seamlessly with the ethereal ambience.

Among the Diggers, a brotherhood united by the quest for fortune, attire paints a diverse tableau. Twilled shirts, each a distinct shade, blend harmoniously with moleskin pants, suit jackets, and silken vests—a medley of origins and aspirations. Sailor uniforms mingle effortlessly with the badges of the police force, a silent testament to the patchwork of lives lured by the seductive call of gold.

Some seek shelter from the unrelenting sun beneath the brims of top hats, while others opt for the pragmatic allure of cabbage tree or fedora hats. Boots of various lengths—knee-high, riding, or simple shoes—stir the earth beneath them, a dance amidst the dust. Many shoulder the weight of musket pistols or Colt revolvers, a reminder that survival in this realm requires fortune's favour and the means to defend it.

Within this vibrant tapestry, Bill Brody emerges—a figure pushing a wheelbarrow burdened with the weight of potential riches. His progress through the ranks of Diggers is a testament to his unwavering resolve, every movement a dance with determination and strain. His gait, marked by a limp and a hobble, tells a tale of battles fought within his flesh from a past altercation. Yet, with each step, he defies the odds, inching forward with a resilience that refuses to surrender.

As he approached the water's edge, removing his hat signals a brief pause, a fleeting reprieve from the unforgiving sun. A well-worn rag brushes across his forehead, a gesture that carries the weight of countless exertions. The harsh sun casts shadows of fatigue upon his features, a testament to the cost of his endeavours.

Bill shovels earth into his prospecting pan with a hand that balances skill with weariness. The pan is a bridge between him and the dreams he holds close. The twinge of pain that shoots through his gammy leg, a relic of past struggles, is a whisper compared to the chorus of his determination.

Within the earth's embrace lies a tapestry of secrets, and Bill is resolute in his decision to unravel them, regardless of the toll upon his body. Yet, even the most unyielding spirit must reckon with its limitations. The contents of the pan—glimmers of possibility and the harsh reality of disappointment—become too heavy to bear. With a forceful motion, Bill casts the pan aside, its contents joining the realm of rejected dreams.

Bill's descent to the earth, surrendering onto the soil that harbours his ambitions, is a symphony of sacrifice and resilience. His body, wearied and battered, finds solace in the embrace of the dirt—the same earth that has borne witness to countless dreams.

In this singular moment, amidst the chorus of unwavering spirit and the backdrop of hope, Bill Brody embodies the essence of those on the goldfields who surrender defeated. A realm where aspirations and reality converge, where the pursuit of treasure bears testament not only to the allure of metal but to the indomitable spirit of those who dare to reach beyond their endurance and seek relief in the shimmer of destiny itself.

Chapter Forty-Two

The main road in Ballaarat stretches wide, flanked by rows of tents transformed into makeshift grog shops, hardware stores, and eateries. Facades of tin and wood adorn the fronts of these provisional establishments, creating a vibrant tapestry of activity.

Beyond a timeworn grog shanty, a collision of lives unfolds. Two Diggers' senses, dulled by intoxication, become entangled in a fervent brawl. Bill Brody faces off against his opponent, both men with moleskin trousers rolled up to their knees. Their white long-sleeved undershirts stand as stark contrasts against the rugged setting.

In a raw display, their fists meet in a rapid exchange, drawing an excited crowd of diggers into the heart of the dirt road. Bill Brody's stance is shaky and uneven as he raises his knuckled fists in defence. With a forceful right-handed uppercut, he sends his opponent sprawling, unconscious.

Cheers erupt from the crowd as currency exchanges hands under the watchful eye of a vigilant gaming bookie. Among the jubilation, the excited diggers roar their approval raucously, "HOORAY! WELL DONE BRODY!"

As the elation subsides, Brody, wearied and bearing battle scars, retrieves a rag from his pocket. He gently tends to the cuts and bruises that mar his face, the remnants of his fierce encounter. Amidst the dispersing crowd, a figure of authority emerges. The Police Constable, dressed in a goldfield uniform—dark blue twill jacket with a high collar, yellow cuffs, and blue twilled trousers adorned with yellow stripes—presses through the gathering to assess the situation. Atop his head sits a blue peaked cap.

Approaching with measured steps, the constable directs his attention to Brody, who is cheered on by a chorus of congratulatory pats from fellow Diggers.

The police constable's voice is commanding, "ALRIGHT, ALL OF YOU! Disperse immediately, or face the prospect of being escorted back to Police Hill without hesitation!"

Reluctantly, the crowd complies, their discontent murmured as they retreat. The constable singles out two onlookers, pointing with authority, and addresses them. "YOU TWO! Unless you wish to be charged with fomenting unrest, you will assist in carrying the unconscious man to Police Hill, where Commissioner Captain Dana awaits."

The constable then shifts his gaze to Bill Brody, and with a tone of stern command, he inquires, "You, sir... what's your name?".

"Bill Brody"...

The police constable responds gruffly, "Then you will accompany me to face Captain Dana for the charge of Affray. Tidy your appearance; strive to present yourself respectably."

Bill Brody finds himself shackled and led behind a chestnut horse. A rope tethered around his midsection, he navigates awkwardly due to his gammy leg - the Constable rides his horse leisurely.

Perched atop a hill, the Police Camp commands a view of the bustling tent city below. A prominent white tent takes centre stage, flanked by a row of tethered police horses. Adjacent to a lofty flagpole, three Aboriginal Troopers—known as 'Traps or Joes'—stand in sentinel, symbolizing authority.

The mounted constable, leading the way with Brody, arrives at the entrance of the police tent. A firm tug on the tethered rope propels Brody forward, his movements uncertain. The tent's flap parts to reveal a man of stature. Captain Dana, with a commanding presence—an elevated brow, penetrating dark eyes, and a robust physique—steps forth. His full beard and drooping moustache accentuate his air of authority. He wears a blue cotton uniform, its high neck collar adorned with epaulettes and ceremonial regalia that marks his rank as Captain.

Captain Dana's gaze settles on Brody and the Constable. To the constable, saluting, he enquires, "Who is this, Constable? And what charge does he bear?"

The police constable replies, "This is Bill Brody, Sir! Accused of Affray. He and another man are the cause of turmoil in a street fight. The other party is en route, Sir, albeit in a less robust state."

The Captain's focus shifts to Brody, his scrutiny penetrating, raising an eyebrow. "Was the confrontation equitable, Constable? Were they evenly matched?"

Police constable, "Certainly, Sir!"

The Captain then turns his attention to Brody, his manner composed. "And what transpired to lead to this Affray, Mr Brody?"

Brody chooses his words, "Excessive alcohol, Sir."

Captain Dana smiles, "Do not presume to underestimate my capacity to discern, Mr Brody."

Body nervously, "He belittled me, Sir. Questioned my worth. My gammy leg prevents me from engaging in gold prospecting. Before this pursuit, I managed Ercildoune Station in the Buninyong District."

Captain Dana, with interest, asks, "Given your leg's condition, can you still ride?"

Brody," Certainly, Sir. I adapt the stirrups to accommodate my gammy leg."

Captain Dana smiles; "Your leadership attributes intrigue me, Brody. Your gammy leg appears not to hinder your fighting spirit."

Brody, with conviction, "Indeed, Sir. In a fair contest, I can hold my ground against most men."

Captain Dana nods, “I need a leader for my Aboriginal troopers tasked with collecting license fees across the diggings. My white officers have deserted their posts for the goldfields.”

Brody resolute, “It would be an honour to serve in such capacity, Sir. I assure you I will discharge my duties with the utmost respect and efficiency.”

Captain Dana nods again, “Constable, record Brody's measurements and ensure he is properly attired without delay. One final directive, Brody. Maintain sobriety; drunkenness shall not be tolerated among my men while on duty.”

Brody, with determination, “Understood, Sir. I pledge to uphold the highest standards of professionalism.”

The constable then offers a salute, guiding Brody away.

Chapter Forty-three

Beneath the brilliance of the sun's relentless gaze, the Diggers labour ceaselessly within the depths of the East Ballaarat gravel pits. Their toils unfurl as they delve into the earth, carving deep shafts that pierce through soil layers, reaching for the coveted blue clay—a telltale sign of the gold hidden further below. Primitive windlasses stand sentinel, their creaks and groans adding a rhythm to the air as dirt-laden buckets rise and fall in an orchestrated dance. Beside certain shafts, canvas sails unfurl and billow, ensuring a steady flow of fresh air into the subterranean labyrinth. The scene vibrates with the raw energy of men driven by their relentless pursuit of precious golden fortunes.

Bill Brody's attire has transformed, now adorned with the official Police uniform that marks his elevated rank—a Sergeant Trooper distinguished by the three bold yellow stripes tracing his arm sleeves. Unwavering determination, he guides his mount towards the bustling gravel pit diggings. Three Aboriginal Troopers follow closely, their presence emblematic of authority and the law they uphold.

A resounding cry of 'JOE! JOES! TRAPS!' reverberates through the air, a warning that sends Diggers lacking the required monthly Goldfield Licence scrambling to the bush for shelter, desperate to elude the watchful eyes of the troopers. Meanwhile, those bearing valid licenses continue their relentless efforts, accompanied by the rhythmic clank of windlasses and the muffled camaraderie of their fellow diggers.

In a dramatic gesture, Brody abruptly halts his mount at the edge of the first shaft, raising a cloud of dust that envelops him in an ethereal veil. The hooves of his steed echo with determined thuds as they meet the earth. Swiftly, the trio of Aboriginal troopers dismount, their movements choreographed with authority honed through practice.

Within the heart of the earth, one of the troopers ventures into a shaft, a fleeting silhouette against the dimly lit interior. Simultaneously, the other two troopers begin a methodical inspection, their unwavering gaze assessing the licensed diggers stationed at their respective windlasses. Emerging from the shaft depths, the trooper's head reappears, his grip firm on the collar of a young digger, scarcely in his adolescence and aged around fourteen. The youth's face is smudged with dirt, his wide eyes a canvas painted with fear and uncertainty.

Turning towards Brody, the trooper speaks, "Him no ticket, Boss! Hiding like a scared rabbit."

Brody's response is swift and resolute. "Cuff him and secure him with rope. Hand me the end of the rope." His voice carries an air of command, met with the troopers' prompt compliance.

As the youth is restrained, the troopers turn their attention to the licensed diggers nearby, their actions meticulous and thorough. They collect and scrutinize each license with practised efficiency—a visual affirmation of compliance with the mandatory licensing requirement.

The troopers navigate the labyrinthine landscape of shafts, disappearing into one after another, ensuring that the rule of licensing extends to every corner of the diggings. Their presence is a testament to authority and a reminder of the consequences that befall those who stray from the bounds of legality.

Under the relentless sun's warm embrace, Brody guides a trio of hand-cuffed diggers in a sombre procession. The rope tethering them to his sturdy mount stretches taut, each step resonating with a quiet acceptance. The three Aboriginal Troopers follow closely, their mounts guided by practised hands. The lengthening shadows of the late afternoon mirror the solemnity of the occasion.

Approaching the heart of authority, the entrance flaps of the Police Commissioner's tent stand wide open, unveiling an interior tableau. Positioned around a table, Mr Doveton, the Goldfield Commissioner, sits with an air of distinction. Youthful features belie his position of power, his elaborate uniform adorned with intricate embroidery and a ceremonial sword at his side. Beside him, Captain Dana, the Police Commissioner, exudes an aura of control and confidence.

As Brody nears the Commissioners, he executes a salute—a gesture of respect and a symbol of his commitment to the hierarchy. "Three more prisoners, sirs, ready to be logged," his voice carries the weight of his responsibility.

Mr Doveton responds promptly, acknowledging the accomplishment. "Excellent work, Sergeant Brody! This will send a clear message that license fees cannot be evaded. Do the prisoners offer any explanations for their actions?"

In response, the first cuffed digger steps forward, a mix of respect and nervousness in his voice.

"I just arrived yesterday, sir. I was unaware that I needed a license," his explanation hangs in the air.

Mr Doveton's patience wanes, his tone bordering on dismissive. "Nonsense! It is common knowledge on the goldfields. Obtaining a license is the first step for anyone. And what about you, prisoner number two?"

The second cuffed digger hesitates, his words trailing with uneasiness, "At Father Smyth's request, I was merely visiting the diggers at the Gravel Pits. I am not a miner myself. I was to inform them about a religious service on Sunday at Bakery Hill."

Captain Dana intervenes, his voice firm and unwavering. "Ridiculous! Whether seeking gold or not, everyone must possess a license. We cannot make exceptions based on religious or political grounds. And what is your excuse, prisoner number three?"

The youngest of the trio speaks with a mix of innocence and fear, his youth amplifying the gravity of his words. "I ain't got no money, Sir. Used every penny to get here. I've joined Grey's Mob. Grey says we'll hit pay dirt tomorrow, and he'll get me a license then."

Captain Dana's tone becomes unyielding, "Rubbish! I will have all three of you chained to the logs as prisoners unless you pay the five-pound felony charge and your thirty shillings miner's license fee. Every person on this goldfield must obtain a license before beginning work, regardless of finding gold. Do you have the full amount, or is someone willing to pay on your behalf... immediately?"

In unison, the roped diggers respond with collective desperation, their voices mingling in helplessness. "No, Sir!" their words form a chorus of surrender.

Captain Dana's verdict is resolute, his decision final. "Very well, Sergeant Brody. These three will join the others chained to the logs. They will be held here for seven days unless their fines and fees are paid in full. After that, they will be expelled from the goldfield to return to Melbourne, Geelong, or wherever they came from."

Brody's response is immediate, his salute compliance. "Understood, sir," he acknowledges, his words carrying the weight of his commitment to upholding the law.

Chapter Forty-Four

A single white canvas tent emerges amid Main Road's bustling encampment, offering a glimpse into its interior. Black liquor bottles and sturdy tumblers grace a table as several diggers and Bill Brody are seated. An air of intoxication hangs heavy, with Brody still clad in his uniform—a stark contrast to the revelry surrounding him.

"Thanks for the drinks, mates! The next round's on me... or maybe not, HA! You better keep your noses clean while I'm away, or I'll have me Blackfellas shut down this illicit grog shop for good! I'm heading back to the Little Bendigo District to reunite with me, missus," Brody's words tumble out with a mixture of slurring and laughter. His movements, however, betray his inebriation as he struggles to rise from his seat and unsteadily makes his way toward the exit.

A chorus of mumbled responses wafts through the tent: "Bugger off then, mate!" - "Who'd wanna be with yuh, anyway? "You're a bloody disgrace!"

Outside the tent, Brody maneuvers to mount his horse, tied nearby. With his left foot in the left stirrup, he awkwardly swings his stiff right leg over and sets off along Main Road, Ballaarat. His posture reflects his intoxicated state—slouched and unsteady.

The scene dissolves, and Brody guides his horse up a dirt track leading to a miner's hut within the Ballaarat District of Little Bendigo, about four miles from the bustling Main Road. The humble abode echoes the simplicity of a shepherd's dwelling, with split log walls allowing slivers of sunlight to filter through. The rough-barked roof and pounded dirt floor imbue it with rustic charm. Sacking partitions divide the interior into three distinct spaces, where wooden crates and raw timber fulfil the role of furniture. Over an open stone fireplace, Alice, Brody's wife, tends to the evening meal within a heavy-based pot.

Brody bursts in, swinging open the front door, and stumbles inside. Engrossed in her task, Alice startles at his abrupt entrance, her trembling hands a testament to the turbulence his return lately brings.

"Where's me dinner... Woman? Look at yuh... Where's the beauty once proud to say I Owned?... AH! Turning into nothing but a Bush Hag since comin' to this district," Brody slurs, bitterness dripping from his words.

Alice halts her activities, her attention now firmly on her husband. Concern is mingled with trepidation in her gaze as she turns to face him.

"That's because of your return to drinking and gambling. There's no money left for Levi and me to buy anything nice. We're fortunate to have food on the table, thanks to my laundry work," her voice bears the weight of weariness as she responds.

"Hold your tongue, Woman!" Brody snaps, his anger immediate and palpable.

Gathering a flicker of courage, Alice perseveres, "Bill, we can't continue like this. You've grown bitter over not being able to prospect with the other miners. Returning to the grog only makes things worse. You have stable employment now—you must give up the drink and gambling!"

Brody's anger ignites, and a backhanded slap crashes onto Alice's face. She stumbles against the table, collapsing onto the ground. Brody's frustration morphs into a darker shade, his kicks landing on her as she curls into a protective fetal position.

"Get up and get me dinner... NOW! Where's that boy of yours... he should be here doing his chores," his voice drips with menace as he asserts his dominance.

Alice rallies, her determination greater than her fear. She gathers herself, rising shakily, and moves towards the fireplace. Brody reclaims his seat at the table, asserting his authority with a menacing presence.

"He finished his chores after school and went to Snake Gully for some gold prospecting. He should be home any minute. Bill, you have to stop beating him. If it weren't for me, the boy would have run away by now," Alice's words brim with concern and desperation, her plea echoing countless previous instances.

"Lazy mutt only thinks of himself. The boy wants to go to Tonkin's school only to avoid work," Brody scoffs, bitterness lacing his tone.

"No, Bill... I want him to have a better future and make something of himself. That's why I work hard to pay the school fee," Alice's voice blends determination and sorrow as she counters his sentiment.

"Shut your mouth, Woman, or I'll shut it again for yuh! Make something of himself, will he? Not like me - Oh! No! I'm now reduced to half a man by this gammy leg, got when trying to defend your and Dan's honour from the sins yuh did commit!" Brody's words drip with resentment and pain, his bitterness unchecked.

"Bill... STOP! - You've turned into such a brute!" Alice's plea rings with fear, her voice reflecting her desperation. Alice raises the bottom of her apron, wiping away a tear—a silent testament to the shadows that have enveloped their life, casting darkness over the love they once shared.

Chapter Forty-Five

The Little Bendigo school unfolds within the confines of a timeworn and weathered large tent, its appearance echoing the passage of time and the trials it has witnessed. Grime and decay cling to its fabric, a testament to years of use. Nearby, a tall flagpole stands, adorned with a limp and tattered Union Jack flag that hangs listlessly in the wind.

Amid recess, a gathering of students converges in the gravel front quadrangle, their youthful energy palpable. Among them stands Levi, a figure distinct in demeanour, drawn into a confrontation that promises to stir the air with tension.

Danny Briggs, known by the moniker "Fatty Briggs," assumes a central role in this brewing conflict. His stout frame and confrontational disposition set him apart. With a venomous glint in his eyes, he addresses Levi with a promise of violence. "I'm gonna smash yuh teeth in, Brody."

Levi, facing Danny Briggs, counters with a measured calm that belies the mounting tension. "What's got you all riled, Danny?"

A smirk tugs at the corners of Danny's lips as he delivers his taunting words. "Yuh think you're smarter than the rest of us... Mr Know-it-all. You're nothing but Stinky, the drunk police trooper's bastard son!"

Levi's response is swift, his words honed with an edge of defiance. "Those are fighting words... You're just a fat dumbass, Briggs!"

The scene suddenly turns as Danny positions himself on a log, his improvised chair. Seizing the moment, Levi capitalizes on Danny's unguarded stance. With a well-timed charge, he knocks Danny backward over the seat. Danny lands awkwardly, his heels atop the log, while Levi vaults over, his knees pressing into Danny's shoulders, immobilizing him. A pent-up anger is released as Levi's fists unleash a torrent of blows upon Danny's fleshy face. Each strike carries the weight of resentment, a response to the pain inflicted by Danny's cutting words.

A cry filled with desperation escapes Danny's lips. "Stop, you bastard! Help! Get him off me! He's gonna kill me!" The commotion attracts a crowd of onlookers, their voices blending into a rhythmic chant that rings in the air: "FIGHT! FIGHT! FIGHT!"

Levi's rage flares, stoked by the fervent cries that encircle him. Yet, an unexpected sting pierces the chaos. Searing pain radiates through Levi's ear, neck, and back as Mr Tonkin, the schoolmaster, intervenes with a long cane. Each strike lands with calculated force, forcing Levi's retreat. Tonkin seizes Levi by the collar, wrenching him away from Danny's grasp.

"LEVI BRODY! You have gone too far this time! You are expelled from this school for good. If you dare to return, your father and the Police Commissioner will be informed of this incident. Do you understand, young man?" Tonkin's words carry the weight of authority, a pronouncement that leaves no room for negotiation.

Levi's fiery glare meets Tonkin's stern gaze, a confrontation that simmers with unbridled anger.

"GIVE ME BACK MY SHILLING PAYMENT THEN... YOU WRETCHED OLD COCKROACH. I HATE YOU AND YOUR DAMN SCHOOL," Levi's words cut through the air like daggers, each syllable dripping with bitter contempt.

Levi's hurried steps propel him across the open countryside as the scene shifts. The ground beneath his feet bears witness to his frantic escape, a flight from his troubles and a quest for solace. With unmatched swiftness, he dashes forward, leaving behind the weight of his burdens, if only temporarily: *"I can't go straight home. Ma will figure it out. Old Tonkin never gives us a break unless we're on the verge of keeling over. I'll go down the dirt track to Snake Gully, my haven. It's not far from home,"* Levi's thoughts guide his movements, providing direction in a sea of uncertainty.

The sanctuary of Snake Gully embraces Levi, its shady gum trees gleaming white in the sunlight's embrace. Tall grass trees stand sentinel, their dark forms adding a mystery to the landscape. The scent of eucalyptus fills the air, a natural balm to Levi's senses. Amid this sanctuary, he discovers a respite from his troubles. Levi's secrets find concealment beneath a dense canopy of blackberry bushes—his short-handled shovel, a rusty tin pan for gold prospecting, and a ceramic ginger beer bottle for storage.

The gully cradles a clear creek, its winding path a testament to nature's artistry. After heavy rains, the stream relinquishes a bounty of gravel. Levi seizes his tools, advancing to the water's edge. His movements are practised, a dance of familiarity as he scoops up grit, swishing and shaking it in the submerged pan, muddying the water. Levi manipulates the pan precisely, sifting out the lighter materials until only dark mineral sands and glimmering gold fragments remain. With careful precision, he collects the precious remnants, depositing them into the ceramic ginger beer bottle—a vessel cradling his secret treasure, a vessel bearing the promise of a new life beyond the struggles of Little Bendigo: "*As this bottle fills to the brim, I'll know the day of my journey's beginning approaches. I'll follow the path this gold illuminates, perhaps all the way to the Swan River Settlement in Western Australia,*" Levi's whisper weaves dreams with the gleam of gold.

Amid Snake Gully's tranquillity, Levi finds a moment of serenity. Tenderly, he buries the ceramic bottle beneath the earth's embrace, sheltered by the blackberry bushes, alongside his aspiration tools as he prepares to journey home.

Chapter Forty-Six

The sun dips lower, casting its warm, golden brushstrokes across the landscape. Levi's steps quicken, his feet guiding him along the homeward path. The waning light embraces him, and within its fading embrace, his thoughts are consumed by a singular figure—his mother, Alice. Contemplation weaves through his mind, a tapestry of her beauty and the hardships etched into her being: *"To think of my mother, Alice Brody, is to contemplate the very essence of beauty within Ballaarat,"* Levi murmurs, his voice carrying a tender secret. *"A truth that transcends my role as her sole child. Ma's hair cascades like jet-black silk, an aura of ethereal radiance gracing her countenance."*

Levi's voice blends admiration and curiosity, a symphony of emotions as he dissects his mother's choices. He punctuates his thoughts with a kick at the earth, his foot painting punctuation marks in the dirt. Fists carve arcs through the air, a choreography of contemplation: *"Why did she choose him, Bill Brody, as her partner? What drove her heart to his when there were gentlemen in Geelong who could have adorned her life like royalty?"* His words resonate, carrying both inquiry and assertion.

Levi's gaze holds a swirl of emotions—admiration entwined with sorrow, a look that peers into a horizon laden with concealed dreams: *"Someday, Ma, I'll craft a reality where those tattered rags are but a memory,"* Levi's declaration is fueled by a fire of determination, his eyes ablaze. *"We'll escape this place, finding a haven where you'll reign as the queen you truly are. A promise, Ma."*

As the sun's glow surrenders to the horizon, the symphony of Levi's thoughts unfolds, a crescendo of dreams and commitments.

Levi's strides guide him to their modest abode. The fading light casts a muted glow, revealing Alice's silhouette, waiting. Their entrance is marked by the dance of candlelight, painting gentle shadows around them. His eyes catch the tear stains that mar his mother's gaze.

"Ma, it seems Jimmy Crockett hasn't kept his silence... about my school troubles," Levi admits softly, the weight of uncertainty heavy in his voice.

Alice's eyes reflect sorrow and concern, mirroring their shared love and fears. "Levi, why? What led you there? I can't continue protecting you with falsehoods. Bill, your stepfather, will learn of this incident," Alice's voice trembles with apprehension.

Tears find refuge in her apron's folds, vulnerability etched on her features. Levi understands they must brace for Bill Brody's return, a storm he is all too familiar with.

Levi's gaze questions, his eyes seeking answers that have eluded him. "I wish you'd answer the questions that haunt me," urgency colours Levi's voice, a plea for understanding. "The truth about my stepfather's accident, the story behind his gammy leg, the identity of my birth father. Why Bill Brody?"

Alice's words emerge softly, a caution to temper the unspoken queries. "Hush, Levi. Those words wound me, too. The time will come for me to reveal all," Alice responds, tenderness woven with resolve.

Shadows play witness to family ties, a mother and son linked by love and hidden truths.

Levi's voice rises anew, his thoughts shifting to Bill Brody, a figure of authority with little respect. "The man's a disgrace, a police trooper turned rogue," Levi's disdain is palpable, each word an indictment. "Most Ballaarat Diggers scorn him, ranking him no higher than blackfella troopers or ticket-of-leave convicts he commands on the goldfields."

Alice's voice interjects, a voice of reason amid turbulent waters. "But it's his duty, Levi. Without the fees he collects, his role would vanish."

Levi's voice sharpens, critique laying bare the complexities of Brody's alliances. "Respect eludes him in Ballaarat and Little Bendigo. Only sly grog shanty scoundrels revere him, plying him with liquor for a favour," Levi's words bristle with frustration and observation.

Alice's voice adopts a practical tone, a solution offered amidst trials. "Friday is your stepfather's night of heavy drinking. It might be wise to be away when he returns. Seek refuge with Ma Crockett. She'll understand. Take this fresh loaf of bread, a gift to share."

Levi accepts the offering, a bittersweet recognition of their reality. In their exchange, a symphony of unspoken words binds them, a connection forged in shared struggles and the dreams they both hold.

At this moment, Levi grasps the fragile strength within his mother's resolve. The dance of candlelight and shadows lingers, echoing promises and burdens unspoken.

Chapter Forty-Seven

Beneath the serene glow of the moon, Levi's steps carry him toward the Crockett cottage, his journey a contemplative one. The soft rustling of leaves adds a gentle rhythm to his movement, a melody of solitude. Each kick at the earth becomes a release, a way to cast off the weight of pent-up frustrations into the embracing night.

In stark contrast to the humble Brody shack, the Crockett cottage is a beacon of progress in the evolving goldfields. It boasts three well-constructed rooms on sturdy floorboards, its roof gleaming like molten silver beneath the moon's luminous touch. Designer wallpaper adorns its interior walls, a testament to refinement, while the exterior showcases the raw beauty of tree-sawn planks.

As Levi nears, Ma Crockett is perched outdoors, seated upon a log, her presence a comforting silhouette against the night. A short white clay pipe rests between her lips, ember casting a warm glow.

The marks of motherhood shape Ma Crockett's figure, a testament to her role in nurturing six children and the promise of more. Her hair is an unruly cascade, a nest of disarray reminiscent of a magpie's nest flipped upside down. Her apron, adorned with signs of constant use, is a testament to her ceaseless work.

"Levi, what brings you here after the uproar at school?" Ma Crockett's voice is resolute, laced with concern. "You could have inflicted grave harm upon Danny Briggs. Thankfully, his father is away, tending to cattle in Adelaide. Otherwise, the commotion stirred by your actions would be undeniable."

Levi's response carries a blend of vulnerability and honesty. "Ma's troubled for me, hence the request to spend the night again. It's Pa's evening for indulging in strong spirits. After today's school incident, I might be unsafe if he crosses paths with me."

Ma Crockett's words are pragmatic and empathetic. "You're welcome to stay the night. Go inside. Just avoid any confrontation with Jimmy about revealing your secret. Your Ma was anxious for you, and Jimmy let the cat out of the bag. Your Pa will likely succumb to the drink once he realizes you're not home."

Levi presents the loaf of bread he brought as a gift, handing it to Ma Crockett before entering the cottage. There, he's met by Jimmy Crockett and his five siblings — two boys and three girls — all seated around a table. Jimmy, Levi's contemporary, and his siblings fix their gaze on Levi's entrance. The girls shyly avert their eyes, mirroring their mother's demeanour in miniature.

Levi's voice, filled with playfulness, breaks the quietude. "Why the scrutiny, everyone? I assure you, I'm not an axe murderer... BOO! Your Ma invited me in. She's right outside, safe and content."

With the fluidity of a curtain being drawn, the scene transitions. Inside the cottage, Levi and the Crockett family gather around a long, polished table in the dining room. They partake in a hearty stew, its aroma enveloping the room in an inviting embrace. The clinking of utensils and occasional contented sighs punctuate the tranquil atmosphere.

Levi's voice carries gratitude as he savours the flavours. "Ma Crockett, this beef stew is a revelation. Such tastes are a rarity for me, save for Christmas Day. It's a luxurious indulgence, you see. My Stepfather only grants it on Christmas Day when the gambling dens and grog shacks are shuttered for two days. Otherwise, mutton is the staple, the most economical meat in these parts for him."

Ma Crockett's response reverberates with warmth and hospitality. "Enjoy it to your heart's content, Levi. There's ample for all. Pa Crockett will partake later tonight upon his late return from work."

The savoury meal draws to a close, and Ma Crockett, her brood, and Levi gather outside the cottage, settling onto weathered logs beneath the gentle caress of moonlight. The night wears a warm, balmy cloak, and the air carries the hushed cadence of tranquillity. Ma Crockett tends to her white clay pipe, coaxing it to life, the smoke's tendrils spiralling into the night sky's velvety expanse.

"Bedtime for you young'uns," Ma Crockett proclaims, her voice a blend of authority and tenderness. "The hour's grown late."

A small voice from the youngest child interrupts, piercing the stillness. "But Ma, what of Jimmy and Levi?"

Ma Crockett's eyes twinkle with knowing. "Jimmy shall spin you a tale before slumber, and Levi, well, he's accustomed to bedding beneath the dining table."

A protest emerges, carried on the wings of a young voice. "Unfair, Ma! It's far too warm to sleep indoors!"

With a magician's flair, a wooden spoon appears from Ma Crockett's apron, and the children, including Jimmy, hasten indoors, drawn by the promise of bruised buttocks. Ma Crockett's hand extends, a gentle yet persuasive pull as Levi prepares to follow.

"Stay a spell, Levi," she suggests, her tone imbued with intention. "There's something we ought to discuss. Let the young'uns settle into Jimmy's tale."

Taking his place on a nearby log, Levi settles in, awaiting the conversation that hangs in the air.

"You've grown swiftly, Levi, perhaps too swiftly," Ma Crockett commences, her gaze unwavering, an anchor in the gathering night. "Jimmy remains a lad in comparison. Your Ma's heartaches are shadowed by your Pa's presence. She comprehends that while immediate education may not be a necessity, your yearning for it is undeniable."

A moment of contemplation graces their dialogue as Ma Crockett tends to her pipe, coaxing its ember to life. "Education won't fully bear fruit until Ballaarat burgeons," she continues, her words heavy with insight. "Pa Crockett sees growth on the horizon, especially with the arrival of Mr Urquhart, the Government Surveyor, from Melbourne later this year. His vision entails elevating the town upon the plateau, safeguarding it against flooding. And you, dear Levi, could lend a hand to your Ma and Pa in the meantime. Assist Pa Crockett in tent-crafting or at a hotel seeking a strong and willing lad."

Levi's unwavering voice adds to the discourse. "Ma yearns for my education, a chance to ascend, perhaps even boarding in Melbourne. She dreads the echoes of my stepfather's path, marked by affliction and bitterness. She envisions a future removed from the mines. Without her aspirations, I'd be in the goldfields, panning for more treasure. I reckon my skills match those of any Digger out there."

A shadow of concern tints Ma Crockett's features, her maternal wisdom guiding her words. "Undoubtedly, Levi, unless your Pa's temper and recklessness smother your potential prematurely. Your struggles at school signal a drift from Rev Hastie's teachings. If you could bring home earnings, your Pa might relent. I fear you'll be caught in his cycle. His severity knows no bounds, a temper even more extraordinary for a police trooper. Whispers hint at confessions to a higher power, which may encompass lives snuffed out. There's talk of missing Chinamen and Aboriginals in our midst and conjecture fingers your Pa."

Deep in thought, Levi rises from his seat, carrying the weight of their conversation and the shadows of uncertainty. "I'll join Jimmy inside, bed beneath the dining table," Levi proposes, his voice a blend of resignation and readiness to withdraw.

But Ma Crockett's voice, as gentle as a summer breeze, intervenes. "Not tonight, Levi. You and Jimmy can rest beneath the stars on your swags. Just heed the quietude and watch for mosquitoes. Those bloodsuckers are a plague come nightfall."

With a nod, Levi accepts the offer of the open sky, a balm for the concerns that burrow within his heart. As he lies beneath the tapestry of stars, he contemplates the path forward, a journey marked by both the illumination of hope and the uncertain haze of the unknown.

Chapter Forty-Eight

Beneath the shroud of night, Levi and Jimmy slumbered in peaceful repose. However, the serenity is shattered by the rustling of twigs, jolting them awake. Levi nudges Jimmy, urgency in his gestures. "Jimmy," his voice is a thread of alertness, "there's someone out there, perhaps someone nosing around the chicken coop. We need to drive them off."

Levi sits up on his sleeping sack, infusing his tone with authority. **"Clear off, you lot!"** he commands, his voice low and menacing. **"I'm armed, and I won't hesitate to fire!"**

A ghostly figure emerges from the shadows under the quarter moon's light. Levi's eyes adjust, revealing the looming form of a horse and rider. Time seems suspended as the rider guides the horse forward; the Grey steps cautiously and hesitantly.

As the figure draws nearer, Jimmy, still half-roused, scrambles over Levi, seeking refuge. The rider expertly maneuvers his horse, keeping his distance. About ten paces away, his obscured face remains fixed on them. Levi and Jimmy watch, captivated by the unfolding scene.

The rider's features sharpen with each stride; a cap and dark uniform coalesce into a stark image. "Jimmy, step away," the rider's voice is a harsh command. **"Get indoors—now!"**

Jimmy hurries toward the cottage door, finding solace in Ma Crockett's embrace. The door creaks open, revealing the inquisitive faces of Ma Crockett and her younger children peering out to the side of her night-shirt.

The Grey halts, and the rider's arm rises, followed by a crack reverberating into the night. The arm readies for another strike. Ma Crockett guides her children away, disappearing from view.

"Did you dare defy me, my foolish son?" the rider's tone drips disdainfully. "I've wasted money on your education only to watch you squander it. Do you think you can idle while others toil for their bread? Kneel and accept the consequences like a man. It'll toughen you up, mould you in my image—of Bill Brody, the most ruthless trooper in town."

Fear courses through Levi as Brody advances. Suddenly, the whip's crack splits the air, lashing Levi's cheek. Blow after blow falls, inflicting pain and leaving bloodied trails. Levi winces, teeth clenched against the agony.

Determination kindles within Levi, and he rolls away, striving to escape the whip's reach. Yet Brody persists, wielding the whip-like an instrument of torture. Levi's resolve is unyielding, his spirit unbroken by the torment.

The whip's merciless assault continues until a shout rends the night. Mr Crockett intervenes, attempting to halt the brutality. "BRODY! Cease, man! You'll kill him!"

Brody's gaze momentarily shifts to Crockett, the whip's grip loosening. "Is that so, Crockett?" Brody's voice is laced with malice. "Perhaps I should finish the job well if destined for the gallows. Maybe you should keep your nose out of others' business before your luck turns sour."

Brody redirects his attention back to Levi. "YOU!" his command drips with venom. "**Levi!** Return home, lad, where your Ma and I await you!"

Levi, battered and bruised, hesitates. In that instant, a decision crystallizes. Summoning his strength, he defies Brody's directive. Ignoring the pain, he runs, vanishing into the night's embrace. *"I won't comply,"* he whispers, his resolve unshakable. *"I won't endure his brutality tonight. Snake Gully shall offer refuge."*

He follows the dirt road, his body a canvas of pain and uncertainty. Eventually, he reaches the well-trodden path leading to Snake Gully, maneuvering through dense undergrowth. Prickly branches claw at his legs, and twigs lash at his face, but he perseveres. Finally, he arrives at the concealed alcove beneath the sprawling blackberry bush, where his precious prospecting tools are hidden.

Levi takes a moment to steady his breath, the weight of his actions and the physical ache bearing down. He has challenged his stepfather's authority, choosing a divergent path. He contemplates the repercussions as he rests in his hidden enclave, unsure if his defiance will trigger Brody's pursuit.

Beneath the embrace of the blackberry bush, Levi lies ensconced in patient silence, the night unfurling its tapestry of secrets. The rhythmic cadence of hoofbeats weaves through the air, a distant echo that crescendos as a horse charges along the dirt track. The symphony of sounds culminates at the ridge, the abrupt halt seizing Levi's attention like a vice. *"Darn it,"* he mutters, the weight of realization settling upon him. *"This wasn't in the script."*

A voice, a blade slicing through the night's cloak, shatters the calm, **"LEVI! LEVI! Come here, boy,"** the words cut through the air, heavy with anger and menace. "**Or I'll unleash my fury upon ya, carve you to the bone. You wish your Ma to bear the brunt of your defiance? Show yourself, else I'll extract a reckoning."**

Levi listens, ensconced in his leafy refuge, his mind a tempest of thoughts. *"Advance... shield Ma... face the onslaught. Or bide time, veiled?"* he ponders. *"Wait for that window, strike and flee. Let Brody believe retribution from natives was at hand—waddie sticks justice."*

Immovable, Levi muffles any sound that might betray him. Brody's footsteps, heavy and impatient, traverse the vicinity, intermingled with curses and the rustle of leaves.

"Levi, you miscreant!" Brody's voice reverberates, frustration and wrath swirling. **"Reveal yourself, or I'll turn the scrub into a sieve. Tempt me not to augment your pain. You've earned naught else."**

Levi gauges his timing, locked in silent communion. Brody vents his vexation, a prelude to Levi's gambit. Then, an anguished cry—**piercing, raw**—shatters the night's facade.

Levi tenses, his pulse a thunderous drumbeat. He emerges from his verdant sanctuary, cautiously tracing the source of upheaval. A gaping maw—a mineshaft—yawns before him, Brody's torment entwined within its depths.

"**ARRH!** Me Legs... Damn, You!" Brody's lament resounds, a symphony of agony and ire.

Levi inches closer, supine at the precipice, gazing into the stygian abyss. The void absorbs all light and detail, a chasm of uncertainty.

"Who lingers? Levi?" Brody's voice trembles, wounded vulnerability surfacing. "Speak, lad!"

Levi grapples with his dilemma, words a pendulum, then silence.

"Answer me, curse you!" Brody's tone flickers, a blend of urgency and ire. "Who stands there?"

Levi retreats and silences his guardian, his weapon.

"Levi, speak, in God's name!" Brody's plea weaves desperation. "Who's there?"

Levi recoils, the art of silence his refuge.

"Levi, if you're there, heed my plea!" Brody implores. "Lend a hand. My leg's in agony, maybe fractured. Seek aid, summon Crockett, fetch a rope. Move, boy!"

Levi's mind churns, options churning like tempestuous waves. He disengages from the precipice, mapping his next step.

"Levi, I'm wounded," Brody's voice trembles, a nuance of vulnerability emerging. "Aid me, son. Lend a hand, and reward shall follow."

Levi retreats, his path evident. He ascends the gully's crest, abandoning Brody's cries to the night. At the zenith, Brody's grey mare beckons, reins tethered. Levi unhitches, and a sharp slap urges the mare towards home. The haunting cries from the abyss persist.

"Hey! Someone... Aid me!... Help!" Brody's voice begins to dwindle as the mare vanishes.

Levi marches on, resolute in his choice. Brody's destiny lies in the past, Levi's journey obscured by the enigma of the nocturnal tapestry.

Chapter Forty-Nine

Levi's footsteps reverberate through the earth, a rhythmic pulse propelling him toward the sanctuary of his home. He swerves from his intended path, ascending a ridge that conceals him from prying eyes. As he nears the cabin, the grey mare's presence greets him, a silent testament to his tumultuous journey. The cottage's welcoming walls echo with Mr Crockett's voice.

Crossing the threshold, Levi finds Alice rushing towards him, her arms a lifeline as they enfold him. Her kiss lands on his bloodied face, a balm for the wounds both seen and unseen. Worry etches lines of raw emotion across her features.

"Levi, my precious boy," she breathes, her voice a symphony of relief and apprehension. "Where have you wandered? Mr Crockett shared your confrontation with your father. I've been consumed by worry... Why did you not heed his counsel and return home? I would have sheltered you from his wrath."

"He holds no claim as a father," Levi retorts, his words laden with defiance. "I sought solitude, refuge at Rotten Gully, to escape his grip. But where has he gone?"

"Have your paths not crossed?" Alice inquires, concern knitting her brow. "He believed he knew your destination and set off in haste."

Amidst their conversation, Mr Crockett's voice intrudes. "I shall venture outside, endeavour to soothe him on his return," he suggests, unwavering in his resolve. "Levi, your presence will fan the flames of his temper. Ensure the door is bolted firmly behind me."

Crockett's exit is swift, his reentry swifter. A knock heralds his return, his expression a tableau of gravity. "Alice," he addresses her, his tone laden with weight, "do you possess any inkling of his whereabouts? Brody's horse awaits, saddled, yet he has vanished. A fall, perhaps, muddled by grog. Else, his rage would have torn him through these doors."

Crockett's determination remains resolute. "I shall commandeer his horse, scour until dawn," he declares. "Should he elude my pursuit, I will beckon the police commissioner and summon Black Trackers to his trail."

Alice's response drips with regret. "I know not his chosen path," she admits, her concern for Levi eclipsing any notion of Brody's flight.

At the threshold, Levi and Alice stand, witnesses to Crockett's departure. Night enshrouds him, a cloak of obscurity. His figure recedes, dissolving into the moon's soft glow. Two figures stand, adrift in a sea of uncertainty. The hush of the night wraps around them, bearing hope for the safety of both Brody and Crockett within its enigmatic embrace.

Within the confines of their modest cabin, Alice and Levi find themselves seated around the well-worn dining table. Their countenances are marked by the weight of profound concern, each line etched with the gravity of the previous night's events. The atmosphere is thick with unease, the events of the past hours hanging heavy in the air.

"Levi," Alice's voice emerges, a blend of contemplation and anxiety. "I can't shake this apprehension retarding Bill's whereabouts and the potential consequences his actions might unleash. There's a haunting possibility that he's met with harm, perhaps lost in the vast labyrinth of the Little Bendigo goldfield. Those old mineshafts scatter the land, and the peril is all too real."

As her words linger, a sudden sound breaks the stillness—a rhythmic galloping that captures their collective attention. Swiftly, Alice and Levi rise from their seats, a shared urgency propelling them out the door. Their steps echo with palpable haste. Out in the open, a scene unfolds: Crockett sits astride Brody's grey mare.

His visage communicates myriad emotions, painted with shades of disappointment and deep concern.

Addressing Alice, Crockett's voice bears the weight of his efforts. "Alice," he begins, a sigh underscoring his words. "I've scoured a two-mile radius from here, calling out for Bill. But there's been no trace of him. I'm setting a course for the Police Commissioner, Captain Dana. It's time to inform him of Trooper Brody's inexplicable absence. We'll seek the aid of the Black Trackers to assist in the search."

His words hang in the air, carrying a gravity beyond speech. Crockett spurs the mare forward with a nod that speaks volumes, setting her into motion. Dust swirls in the wake of his departure, leaving an unsettled silence. Alice retreats into the cabin, her troubled thoughts evident in the furrow of her brow.

Outside, Levi remains, his gaze following Crockett's vanishing silhouette until it merges with the landscape—a lone figure against the canvas of uncertainty.

His thoughts turn inward, a meditative contemplation of the unfolding events. *"Crockett's dedication is unwavering,"* Levi murmurs to himself, his words a mere echo carried away by the wind. *"He's covered every inch, from Snake Gully to parts beyond. Yet, the absence of Pa's response... troubles me deeply. Crockett's voice should've carried for miles on a night as hushed as this. But the stillness remains unbroken. Is he incapacitated, or perhaps..."*

A surge of emotions courses through Levi's veins, a tide of conflicting sentiments that intertwine and clash. *"But I can't wish him death,"* Levi confesses, the admission heavy on his tongue. *"For my sake, but more so for Ma's. Despite his wrongs and trespasses against us, a portion of Ma's heart still holds him. He was her refuge when she was adrift, and their history is a tapestry woven with secrets I've yet to untangle."*

Amidst the tumult of thoughts, unanswered questions linger like shadows, casting uncertainty over Levi's mind. The complex interplay of emotions—resentment juxtaposed with an unexpected empathy—shapes his perspective.

Standing in the embrace of the night, Levi grapples with the enigma of Brody's disappearance and the intricate web of emotions that tether them together. The air is dense with unspoken words, and at that moment, he confronts the profound enigma of their shared journey.

Chapter Fifty

Under the high noon sun, the shack stands as a solitary outpost against the vast expanse. A dust cloud billows on the horizon, heralding the arrival of two mounted figures. The horses they ride possess a regal stature, distinct from the common breeds of the district. Clad in dark blue tweed jackets with high collars and matching trousers adorned with gold stripes, the black troopers' attire contrasts sharply with the rough-hewn backdrop. Their presence is one of confidence and authority, flat-jack hats partially concealing their wiry black hair.

Of the two, the taller trooper, his bearing commanding, directs his gaze towards Alice. "G'day, Missus," he addresses her with a tone that demands attention. "We've come in search of Boss. I am Trooper King, and him Trooper Bill. We'll find'em, Boss, return him real quick. No need'em worry, Missus. We best trackers."

Alice finds solace in Trooper King's demeanour, and her expression reflects her approval. With a fluid motion, Trooper King dismounts from his grey horse and lowers himself to the ground, studying the hoof marks etched into the dusty terrain.

"See here," he points, his finger tracing the markings. "This one, him arrive at hut, with no rider. This one, him headin' for Ballaarat. We'll be followin' this one - return and try another if no find boss first time."

With his assessment complete, Trooper King remounts his horse with a swift kick and a flick of the reins, setting both troopers in motion. Their departure kicks up a cloud of dust as they ride off, their figures gradually disappearing on the horizon. Trooper King offers a parting salute, a gesture of respect that lingers in the air even after they're gone. Alice and Levi remain there, their thoughts rife with the uncertainty the trackers' search might bring.

"They will find him, Levi," Alice offers, her voice carrying a note of reassurance. "But what will be his condition when they do? Will he be wounded, his legs broken? Or, Heaven forbid, will we receive news of his passing?"

With a gentle lift of her apron, Alice dabs at a tear that has escaped, her concern for Bill Brody evident in the depths of her eyes.

The day wears on, and the hut's interior is illuminated by the warm glow of the fire. White smoke spirals from the stone chimney, while outside, Levi's exertions have brought sweat to his brow as he chops wood. In the distance, a familiar sight emerges—an approaching dust cloud, signalling the return of the black troopers.

Within Levi's mind, uncertainty simmers, and his thoughts split between the possibility of their bearing Brody and the potential outcomes that may entail. *"I can't spot him yet,"* Levi mutters to himself, a note of frustration evident. *"Damn it. I'll need to concoct a tale and make it seem like I stumbled upon him at Snake Valley. My heart's racing, and my stomach feels in knots. I'm on the verge of retching—ugh!"*

The two black troopers swiftly drew nearer, their horses kicking up dust in their wake. Levi shifts closer, his intent to offer assistance evident. Trooper King, his passenger resembling Brody, arrives. Brody's arms are clasped tightly around King's waist, his head resting heavily upon the trooper's shoulder.

"Help 'im down, Boy!" Trooper King directs Levi, his voice carrying authority. "We've got Boss, don't need worry. Boss ain't too hurt; just felled asleep down big hole. We get him home safe and sound. I'll tell Big Boss Dana, too. We're goin'—hurry! Tell'em Boss will drop by in one day or two." With a swift release, Trooper King lets go of Brody's arms and gives his face a gentle slap to rouse him.

"Huh? What's yuh want?" Brody mumbles, his words slurred.

Levi lends his strength, guiding Brody to dismount. Brody's stiff leg swings over the horse, and he slides down, clutching King's jacket. Levi offers his shoulder, and Brody rests an arm upon it. They go towards the cottage door together, where Levi quickly kicks it with his boot. As the two trackers gallop away toward Ballaarat Police Camp, Alice emerges from the hut. Together, they assist Brody to his bed. Alice gazes upon Brody's battered appearance, her worry palpable.

Levi's voice breaks the silence. "The Black Troopers found him trapped in a mineshaft at Snake Gully. They believe he's not too seriously hurt, that he simply fell asleep due to the drink when he couldn't get out. He's still dazed, Ma. I don't think he realizes he's home."

Alice offers her thoughts, her voice a mix of concern and relief. "We'll let him rest and heal. When he awakens, I'll explain everything to him. And as for you, Levi, you can tell him you weren't anywhere near Snake Gully when he fell. That's the truth, isn't it?"

Levi nods, averting his gaze as he carries the weight of the situation. Alice's voice is a mix of tenderness and conviction. "Levi, you understand that you won't be able to continue attending Mr Tonkin's school, don't you? But there's another option. General Williams has set up a school at Bentley's Hotel. You could walk there."

Levi responds, his voice resolute. "Ma, I spoke with Ma Crockett yesterday. Mr Crockett said he'd take me on as his apprentice in tent-crafting. He's got plenty to do. I can continue my education later on my own terms."

Alice's smile is warm with approval. "That's a fine plan, Levi. It'll lift your Pa's spirits. We'll talk to him once he's fully recovered."

Chapter Fifty-One

` In the heart of the shop, Mr Crockett and Levi stand side by side, their focus unwavering and intent. The shop occupies a spot along Main Road in Ballaarat, its robust timber facade commanding attention from passersby on the dirt road. A declaration of craftsmanship and durability hangs above in bold letters: **"CROCKETT'S TENTS** - ***Made To Last***." At the rear, a lean-to extends, its roof adorned with wood shingles that shelter the space below. Crockett and Levi unite their efforts in this enclave of canvas and creation.

Upon the ground sprawls a canvas expanse, its surface etched with a meticulously traced pattern. Levi holds a pair of shears, sturdy blades poised for their purpose.

Levi's voice weaves through the air, reflective and open. "My stepfather is on the mend," he observes, a mix of candour and insight lacing his words. "Though his bones remain unbroken, his body carries the aches and bruises of his own recklessness. The weight of his actions that night has caught up with him. Curiously, the aggression that once marked his interactions with me has vanished. He's even extended an apology for his behaviour."

Crockett acknowledges Levi's words with a nod, a shared sentiment lighting his eyes. "That's reassuring news, Levi."

The conversation thread continues, Levi's voice flowing like a steady current. "His perspective has shifted. A commitment has emerged, pledging against raising his hand against Ma or me again. Even his habitual Friday night revelry has dwindled, though he still finds solace in a drink on quieter days."

Crockett's response is measured, his voice a compass of moderation. "We can only hope he holds steadfast, Levi."

Levi's introspection continues to unfurl. "We've embarked on a path of reconciliation, a family dialogue aimed at smoothing the wrinkles in our relationships. We've held up a mirror to our mistakes and missteps. Yet, in the depths, the wellspring of genuine affection remains uncharted."

Crockett's wisdom resonates, his tone steady as an anchor. "The emotions themselves matter less now, Levi. You've realigned the balance through your efforts and your contribution to the household. His resentment carries less weight."

Levi's voice evolves, a testament to transformation. "Even in his moments of inebriation, his demeanour has softened. A touch of gentleness has replaced the harshness. It's lessened the burden on both Ma and me. And for her sake, I now address him as 'Pa.'"

A ripple of shared amusement courses through their exchange, Crockett's words tinged with lightness. "The 'bush telegraph' hasn't been silent, Levi. News of Trooper Bill Brody's confrontation with you, fueled by alcohol, has echoed. He emerged from the clash with more than just a bruised ego."

Their laughter converges, a harmony forged in shared understanding. Amidst the rhythm of their labour, a tapestry of peace is woven, each stitch a testament to the resilience of family bonds rekindled.

In the Gravel Pits Goldfield of east Ballarat, a tapestry of labour and aspiration unfurls like a vivid mosaic before the eyes. Diggers are sentinels of tenacity, each engaged in unique pursuits that harmonize into a symphony of ambition. Solitude and companionship intermingle as figures work in pairs or groups, forging unity within their collective endeavour. Against the canvas of earth and sky, shanty huts and makeshift tents punctuate the landscape, marking the rhythm of life etched onto this canvas.

Levi, a lone figure atop a hillock, takes mid-day refuge from his tent work and observes the scene below, his eyes tracing the dance of determination woven into every movement.

"*The life of a gold digger,"* Levi murmurs to himself, his voice a quiet cadence within the bustling tableau, *"is a testament to versatility. They must master myriad skills – from felling trees and hewing planks for shafts to excavating gravel and erecting shelters. Their tasks range from sewing garments to chopping wood, a symphony of exertion under the harsh embrace of nature. Endurance, spirit, and vigour are their companions, sustained for three arduous months just to yield a glimmer of gold and a touch of rheumatism."*

Yet, amid this tableau of labour, an unexpected interruption shatters the tranquillity. A procession of Redcoat Troopers, their regal mounts charging forth from a nearby gully, injects urgency into the scene. A sea of blue-coated policemen, both on foot and horseback, trails behind a formidable force, including Aboriginal Troopers and 'Vandemonians'. Musket rifles gleam, bayonets poised in resolute readiness.

From the diggers, a collective cry rises, a chorus of warning. "JOE! - JOES! - TRAPS! **The Traps and Joes are coming!"**

In a swift response, those lacking valid mining licenses scramble to find sanctuary, seeking refuge in gullies or retreating into their subterranean shafts. The license holders stand resolutely, facing the oncoming troopers with determined gazes.

Redcoats maintain their mounted positions, circling shafts like vigilant sentries. Horseback police troopers surge towards escapees, chasing them from nearby gullies. On foot, blue-coated policemen methodically inspect licenses, confiscating and scrutinizing them. Some descend into the shafts, extracting diggers by their shirt collars.

Amid this orchestrated upheaval, Bill Brody stands tall, draped in his blue coat uniform, a figure of authority amidst the Redcoats. "Efficient work, gentlemen!" Brody's voice resonates, a command echoing through the chaos. "Shackle the ones without valid licenses and keep them together."

The offenders line up before Trooper Brody, their expressions a blend of defiance and frustration. Led away in procession, Brody takes the lead, his form a beacon guiding their march.

Amidst this tumultuous stage, the diggers left behind voice their outrage and dissent, a chorus of protest and anger. "Nothing but harassment! - Down with the red toads and blue rouges! - Your reckoning will arrive sooner than you think!"

As the turmoil unfolds, Levi watches from his elevated vantage, his heart a tempest of emotions. *"PA!"* he mutters inwardly, eyes ablaze with indignation, *"You and your cohort tarnish the honour of these diggers. Their toil enriches Victoria and Melbourne Town, yet their reward is harassment. Millions in gold, earned through sweat and sacrifice, headed towards the coffers of Melbourne's elite, yet these diggers are denied a political voice in shaping their destiny."*

As the scene fades, its impression remains as indelible as the marks on Levi's heart.

Chapter Fifty-Two

Levi and Mr Crockett collaborate, constructing a new tent at the back of the tent store. Their labour orchestrates a symphony of purpose.

"The discontent among the miners has simmered for weeks," Crockett's voice carries the weight of observation, "a chorus of protest against the exorbitant license fees and the relentless intrusion. John Humffray's 'Ballarat Reform League's Charter' has rallied their cries. The Melbourne Board of Inquiry denies their plea to reduce the mining fee to ten shillings. Thirty shillings a month is an oppressive burden for those who have yet to strike gold."

Levi's response resonates with empathy, his voice touched by personal experience. "No surprise there," he remarks, a tinge of understanding colouring his words, "the heightened checks and ceaseless harassment by the redcoats and police have ignited a fire of resentment among the diggers. I've seen it firsthand."

Crockett's agreement is palpable in his voice. "Indeed, the visit of Governor Sir Charles Hotham provided a glimmer of hope. Some loyal diggers hailed his arrival, yearning for change. They showcased the success of the fortunate few, but upon his return to Melbourne, he seemed convinced that luck smiled upon every digger – a view that fails to address their grievances."

Levi interjects, his voice sombre. "The tragic demise of young miner James Scobie has only stoked the flames. The Police Magistrate absolved James Bentley, proprietor of the Eureka Hotel, of any wrongdoing. Even though Martin accompanies Scobie when they leave the hotel premises and swears Bentley murdered his mate.

Crockett picks up the narrative thread, his voice unwavering. "Accounts tell of Bentley, his wife, and Fletcher pursuing them. Accusations were flung that Scobie had purposely broken a hotel window, Martin, his mate, was felled, and it's believed Bentley delivered the fatal blow with what Martin described as a battle-axe. A doctor was summoned, but Scobie had already passed."

Levi's voice carries a hint of lament. "If only Scobie had made it back to his tent."

Their conversation flows, and a figure enters the scene – a man of presence, marked by his commanding aura. A broad-brimmed hat conceals fiery hair, while a robust red beard and moustache obscure his face, hiding scars save for one beneath his left ear. Authority emanates from his very being.

"Good day, Mr Raffaello Carboni," Crockett's greeting bears a touch of recognition. "Another order for tents, I presume?"

Raffaello's response is affirmative. "Indeed, Tom. More compatriots will arrive from Rome by the end of the month. They'll require five more tents."

Crockett acknowledges the request. "We appreciate your continued patronage, Sir. I'll initiate work on them within the week."

Raffaello's demeanour shifts, his words shedding formality. "I'm a man of labour, Tom. 'Mr.' and Sir are titles best suited for Ballaarat's elites, striding about in their grand coats and top hats. Call me Raffaello."

Crockett assents, a shared understanding evident. "Certainly, Raffaello. Levi, did you catch that?"

Raffaello turns his gaze to Levi, his expression softened by familiarity. "And who might this sturdy young lad be, toiling alongside you, Tom?"

Crockett introduces Levi, their connection bridging the gap. "Levi Brody, my apprentice," Crockett states proudly.

Raffaello's voice is touched by emotion. "Levi, you remind me of my son Antonio in Urbino, Italy. He's of your age. I hope we cross paths more often. A young presence eases the ache in my heart, a reminder of my distant family."

Levi responds with sincerity. "I'd be honoured, Sir... or rather, Raffaello."

Raffaello's passion deepens. "Splendid! Until my homeland breaks free from tyranny, I cannot return. I fought alongside Mazzini and Garibaldi, seeking to liberate Italy from Austrian sway. After the fall of the Roman Republic in 1848, I fled to London. And here I stand, in Ballaarat, pursuing gold to fund my eventual return when the stars align."

In this convergence of lives, Crockett, Levi, and Raffaello are witnesses to each other's stories and dreams, a testament to the enduring pursuit of a brighter horizon.

The Eureka Hotel stands engulfed in a tempest of chaos, its façade echoing the fervent demands of the angry mob. Trooper Bill Brody, alongside his Vandemonian foot police, forms an imposing barricade at the entrance, effectively shielding James Bentley and his staff from the maelstrom outside. The uproar of the crowd's shouts reverberates through the air, a symphony of anger and frustration.

Amidst this tumultuous chorus, individual voices rise like distinct notes: **"Come out, you coward, and face justice!" "Yer a murderer Bentley – a dog!" "Come out, or we're comin' in!"**

James Bentley emerges from the heart of this uproar, a portrait of defiance, his demeanour impervious to the accusations hurled like stones. A veneer of dismissiveness coats his features as he stands in the shadow of Sergeant Brody, his gaze casting down from a perch of superiority. His voice carries with unwavering conviction a challenge tossed to the elements. **"Get lost! I've been exonerated by the inquest! I owe no explanations to you, a mob of ruffians!"**

The mob's anger swells, fed by suspicions of Bentley's undue sway over the Magistrate. In the distance, the measured cadence of approaching Redcoats becomes discernible.

"We Know You've Bought Off The Magistrate, Bentley!" the mob's uproar rises, dissent now surging into an unstoppable crescendo.

Amid this unrest, several Diggers surge forward, hands clutching gravel harvested from the road. These small stones transform into missiles, crashing against the windows with a cacophony of shattering glass. Swiftly, the blue-coated police retreat within the hotel's confines, Bentley and Brody leading the retreat towards the rear. Trooper Brody guides Bentley toward a horse, already saddled and waiting in the stable's shadows. With purposeful resolve, Bentley mounts the steed and spurs it into a gallop, leaving the mob behind.

Jubilation courses through the crowd as they witness his escape, their triumph tangible on the night air. Meanwhile, at the rear, the Redcoats assemble, forming a disciplined line, poised to restore order – yet, faced with overwhelming odds, they opt for cautious restraint over open confrontation.

Amid the surging elation of the mob, voices meld into a unified chant: **"Bentleys Fled!" – "The Hotel Is Ours!" – "The Redcoats Are Here!" – Show them Our Force!"**

Pandemonium erupts within the hotel's interior as Diggers storm through the entrance, a tempest of rage and disorder. The space becomes a canvas for their fury as furniture and fixtures are flung through windows and doors. Amidst the upheaval, the hotel staff are shepherded into the side alley by Brody and his men, powerless witnesses to the overwhelming tide of anger. At the rear of the crowd, the small contingent of Redcoats maintain their vigilant stance, a token presence against an insurmountable throng.

Amid the escalating chaos, a shadowy Figure emerges, igniting the side wooden panels in flames. Two Diggers wrestle a barrel of

Port, intent on rolling it through the entrance. But a swift swing of an axe cleaves into the barrel, spilling its contents across the ground and accelerating the fire's voracious spread. Another pair of Diggers overturns a rain barrel, rendering it useless as a tool against the inferno. The flames embrace the opportunity, sweeping hungrily through the aged wooden structure.

The mob bursts into triumphant cheers, a chorus of victory and vindication that echoes in the night. **"Justice is served! Do you hear us, Brody and you red toads?"** Their voices resonate, a testament to the fierce determination fueling their actions. Amid the fiery dance and crackling flames, the night witnesses the fervour driving their pursuit of justice.

Chapter Fifty-Three

Amidst the brilliance of Ballaarat riches, on November 30th, 1854, a congregation of Diggers burgeons under the sun's embrace, united by a single purpose. The emblem of their cause, the Southern Cross Flag, emerges on the flagstaff at Bakery Hill, its origins tied to the Canadian miner, Captain Henty Ross of Toronto.

In a twist of irony, Captain Ross is the flag's architect and protector. His grip tightens around a gleaming sword, a sentinel encircled by rifles held steadfast by a dedicated division. Within this assembly, Peter Lalor, Commander-in-chief, claims a position atop a stump. His left-hand cradles a rifle, its butt end resting against his foot, while his right hand, draped over his heart, symbolizes determination and proclamation.

Lalor's voice resonates with unwavering conviction, each word bearing weight. "My duty here is to oversee the oath, binding you to the cause embodied by the Southern Cross. Not distinguishing this emblem is betraying the core of courage. Listen well. Those who cannot uphold this oath must depart this assembly promptly. Divisions, armed and ready, gather around the flagstaff."

With synchronized movement, five hundred armed diggers surge forward, determination palpable in each stride. Captains from diverse divisions salute Lalor, a salute brimming with military honour. Then, in a moment of solemn gravity, Lalor kneels, his head uncovered, his right hand extending towards the flag, a gesture of commitment as he utters: “WE SWEAR BY THE SOUTHERN CROSS TO STAND TRUE TO EACH OTHER, TO FIGHT FOR OUR RIGHTS AND LIBERTIES!"

The mob replies, their voices suffused with determination, "AMEN!"

Raffaello's voice surges with fervor. "Gentlemen soldiers, if firearms elude your grasp, let six-inch blades atop poles become your weapon. Let those blades pierce the heart of tyranny!"

In response, the angry mob releases fervent cheers, a symphony of unity resonating through the air. Lalor stands tall, a beacon of determination. "For those who pledge to protect the flag, let your mining licenses be reduced to ashes. This conflagration signals our unyielding resolve to safeguard our liberty – even if it necessitates force until our demands are met."

With ardour, the crowd ignites their licenses, the flames an unequivocal declaration of their defiance. Amid this fiery spectacle, John Humffray steps forth, a figure of stature with wavy black hair and a meticulously groomed beard. His voice commands attention as he advances.

Humffray's words echo a call to unity. "GENTLEMEN! - GENTLEMEN! The power of the press can eclipse the might of a revolver. Let us repose faith in the 'Ballarat Reform League's Charter' until our aspirations materialize."

From within the mob, voices of dissent surge. "TRAITOR!" - "YOUR CHARTER HAS FAILED US!"

Tensions swell within this ocean of divergent viewpoints. The scene captures the intricate interplay of passion and discord. Amidst the tempest of differing opinions, the steadfast commitment of the diggers to their collective pursuit of justice and freedom remains unshaken.

Restlessly, Raffaello paces back and forth, his agitation expressed through his sweeping gestures. Levi occupies a makeshift seat crafted from a log, his attention thoroughly captivated by the conversation unfolding before him.

Raffaello's voice carries animation and fervour, his words weaving a tapestry of vivid imagery. "Levi! The air at the meeting was charged and vibrant with energy. An assembly of countenances adorned with distinctive features and hues – a mosaic of men harbouring their stories. Their eyes ignited with fervent passion as they gazed upon the emblem of the Southern Cross. It was a scene evoking the spirit of the Crusaders in the heart of Palestine! Five hundred right hands extended towards that very emblem!"

Levi, his tone nostalgic, responds wistfully. "Oh, how I wish I could have been present to bear witness to such a monumental moment!"

Raffaello's words flow lyrically, like a river's gentle current. "Our flag soared with majesty, akin to a summit's peak. An impressive mast, stretching eighty feet high, straight as an arrow in flight. No standard from the old realms of Europe could rival the elegance of the Ballaarat Miners' Southern Cross flag. Against a canvas of blue, a radiant white cross adorned with five stars akin to those gracing our southern celestial dome stands as a symbol of purity and nature, unburdened by other extraneous emblems or symbols. Amid those armed men, the tenacious gold diggers hailing from diverse languages and shades, the sight of our standard held an entrancing allure!"

Levi inquires about the potential government response. "Do you believe this fervour will compel the authorities to heed your cause and bring about change? Or do you fear a sombre end?"

Raffaello's uncertainty is palpable as his words echo. "Levi, I cannot predict. I traversed a staggering 16,000 miles in search of refuge from the tyranny of the sword, only to be exploited on my first day at the Ballaarat goldfield. Amidst the rustling undergrowth nearby, a clamour emerged as I toiled in the soil. 'What's the matter? Your license, mate!' Such were the brusque words of a towering figure, a Vandemonian tough armed with carbine and bayonet. I simply presented my license, and he moved on. Levi, that exchange shook me to my core. The emotion is difficult to convey unless one has tasted it amidst the Gravel Pits of Eureka. That echoing call of JOE! – JOE!"

Pausing to light his pipe, Raffaello takes a contemplative puff before resuming. Raffaello's voice becomes a symphony of frustration and determination.

"To subject upright men to degrading and repugnant license searches is an affront. Some troopers exhibited a modicum of civility – yes, they bore the burden of their duty with a measure of shame. Yet within their ranks festered souls driven by malevolence, deriving pleasure from their actions, blinded by their insatiable greed, unable to witness the abundant piles of gold-laden soil left untouched."

Levi chimes in, his voice laced with empathy. "I have personally borne witness to those injustices, Raffaello."

A note of indignation resounds in Raffaello's voice. "Are the diggers to be treated as mere hounds or savages, hunted down without mercy? Must they emerge from their shelters and tents like prey under Pellissier's African approach, summoned by the hounds of the executive? Has the attire of a digger now become a symbol of inferiority and shame?"

Levi responds with unwavering conviction. "No, Raffaello – the Diggers are the backbone and the wealth of our land, deserving the same right to vote as the Squatters and landowners."

Acknowledging Levi's familial connection to the troopers, Raffaello expresses his feelings. "Levi, I know your father is a leader among those troopers, one of the 'Joes'! My heart aches for your predicament as you find yourself in a complex position. Nevertheless, any insight you can offer regarding the plans and conspiracies of these 'Joes' and 'Traps' against the diggers' cause would be of immense value."

Levi pledges his unwavering support. "You can rely on me, Raffaello. I shall keep a vigilant watch and a keen ear on my Pa. You shall be promptly informed if he should boast of any corrupt schemes to thwart your uprising, as he often does in his drunken ramblings to my mother at night."

With gratitude, Raffaello acknowledges Levi's dedication. "You are a steadfast friend!"

Their exchange resonates like a well-composed symphony, echoing with the notes of their unwavering commitment to the pursuit of justice and freedom.

Chapter Fifty-Four

Raffaello finds himself amidst the attendees at Diamond's Store on Main Road, the carefully selected venue for a meeting of utmost significance. Raffaello meticulously places black bottles and tumblers on the table as the proceedings loom, each movement deliberate and purposeful. His actions are imbued with strategic intent, ensuring that any unwelcome intruders remain blinded to the impending formalities.

Within this charged atmosphere, Lalor, the esteemed leader, stands before the assembly. His voice carries an air of authority as he addresses the gathered individuals.

"Gentlemen, as your designated leader, I have convened this assembly of captains for a momentous war meeting. Among us are representatives spanning diverse nationalities and key figures intimately connected to our Movement."

The mere mention of specific names evokes a tangible response – a collective raising of hands in acknowledgment, a visual testament to the shared commitment of these individuals. Lalor continues to speak with an aura of gravitas.

"Our ranks include Edward Thonon, entrusted with the representation of the Prussian diggers; Vern, symbolizing the

German contingent; Patrick Curtin and John Manning, embodying the spirit of the Irish; Captain Ross, an embodiment of Canadian resolve; and, naturally, James McGill, serving as the resonant voice of the American participants."

Stepping forward, Raffaello seizes the opportunity to address the assembly. "Gentlemen, we have convened under the able leadership of Peter Lalor, who has assumed the mantle of Commander-In-Chief for our armed forces. While his prior experiences in military matters may be limited, I harbour unwavering faith in his leadership. Manning may have recommended me due to my past experiences combating Austrian forces, but I modestly declined due to my exhaustion from the previous winter. My allegiance lies resolutely with Peter Lalor. The essential essence of trust between soldiers and their leaders resonates profoundly. While respect might be accorded to an outsider on the goldfields such as myself, the collective recognition of the most deserving leader within our ranks prevails within the British assembly segment."

Lalor responds with gratitude. "I appreciate your faith in me, Raffaello. I have entrusted Vern with the crucial task of formulating our military strategies for the impending stockade. Vern, I implore you to elucidate our meticulously crafted plans."

Vern, a figure of physical prowess and esteemed within the community, rises from his seat, commanding the room's rapt attention simply through his presence. With a commanding demeanour, Vern takes centre stage.

"Gentlemen, our strategy is comprehensive, centring around constructing an imposing stockade that will span a considerable acreage within the Eureka gravel pits. This fortified structure, a bastion of defence, will extend along old Melbourne Road, ultimately connecting with the expanse of Warrenheip Gully. Erected from durable slab hurdles and timber, methodically positioned and raised four feet off the ground, it shall serve as an impregnable barrier against the onslaught of mounted cavalry."

The room seems to pulse with collective determination as every individual absorbs the intricate details of the strategy before them.

Raffaello finds himself outside his tent, seated upon a simple log that serves as a makeshift seat. He deftly wields a knife, expertly carving into a piece of wood. His movements are rhythmic, and he seems fully absorbed in this meditative act. Nearby, Levi joins him, settling onto another log.

Raffaello's tent is strategically positioned upon the hillside to the west of the stockade and provides an unobstructed view that overlooks the ongoing activities below. Together, they observe the diggers as they gather purposefully, meticulously arranging timber slabs to reinforce the burgeoning barricades.

Amidst this tableau, Lalor's authoritative presence is evident as he orchestrates the proceedings, offering instructions to different divisions and expertly organizing their positions around the intricate network of trenches that will serve as their defensive strongholds. Vern, the designated defence leader, shadows Lalor closely, absorbing each directive with unwavering focus.

Amid this contemplative scene, Raffaello's voice finally breaks the silence. "They claim Vern, the German, hails from Hanover, yet his grasp of the language is more confounding than a blend of English and French. I can fluently converse in nine languages. I suspect Vern's origins might be more inclined toward Mexico and Peru. His vanity and boundless ambition render him an improbable candidate for a role in military leadership."

Curiosity gleams in Levi's eyes as he seeks clarification. "What prompts you to hold such an opinion?"

Raffaello's tone carries a trace of scepticism. "My reservations stem from the effectiveness of Vern's defensive tactics, shaped by my own experiences in warfare. Despite my attempts to offer insights, his obstinacy continues to prevail. Vern commands individuals possessing minimal military expertise to confront disciplined soldiers, bolstered by hordes of traps and police troopers. The current design of the stockade renders it disturbingly vulnerable, featuring inadequate defences and a paltry force."

Levi's interest is genuine as he probes further. "Can this situation be rectified?"

Raffaello's voice conveys a mixture of resignation and determination. "Hope and prayer, Levi. The captains must take it upon themselves to train the diggers representing our respective nationalities. In my group of twenty-five Italians, the majority lack firearms. Accordingly, I am organizing a pike unit to face any mounted Redcoats who attempt to breach our defences. Symbolism holds more weight than a strategic advantage in this case – it's a testament to our resolute spirit above all else. Our primary aspiration is that our unwavering determination will compel the current Goldfield Commissioner to step down, thereby paving the way for a peaceful resolution and equitable treatment."

Levi's contribution is crucial as he shares the information he has gathered. "Last night, I overheard my father boasting to my mother in his inebriated state. He revealed that the Goldfield Commissioner has issued orders for police troopers and Redcoats to conduct license searches tomorrow. The aim appears to expose those deliberately destroying their licenses."

Raffaello acknowledges the gravity of the revelation. "Well done, Levi. I shall promptly relay this development to the executive. Now, you must depart. Caution is our watchword; we must avoid being seen together. The presence of spies is pervasive, and safeguarding the confidentiality of our plans and discussions holds paramount importance."

With an unspoken understanding of the immense stakes at play, a mutual nod passes between them before they go their separate ways.

Chapter Fifty-Five

Levi arrives at Raffaello's tent, finding him amid preparations to head off to the stockade. The progress on the fence is apparent – the hurdles have been arranged to form a rounded barricade. White tents are scattered across the landscape inside the stockade, giving the area a bustling feel. A vigilant Digger, easily recognizable by his cabbage-tree hat, stands watch at the entrance. Armed with a musket rifle and a Colt revolver, he exudes an air of alertness.

"Levi, why are you here at this hour? Aren't you supposed to be at work?" Raffaello asks as he approaches.

Levi looks up and responds, "I told Mr Crockett I needed to run some errands for Ma. But I have important information for you. Over a hundred Redcoats from the Twelfth Regiment have set up camp at the base of the Black Hill. Word is they are planning to attack the stockade any day."

Raffaello nods thoughtfully. "You can join me; we're about to inform the Council. They're gathering in the council tent within the stockade."

Levi raises a concern, his brows furrowing. "Do you think the Eureka Committee will still trust me after I provided them with false information about the license check?"

Raffaello offers reassurance, his voice steady. "If the new Goldfield Commissioner, Mr Rede, had carried out that license check as planned, he would have faced hostility from the Eureka diggers. The fact that it didn't happen works in our favour. Trust me, they'll understand."

Approaching the Stockade Gate, Raffaello leans in and whispers the password. "Vinegar Hill," he murmurs.

The Duty Guard acknowledges their entry. "Enter, gentlemen!"

Guiding Levi, Raffaello advises, "Find a tent and keep a low profile while I attend the council meeting." They make their way deeper into the stockade. Raffaello heads towards a giant tent among the cluster, leaving Levi to enter the nearest tent to observe the activities quietly.

Outside, a skilled Blacksmith, possibly of German or American origin, hammers away, crafting six-inch pikes. A small crowd gathers, waiting for their turn to make a purchase. Confident in his work, the Blacksmith proclaims, "These pikes will do the trick against those Red Toads and Blue Rogues, mark my words! I've supplied similar ones to rebels during the Wars of Mexico."

A bystander nearby shares a whisper with his companion, "He's definitely making a profit. Watching his rugged craftsmanship is interesting, though I doubt those pikes can pierce anything tougher than a possum."

In the camp, diggers gather for daily drills involving pikes and rifles. Levi's attention is drawn to Raffaello, who leads a group of foreign diggers through their routines.

Later in the day, the gravel pits come alive with noise as the Creswick Mob arrives. Their presence causes a stir among the diggers. This group of worn and dusty diggers marches toward the stockade. Having left their claims at the Creswick Goldfield, they've journeyed along the Miner's Track to Ballaarat. Signs of their trip are evident, and their dishevelled appearance hints at encounters with illicit grog shops.

Curiosity piqued, and Levi rushes out of his tent to witness the scene. At the forefront, Lalor and Raffaello move towards the front gate to greet the incoming mob. "What's the reason for this gathering, Diggers?" Lalor inquires.

Stepping forward, the leader of the Creswick Mob stands tall. "We've heard about the impending battle you're facing and have come seeking Work, Honour, and Glory! We're prepared to fight, even willing to sacrifice our lives for the cause!"

Raffaello nods appreciatively, responding, "While your enthusiasm is commendable, let's clarify things. Whoever passed on this information to you might not have been entirely accurate. We value your eagerness and your offer of assistance, but accommodating, feeding, and arming such a large group presents challenges for the Eureka Council."

Lalor chimes in, "You and your group are welcome to enter and refresh yourselves. However, unless you've arranged sustenance within the town, it might be wise to consider returning to your starting point."

Acknowledging this reality, the leader of the Creswick Mob expresses disappointment. "This is unfortunate news and will likely dampen our spirits. Some of us have connections here who might offer support, while the rest of us will head back today after replenishing ourselves for the journey."

Amidst the collective murmurs of the Creswick Mob, they enter the stockade. Their arrival prompts a break in the drills as fellow diggers extend a warm and hearty welcome.

Chapter Fifty-Six

Levi emerges from his room, his steps carrying him into the welcoming embrace of the kitchen area. Bill Brody, his stepfather, already occupies the space, and the air is infused with the aroma of a simple breakfast. The room emanates a humble charm, reflecting the family's unpretentious lifestyle.

"Morning, Levi. Sleep well?" Brody's voice resonates with a gentle greeting that breaks the morning silence.

"Morning, Pa. Yeah, I slept alright. Heard you talking to Ma. What's this emergency you mentioned?" Levi's curiosity wells up, prompting him to seek answers.

Balancing his steaming coffee cup in his hand, Brody exhales a sigh that carries the weight of brewing concerns. "Seems like things are escalating. The police and the redcoats have been called in for some urgent matter. I've been assigned to the Police Camp for the weekend."

Levi's brows knit, his thoughts forming questions. "Is it about the diggers and the stockade?"

"Very well could be. Tension's been growing like a storm cloud. Authorities are getting jittery about the stockade situation. They're gearing up for what might come," Brody responds, painting a picture of uncertainty.

In seamless succession, Alice, Levi's mother, enters the kitchen, the threads of conversation weaving around her presence. "I hope it doesn't come to that. The thought of violence... It's unsettling."

"We're doing our best to keep order, Alice. Safety is a priority. Let's hope it doesn't escalate into a full-blown clash. But we've got to be ready, just in case," Brody's voice resonates with a mix of determination and concern.

After a brief exchange, Brody shoulders his saddlebags and musket rifle, ready to face the day's duties. Levi trails behind him, stepping out into the open air. As Brody walks away, Levi's pace quickens, drawing him back inside the hut. There, a surge of excitement propels his words as he confronts Alice.

"Ma, Pa said I can go camping at Snake Gully, do some prospecting. It's a way to stay away from the chaos and keep busy. He'll let Crockett know I won't be in until the Eureka affair blows over," Levi shares, his eyes gleaming with the prospect.

Alice's voice carries the wisdom of a mother's perspective. "Remember, you're still expected back each afternoon to lend a hand with the chores."

Levi's enthusiasm is unbridled as he assures her, "Of course, Ma. I'll pack up and head out right away!"

Alice adds, "And what about a good breakfast?"

"Plenty of bread, some dried beef, and cheese will do to take with me," Levi responds, his eagerness evident.

With haste guiding his actions, Levi assembles a change of clothes and gathers his food supplies. The kit bag becomes a repository of essentials, accompanied by his trusty hat. Without hesitation, he bolts out of the hut. Yet, his course defies expectation; instead of veering towards Snake Gully as he had mentioned, he turns and sets his sights on the path leading to the Eureka Stockade.

Moments pass, and Levi finds himself at the stockade's front gate, a sentry named Ben stationed there. The vibrant hum of activity within the stockade's walls captures his attention. “G'day, Ben! 'Happy days'!" Levi's cheerful greeting hangs in the air.

A chuckle erupts from Ben, a hearty response to Levi's error. "That's last night's code, you scamp! What's your business?"

Levi's contrite tone follows. "Apologies, Ben. Got some crucial intel for Raffaello."

Ben's nod grants permission, his gesture allowing Levi to enter. Yet, a reminder lingers. "Remember to stay updated on the passwords, lad."

Stepping within the stockade's confines, Levi maneuvers through the bustling scene. His destination is Raffaello, the heart of activity amidst the fervour. Raffaello commands a division of twenty-five men, each movement deliberate and precise.

"PIKERS! READY TO RECEIVE CAVALRY! CHARGE! PIERCE THEIR MOUNTS' FLANKS! DRAW THEM FROM UNDER THEIR TAILS!" Raffaello's voice surges, shaping the drills with authority.

Levi ventures closer, capturing Raffaello's attention amidst the drills, "Raffaello! Got crucial news to share."

With the drills momentarily stilled, Raffaello inquires, "MEN! STAND DOWN! - Levi, what have you learned?"

In hushed tones, Levi transmits the intelligence he's gathered. "The Redcoats and bluecoats are on the move and called into for an overnight emergency, with more troops anticipated to arrive in force within the day. We need to stay vigilant, ready for whatever's coming."

Raffaello's expression shifts, absorbing the gravity of Levi's words. "Thank you, Levi. This is vital information. Our preparations must continue, defences fortified."

As Raffaello resumes his command, Levi retreats slightly, absorbing the drills and the unwavering determination radiating from the diggers. In that charged atmosphere, purpose and resolve intertwine, forging an indefatigable collective spirit in the face of uncertainty.

Chapter Fifty-Seven

Levi stands beside Raffaello's tent from his vantage point, his gaze fixed on the flurry of activity that envelops the stockade. Old colonial-looking men dart back and forth, a choreography of urgency. Some carry canisters of gunpowder and bags of shot, while others transport firearms and boxes of caps. The air hums with a sense of purpose as they press store owners for help, preparing for an unseen storm.

Amidst this orchestrated chaos, one sight arrests Levi's attention. With an audacious nonchalance, a fella peddles nobblers from a keg of brandy slung around his neck. The act's audacity forces Peter Lalor to intervene, banishing the rogue from the stockade. The spectacle of commerce amidst preparation resonates, juxtaposing the mundane and the impending turmoil.

Levi's focus shifts to another corner of the stockade, where a distinctive group has assembled. The 'Independent Californian Rangers Revolver Brigade', as they are known, exudes an air of rugged determination. Armed with Colt revolvers and Mexican knives at their hips, they are a testament to a readiness that borders on defiance. James McGill, a figure moulded by a former military academy attendance, orchestrates their drill, a symphony of precision.

Levi muses, his thoughts tracing the lines of discipline etched into their bearing. *"To consider the scene they conjure. Under James McGill's guidance, the Independent Californian Rangers Brigade possesses an undeniable presence."*

McGill's commands resound, punctuating the air with authority. **"All Fall In For Drill! Pick up your rifles. - Shoulder Arms! — Order Arm! — Ground Arm! — Stand At Ease!"**

Yet, even within this orchestrated symphony, a dissonance emerges. McGill storms towards a digger whose response lags, his words a whip of reproach. **"YOU ARE A DROWSY DIGGER! GET YER ACT TOGETHER, OR I DON'T WANT YA IN MY BRIGADE!- UNDERSTAND!"**

The drowsy digger's resounding reply, affirmation and deference, echoes in the air. **"YES, SUH!"**

Amidst this blend of discipline and urgency, Raffaello emerges from the heart of the stockade, his steps leading him towards his tent. Here, Levi waits, a silent witness to the ebb and flow of activity.

The twilight casts elongated shadows as the day gently fades into the evening. Within the confines of the stockade, the training drills continue. Amidst the dusky backdrop, Father Patrick Smyth, a Catholic Priest, enters his countenance a tapestry of earnestness and anxiety. He approaches Lalor and Vern, the German, a concerned guardian watching over the drills. A young digger named Jimmy accompanies them, an emblem of youthful vigour in these tumultuous times. Father Smyth's concern revolves around the diggers, their struggle and the shadows that loom.

"Mr Lalor, I wish to speak to the men under arms who belong to my congregation regarding the hopelessness of the diggers' struggle," Father Smyth declares, his voice a resonant note of conviction.

Lalor, grounded in his resolve, responds with respect and pragmatism. "I won't deny a man of the cloth the opportunity to address his flock. These diggers have taken an oath to the cause, and I don't believe you will change their minds."

Vern, a pillar of fairness, adds his perspective. "As a Protestant, I also grant permission for my men to hear what you have to say - to be fair to all. Any man swayed by your words will be free to leave the stockade. Young Jimmy, spread the word that a meeting will occur immediately."

With a crisp acknowledgment, Jimmy sets out to disseminate the meeting news. The diggers gather, their faces reflecting the seriousness of the moment. Father Smyth stands before them, a bastion of resilience.

"The government camp is heavily armed, with around seven or eight hundred soldiers. I have received reliable information that reinforcements from Melbourne are on their way to Ballaarat. It is foolish, lads, to stand against such forces. This path leads to needless bloodshed. I remind you all that you are Christians! I urge every member of my congregation to attend tomorrow's Sunday Mass. That is all I have to say on the matter. Now, it is up to each man's own judgment. May God be with you!" Father Smyth's words resonate a declaration both bold and sombre.

Father Smyth exits the stockade without waiting for the diggers' response, carrying the weight of the evening's revelations. The diggers huddle, their voices a mix of contemplation and deliberation. Vern's gaze shifts towards Lalor, capturing the nuances of the moment.

"Father Smyth's passionate counsel, though heartfelt, may find barren ground," Vern observes, his words a reflection of both spoken and unspoken realities. Seizing the moment, Lalor steers their focus towards the task at hand. "While the men are here, let McGill read the Independent Californian Rangers Brigade their general orders for the night. They must take up their positions in the fire pits as sentries."

With authority commanding respect, Vern states, **"McGill and the Independent Rifle Division, step forward and prepare yourselves for night duty - MOVE!"**

The Californian mob led by McGill respond promptly, a testament to the unity that pervades these uncertain times. They parade before Vern; their commitment is palpable. "Gentlemen, before the committee adjourns for a war council, we have received reports from a few diggers that Melbourne Road is teeming with fresh reinforcements. They believe an attack from the military is imminent. Even the Devil himself would hesitate to strike on the Sabbath Day tomorrow, fearing the wrath of God Almighty - but we can't trust these Redcoats! Hold fast to your courage, lads, and fear not! For I lead you to either Death or Glory!"

Vern's voice carries the weight of leadership, a rallying cry that resonates within the hearts of those gathered. As twilight deepens into the night, the stockade becomes a crucible of conviction, a testing ground for courage in the face of adversity.

Chapter Fifty-Eight

Levi's footsteps echo through the dimly lit streets of Ballaarat as he navigates his way to a Main Road bakehouse. The late hour has prompted most shops to close their doors, but he manages to secure a loaf of bread just before the final shutters are drawn. The night embraces him, its cool fingers weaving through his thoughts that whirl like leaves caught in a gust. However, his journey turns unexpectedly when he stumbles upon a disturbing scene outside D.Y. Connor's store. Under the muted glow of the streetlamp, he witnesses a confrontation that sends a shiver down his spine.

Before him, a group of four armed Vandemonian rogues stands before the store, their intent clear and ominous. Their words slice through the night air, a chilling prelude to the unfolding drama.

"Storekeeper, we're here on business from the Eureka Committee. We need powder, shot, and food for the stockade," declares one of the rogues, his voice dripping with authority.

Connor, a man of resilience, holds his ground, his voice a mixture of weariness and defiance. "Eureka Committee be damned... It's more likely you're here for your own selfish gain. I've already done my part for their cause."

Yet, the Vandemonians remain undeterred, their threats casting a heavy pall over the scene. "Well, then we'll have to help ourselves, old man. Keep your hands visible and stay right where you are, or you'll end up in the cemetery."

In a swift and unsettling motion, the rogues take hold of the store's provisions, their actions a testament to their power and intent. They seize fine Yorkshire ham and coffee, their hands showing no hesitation in claiming what they desire. And then, with a final blow, they snatch the cash box, its weight an emblem of the authority they wield. Levi stands frozen, an unwitting witness to this audacious act of intimidation. His heart pounds with fear and urgency, pushing him into action. He pivots on his heel, his steps guided by instinct and the dire need to act. He rushes back through the darkened streets, his mind racing to inform Raffaello of the unfolding catastrophe.

The moon casts its ethereal glow upon the stockade, a soft radiance that paints shadows upon the canvas of the night. It is a few minutes before midnight this Saturday night, and the atmosphere is deceptively calm. Most diggers have found solace in sleep or gather around the warmth of a crackling fire. The camaraderie that binds them becomes a comforting balm for their weary souls.

Levi's urgency drives him forward until he spots Raffaello seated outside his tent, a sentinel at night. Without hesitation, Levi approaches, his words tumbling out in a torrent of worry. "Raffaello... something terrible is unfolding on Main Road. Vandemonians are ransacking Connors's store in the name of the Eureka Committee."

Raffaello's face darkens with concern, his mind swiftly assessing the gravity of the situation. "Damn, I had a feeling this might come to pass. The reputation of our cause hangs in the balance. We must inform Lalor immediately and organize a patrol for Main Road."

With shared purpose, they navigate the night, their steps carrying them through the sentinel-guarded entrance of the stockade. Guided by the moonlight, Raffaello engages in a brief and tense exchange with the sentry, their voices low and urgent. "Good evening, Thonon. How fares the night?" Raffaello's tone blends courtesy with a keen inquiry.

Thonon, the sentry, offers a glimpse into the challenges surrounding them. "We could use more hands. Many diggers have sought refuge in their family homes for the night, upholding the sanctity of tomorrow's Sabbath. The Independent Californian Ranger's Rifle Brigade is out intercepting rumoured reinforcements from Melbourne. Neilson and his division have embarked on a similar mission."

Raffaello's concern deepens, his unwavering faith in the cause intertwined with his sense of responsibility. "I hold Peter Lalor in too high esteem to believe he would endorse actions of such recklessness. I must speak with him."

Thonon's voice resonates with both duty and empathy. "Peter is seeking rest for an hour or two. He sleeps, exhaustion weighing him down."

With a nod of gratitude, Raffaello acknowledges the reality they all face. "I understand, Thonon. I wish you strength. Both young Levi here and I have scarcely known rest since Thursday night. Tomorrow will usher in its own set of trials."

As they emerge from the sentinel-guarded gate, the night envelops them in a hushed stillness. Their return to Raffaello's tent is marked by weariness and determination, each step carrying the weight of the events that have transpired. Collapsing onto canvas stretchers, they surrender to the embrace of sleep, exhaustion claiming them as the night deepens, whispering of the challenges yet to unfold.

Chapter Fifty-Nine

"EUREKA STOCKADE BATTLE - Sunday, December 3, 1854".

The pale light of Sunday morning abruptly awakens Levi, the dawn breaking with a sense of foreboding that chills his heart. Urgency surges through his veins as he rushes outside, only to be met with a scene that defies comprehension. Gunshots crack the air, their echoes mingling with the haunting call of a bugle, piercing through the fabric of tranquillity.

"FORWARD," the command reverberates, and a formidable tide of redcoats, nearly three hundred, emerges from the gully to the west of the stockade. Levi's heart races as overshots whistle past him, the battleground unfolding like a tempestuous storm. Amidst this maelstrom, Raffaello's tent is a fleeting landmark, and Levi seeks refuge outside beside the unyielding stone chimney. But Raffaello, his stalwart companion, is conspicuously absent.

To the north, Captain Ross's Canadian division seeks cover behind the assembled fence of slabs. In contrast, Thonon's division forms a resolute line confronting the southern front, facing the gully with unwavering determination. In response to the approaching military force, the three divisions of diggers stand defiant, their resolve unwavering as they return fire against the encroaching onslaught. Yet, the redcoats maneuver and adapt, their movements guided by the stern commands of a Redcoat Sergeant. "FORWARD! KEEP YOUR LINE!" The sergeant's voice is a thunderous declaration of authority.

Amid the cacophony, a group of about twenty to thirty members from the Independent Californian Rangers' Brigade, who had maintained a watch throughout the night, occupy strategic positions in rifle pits within the lower precincts of the stockade. Chaos extends to Vern's German division, which hastily shifts and repositions itself to the eastern flank, obscured from Levi's view by the labyrinthine maze of tents.

Then, a young Regimental lad stationed by the gully emits bugle notes. The redcoats react with remarkable cohesion, forming ranks in perfect synchrony. A soldier at the head of their advance directs their fire toward Vern's division, their movements choreographed like a deadly dance.

"FIRE AT WILL ON ALL MOVING TARGETS!" The leading soldier's voice cuts through the din, his command resounding as a battle cry.

Levi watches, his senses ensnared by the tumult as the air is punctuated by the erratic trajectories of stray musket balls. Amidst this chaos, another tableau emerges, searing itself into Levi's consciousness. A young American Digger, wounded in the leg, commands a small band of men within fire pits to the north. Undaunted by his injury, he exhibits an indomitable spirit, his determination driving him to hop on one leg as he stands steadfastly by Captain Ross's side.

Dragoon Troops, converging from the north and south, charge with unrelenting vigour, their bayonets poised with lethal intent.

Perched atop the makeshift barricade within the stockade, Peter Lalor stands as a beacon of unwavering resolve. With a signal, he directs the pikemen under Raffaello's command to advance, their steadfast march a testament to their determination. But in the blink of an eye, Lalor flinches, his grip on his left shoulder weakening as he collapses to the ground. The military's musket fire scythes through the air, cutting down diggers who dared to raise their heads above the barricades.

In this chaotic tableau, musket balls dance a deadly ballet, bodies convulse and fall within the stockade, and Levi watches in visceral horror, his heart weighed down by the helplessness of the moment. An inarticulate scream reverberates within him, a silent echo of his mind's torment. He instinctively covers his ears, seeking refuge from the deafening symphony of violence that envelops him.

Yet, even as he recoils, his feet remain anchored to the ground, his gaze transfixed by the nightmarish panorama that unfolds before him. He struggles to process the enormity of the brutality before his eyes. *"I can't run!... I've got to stay... I'm an independent witness to these horrors,"* he murmurs to himself, his voice a fragile affirmation of his resolve to bear witness to the truth.

Captain Ross, a figure of authority, falls victim to the chaos, a gunshot striking him in the groin. He lingers for a fleeting moment, stunned by the searing pain, before collapsing onto his knees and curling into a fetal position. Thonon, the sentinel of the south, is struck in the throat, his cough choked with blood.

Levi flinches and instinctively dives for cover as musket balls whiz past him, tearing through canvas and fabric, their trajectory a stark reminder of the battlefield's unyielding brutality. Bullets punctuate the air, slamming into the chimney beside him with a resounding impact, the echoes of attack reverberating like an ominous drumbeat.

In the heart of the chaos, the pikemen stand steadfast, their faces etched with determination. Arranged in double file and facing old Melbourne Road, they are a formidable barrier, armed with their long pikes to confront the advancing cavalry. Unwavering, they hold their ground, a symbol of defiance etched into their stance. But then, a command reverberates, guiding the rear ranks of the Redcoats into motion.

"CHARGE!" The officer's proclamation is a clarion call to action, a surge of movement that mirrors the ferocity of battle. The troopers charge forward, bayonets glinting with a deadly sheen, their determination an unbreakable force. The Foreign Pikers within the stockade respond with resolute valour, their actions a testament to the indomitable spirit of the diggers. Yet, outnumbered and overwhelmed, they soon find themselves yielding ground, their heroic stand bending to the inexorable tide of battle.

In the heart of the turmoil, Raffaello stands resolute, his sweat-soaked form a beacon of unwavering defiance. He confronts the onslaught of redcoats with fierce determination, his voice rising above the chaos as he urges his fellow diggers to fall back. "RETREAT! RETREAT! THIS DAY IS DONE, BOYS. NO MORE WIDOWS SHALL WE MAKE!" His voice, a blend of command and compassion, resounds through the tumult, a reminder of the toll that this battle exacts on both sides.

With his pike as shield and weapon, Raffaello moves with fluid grace, carving moments of respite for his comrades to regroup and seek safety in the heart of the stockade. But the redcoats' victory, stoking a cruel zeal, show no quarter. Bayonets thrust into fallen and wounded diggers, transforming the battlefield into a canvas of relentless brutality.

Amidst this unfathomable horror, the Southern Cross, a symbol of the diggers' aspirations for justice, is torn down. The exultant cheers and laughter of the redcoats morph the tragedy into a grotesque carnival. "HURRAH! HEY! HEY! HA... HAR!" The triumphant cries of the Redcoat bullies echo through the air, their jubilation a stark juxtaposition against the grim tableau.

Levi's gaze locks onto a trooper, his figure looming like a harbinger of doom. With matches ablaze, he sets a corner of the Diamond store alight, where diggers had convened for their council. The Police Troopers on horseback join this orchestrated onslaught, descending upon the chaos with a voracious appetite for destruction. Flames consume the tents, the conflagration devouring even those that shelter the wounded.

"Terrible Howls and Yells" fill the air, a cacophony of malice that underscores the troopers' cruelty. Acting with abandon, they lash out, brutalizing those who surrender, turning them into captives in their fight for freedom. The wounded, ensnared by the flames, meet a grim fate, their agonized cries mingling with the chaos. Troopers scatter, leaving trails of devastation in their wake, while others pursue those who dare to escape. Raffaello's neighbouring tent succumbs to the inferno, its destruction a poignant symbol of the battlefield's unyielding cruelty.

Chaos reigns supreme, and the diggers' dreams of liberation and justice are trampled beneath the inexorable march of authority. Amidst the tumult, Levi seeks refuge within Raffaello's tent, the chaos outside mirrored by the turmoil within his heart. He collects scattered manuscripts and papers within the bedlam, their significance not lost. Levi urgently secures them in a concealed compartment beneath Raffaello's canvas stretcher bed.

Determination fuels his steps, compelling him to confront the grim reality he has witnessed. Yet, his path is abruptly intercepted by Sub-Inspector Carter, a pistol aimed with intent. Levi is ordered to join a group of prisoners, his helplessness palpable in the face of authority.

"YOU... LAD! FALL IN BEHIND THESE MEN... NOW!" Carter's command hangs in the air, its weight inescapable.

Levi acquiesces, a mixture of fear and resignation coursing through him. Yet, as the procession moves forward, Levi seizes a fleeting opportunity to address Captain Thomas, a figure of authority standing amidst the gully. "SIR!.. SIR! I wasn't fighting in the stockade. Why am I a prisoner?" Levi's voice quivers, his words an embodiment of his innocence.

Captain Thomas regards Levi with a measured gaze, a touch of compassion lingering in his features. His sword extends a gesture that carries a recognition message as it touches Levi's shoulder.

"If you are an honest digger, I don't want you. You are free to return to your tent." Captain Thomas's words are a lifeline, a testament to his ability to discern truth amid the chaos.

Grateful for this unexpected reprieve, Levi makes his choice. Defying the safety of Raffaello's tent, he steps into the heart of the aftermath. The wounded await his aid, a chorus of suffering that demands his response. Amidst the landscape of agony, he is beckoned by Doctor Carr and Father Smyth, their faces etched with concern.

"Dr Carr, where is Dr Kenworthy? Humffray's notes mentioned his presence here." Father Smyth's voice holds a note of urgency, a concern for those in need.

Dr Carr's reply carries a tinge of uncertainty. "I do not know, Father. And where is the Protestant Priest? Many among his flock need solace."

The weight of their duty bears down upon them both. "It matters not, Doctor. Threats from the troopers have forced me to abandon my sacred role. Our immediate priority is to tend to the wounded."

As the scene fades, Levi stands amidst the chaos and resilience, a witness to the aftermath of a battle that has etched its mark upon history's canvas.

Chapter Sixty

The battlefield is a scene of chaos and despair. Diggers from outside gather within the stockade, but their apathy is striking. They show little concern for the fallen as they congregate within the battle-torn area. Amidst the turmoil, a surge of troopers, led by the formidable Bill Brody, emerges with swift precision. They disperse the curious onlookers through mere gestures and the ominous glint of pistols.

The diggers near the wounded offer no resistance, quickly dissipating. Some seek refuge within tents, and others crouch behind chimneys or huddle beneath stretchers. A few unfortunate souls who escaped the turmoil outside willingly submit to being shackled by the despised police traps under Brody's command.

Levi remains knelt beside a wounded digger, cradling a pannikin of water. His gaze intently follows the troopers as they expertly guide the curious diggers away from the scene. Amidst this orchestrated chaos, Levi's thoughts turn inward, his contemplation focused on the glaring apathy of his fellow diggers. Their absence at this critical juncture echoes somberly within him, a disheartening reflection of solidarity lost. *"Amid the diggings, the mere utterance of 'Joe' once held the power to keep the troopers at bay. But now, those very diggers who once stood united are conspicuously absent. The camaraderie that once fueled their fervour is now obscured."* Levi's heart aches at the stark reality – the gallant souls who once fought shoulder to shoulder have vanished into the shadows, leaving their comrades to face peril alone.

Levi's purposeful movements take him to another fallen digger, his actions momentarily interrupted by the arrival of Trooper Brody on horseback. Brody's gruff tone carries an air of command as he addresses Levi's presence amid the chaos.

"Levi, what in the hell are you doing here, boy? Get home, or you'll end up in jail and swing from the gallows like the rest of 'em."

Levi's response is fervent, driven by a sense of duty and compassion. His voice trembles with determination and urgency as he pleads, "Pa, let me lend a hand to bury the dead – it's the Christian thing to do. I'll return home when the job's done! Please..."

Brody's reticence hangs in the air as he spurs his mount and turns away, signalling the continuation of his grim task. Once held high by its rightful bearers, the diggers' standard is now desecrated as it's discarded and trampled upon. The sight is a stark reminder of the blatant disregard for the lives and ideals that were once cherished.

The scene is disarray and turbulent as redcoats continue their relentless rounding up of diggers outside the stockade. Many are wounded, their steps marked by the telltale drops of blood. Some move with limping gaits, prodded forward by the soldiers' bayonets. The soldiers are a frenzied bunch, their agitation palpable as they brandish swords and raise their voices in excitement and exultation.

"We have woken up, Joe! And sent Joe to sleep again!" Their triumphant shouts pierce the air, a mocking refrain that dances on the edge of jubilation.

Flames consume many tents surrounding the outside of the stockade, a vivid reminder of the destruction that has swept through the once bustling camp. Levi intends to enter one of the tents to search for wounded souls before the fire claims its prize. But an anxious and urgent cry ripples through the air, interrupting his course. **"The troopers are coming again!"**

Troopers arrive with purpose, their carts poised to collect the fallen bodies. Levi counts, his heart heavy, as fifteen lifeless figures are unceremoniously heaped into a single cart. Others lie nearby, their faces turned upwards, their pallor a chilling reminder of the lives extinguished. Some still cling to the fragile thread of existence, their wounds seeping or spurting blood with each laboured breath.

Among the fallen rest a man, his stature robust, about forty years of age, a pike by his side. His body bears the brutal marks of battle

– contusions on his head, gashes across his brow, a bayonet wound etched beneath his ear. Fifteen scars of his ordeal are etched across his frame, a testimony to the fierceness of the battle around him.

Amidst the grim scene, weeping women approach. Their hands offer solace in the form of handkerchiefs, bed linens, and matting, a tender gesture to cover the faces of the deceased. Amidst her tears, one woman turns to a digger standing nearby, her voice a poignant blend of fear and sorrow.

"Oh, God! Sir, it's a sorrowful sight for a Sabbath morning. I pray that heaven will never again bear witness to such horrors. My soul recoils at the brutality a heartless government employs in the name of the law."

Amidst the sorrow, a poignant image emerges – a small terrier perched atop a man's chest amidst the corpses. Its mournful howl echoes an ode to the fallen. Even as the bodies are moved, the terrier remains steadfast, a loyal companion to its fallen master.

Levi's attention shifts, drawn to a wounded digger who crawls out from a tent on the fringes of the scene. His urgency is palpable as he rushes to the digger's side, his determination unwavering. Their eyes meet – the wounded diggers filled with pain, Levi's with compassion.

"I was wounded and surrendered my sword... the Trooper still shot me as I lay on the ground," the wounded digger's words are punctuated by the rasping of his breath, his strength waning. Levi bears witness to the wounded digger's final moments, his life slipping away like grains of sand through an hourglass. Beside him lies another fallen figure, a stark reminder of the cost of this conflict.

Levi's gaze shifts to a poor woman and her children, standing near a tent, their faces etched with fear and confusion. Levi, driven by his innate compassion, approaches them. His voice carries reassurance amid the turmoil.

"The troopers surrounded our tent and pierced it with their swords... took away my husband. What am I to do?" The woman's voice trembles, a reflection of her vulnerability.

Quick thinking guides Levi's response. "Father Smyth – quick, take yourself and your children to him for help. Be quick!! See him over there," Levi points out Father Smyth, providing a lifeline amidst the chaos.

Levi then shifts to an old man consoling a distraught woman near a burnt-out tent. The old man guides the woman and her four young children away, their vulnerability a poignant reminder of the innocence caught in the crossfire. Approaching the old man, Levi offers his assistance.

"Mr Crouch, do you need help?" Levi's voice is laden with concern, his intentions genuine.

Mr Crouch's response is measured, highlighting his self-sufficiency. "No, Levi. But I came here to help Mrs Haslam," he replies, his voice blending empathy and determination. He recounts the harrowing tale of Mr Haslam's suffering – the sudden onslaught of bullets, the merciless shooting by a trooper, the agony of handcuffs, left to his own fate and the agonizing wait for a blacksmith's intervention.

Levi's determination remains steadfast, and he soon finds himself drawn to the presence of Dr Carr within the fallen barrier. Amidst the tumult, the doctor's instructions are clear – Levi is to assist in gathering stretchers from the tents, a crucial step in converting the London Hotel into a makeshift haven for the wounded. Another urgent task awaits Levi – retrieving Dr Carr's surgical instruments from Dr Glendinning's hospital on Pennyweight Hill.

In a swift transition, the scene shifts, and Levi returns with the needed instruments, accompanied by Dr Glendinning. The urgency in Levi's actions is palpable as he hands the surgical bag to Doctor Carr. The stakes are high, and the race against time is relentless.

"Levi, Father Smyth needs more help. He's in the stockade with two others. Find him," Dr Carr's instructions cut through the chaos, and Levi responds with swift determination. Guided by his instincts, he locates Father Smyth within the stockade, the atmosphere of caution and secrecy.

Levi's presence is met with an air of urgency as Father Smyth and his assistants reveal their plan. "Quick, Levi, help them move this man to a safer location, away from prying eyes. Take him to the bush until dark. Return with my assistants later tonight and transport him to my manse at Ballarat East. Troopers are checking all vehicles for the wounded and escapees," Father Smyth's words are a lifeline, a beacon of hope amidst the turmoil.

Levi's resolve remains unshaken as he assists in uncovering the wounded man. With a shared purpose, they prepare to move him, their determination a testament to their unwavering commitment. As they lift the hurdles that conceal the injured man, a revelation strikes Levi with astonishing force – the wounded man is none other than Peter Lalor, the commander of the rebellion forces. Levi's voice trembles as he relays this momentous discovery to the group.

"This is Peter Lalor! I saw him fall during the battle and assumed he had been captured or killed," Levi's words carry a mix of awe and disbelief, a reminder of the unpredictable twists that life can take.

Peter Lalor's condition is grave, his injuries a stark testament to the brutality of the battle. A fresh bloodstain marks his left shoulder, indicating the pain he endures. Lalor's presence looms large despite his unconsciousness, symbolising resilience amidst the chaos.

Levi and the two attendants carefully handle Lalor, lifting him onto a makeshift stretcher. Their movements are deliberate, their purpose unwavering. Together, they navigate the terrain and enter the bush shelter below the gully. With branches as their shield, they carefully conceal Lalor, a fragile ember of hope amidst darkness.

Chapter Sixty-One

The moonlight casts a pale glow as Levi and the two attendants of Father Smyth return to their clandestine mission. Their steps are silent, guided by a sense of urgency and purpose. With practised precision, they carefully lift Peter Lalor's limp form and place him in a dray wagon. A canvas cover conceals their precious cargo, shielding him from prying eyes. Together, they embark on a journey through the night, fraught with significance and uncertainty.

Their destination is Father Smyth's refuge, the manse at St. Alypius Church in East Ballaarat. Here, two surgeons, Dr Doyle and Dr Glendinning, await. The room is filled with anticipation as the attendants carry Lalor inside. The flickering candlelight dances upon their faces, casting shadows that echo the gravity of the situation.

Dr Doyle's voice cuts through the stillness, delivering the harsh reality they must confront. "It appears Lalor has received a musket ball in the left shoulder, together with two smaller bullets that have shattered his upper arm. His blood loss would've rendered him incapable of further action on the battlefield. We have no other option but to amputate his arm to save his life."

Dr Glendinning administers laudanum, a merciful sedation that veils the pain that awaits Lalor. The room's occupants exchange glances laden with trepidation and resolve. Dr Doyle's directive follows, acknowledging the need for privacy in this dire hour.

"Father Smyth, Levi, and one attendee should leave the room before we commence the operation," he states, his words hanging heavy in the air.

Levi's voice, a blend of determination and empathy, pierces the silence. "Doctor, please allow me to help with Mr Lalor's operation. I helped to recover him from the battlefield and believe I'm owed the honour of assisting him further."

Dr Doyle's gaze settles on Levi, a mixture of admiration and disbelief in his eyes. "You are unbelievably fearless, Levi, for your age. I've never seen anything like it. You can help restrain Mr Lalor's legs during the procedure. If you would be so kind as to hold his upper body, Dr Glendinning, we will proceed."

Levi's role is defined, and his purpose is clear amidst the uncertainty. Dr Glendinning takes his place, ready to support Lalor's upper body. Levi stands resolute, his heart a cacophony of emotions – anxiety, empathy, and an unyielding determination to stand by Lalor's side.

Amidst the tension, Lalor's semi-conscious voice, a spirited declaration, cuts through. "Courage! Courage, doctor! — Take it off!" His words reverberate, a rallying cry that defies the impending darkness.

Dr Doyle, steadied by Lalor's spirited encouragement, takes up the bone saw. Levi's watchful eyes capture every movement, every nuance. The doctor's hands waver only slightly as he initiates the gruesome task, his resolve unshaken. Lalor's resilience and the doctor's determination intertwine at that moment, transcending pain and fear.

The sun rises on a new day, shining gentle light upon the goldfields. Levi's presence is a testament to unwavering resilience. Alongside Mr Crockett, they work in tandem, repairing a tent at the back of the shop. Each stitch and tug of the fabric carries a sense of purpose – a small act of normalcy from the previous turmoil.

Mr Crockett's voice breaks the rhythm, his words heavy with the weight of recent events. "Levi, it is a tragic day when such events occur on a Sabbath. I heard Captain Ross of Toronto fell victim to the violence, and Vern the German met a grim fate."

Levi's response carries the weight of firsthand witness. "It was a horrifying sight, Mr Crockett. I witnessed it all – both the battle and its aftermath."

Their conversation shifts, revealing the human cost of the conflict. Mr Crockett's words paint a picture of loss and despair. "A man I saw walking along Main Road spoke of his inability to hold on much longer. They shot his brother right beside him."

Levi's voice resonates with empathy, acknowledging the gravity of the situation. "A long list of casualties is yet to be accounted for, Mr Crockett. When families and friends learn the extent of the tragedy, there will be voids that cannot be filled."

The conversation takes a darker turn, delving into the broader implications of the Eureka massacre. Mr Crockett's words reflect a sense of hopelessness, a stark reflection of the disillusionment that prevails.

"I fear that the massacre at Eureka is only a skirmish if things don't change," Mr Crockett's voice is tinged with resignation. "Breathing the blood-tainted air of the diggings has become unbearable."

Levi's response holds a firm resolve, a reflection of his own convictions. "According to Pa, the count stands at twenty-two Diggers dead, including one woman and six soldiers. Many more are wounded and suffering."

Their exchange shifts, turning toward a mutual acquaintance – Raffaello Carboni. Levi's words echo with a mixture of concern and determination. "Father Smyth told me he was knocked insensible during the battle but is otherwise unharmed and imprisoned at the Trooper's Barracks."

The morning light continues to paint the scene, a tableau of resilience amidst adversity. In the quiet moments of labour and conversation, the strength of their bonds shines through, a testament to the indomitable spirit that refuses to yield.

Chapter Sixty-Two

The small room within the Trooper's barracks pulses with anticipation, an air of uncertainty and unwavering resolve mingling. Levi occupies a corner, his demeanour a mix of eagerness and concern as he awaits Raffaello's arrival. A soldier acts as a reluctant usher, guiding Raffaello into the room. The clinking of chains accompanies Raffaello's every step, a sombre symphony of restraint. His appearance is a testament to the trials he's endured – hands weighed down by manacles, an iron ball an inescapable companion to his legs, and the tattered remnants of his once-proud attire. The iron ball finds its designated spot on the floor, a heavy symbol of captivity and defiance.

"Hello, Raffaello," Levi's voice punctuates the charged atmosphere, a blend of relief and concern evident in his words. "I'm glad you are alive and not severely injured."

Raffaello's response is imbued with a weariness that only fortifies his spirit. His voice carries the weight of trials faced and hardships endured. "Hello, my good angel. Thank you. Physically, I'm unharmed, but my pride has taken a severe blow. These rogues tore down our clothes to the undershirts and treated us disrespectfully."

The resilience in Raffaello's spirit refuses to be extinguished, even in the face of adversity. Amidst the turmoil, he finds solace in acknowledging the support he's received. "Father Smyth informed me that you hid my writings and accounts journal from the officials. Well done, lad."

As the conversation deepens, the uncertainty of their fate casts a shadow. Levi's concern deepens as he treads on the fragile ground of their future. "What do you suppose will happen to you all now?"

Raffaello's response holds a mix of acceptance and determination, his voice reflecting the weight of their situation. "One hundred and thirteen Diggers were taken prisoner, and only thirteen of us stood before the magistrate and were found to have a case to answer as the leaders of the rebellion. We will be sent to Melbourne Gaol, facing a jury at the Melbourne Courthouse. If found guilty, there is a chance we will hang!"

Levi's heart bears the burden of their impending fate, a heaviness reverberating through his voice. "I've heard that there was a rally in Melbourne, and the newspapers are expressing sympathy for your cause and criticizing the Governor's harsh actions."

The disparity between different regions surfaces in Raffaello's response, his words tinged with bitterness. "Perhaps that is the case in Melbourne, but in Ballaarat, not a word of protest has been voiced. The treatment we receive as prisoners should be brought to John Manning's attention at the 'Ballaarat Times.'"

Levi's commitment to truth and justice is unwavering. His voice carries a determination that underscores his resolve. "Certainly. What shall I tell him?"

The recollection of mistreatment in prison carries an undercurrent of raw vulnerability in Raffaello's words. "I just wanted to keep my waistcoat because it contained money and important papers in the breast pocket. However, they tore my clothes into rags. When I tried to protest, they kicked and knocked me down before throwing me naked and senseless into a lock-up."

Levi's response manifests his indignation, an assertion that echoes through the room. "Those brutes! I'll make sure Manning knows about the mistreatment. Is there anything else?"

Raffaello's narrative unfolds further, painting a vivid picture of the harsh reality they faced. "Tell Manning that the prison was unbearably crowded. Our groans and howls reached Commissioner Rede. The doors opened around two o'clock in the morning, and they transferred us to a spacious and well-ventilated room in the camp storehouse."

A glimmer of unexpected empathy emerges amid the darkness. Raffaello's voice is softer as he recounts an instance of humanity amidst cruelty. "Despite the circumstances, Commissioner Rede personally visited us and appeared to empathize with our situation."

As the conversation navigates deeper, Levi's inquiries delve to the core. "Is that all?"

The weight of their suffering is evident in Raffaello's voice, a mixture of pain and unyielding determination. "No! The following day, around ten o'clock, they ordered us to form four rows. The camp officials and their lackeys revelled in their power. They treated us like prey, numbering and singling out a few as examples for their twisted purposes."

A pause envelops the room as Raffaello gathers his strength to continue, a vulnerability underscoring his words. "Identified by my red hair, fizzing red beard, and fizzing red mustachios, my name was taken down by an armed ruffian and an anonymous scribbler, followed by the black American rebel to front the Magistrate with eleven others. All thirteen are now reserved as rebel leaders to go to trial in Melbourne charged with the act of High Treason!"

In the face of such adversity, compassion blooms anew. Levi's voice softens, reflecting his empathy for his friend's plight and the injustice they all endure. "The reward for Peter Lalor's capture will never be collected due to public sympathy. Lalor remains concealed at Father Smyth's manse in Ballarat East and will need time to recover over many weeks."

Raffaello's response encapsulates the essence of their enduring spirit. It's a blend of acceptance and hope, a testament to the resilience that defines them. "It is best, Levi. If we thirteen State prisoners are to hang, then at least our Commander-In-Chief can continue our fight for justice - even with one arm."

Their voices resonate in the shadows of their trials, a chorus of determination and resilience that is a testament to their unbreakable spirit.

Chapter Sixty-Three

"7th OF DECEMBER (THREE DAYS AFTER THE BATTLE) - 100 PRISONERS ARE LIBERATED EXCEPT THE THIRTEEN RESERVED TO RATIFY AND VALIDATE THE ACT OF TREASON."

The pale light of Tuesday's dawn filters through Levi's window, gently rousing him from his slumber. A heavy air hangs over the day, laden with significance. His thoughts, however, are not bound within the walls of his room; they drift toward the prisoners held captive within the confines of the compound. With a determined resolve, Levi rises from his bed, ready to embrace the tasks.

Beyond the walls of the compound, a tableau of activity unfolds. Thirteen State prisoners, now symbols of resistance, stand on the precipice of a journey that will shape their destinies. Levi arrives just as Captain Thomas, an imposing authority figure, orchestrates the proceedings with a commanding presence. An observer of this poignant moment, Levi watches in solemn silence as Captain Thomas addresses the prisoners.

"PRISONERS! If any of you dare stir a finger or utter a word, especially on the diggings, heed my warning... those transgressors will be shot on the spot! You are under my jurisdiction for transit to Melbourne Gaol."

The weight of Captain Thomas's words hangs heavily in the air, a testament to his power and the gravity of their situation. Despite the harsh decree, the prisoners stand unwavering, their spirits unbroken.

Among them, Raffaello's voice emerges as a beacon of defiance. "GOD SAVE THE QUEEN!"

Sergeant Bill Brody – an embodiment of restraint, strides towards the defiant prisoner Raffaello Carboni and tightens his shackles. The clinking of chains serves as a stark reminder of their captivity. Bound alongside the Mulatto American Rebel, they are positioned at the forefront of a cart. Captain Thomas's instructions echo, underscoring the fragility of their circumstances. "**Guard!** If either of these two attempts to turn their heads – shoot them without hesitation!"

And so, the journey begins. The convoy sets forth along the old Melbourne Road, a caravan of uncertainty traversing the landscape. Troopers, symbols of authority, flank the carts with swords drawn and carbines ready. Linked by chains, the prisoners embody resilience, facing adversity with unyielding determination. Once leaders labelled rebels, they're now prisoners embarking on a path leading to Melbourne Gaol.

Raffaello's gaze lingers on the familiar landscape amid this movement – the Eureka gravel pits. A fleeting moment of introspection washes over him, a melancholic reflection on the past. The tent that once bore meaning, a testament to his pursuit of justice, now stands abandoned and forgotten.

"Raffaello, my friend," Levi's inner voice carries empathy and camaraderie, *"the perception of Ballaarat toward your actions at the Stockade is crystal clear. Although not totally alone in that moment. I am the only independent witness present on Main Road as they led you away."*

As the journey unfolds, the landscape transforms, bathed in the sun's golden hues. The prisoners, symbols of defiance, traverse the distance while vigilant Dragoons guard them from all directions. The horses that pull the carts possess an air of duty, steadfast in their charge.

Hours drift by, and the convoy arrives at Bacchus Marsh Gaol. Anticipation fills the air as the prisoners – symbols of rebellion – are ushered into a holding cell, a temporary sanctuary amidst their journey. Captain Thomas's voice, unexpectedly touched by compassion, addresses them again.

"Prisoners, your behaviour during our ride to the Bacchus Marsh changeover has been commendable. A glass of ale and damper bread with cheese shall be offered to you."

But the journey remains unfinished. As day gives way to night, the convoy reaches the imposing structure of Melbourne Gaol. The prisoners, transferred from one authority to another, find themselves in the hands of the turnkeys. Captain Thomas's duty fulfilled, the prisoners now stand before the gaol governor.

"Governor," Captain Thomas's voice resonates with authority, "these thirteen men are the Rebel leaders of the Eureka Stockade, charged with High Treason. Their conduct throughout the journey has been exemplary."

In the presence of the gaol governor, the prisoners stand as embodiments of resistance, their garb belying their destiny. Their fate, a riddle shrouded in uncertainty, is sealed within these walls. As the heavy cell door closed behind them, their thoughts turned inward. While sleep may elude them, their minds brim with memories, regrets, and a determination that remains unshaken, even within the darkness of their confinement.

Within their cell's confines, they confront their shadows, grief, and unyielding commitment to the cause that propelled them to this juncture. The physical and metaphorical journey marches on – a testament to their enduring spirit and resolute determination.

Within the dimly lit holding cell of the courthouse, an atmosphere of desolation hangs heavy. Raffaello, the Italian and Joe, the mulatto American, share a sombre bench, their expressions reflecting a mixture of melancholy and resignation. The weight of their impending trial bears on them, suffusing the air with tension.

"It's been said that the government intends to make an example of us, condemning us to fifteen years in the hulks," Raffaello's voice carries the burden of acceptance, his words echoing the sentiment of defeat.

A letter from Mr Lynn, their solicitor in Ballaarat, serves as a tangible reminder of their dire circumstances. "Mr Lynn's letter reveals the elusive nature of defence funds from those lucky prisoners released. With available resources, we've gathered only two hundred pounds from our fellow state prisoners. Joe, what fate awaits us at the end of this arduous journey?"

Joe's response is a blend of uncertainty and determination. "If the jury finds us innocent, we'll vanish into the gravel pit diggings again. But if the jury's verdict isn't in our favour..."

With a knowing gesture, Joe paints a vivid picture – bowing his head and emitting an eerie whistle, his thumb pressing against his windpipe and collarbone.

"Joe, your message is as clear as crystal," Raffaello acknowledges with a solemn nod.

"And we're fortunate," Joe's tone takes on a glimmer of hope, "to have Mr James Macpherson Grant on our side."

Raffaello's response is laden with theatricality, encapsulating the gravity of their situation. "Indeed! Grant stands as a man of substance, a Scot whose wisdom has been honed by experience. His stature mirrors his competence – a sharp legal mind familiar with every intricate detail of his craft. His forehead is the canvas of astuteness, and his gentle demeanour reassures us of his unwavering support in our time of need. His eyes, windows to his soul, betray his disdain for oppression. His nose, an emblem of truth, speaks against deceit. And his manners, truly those of a gentleman, mark him as the ally we so desperately require, Joe!"

Grant enters the holding room as if summoned by their discussion, a beacon of hope amidst their tribulations. "Gentlemen, take heart! There is no need for trepidation. The day of your liberation is imminent... for each of you!" Grant's proclamation resonates with optimism. "I've secured the services of Mr Aspinall, a defence barrister of exceptional skill. The tide of sympathy sways in your favour."

Raffaello's gratitude emanates through his words. "May God's blessings be upon you, Mr Grant!"

Grant's assurance continues, carrying a message of solace and deliverance. "The tempest has subsided for the one hundred stockade prisoners released in Ballaarat. They count themselves fortunate to have escaped more severe consequences. They've returned to their diggings with renewed spirits, reigniting the flames of better times. And you, too, shall soon find respite in the familiar embrace of the gravel pits. An angel, embodied by Mr Aspinall, descends to secure the release of all remaining state prisoners."

Amidst the shadows of uncertainty, a glimmer of hope pierces through, extending its hand to Raffaello and Joe. This hand is woven with the steadfast support of Mr Grant and the promise of a skilled advocate. The path before them is illuminated by the prospect of redemption, offering a chance to emerge from despair and embrace a future unshackled by chains.

Chapter Sixty-Four

" TWO DAYS EARLIER"...

Levi's home emanates a sense of warmth and belonging, an oasis of familiarity where the presence of his mother, Alice, is a balm to his soul. Their connection is palpable as they engage in a heartfelt conversation that captures their bond.

"Ma," Levi's voice carries a mixture of excitement and contemplation, "an extraordinary opportunity has presented itself. George Bugslag, having witnessed my aid to the 'Eureka Boys,' has offered to take me to Melbourne in his supply cart. He insists it is free of charge as a token of appreciation. We are set to depart this very afternoon."

Alice raises an eyebrow, her maternal concern evident. "But what about your responsibilities with Mr Crockett?"

Levi responds promptly, his conviction unwavering. "Mr Crockett is well-informed about my plans and fully supports them. He recognizes the significance of this journey – a chance for me to revisit my birthplace and reunite with Pa, especially now that he is stationed there for the Eureka Trials."

Alice's gaze remains fixed on her son, a perceptive glint in her eyes. "Yet I sense that your true motivation lies in supporting Mr Raffaello Carboni. Promise me that you will take the time to see your father amidst your commitment. If you pledge to do so, you have my blessing."

Levi meets his mother's gaze, sincerity radiating from his eyes. "Absolutely, Ma. I will make it a point to visit Pa."

The scene shifts and the road to Melbourne unfurls before them, bathed in the soft afternoon glow. George Bugslag's cart arrives at the cabin, drawn by a pair of robust horses. Levi assumes his place beside George, the impending journey infused with purpose. The landscape unfolds as the cart sets off – a canvas of countryside vistas and quaint settlements.

Levi breaks the silence, expressing his gratitude to George. "George, I can't express enough how thankful I am for this opportunity to accompany you. My primary objective is to visit Raffaello and offer him my unwavering support throughout the trials."

George's response is filled with understanding and warmth, a testament to their camaraderie. "I witnessed your actions at Eureka – your dedication to aiding the wounded and injured. It's an honour to extend this invitation to you, Levi. In times like these, we must stand by our mates. Raffaello is a man of integrity, deserving all the backing he can get."

As the wheels of the cart roll onward, Levi and George's conversations become more than mere words – they become threads that weave together their past experiences and the events that have shaped their present. The road to Melbourne transforms from a physical passage to a symbolic journey of solidarity and friendship, a testament to their commitment to stand by those who need it most.

The courtroom is charged with solemnity as Justice Barry presides over the proceedings, clad in the regalia of his position – robes flowing majestically, a grey wig crowning his head. The Clerk of Court occupies a place before him, the air heavy with anticipation. Amid the spectators, Levi sits in the second row of the civic gallery, his gaze unwaveringly fixed on the defendant's box where Raffaello sits. Raffaello's countenance reflects a fusion of determination and weariness, a mirror to the weight of the trial he faces.

Standing before the jury box, Mr Aspinall commands attention as he delivers his opening address to the twelve male jurors. Their expressions form a spectrum of emotions – curiosity, scepticism, and an innate sense of duty.

"Gentlemen of the Jury," Mr Aspinall's voice resonates, "our objective is to dismantle the charge of high treason by unveiling its inherent absurdity. Even the most seasoned legal minds have struggled to decipher its true meaning. The British legal system boasts of Urbis et Orbis terrarium – the past's delivery of traitors to the notorious English executioner, Jack Ketch, under the orders of King Charles II. Their heads spiked atop a post at the city gates to be gawked at and pecked over by crows. This gruesome spectacle aimed to instil fear and loyalty, employing brutality as its tool."

Levi's attention shifts to the jurors, observing their reactions – widened eyes, uneasy changes in their seats – as Mr Aspinall's words wash over them. The courtroom seems to collectively hold its breath, the air charged with anticipation. Mr Aspinall persists, his arguments artfully dismantling the very foundation of the high treason charge.

"This charge against Raffaello Carboni and his fellow rebels is utterly baseless," Mr Aspinall asserts with unwavering conviction. "It serves as a means to silence the voices of the oppressed, denying their fundamental rights. The diggers at Eureka were not traitors; they were individuals driven to desperation by injustice. Their actions were rooted in a fervent desire to address longstanding grievances."

Levi focuses on the jury, his gaze tracing their evolution from scepticism to contemplation. The courtroom scene transitions seamlessly, capturing Mr Aspinall's fervent delivery of his closing address. As Mr Aspinall concluded his address, the collective attention of the courtroom shifted to the jurors. Still seated in the felon's dock, Raffaello wears a blend of hope and apprehension. The jury retires to deliberate, the fate of Raffaello Carboni resting squarely in their hands.

Time passes, and the hours are marked by anxiety and anticipation. The jurors eventually reenter the courtroom, their demeanour bearing an air of assurance.

Justice Barry addresses them. "Gentlemen of the Jury," his voice carries gravitas, "have you reached a unanimous decision?"

The Head Juror responds with authority. "We have."

A hushed tension envelops the room as the pivotal moment unfolds. Justice Barry's voice, imbued with solemnity, pierces the silence. "Is the prisoner at the bar guilty or not guilty?"

With a firm and unwavering voice, the head juror responds, **"Not guilty!"**

A collective sigh of relief sweeps through the courtroom. Raffaello rises from the felon's box, his shackles removed. Levi springs forward, embracing Raffaello in an exuberant hug. The courtroom erupts into a jubilant celebration; a photographer scrambles to set up his camera to capture the scene. Raffaello's trial concludes with an overwhelming triumph, a victory that resonates with vindication and justice achieved.

Chapter Sixty-Five

The courthouse doors swing open, allowing Raffaello to step out into the warm embrace of daylight. Freedom beckons, and a fervent crowd of supporters await him as he emerges. Cheers erupt from their lips, mingling with the applause that fills the air. The collective joy and relief are tangible as they celebrate Raffaello's hard-fought vindication.

With purposeful steps, Raffaello moves forward, his gaze fixed on the crowd before him. His voice carries a mixture of gratitude and emotion as he addresses the assembled supporters, his words reaching every corner of the street.

"Friends!" His voice resonates through the crowd, each syllable infused with heartfelt sincerity. "This victory is not mine alone; it belongs to each of you who stood unwaveringly by our side. I am humbled by your relentless support and your unwavering faith in the cause we fought for. Let this triumph stand as a symbol of hope – a testament to the power of unity and unwavering determination."

The crowd responds fervently, their jubilant voices blending into a harmonious chorus that echoes through the bustling streets. Raffaello's voice rings out again, with unwavering intensity, as he shares his sentiments.

"Thank you, people of Melbourne! Your steadfast support and friendship have been my guiding light through these trying times. Together, the diggers have proven that the spirit of the people cannot be suppressed, and the pursuit of justice is worth every sacrifice."

The crowd's cheers and applause crescendo, the energy swelling in the air as they revel in the moment of victory. Amidst the euphoria, Levi rushes forward, his hand lifting Raffaello's arm in a triumphant gesture before the crowd. He turns to Raffaello, his voice carrying over the cheers.

"Raffaello, my friend, your courage and resilience have been remarkable. It's been an honour to stand by your side and witness this historic moment. Your fight for justice will inspire generations to come."

The connection between Raffaello and Levi is palpable – a shared journey of trials and triumphs, friendship and solidarity. Their exchange is more than words; it's a testament to their bond through adversity. Raffaello nods in acknowledgement, his eyes reflecting a deep understanding and gratitude for their shared experiences.

"Levi, there are matters I need to attend to," Raffaello's voice carries a sense of purpose. "I'll be staying at the Criterion Hotel. Meet me there. Tomorrow afternoon, we'll journey back to Ballaarat with Mr Bugslag."

Levi's agreement is swift and resolute. "Agreed. It will also allow me to visit my Pa, as I promised Ma."

As the congratulatory gestures and pats on Raffaello's back continue within the crowd, they navigate their way, their expressions mirroring a blend of triumph and anticipation.

Raffaello and Levi, seated in George Bugslag's cart, return to Ballaarat the next day. The journey's toll is evident on their faces, etched with the weariness of their challenges. Levi breaks the silence, his gaze fixed on the familiar landscape ahead.

"We'll be back at your tent near the Eureka gravel pits soon," he remarks, a glimmer of reassurance in his voice.

Raffaello's reply carries a mix of fatigue and unyielding resolve. "Four months of confinement have dampened my eagerness to return, Levi. The Diggers who managed to escape prosecution left the thirteen state prisoners without support – both financial and moral. I don't expect a grand welcome."

As the cart approaches the gravel pit diggings, a remarkable scene unfolds. Every digger ceases their work, tools abandoned as they rush toward the carriage that carries Raffaello. With hats in hand, they wave them jubilantly, their cheers ringing like a triumphant chorus.

"Hurray! Welcome home!" - "You are a bloody hero!" - "I'll buy you a drink, mate... any day!"

Raffaello, invigorated by the outpouring of support, stands tall on the cart. His acknowledgement is wholehearted, a wave of his hat expressing his gratitude and shared camaraderie. His voice, strong and unwavering, rises above the crowd as the cart maintains its leisurely pace.

"Thank you, my friends! Our battle isn't over – together, we've stood for justice and liberty."

As the cart continues its journey, Raffaello and Levi disembark, their weary bodies craving rest. However, their anticipation transforms into shock as they approach Raffaello's tent. The scene within is chaotic – belongings are strewn about, and order is replaced by disorder.

Raffaello steps into the tent; his disbelief is evident in the furrow of his brows. "Levi, my neighbours have betrayed me, shattered my trust. Everything of value is gone – even my cherished gold specimens, symbols of my struggle."

Levi's voice carries a mix of indignation and determination. "This is an act of betrayal, Raffaello. We must uncover those responsible and ensure they face the consequences."

Raffaello's resolve remains unshaken, his spirit undeterred even in adversity. He retrieves his journal from beneath the stretcher, brushing off the dirt before he opens its pages. "My account book shows I had forty-nine pounds on that fateful Sunday. Now, it's all vanished. I can only hope that the gold dust and my clothes – confiscated by the police – remain at their barracks. Tomorrow, I'll confront them and demand answers."

Levi's determination mirrors Raffaello's and their unwavering commitment to justice. "We won't let them extinguish your hope, Raffaello. We'll confront the authorities and reclaim what rightfully belongs to you. As a Eureka Digger, your spirit will remain unbroken."

In their shared determination, since the cheering crowd and the chaos of betrayal, Raffaello and Levi stand firm, ready to face the challenges ahead.

Chapter Sixty-Six

Levi walks alongside Raffaello through the vibrant streets of Ballaarat. The town's atmosphere crackles with anticipation, mirroring Raffaello's unwavering determination to reclaim what was unjustly taken from him. Their footsteps lead them to the Police barracks on Camp Street, where Raffaello's gaze fixates on a constable with distinct Vandemonian features – the key to unlocking the truth he seeks.

"Excuse me, Constable," Raffaello's tone is courteous yet firm. "I was apprehended on the day of the Eureka affair. Raffaello Carboni is my name. I wish to inquire about my confiscated belongings – money, a small bag of gold dust, my mining license, and a pair of new watertight boots."

With a nod, the constable acknowledges Raffaello's presence, maintaining professionalism. "Ah, Mr Carboni, I remember you well. Allow me a moment to consult the records book and gather information about your missing items."

The constable's fingers navigate the pages of the records book with practised efficiency, tracing lines of text as he searches for answers. "Regrettably, Mr Carboni," the constable's voice carries a touch of empathy, "the records indicate that on the day your possessions were seized, they vanished alongside those of others, disappearing into thin air along with Gaoler Nixon. The man has vanished without a trace. Nevertheless, there is a silver lining. Upon learning of your mistreatment, Inspector Foster entrusted your small bag of gold dust and gold license to Father Smyth for safekeeping."

Raffaello's expression reflects disappointment and acceptance, absorbing the weight of the unfortunate news. "While that may provide some solace, Constable, my loss still amounts to around thirty pounds."

The constable's sympathetic nod acknowledges the gravity of Raffaello's situation. "Certainly, Mr Carboni, it is indeed regrettable. However, there is positive news to share. The government has introduced an alternative form of licensing known as the 'Miner's Right,' requiring a mere two pounds annually. Furthermore, the monthly gold tax has been abolished, and a general amnesty has been granted to the three miners arrested for the Bentley's Eureka Hotel Fire."

Raffaello's response is genuine and heartfelt, reflecting a blend of gratitude and relief, and he whispers to Levi, "That is indeed heartening news! It signifies that our pain, struggles, and the sacrifices of those who laid down their lives were not in vain."

Levi and Raffaello exchange glances, their eyes alight with hope as they find comfort in the positive strides made amidst Raffaello's hardships. With their conversation concluded, they step away from the constable and the police barracks, leaving the shadows of uncertainty behind. As they walk, their shared optimism shines like a beacon in the face of adversity – a glimmer of hope amidst the unknown.

The scene transitions to Raffaello's tent, bathed in the soft glow of daylight. He stands outside, conversing with John Humffray, a fellow activist and kindred spirit who grasps the significance of their struggle.

"Congratulations on your return, Raffaello," Humffray's voice brims with genuine warmth, his eyes reflecting their shared triumph. "The bold actions of the Eureka Diggers have borne profound consequences, even amidst the pain and loss."

Raffaello meets Humffray's gaze, a bond of understanding passing between them. "Our actions were driven by necessity, John. The inaction of the 'Committee's Charter' left us with little recourse. We couldn't have foreseen the severity of the Governor's response to our unity."

Humffray nods knowingly, recognizing the complexity of their journey. "Those days are behind us now, Raffaello. The government has granted the Diggers political representation, acknowledging their rights and affording them an equal voice alongside the established elites."

Determination gleams in Raffaello's eyes, a spark of hope amidst their challenges. "And what of Peter Lalor? What has become of him?"

With a solemn tone, Humffray imparts his knowledge. "Thanks to overwhelming public support, the reward for Peter Lalor's capture went unclaimed. He found refuge in Father Smyth's manse in Ballaarat East, hidden from the authorities for weeks. He was then covertly transported to Geelong, remaining there until the storm subsided. It appears the authorities have ceased their pursuit."

Raffaello's words resound with pride and conviction. "And rightfully so! Lalor deserves to be hailed as a hero for our accomplishments."

Humffray's agreement is palpable in his voice. "Absolutely. With the impending State's general elections proposed by London, where Digger representatives will be chosen, I intend to nominate Peter Lalor as the representative for Ballarat East. As for myself, I have aspirations for office."

Raffaello's response is swift and resolute. "You both have my unwavering support, John."

Humffray's words resonate with purpose and optimism. "The uprising has ignited a movement for change, compelling the government to acknowledge the power and rights of the people. The impact of this movement will extend far beyond the Diggers, reshaping the entire Nation."

As Raffaello and Humffray share their dreams of a brighter future, their words weave threads of hope, stitching together the fabric of a transformed society.

Chapter Sixty-Seven

"BALLAARAT 1856"...

Levi, a sixteen-year-old caught between youth and maturity, is perched on a rough-hewn log outside his humble home. The diary on his knee becomes a canvas for his thoughts, his pencil etching his inner monologue onto the pages, releasing his musings into the world:

Dear Diary," Levi's voice whispers softly as if sharing secrets with an old friend. His words resonate, carrying his reflections beyond the confines of his thoughts. *"Raffaello's triumphant 'Not Guilty' verdict from the British Jury has woven him back into the fabric of Ballaarat's society. Amidst the complexity of existence, he found solace amidst the exultant cheers that echoed through the Adelphi Theatre. His notes of 'When Ballaarat unfurled the Southern Cross' lingered in the night air, a testament to his unyielding spirit."*

Levi's gaze turns inward, his eyes carrying a reflective glimmer. *"In the warm embrace of the noble-hearted Carl Wiesenhaven, steward of the Prince Albert Hotel, Raffaello discovered an anchor in turbulent seas. He found solace and refuge within Carl's benevolence – a sanctuary amidst life's storms."*

With unwavering focus, Levi's pencil moves, capturing moments in charcoal. *"As fate spun its threads, Humffray and Lalor ascended as the Diggers' Representatives in the Victorian Parliament. Their elevation stands as an embodiment of steadfastness and unwavering dedication."*

A tender smile graces Levi's lips as he records a tale of devotion. *"Alicia Dunne, who nursed Peter Lalor's wounds during his fugitive days in Geelong, became his partner for life. The vows exchanged at St*

Mary's Church, Geelong, on July 10th symbolize unwavering loyalty and resilience."

The diary pages turn each movement of Levi's hand into a brushstroke on the canvas of history. *"On the 14th of July, a public assembly gathered at the famous Bakery Hill. Their purpose was to elect a cadre of esteemed figures to the local court, embodying the legacy of the Eureka Stockade. United in purpose, the public's choice fell upon Raffaello Carboni, casting him as a sentinel of justice."*

The diary closes with a soft sigh, capturing Levi's introspection. The chronicle of events born from the Eureka rebellion remains a living testament to the indomitable force of hope and justice.

The scene shifts, the dawn of a new day casting a golden hue over the landscape. Raffaello and Levi stand on the bustling boardwalk of Main Street, the world alive around them. The morning sun paints them in a warm glow, a tableau of mixed emotions as they await the arrival of the coach that will bear Raffaello away from the goldfields back to the distant shores of his European homeland.

Raffaello's voice resonates with conviction, his words carrying a weight of finality. "Levi, in your companionship, I've found the bond of a son. Amidst the tumultuous trials of the goldfields, your loyalty and unwavering presence have been a beacon of light. The moments we've woven together will remain etched in my heart."

Levi's response is a blend of gratitude and emotion, his words echoing in the morning breeze. "And you, Raffaello, have been a guide, a mentor shaping my path in ways beyond measure. Your wisdom and guidance will be my compass as I embark on my own journey."

Anticipation hangs in the air, accompanied by a touch of melancholy in Raffaello's voice. "Soon, Melbourne will be my starting point, the first step on a journey back to Europe. The place I leave behind, Ballaarat, is unlike any other – a tapestry woven with rebellion and the pursuit of justice. Its essence will linger even as time sweeps away my presence."

A magnificent Cobb and Co. coach, a grandeur of six horses in tow, emerges into view. The driver, a rugged colonial figure sporting a cabbage tree hat, eases the carriage to a stop beside Raffaello and Levi. The carriage guard, deft and efficient, attends to luggage and belongings.

Raffaello's words ring with finality, a farewell laden with significance. "Levi, my young friend, our paths diverge from this juncture. I bid you farewell, trusting that the path ahead will lead you to remarkable discoveries."

Levi's eyes glisten, his farewell heartfelt and sincere. "Thank you, Raffaello. Farewell, my dear friend. Remember to chronicle your adventures in your letters."

With a wave, a gesture of both eagerness and sorrow, Levi watches as the coach sets into motion, carrying Raffaello away. His teary eyes mirror the blend of emotions in his heart, a bittersweet kick against the boardwalk a testament to the courage it takes to move forward. As the coach disappears down the road, a new chapter unfolds for both Raffaello and Levi. Bound by fate, their stories now embark on separate but equally meaningful journeys, forever intertwined by the echoes of their shared past.

Chapter Sixty-Eight

The relentless summer sun paints Main Road in Ballaarat in an unforgiving blaze, casting a swirling veil of dust over the thoroughfare. What was once a familiar path now becomes a gritty realm, a canvas etched with the frenetic energy of a bustling community. A vibrant tapestry of businesses unfolds along this road between Eureka and Esmond Streets – a lively ensemble of shops, hotels, and theatres, each contributing to the grand spectacle.

Upon this bustling stage, people traverse the long stretches of rough timber boardwalks, their steps purposeful and determined. The street pulses with activity, a symphony of pursuits and identities intersecting. Bearded men intermingle with the more polished, distinguished by top hats and tailored coats, some adorned with high-knee boots. Meanwhile, women shoppers adorn themselves in outspread crinolines and bonnets, their unique coal shuttle-shaped headwear carving out an unmistakable silhouette.

The air itself hums with the harmonies of commerce and life. Shopkeepers stand at their makeshift stalls, fashioned from canvas, softwood, and repurposed packing cases. Their voices rise in enthusiasm, their calls crescendoing as they beckon passersby to explore the treasures within. On occasion, they adopt the role of enticers, coaxing reluctant souls into their domains, ensuring that the spectrum of wares on display doesn't go unnoticed. Amid this lively orchestra, the figures of Diggers emerge – recognizable in their rugged attire, red or blue twilled shirts, sans coats, clay-stained moleskin trousers tucked into high boots.

Amid this symphony, fortunate Diggers who've struck gold celebrate their newfound prosperity. Bedecked in resplendent pink silk waistcoats adorned with weighty gold chains, they flaunt their triumph with exuberance and inebriation. Cuban cigars dangle languidly from their lips, with additional ones finding shelter in waistcoat pockets – an emblem of their elevated stature.

However, the surface of the main road lies in deeper layers. Amid the glimmer of commerce lies the shadowy underbelly. With a staggering ninety-four licensed hotels and concealed grog shops tucked away in enclaves like Esmond Street and Arcade Streets, the street transcends commerce to become a playground for the murkier aspects of human nature. Thirsty diggers seek solace in these haunts, while shrewd opportunists capitalize on their intoxication, leading them astray into dens of vice. Certain women exploit their vulnerability, making off with more than just gold – robbing them of their possessions and dignity.

As the sun dips below the horizon, a ritual unfolds – a procession that underscores the worth of what's being guarded. A gold escort, heavily armed, marches down the road. Guided by Bill Brody's watchful eye, two bearded troopers lead a wagon with thousands of ounces of precious metal. Riding alongside, additional escorts stand vigilant, carbines poised, their presence a deterrent to lurking bushrangers who might seek to seize the valuable cargo on the road to Melbourne.

And then, as the day fades into twilight, a trumpet's clarion call pierces the air. It's a signal heralding the arrival of the Geelong mail coach. Ned Devine, his ever-present Cabbage Tree hat, guides the horses with expert precision, his position atop the coach commanding reverence. A guard at the rear blows the trumpet, alerting all to the coach's swift approach. The galloping procession leaves a trail of excitement and anticipation in its wake, a fitting crescendo to the ongoing symphony of Main Road – a thoroughfare that pulsates with life, commerce, and the myriad shades of human endeavour.

The quiet interior of Crockett's shop is alive with purposeful activity. Mr Crockett and Levi stand side by side, absorbed in assembling a new tent. Their hands move with practised precision, weaving fabric and securing seams. The tent begins to take shape under their skilful touch, a testament to their craftsmanship and unspoken bond.

Levi's voice breaks the rhythm of their labour, tinged with excitement. "Mr Crockett, a letter from Turin Town in Italy has reached me. It's from none other than Raffaello Carboni."

Intrigue lights up Mr Crockett's eyes as he responds, "Well, Levi, don't leave me in suspense. What tidings does Raffaello bring?"

Levi reaches into his back pocket, retrieving the letter that has travelled such a distance. With a gentle touch, he unfolds the pages, his gaze scanning the inscribed words: "In his letter," Levi begins, *"Raffaello recounts how he utilized the gold he had earned in Ballaarat to secure passage on the ship Impératrice Eugénie. His voyage led him through the enchanting lands of the East, where he explored remarkable places like Jerusalem and Bethlehem. From there, Raffaello returned to Italy, making stops in London and Paris. In Milan, he lent his linguistic talents as an interpreter to the French army, an endeavour that earned him a commemorative medal. Now, he resides contentedly in Turin Town with his family, his heart filled with gratitude for the French triumph over the Austrians – a victory that ensured his safe homecoming."*

A warm smile graces Mr Crockett's features as he responds, "Truly heartwarming news, Levi. I'm thrilled that Raffaello has found his way back and is flourishing."

Levi's voice takes on a more contemplative tone as he continues, "His letter concludes with a verse that lingers in my thoughts: *'My right-hand shakes like a reed in a storm; my eyes swell from a flood of tears. I can control the bitterness in my heart and say, 'So far shalt thou go,' but I cannot control its ebb and flow — just now is the Spring tide.'"*

The weight of Raffaello's words hangs in the air, a poignant reminder of life's complexities that touch Mr Crockett and Levi. With calm wisdom, Mr Crockett speaks, "That verse captures the essence of Raffaello's journey through life's tempests. It speaks to the balance we strive to maintain – to assert control over our emotions yet acknowledge that their currents are beyond our mastery. A sentiment that resonates deeply, especially when facing life's challenges."

Levi's nod is thoughtful, his gaze distant yet purposeful. "Absolutely, Mr Crockett. Raffaello's words encapsulate the rhythm of existence – the undulating highs and lows that define our paths. His journey is a testament to the strength that resides within him."

Reinvigorated, they return to their work, the letter from Raffaello serving as a thread that binds past and present. As the tent materializes under their hands, the echoes of friendship and resilience reverberate through time, a tribute to the enduring bonds forged amidst the goldfields of Ballaarat.

Chapter Sixty-Nine

The gully is bathed in the warm embrace of the sun's descent, a cascade of golden light that blankets the landscape in a soft, radiant glow. Amidst this tranquil tableau, Levi's unwavering dedication yields its fruit. His keen eyes catch a subtle glint in his pan – a delicate collection of shimmering gold specks.

A triumphant exhale escapes Levi's lips as he exclaims hushedly, *"Yes! Another discovery made!"* With meticulous care, he gathers the precious flakes, each delicate piece finding its place within the confines of his ginger beer bottle. Side by side with his prior findings, this humble container now burgeons with an array of golden fragments and minuscule nuggets – a testament to his unyielding perseverance.

In this moment of triumph, Levi grants himself a space for contemplation. His gaze turns inward, and he drifts into a reverie that transcends the boundaries of reality. As the world around him blurs, Levi's consciousness traverses the realm of daydreams.

In this vibrant vision, he stands upon a grand stage, a sea of fellow diggers stretching before him like an undulating tide. His voice, a beacon of confidence, resonates as he addresses the crowd. His words, a reservoir of inspiration and aspiration, flow like pure motivation. With resolute conviction, Levi declares to the imagery, *"I embarked with a simple pan and a dream. Through unyielding determination and ceaseless effort, I unearthed my fortune from these gullies."*

Thunderous applause erupts from the assembled crowd, a symphony of admiration and respect that infuses the atmosphere with warmth and affirmation. Levi's voice touched with a profound sense of pride, continues its journey, *"Armed with newfound prosperity, I bid farewell to this place. My sights are set on the distant horizons of Western Australia, where the settlement of The Swan River awaits." The applause swells in volume and intensity, joined by exuberant chants of "for he's a jolly good fellow, and so say all of us" – a jubilant chorus celebrating his achievements with fervour.*

Yet, like the ephemeral dance of sunlight, the daydream eventually wanes, its vibrant hues yielding to the shadows of Snake Gully. Levi blinks, shaking off the enchanting hold of his imagination. A contented smile graces his lips as he tidies his equipment, then walks toward a protective haven – a blackberry bush. With a sense of reverence, he lays the ginger beer bottle beneath the brambles, a secret treasure concealed in the embrace of nature.

Levi's gaze lingers on the gully, expressing gratitude for the opportunities it has bestowed upon him. His voice, a tender whisper, reaches out to the land, *"Thank you, Snake Gully. You've given me hope and the chance to carve my destiny. One day, I shall honour this gift by venturing to the far reaches of Australia."*

With a final, resolute glance, Levi turns away from the gully. A determined spark glimmers in his eyes, an unwavering resolve in his heart. The path ahead beckons, adorned with challenges and imbued with adventures. His quest – is to employ his amassed gold and secure a ticket that will ferry him across the sprawling expanse of this nation.

As the scene dissolves into dusk, a pause of transition and introspection ensues. Emerging from this contemplative interlude, Levi finds himself amidst a new backdrop – the bustling streets of Ballaarat. Main Road thrums with vitality, and his steps mirror his purposeful intent. Amidst the symphony of activity, a familiar figure emerges – the postman. Recognition sparks in the postman's eyes as he approaches Levi's side, handing him an envelope.

Levi's curiosity is roused as he inspects the address: *"Solicitor Adam Lynn, Lydiard Street, Ballaarat."* Uncertainty looms in the air, a weight that bears down upon Levi's thoughts. He scrutinizes the envelope's contents, a sense of unease seeping into his consciousness. As he contemplates the purpose behind this missive, his mind races, fervently hoping for an absence of any connection to criminal matters. Uttering his thoughts into the ether, he reflects, *"What could this entail? I've committed no wrong that warrants the attention of a solicitor save for standing with the Eureka Boys."*

Levi's thoughts drift to the Eureka Rebellion, an indelible moment in Ballaarat's annals where he played a vital role. His musings naturally gravitate toward the comrades who stood united beside him – figures like Peter Lalor and Raffaello Carboni, their names etched into the tapestry of his memory as champions of an unwavering cause.

Lydiard Street-South stretches before Levi, his steps deliberate and purposeful. Clutched in his hand is a notice, a parchment that holds the potential to reshape his life's trajectory. His destination looms ahead – a splendid bluestone building that stands as a bastion of significance. It is the chambers of Adam Lynn, a name that carries weight and consequence. Before he enters, Levi inhales deeply, fortifying himself for the encounter that awaits.

The transition from the street's bustling thoroughfare to the opulent interior of the bluestone building is a sensory experience. The grand portal entry commands attention, drawing Levi to the intricate detailing adoring the archway. Stepping across the threshold, he finds himself in refined aesthetics and architectural elegance. Guided by a hunched figure whose fragility seems incongruent with their surroundings, Levi traverses the corridors that lead him deeper into the heart of the establishment.

The guide's pace slows as they arrive at the doorway to the inner sanctum – the office of Mr Adam Lynn. The room exudes an aura of authority and refinement, a space where decisions of consequence are made. Levi's gaze takes in the opulent surroundings, from the tasteful decor to the imposing presence of Mr Lynn himself. A distinguished gentleman with silver hair, his demeanour radiates dignity and gravitas. Clad in a high-necked waistcoat, a neck-scarf adorned with a gracefully tied ribbon, high-waisted trousers, and an impeccably tailored oversized lapelled coat – all in sombre shades of black – Mr Lynn exudes an air of sophistication. Seated in a commanding chair, his posture reflects years of experience and wisdom as he studies Levi with an unwavering intensity.

In a voice that resonates with authority, Mr Lynn initiates their interaction, his words carrying a sense of expectation, "Master Levi Brody, I presume? Stepson of the infamous mounted police veteran, Bill Brody, and son of Alice Brody, née Riley."

Levi's response is marked by a blend of nervousness and respect, "Yes, Sir! That is correct."

Mr Lynn's gaze, sharp and piercing, maintains its hold on Levi as he imparts the news that holds the potential to alter the course of his life. "Consider yourself fortunate, young man," Mr Lynn asserts, his tone measured and deliberate. "An anonymous benefactor has entrusted me with the oversight of a generous Trust Fund dedicated to your advancement. This fund will cover all expenses incurred during your tenure at 'The Melbourne Academy of Learning'. Your educational journey will commence in a fortnight, and you shall receive a weekly stipend of two shillings. After completing the initial two years, this stipend will be elevated to five shillings. I must emphasize that the identity of your benefactor shall remain shrouded in secrecy. Do you grasp the significance of this?"

Levi's stunned reaction is tinged with eagerness, his voice reflecting a blend of astonishment and enthusiasm, "Yes, Sir! I comprehend the gravity of the situation. But what about my apprenticeship with Mr Tom Crockett? My family's livelihood depends on the income I contribute."

Mr Lynn responds with a calm assurance, "Your generous benefactor has taken your circumstances into careful consideration. I am empowered to employ financial incentives to ensure a seamless transition for you. I shall conduct extensive research and initiate conversations to address potential concerns. In the interim, I recommend that you tend to any loose ends before embarking on this new chapter."

Levi's thoughts swirl with a whirlwind of possibilities, his intrigue heightened by the veil of anonymity surrounding his patron. Summoning resolve, Levi inhales deeply, embracing the enigmatic path that stretches before him. It is a journey illuminated by the promise of a brighter future, guided by curiosity, excitement, and an unwavering appreciation for the opportunities that beckon.

In a hushed voice that carries his inner reflections, he muses, *"Who could this benefactor be? Might it be Mr Lalor, Mr Humphrey, or even some of the Eureka Rebellion comrades who have risen to positions of influence? Perhaps certain Eureka Boys are aware of my yearning for further education. And then there's Raffaello Carboni – the book's author on the Eureka Stockade Uprising. His presence lingers in my thoughts, igniting my curiosity like a beacon."*

With each thought, Levi inches closer to the revelation that awaits him, his journey poised at the precipice of discovery and transformation.

Chapter Seventy

The living room, steeped in rustic charm, becomes the backdrop for an atmosphere charged with eager anticipation. Alice, Levi's mother, unites her hands in a jubilant clap, then presses them to her agape mouth – a reaction that mirrors the mixture of joy and incredulity written across her face. The tidings received from Mr Adam Lynn, the solicitor, have stirred emotions within her that are verge on overwhelming. Positioned before her, Levi reflects her enthusiasm, his countenance aglow with a luminous fusion of happiness and wonder.

Alice's eyes shimmered with unshed tears as her voice trembled with emotion. "Oh, Levi! The dream nestled within my heart – to witness your education – is unfolding right before our eyes. It's almost too much to grasp!" Enveloped by the tempest of feelings, Alice stands rooted, her gaze wide with astonishment, grappling with the disclosure of Levi's enigmatic benefactor.

Levi responds with a smile that speaks volumes, his eyes dancing with their own light of happiness, "It transcends mere words, Ma. Somewhere, beyond our sight, there is faith in me, a longing to extend an opportunity. If only I could unveil the identity of this generous soul."

Bill Brody, Levi's stepfather, Steps into this tableau of familial jubilation. His visage is adorned with a triumphant grin, reflecting the joy within him.

"Well, well, well! Our lad is destined for greatness, it appears," Brody interjects, his voice infused with paternal pride.

He shifts his gaze to Alice, acknowledging her steadfast faith, "Alice, this revelation, it's a validation of what you've always known – that Levi was meant for horizons far beyond the confines of the Ballaarat and Little Bendigo District."

Alice directs her gaze toward Brody, her eyes brimming with tears of pure elation, "Oh, Bill! It's as though our prayers have been heard. Our dear boy, Levi, will finally step into the education he deserves. His efforts, his hard work to secure his future – someone out there is collaborating to turn his aspirations into reality."

Brody's buoyant demeanour mirrors a blend of relief and eager anticipation, reflecting the collective emotions coursing through the room. A wide grin stretches across Brody's features as he replies, "Absolutely, Alice. And to think, this benefactor extends their gratitude even to our financial consideration. It's a situation that blesses us all."

Bound together in a familial embrace, their hearts swell with gratitude and the excitement that comes with the promise of the journey ahead. A profound sense of unity and shared purpose underpins this pivotal juncture.

The scene's hue dims, reminiscent of the fading day, as Levi stands on the wooden boardwalk outside John Alloo's Chinese Restaurant. Now, with eyes moistened, Alice clings to her son in a tender, lingering embrace. The air is charged with the poignant blend of farewells and the thrill accompanying the unknown.

Alice's voice quivers as she imparts her sentiments, her emotions palpable, "Take care, my dearest Levi. Your absence will leave a void. And do remember to write to us – your words will anchor us to your journey."

Levi's voice, touched by emotion, emerges in response, his words punctuated by a perceptible catch, "I promise, Ma. I'll carry your love and support as my compass with every stride. Thank you for everything. I'll make you proud."

As they hold onto one another, an impactful arrival captures their collective focus – a Cobb and Co coach, emblematic of the voyage awaiting Levi. His gaze shifts to the commanding presence of the coach, a swirl of exhilaration and trepidation etching its contours onto his expression.

With a heart full of sincerity, Levi says, "This is it, Ma. The coach will ferry me to Melbourne. May the path ahead be smooth and unobstructed?"

The coach itself stands as a testament to innovation and comfort, an American Concord boasting improved suspension – a harbinger of a journey as comfortable as it is transformative. Six splendid horses, their presence commanding, stand harnessed and poised, an embodiment of readiness for the adventure ahead. The driver, a seasoned and familiar figure, radiates confidence as he addresses the assembled travellers. His voice carries the cadence of an experienced guide, "All aboard! Our destination – Melbourne!"

In this juncture of transition, Levi bestows upon his mother one last lingering embrace before stepping onto the coach. The driver, offering a helping hand, assists with Levi's belongings. Amid the company of fellow passengers, Levi secures his place, his heart a blend of eager anticipation and profound gratitude. As the scene unfolds, the coach stands poised to launch Levi into a future adorned with promise and potential.

The rhythmic percussion of hooves against the earth orchestrates the coach's departure, a harmonious cadence that weaves itself into the very fabric of the atmosphere. With each passing moment, Levi becomes an intimate companion to the coach's swaying motion, a dance that awakens a touch of queasiness within him. Yet, this fleeting discomfort fails to deter him. His attention remains steadfast, firmly affixed to the window's frame. Through the glass pane, he absorbs the evolving panorama of landscapes that unfurl as the coach navigates the vast canvas of the Australian countryside.

The coach's journey culminates in a fresh destination – the precinct of the Albion Hotel's booking office. From the recesses of the coach's rear, a voice resonates, authoritative and echoing.

"Is there a soul present for the lad named Brody, hailing from the enclave of Little Bendigo in Ballaarat and destined for this very place?"

Yet, the proclamation is met with a peculiar silence, an absence of response that leaves Levi somewhat puzzled. His gaze sweeps across the surroundings, a yearning for familiar faces or any semblance of recognition evident in his eyes. A tinge of wry amusement surfaces within Levi's thoughts: *"How fitting – no grand welcome committee here, it seems."*

Emerging from the entrance of the booking office strides a figure of considerable stature, his visage a tempest of vexation. The tall form advances toward Levi, his aura devoid of warmth. The figure's lips part to deliver his words, laden with displeasure, "You must be Mr Levi Brody. Follow me, and bring your belongings along."

Levi clutches his bags, trailing in the wake of this imposing stranger who commands both attention and an air of intimidation. A subtle current of unease courses through him with every step he takes. Levi's response carries a touch of sarcasm, his tone laced with irony, *"Your assistance with these two heavy bags is deeply appreciated, I assure you."*

Chapter Seventy-One

In the wake of their footsteps, a journey commences – one toward the booking office, with Levi a close shadow of this towering figure. This juncture marks the threshold of an untold narrative, an unwritten chapter into which Levi ventures, a blend of apprehension and a readiness to embrace the enigmatic journey ahead.

Amidst the bustling tapestry of the booking office, Levi stands enveloped in a whirlwind of emotions – a potent blend of uncertainty and eager anticipation reflected in his eyes. The absence of his family creates a void, leaving him to ponder the landscape of his nascent existence in this sprawling city. The once-familiar cocoon of security has been left behind.

A purposeful gesture from the tall clerk prompts Levi to traverse the threshold, guiding him behind the counter. Bereft of seating, an intentional absence designed to dissuade loitering, Levi seeks solace on an unassuming box seat within the parcel room, settling in for the wait.

The tall clerk, hands resting nonchalantly in his pockets, observes Levi's presence. His curiosity blooms into words, "And who might be here to claim you, young man?"

Levi's response carries an undertone of uncertainty, "I'm not entirely certain, sir. I'm awaiting collection for transport to 'The Melbourne Academy of Learning'."

A semblance of understanding weaves through the clerk's words, "Ah, The Melbourne Academy, you say? Well, you've certainly kept me guessing. Your attire suggests the kin of a miner more than that of a young gentleman."

Levi firmly confirms his choice of attire as if the option was deliberate, "That's by design. I'd rather not parade my association with the wealthiest and most esteemed gentleman in Ballaarat. One can never predict who might be tempted to liberate the ten gold sovereigns concealed within my luggage."

The clerk's frustration reverberates, an audible exhale echoing his exasperation. A glance towards the front counter is followed by a visible display of annoyance as he retreats to the same.

A sound like that of a soft feminine voice drifts through the air like a gentle breeze carrying a tender query, "Good day, sir. I'm seeking information about Master Levi Brody, who recently arrived from Ballaarat by coach."

The clerk's retort reverberates with disdain, "Indeed, I'm acquainted with him – a source of considerable commotion in the back. Could certainly use a lesson in propriety, if you ask me."

As the clerk vanishes into the back room, Levi's visage contorts subtly, his sidelong grimace a silent commentary on the unfolding scenario. Emerging within the depths is not a female but the youthful figure of Master Crawley, an emissary of The Melbourne Academy. Master Crawley's aura exudes a non-binary grace – raven-black locks cascading down his shoulders, his attire strained at the seams, an ill fit - too short in the arms and legs - that fails to mask his presence.

Master Crawley steps forth, and the atmosphere embraces a tone of formality, "You must be the fresh arrival, Levi Brody."

Mindful of decorum, Levi confirms his identity, "Yes, Sir."

The title carries Master Crawley's introduction, "I am Master Crawley, an instructor at The Melbourne Academy. Collect your belongings, young man, as time is of the essence."

Levi assents by hefting his heaviest bag, but a moment of hesitation ensues with the second. Sensing this pause, Master Crawley assumes responsibility, hoisting one bag by its handle. Thus equipped, they embark towards the exit, a new chapter awaiting.

A sudden stumble momentarily halts their progress, and Master Crawley's voice trembles with discomfort, "You'll have to manage both bags on your own. My back has succumbed to spasms."

Levi's gaze darts towards the source of this revelation, a wince and pout accompanying the declaration. With unwavering resolve, Levi shoulders both bags, propelling them towards the exit, poised for the journey ahead.

Under the open expanse of Bourke Street's sunlight, Levi's hands bear the burden of twin carpetbags. As the weight presses upon him, he directs a query to Master Crawley, a quest for clarity regarding the distance yet to be traversed.

"Pardon me, sir," Levi addresses the Master, "how far lies the Academy?"

Master Crawley supplies the answer, "Approximately a mile. Eastern Hill, beside the Yarra River, marks our destination. A cab stationed at the next corner shall commence our journey."

A row of horse-drawn cabs decorates the corner, their drivers immersed in a card game upon wooden perches. Neglecting the urgency, Master Crawley and Levi approach the closest taxi.

Restlessness surges within Levi, and he amplifies his voice, "Hey! Does anyone claim this languid mare? She teeters on the precipice of surrendering to sheer monotony!"

Startled, the drivers' cards flutter to the ground, their attention drawn to Levi's interjection. From this abrupt incursion emerges a stout cab driver, his ruddy countenance an embodiment of casual nonchalance. Delivered with a sardonic intonation, he queries, "And where to, Governor?"

Levi turns his gaze towards Mr Crawley, a silent cue for affirmation in their tacit exchange.

Master Crawley concurs, "Commence at Buckley and Nunn's Department Store. Later, escort us to the Melbourne Academy on Eastern Hill."

Recognition sparks in the eyes of the stout cab driver, his words tinged with familiarity, "Ah! The new Melbourne Academy of Learning embracing a touch of sophistication now - are we? Since departing the confines of Spring Street, it appears."

Levi rearranges his bags, aligning them for their imminent departure. Shoulder to shoulder, he and Master Crawley embark upon the cab, setting forth on the next phase of their voyage.

The cityscape along Bourke Street is a canvas of transformation, its evolution woven with the prosperity of the goldfields. Amidst this kaleidoscope of change, Buckley and Nunn's Department Store is a testament to grandeur – stucco-style architecture, portico columns framing its entrance, and arched windows punctuating its facade. Their cab navigates the thoroughfare, and as Levi gazes upward, he finds himself entranced by the soaring heights of the buildings. A spontaneous outburst of laughter escapes Levi's lips, rich with mirth, "HA...Har!"

Master Crawley's expression, marked by confusion, casts an inquisitive look at Levi, "What evokes amusement, young man?"

Levi's reply is swift, tinged with sheepish delight, "My apologies, Sir! Looking skyward at the height of the buildings, I was struck by how much I resembled my younger self during a visit to Melbourne with my Pa. He quelled my exuberance with a swift cuff to the head, cautioning, 'Rein it in, Levi. There is no need to broadcast our origins from the Bush to the entire town. We're not signalling the outback to all and sundry!'"

Master Crawley acknowledges Levi's explanation with a measured nod. Their cab arrives at the department store, heralding their impending disembarkation.

Chapter Seventy-two

Inside the expansive realm of Buckley and Nunns Department Store, Master Crawley and Levi cross the threshold. Levi's eyes widen in sheer disbelief as he surveys the vast array of items in this singular space. The master navigates, leading Levi to the drapery and tailor section – an expanse adorned with racks and shelves that bear witness to garments of every conceivable kind. Amid this sartorial sea, a well-dressed, bald assistant with a welcoming smile comes forth.

With a voice that resonates, the bald assistant introduces himself, his smile a testament to his demeanour, "Greetings! I am Mr Bulcher. How may I serve you esteemed gentlemen within the confines of Buckley and Nunns?"

Master Crawley's voice carries an air of intention, "Indeed, we need two complete ensembles for this young gentleman. These outfits shall enable his attendance at the Melbourne Learning Academy. We shall acquire two sets of attire, inclusive of footwear. The lad shall don one set, while the relinquished attire shall find purpose in an orphanage."

Levi's gaze oscillates between Master Crawley and Mr Bulcher, his demeanour marked by an undercurrent of surprise at these instructions.

With a poised nod, Mr Bulcher acknowledges the task, "Ah, I apprehend the purpose. First and foremost, I shall require the young gentleman's measurements." This declaration is accompanied by a gracious bow and a gesture toward the changing chambers.

After meticulous measurements and a thorough fitting, Levi emerges adorned in his freshly acquired school attire. He wears a high-collared white shirt, its generous lapels cascading over a round-necked black vest. Completing this ensemble is a black suit complemented by black lace-up shoes. A white straw Derby Hat adorned with a band of motley hues adds a flourish. Levi's second ensemble, even more daring, showcases black knickerbockers elegantly matched with black tights.

Levi's inner contemplations resonate within his mind, *"This attire would be seen as extravagant back in Ballaarat. It feels as alien as it appears. The journey to adapt to such a wardrobe may be a gradual undertaking if it ever takes place."*

Master Crawley and Levi embark on their return journey to the awaiting carriage. Now attired in his school garb, Levi observes the cab driver slumbering with his hat angled down to cover his face and his horse's long eyelashes closed, their shared repose evident.

Entering the carriage, their voyage unfolds. As they navigate Melbourne's animated thoroughfares, their trajectory carries them from the urban core to the periphery. Eventually, the carriage draws to a halt before an imposing red brick edifice nestled within the vast expanse of Eastern Hill. Standing three stories tall, graced with arched windows and a pitched roof, this edifice unveils itself as none other than The Melbourne Academy.

A congregation of boys, akin in age to Levi, clusters near the portico entryway, all donning akin uniforms. Their demeanour exudes familiarity and confidence in wearing their attire. Master Crawley and Levi disembark, merging seamlessly with this assemblage.

Master Crawley's voice reverberates with command, "Proceed promptly indoors, young gentlemen! Lewis, extend your assistance to Master Levi – he shall require guidance with his belongings and a tour of your shared quarters."

As Levi's gaze meets Lewis's, it is met with a sour countenance. The latter seizes one of the carpet bags and strides resolutely into the building.

Inside the hallowed halls of the Melbourne Academy, Levi and Lewis venture forth into the lobby. Ornate-pressed metal accents adorn this space, accompanied by elaborate cornices that bestow an air of grandeur. Decorative plinths contribute to this architectural tapestry. Light fixtures evoke images of regal palaces, while the blackwood and jarrah parquetry flooring radiate an aura of opulence.

Ascending a flight of stairs and navigating a narrow corridor, Levi and Lewis find themselves at their designated chamber. This compact room houses beds flanking each side of a modest desk with chairs and tallboy dressers standing sentry beside the entryway. The window's whitewashed glass obscures external views. This stark contrast to the opulent lobby encapsulates the essence of their new abode. Levi discards his bag unceremoniously upon the bed adjacent to where Lewis has placed a carpet bag.

Lewis's voice carries an air of authority, "As the head boy, I extend my welcome. Understand your place if we are to be comrades." Lewis's stature exudes humility, crowned with sandy curls that lend him an appealing visage. His demeanour conveys confidence, setting him apart from his peers.

Levi's inner thoughts solidify his self-awareness: *"Seventeen years on, my frame stands wiry, crowned by a crop of prickly jaffa hair. Early life etched in trials and battles, while the echoes of the Stockade Rebellion persist as haunting reminders."* The unspoken declaration resonates; *"My respect for Lewis - he will have to earn! "*

Chapter Seventy-Three

The school bell reverberates through the air, its mellifluous chimes signalling the end of the lunchtime meal. Inside the vibrant expanse of the school's dining room, Lewis and the stout figure of Jimmy Stoddard occupy a table. Their lunch trays sit empty before them, silent testimony to the sustenance they've consumed. Amidst the lively hum of students, each engrossed in their cliques, Levi remains a solitary figure on the outskirts. His gaze sweeps across the social clusters, a mixture of bitterness and disdain shaping his expression. Amidst this contemplative solitude, a voice gracefully interrupts his thoughts.

Jimmy Stoddard, compact and sturdy in stature, divines the emotions that colour Levi's countenance. With an amiable demeanour, he initiates a dialogue, "Don't let the privileged ones trouble your mind, mate." Jimmy's words carry a camaraderie, a bridge from his experience, "I've tread this path for a year and still find myself somewhat detached. But you, you've got potential. Just give it time."

Levi's brow arches, captivated by the intrigue of Jimmy's perspective. In response to Levi's inquisitiveness, Jimmy chuckles softly, "It's my stature, you see. I don't conform to the athletic ideals those chaps uphold. And my grades aren't quite on par with their lofty standards. If not for my Pa's prominence as a Melbourne barrister, I'd likely have been shown the door."

Levi nods in understanding, appreciating the challenges Jimmy faces. Levi's curiosity extends to their culinary experience, "The portions here hardly suffice. How have you managed to maintain your physique?"

A sly grin graces Jimmy's lips, "A generous allowance from home. I've arranged with a local grocer to deliver a pork pie and half a dozen oysters on commencement of our lunch break."

Levi nods knowingly, acknowledging the cleverness of Jimmy's stratagem. With a pensive demeanour, Levi confides a personal dilemma, "Lewis, my roommate, deems me a disappointment. As the head boy, he's steeped in authority. However, it's hard to submit, especially after my ordeals in Ballaarat."

"Ah, Lewis," Jimmy's response emanates empathy, delving deeper into the situation, "Master Crawley holds him in high esteem. He excels academically and commands the rugby field. He's also known to occasionally report students to Mr Batie, the Principal, to uphold his reputation."

Levi sighs, the weight of his predicament tangible. Levi's voice carries the resonance of internal conflict, "I've yet to encounter the Principal. What kind of individual is he?"

"Mr Stuart Batie," Jimmy's tone combines caution and disdain, "Our Principal hails from Edinburgh University in Scotland. And a tyrant he is. The school is modelled on the traditional Scottish educational ethos, where church and learning are intertwined. Beware of him; his authoritarian rule contradicts Christ-like values."

Levi absorbs this portrayal, a vivid depiction of the man who holds the school's reins. "What I miss most," Levi's voice carries a tinge of nostalgia, "is the refuge of my bush sanctuary in Snake Gully at Little Bendigo. Amidst nature, I could find solace and escape from my tribulations."

Jimmy's eyes light up, and an idea takes root, "I have a spot that serves the same purpose. And I believe it could do the same for you. Have you heard of Fitzroy Gardens? It's a short distance from here – a serene haven that might offer the solace you seek."

Levi's curiosity flares, his interest evident. "Fitzroy Gardens?" Levi muses, "It sounds exactly like what I need. Lead the way, Jimmy."

Gathering their belongings, they depart the bustling dining room, fueled by the anticipation of their maiden escapade.

Levi and Jimmy step into the welcoming embrace of Fitzroy Gardens. The symphony of nature – the melodies of chirping birds and the gentle rustling of leaves – envelops them, providing a stark contrast to the hubbub of the school. They traverse winding pathways, immersed in a tapestry of blossoms and the sheltering arms of towering trees.

As Levi breathes in the invigorating air, he reflects, "This place truly is an oasis. I can feel the weight lifting from my shoulders."

Jimmy's smile radiates contentment, "I assured you it would work its magic. When chaos reigns, I find solace, a space to clear my mind."

Levi takes in their surroundings, his eyes reflecting wonder. With a grateful tone, he muses, "This is a world apart from the dusty streets and cramped structures of Ballaarat. It's akin to entering another realm."

Levi's appreciation is palpable as he regards Jimmy; their camaraderie solidified. Amidst shared laughter, Jimmy affirms, "You're absolutely right, mate. Melbourne conceals its hidden gems, and Fitzroy Gardens stands prominently among them. A sanctuary of tranquillity, an avenue for self-discovery."

As they discover a peaceful pondside spot, they settle onto a bench, letting the serenity envelop them. With a sigh, Levi reflects, "It's beyond my expectations to find such serenity in this bustling city. Moments like these make me value the opportunities that led me here."

Jimmy imparts wisdom cultivated through experience, "Levi, this marks the commencement of a new chapter for you. An opening to shed past trials and embrace potential futures."

Levi's nod carries a spark of newfound hope. His words resonate with newfound conviction, "You're absolutely right, Jimmy. This is my chance to redefine my path to chart an uncharted course. No more evading my past or permitting others to mould my identity."

Silence blankets them, the garden's sanctuary enveloping them in a shared renewal, a haven of peace amidst life's tempestuous tides.

Chapter Seventy-Four

The narrow corridor reverberates with a palpable tension, ensnaring Levi, Jimmy, and several other lads as they stand beside Master Crawley, his purposeful stride cutting through the charged atmosphere. But what catches Levi off-guard is the synchronized choreography that unfolds before him. The other lads pivot in unison as if scripted, their backs discreetly aligning against the wall. Their expressions bear a veil of smirks as Master Crawley passes. "Morning, Sir!" The chorus resonates, laden with a veneer of nonchalant respect.

Master Crawley's brow furrows, his gaze sweeping over the row of backs pressed against the wall. He studies each boy's visage with a keen eye. Unbeknownst to him, the lads engage in a playful charade as he moves ahead. Their movements mimic his trademark elegant hand gestures and gait, a silent jest shared among them.

Levi and Jimmy maneuver through this intricate ballet of disrespect, offering congenial smiles as they navigate past Master Crawley. For Levi, however, patience thins, an inner vexation simmering. Swiftly, he clutches the collar of the nearest lad, exerting a firm grip before administering a swift cuff to the side of his head. Levi's voice carries a stern warning, "Show at least a modicum of respect or prepare to face the consequences. Is that clear?"

The lads retreat, their bravado dissolving into timidity as they scuttle toward their impending class. Levi turns to Jimmy, his inquiry tinged with disbelief. "What prompted such an odd display?" Levi's words carry a sharp edge, "Is respect not a consideration here?"

Jimmy offers illumination, casting light on the peculiar situation. "Within the classroom, Crawley commands respect. It's necessary, given that their academic performance hinges on his evaluations across the subjects he teaches. Otherwise, they term him a 'Molly'."

Levi absorbs this revelation as they continue their trajectory down the corridor en route to their next class. Levi and Jimmy find their places in the classroom, the room abuzz with fellow students engrossed in the intricacies of Master Crawley's mathematical discourse. The ambience takes an abrupt turn as Principal Batie makes a grand entrance, his presence underscored by the cane he brandishes.

Principal Batie moves with intent, traversing the aisles, his scrutinizing gaze sweeping over the students' progress displayed on their slate boards. Should a student falter – whether through sluggishness or error – Batie's cane descends with unwavering authority, striking slate and knuckles alike.

Principal Batie's circuitous route brings him to Levi's desk, his piercing stare zeroing in on the incorrectly solved equation. True to his nature, he launches into a tirade.

"What! The Boy from the Bush. Another imbecile – Heaven Forbid!" His voice drips with disdain.

As the cane hovers, poised to strike, Levi holds his ground. With unyielding determination, he meets Batie's challenging gaze, intercepting the descending cane with his palm. The resulting pain courses through him, but Levi refuses to reveal it, maintaining unflinching eye contact with Batie.

Principal Batie registers Levi's audacious defiance, his eyes widening in astonishment, his jaw slackening. A sweeping survey of the room reveals other lads wincing and avoiding Batie's gaze. The realization dawns that the bush boy's audacity won't have immediate repercussions.

Shaken, Batie receives his composure, his attention fixating on Levi. "Come now, Master Brody. Your capabilities surely surpass this,

Lad!" Principal Batie's tone takes a nuanced shift, part reprimand and part begrudging acknowledgment.

Batie shifts his focus to the pale face of Mr Crawley, his voice elevated as he dictates, "I anticipate, Sir! You shall elevate your students' standards beyond their current thresholds!" With that, Principal Batie strides out of the classroom, his exit punctuated by an irksome air that lingers in the wake of his departure.

Chapter Seventy-Five

Beneath the shade of a sprawling gum tree that graces the perimeter of the school's rectangular courtyard, Levi and Jimmy find respite from the rigours of their academic day with a lunch break. Their chosen haven offers solace and camaraderie, a brief escape from the confines of the classroom.

In a scene painted with casual familiarity, a young delivery boy rushes towards them, clutching a small basket. "Here's your order, sir," he announces, his words punctuated by youthful energy. With practised ease, he presents the contents: a savoury pork pie and a parcel swathed in the embrace of a newspaper.

Jimmy, the recipient of this culinary bounty, receives it with a nod of gratitude. His response is swift, spoken with the assurance of a familiar relationship, "Tell Mr Johnson I'll settle my account on Friday," he instructs.

"Very good, Sir!" The delivery boy's response is punctuated by a respectful acknowledgment, a testament to the familiarity that comes with routine. With that, he departs as quickly as he arrives, leaving the two companions in their private enclave.

A sense of haste animates Jimmy's actions. The pork pie vanishes in a flurry of bites, his appetite undeniable. The newspaper-wrapped parcel is unveiled with a fervour that matches his hunger. The contents, six oysters cradled within their shells, offer a delicate indulgence. Yet, in his haste, oyster juice splatters onto the front of his black vest, a testament to his unbridled enthusiasm.

Observing the spectacle, Levi watches in a mixture of disbelief and amusement. He can't help but comment, "Steady, Jimmy. At this rate, you might choke one day!"

Unswayed by caution, Jimmy dismisses the notion with a playful smirk, "No time to waste. We better go to the dining room before we're missed."

"I'll meet you there," Levi offers, his intention clear, "I need to make a pit stop at the privy first."

As their encounter beneath the gum tree concludes, both rise to their feet, their movements synchronized in the silent rhythm of camaraderie. Across the gravel quadrangle, their footsteps echo towards the school's main building.

Jimmy's insatiable appetite beckons him to the dining room, drawn by the promise of a following course. Yet, the threads of destiny weave a different narrative. Principal Batie's path, like a meandering stream, intersects with Jimmy's trajectory within the bustling dining room. The Principal's gaze, typically stern and commanding, narrows with incredulity as it lands upon an unsightly blemish – the stain on Jimmy's vest, a testament to the capriciousness of oyster juice. A swift metamorphosis of colour tinges Principal Batie's complexion, the shock giving way to a fiery flush. In his attempt to articulate his astonishment, his words falter into incoherence.

Unwavering in the face of his shock, Principal Batie seizes hold of Jimmy's earlobe, his grasp unyielding. He proceeds to propel the protesting boy towards his office, the culmination of this chance encounter swiftly spiralling into an unexpected ordeal.

Within the sanctuary of Principal Batie's office, an unforgiving drama unfolds. The cane becomes a conductor of pain, a harsh reminder of authority's weight. Its sharp impact upon Jimmy's form leaves its mark – welts and imprints of crimson and bruised resolve. The boundaries of punishment blur as Principal Batie, unsatisfied with the cane's rigour, realizes the extent of his actions – the rod shatters under the force of his retribution. Yet, the Principal's determination remains unyielding.

The fragments of a broken cane pave the way for an alternative form of chastisement. Principal Batie seizes a sheet of paper, his nibbed pen crafting a message in bold strokes. His resolve is palpable as he retrieves an incongruous piece of clothing from a drawer – a child's pinafore, an emblem of vulnerability. Its imposition upon Jimmy's form is a stark comparison, the mundane attire obscuring his vest.

Yet, the sign pinned to his back transforms this act into a cruel farce. Emboldened letters declare his humiliation: **"Beware! This Boy Is A Pig!"** Principal Batie's voice carries an undertone of disdain as he addresses Jimmy, casting the cloak of degradation upon him.

"You stand as an absolute disgrace. While the source of that mess eludes me, you will bear the weight of this child's pinafore for an entire week. And this sign, affixed to your back, shall serve as a deterrent, a cautionary beacon for your peers. Let it be known, do you understand?"

Bruised, both in body and spirit, Jimmy's voice carries a subdued affirmation, "Yes... Sir!"

As Jimmy re-enters the dining room - a space that once promised sustenance - the atmosphere undergoes an unexpected transformation. His presence becomes a magnet for attention, a spectacle that draws stares and whispers. A puppet in Principal Batie's cruel charade, he navigates the room with a heavy heart.

As Jimmy traverses the room, a well-orchestrated tableau unfolds. The head boy, Lewis, rises from his seat, seizing the role of orchestrator. A gestural directive from him and the room's focus shifts. Every eye is directed towards Jimmy, the bearer of the humiliating sign. Laughter surges forth, an unrelenting wave of mockery and jeering that fills the room.

In this crescendo of cruelty, an unexpected disruptor emerges. Levi stands at the doorway, a figure of defiance and determination. His entrance is a balm to Jimmy's wounded pride. His fierce gaze sweeps the room, encompassing it like a tempest, silencing the laughter and mockery as if he wielded the power to control the very elements.

A silent exchange between Levi and Jimmy carries volumes – a promise of solidarity, a declaration of friendship that transcends humiliation. Lewis, the head boy who masterminded this public derision, quails beneath Levi's unyielding stare, swiftly retreating to his seat. The room responds kindly, the laughter dwindling, the jeers fading into uneasy silence. This chapter ends on a note of defiance, an undercurrent of camaraderie, and a hint of the battles yet to be fought.

Chapter Seventy-Six

A momentous rugby match unfolds under the vast expanse of Melbourne Academy's sprawling grounds. The opposing team, "Melbourne Church of England Grammar School," teeters on the precipice of defeat. On the sidelines, Levi and Jimmy, adorned in their team uniforms, bide their time. As the game approaches its zenith, they await their opportunity to rejoin the fray.

Beneath the sprawling canopy of a gum tree that graces the periphery of the rugby field, Levi steers the conversation, his voice laced with concern and exasperation. "Jimmy, the ordeal Batie subjected you to this past week is an abomination. His malevolence demands restraint. His temperament is more savage than my stepfather's, running rampant like a wild stallion across the highlands. Some folks get agitated for reasons like my Pa's drinking bouts. Others, like me, bear the scars of physical and mental abuse. But Batie is discontent with existence itself. His nature is venomous, an enigma devoid of any discernible catalyst."

Against the backdrop of the rugby match's cacophony, Jimmy listens attentively. His expression oscillates between comprehension and surrender. He responds with an undertone of resignation, "I've been singled out before, and I doubt this will be the last. Yet, the prospect of victory in this match might momentarily quench Batie's hostility."

Levi's determination sharpens, frustration seeping into his words. "If I witness even one more instance of his cruelty, I'll take action. I'll report him to those above him, even if it jeopardises my standing. Batie belongs to that breed of principals who revel in ensuring that no student experiences more joy than they do."

A nod from Jimmy signals his accord. But before their discourse can deepen, Principal Batie's presence intervenes, asserting its dominance. Principal Batie's authoritative voice reverberates across the field, urgency coating his words.

"Brody and Stoddard, back on the field! Stoddard, you're substituting the full-back defender, and Brody, take the left wing. We need an infusion of fresh vigour to seal this victory."

Locked in a shared resolve, Levi and Jimmy exchange resolute glances before ascending from their position. With purpose in their strides, they step onto the field, bearing not only the aspirations of their team but also the weight of their personal battles against injustice. Amid the match's final moments, they are resolute to channel their fervour and create a lasting impact.

Levi and Jimmy, their expressions etched with determination, hastened to their designated rugby field spots. The atmosphere pulses with suspense as the outcome teeters on a precipice.

From the opposing team, a player executes a deft grubber kick, launching the ball over Melbourne Academy's defenders. A collective breath is held as the ball bounces and meanders across the field, racing toward the Grammer's try line. The game's destiny rests on this pivotal juncture.

At the rear defence, robust Jimmy stands poised, arms extended in readiness for a game-altering catch. The ball hurtles towards him, and in a fleeting instant, Jimmy recoils, his eyelids shutting involuntarily. The team watches in disbelief as the ball strikes his chest, veering away beyond his grasp. Capitalizing on the opportunity, an adversary seizes the ball, surging over the try line to clinch triumph.

Batie's emotions erupt from the sideline in a tempestuous surge of anger and frustration. His arms flail wildly as a barrage of acrid insults is hurled toward Jimmy. Batie abandons the game, consumed by his wrath, departing with an incensed and embarrassed Jimmy.

The Academy team congregates around their leader, Lewis. Hushed conversations and fleeting glances are directed at Jimmy, intertwining concern and without compassion. Levi strides toward Jimmy, his demeanour a blend of empathy and determination.

"Pay no heed to their taunts, Jimmy," Levi's voice resonates with unwavering assurance. "If anyone dares to mock, they'll answer to me first. We'll invest time in drills after school to hone your skills. By year-end, you'll stand as a remarkable performer."

Jimmy's gaze reflects gratitude as he replies, "It's not the team that troubles me, Levi. Their jests I can endure. But Batie's vengeance weighs heavily. Consequences loom, like punishments conceived by a deranged mind, that I must endure."

Levi's resolve blazes, his fortitude unshaken. "This might well be the catalyst that propels me to confront him. We'll observe and decide."

With a solemn nod, Jimmy confirms their shared commitment. Levi's comforting hand on Jimmy's shoulder speaks of solidarity, a vow to confront adversity together. As Levi guides Jimmy away from the scene, their camaraderie shines unbreakable against the tumultuous backdrop.

As dawn heralds a new day, its warm hues envelop Melbourne Academy's grounds. The gravel quadrangle buzzes with students, enmeshed in animated conversations, awaiting the clarion call of the first bell. Among the throng, Master Crawley, a vigilant educator, stands watchful, his gaze sweeping over the bustling assembly.

A sudden crescendo of jubilant cheers snags Levi's attention as he arrives at the quadrangle. His gaze gravitates to the epicentre of commotion. Accompanied by Principal Batie, Jimmy appears, garbed in a spectacle of mortification. Pushed forward by Batie's prodding, Jimmy navigates the quadrangle, a tableau of indignity. He dons one of Batie's daughter's voluminous bell-shaped skirts, crowned by a poke bonnet, its bow a symbol of absurdity. Pinned to his back, a sign declares, **"I Play Rugby As A Girl."**

The scene unfurls, a blend of amusement and empathy coursing through the onlookers. An undercurrent of discomfort underscores the spectacle, a manifestation of injustice.

Levi's fury surges as he marches resolutely toward the scene, an avowed intervention on his mind. But Master Crawley's timely intervention arrests his course. Master Crawley grasps Levi's arm, urging restraint. "Easy, Levi," Mr Crawley's voice blends caution and counsel, "Reacting impulsively will worsen Jimmy's plight. Remember, this is momentary. Jimmy possesses the resilience to withstand this humiliation."

Beneath Levi's veneer of indignation, Mr Crawley's words find purchase. His counsel tempers Levi's ire, guiding his focus. The quadrangle's bustling rhythm resumes, heedless of the turmoil simmering beneath the surface.

Chapter Seventy-Seven

Within the hushed corners of Melbourne Academy, Levi stands in the presence of Master Crawley. The classroom's confines hold an air of expectancy. Despite Levi's reputation for a quick temper, Master Crawley perceives a distinct aura around him. It's as if Master Crawley's discerning eye detects untapped depths beneath Levi's brash exterior. There's a spark of hope, a suggestion that Master Crawley views Levi not as a lost cause but as a young man harbouring latent talents. Not the conventional scholarly prowess seen in Lewis, the academy's brightest star, but a different, uncharted aptitude.

In the soft embrace of daylight filtering through the window, Levi occupies a desk, a realm of quietude within the otherwise deserted classroom. Master Crawley's voice resonates with authority as he addresses Levi,

"Levi, your struggles with mathematical equations are evident. I'm prepared to offer you after-school tutoring."

Levi's response carries an undercurrent of reluctant resignation, "Math equations are akin to a foreign tongue for me. I fail to see their relevance in my future."

Master Crawley's words carry wisdom and a hint of understanding, "While that might hold true based on your future trajectory, Levi, remember that these equations are integral to your curriculum here at the Academy. Should you intend to graduate at the end of your tenure, attaining a minimal passing grade is non-negotiable."

Levi's nod conveys compliance, though his retort remains veiled beneath his silence. Master Crawley presses on, his voice etched with unwavering conviction, "Levi, I perceive qualities that could shape you into a society's leader. If you invest in your studies, there's no reason you cannot forge an extraordinary path. One that transcends your origins."

Levi's features reflect solemn contemplation as he responds, "I comprehend, Master Crawley. I yearn to learn. My mother etched the importance of education during my home-schooling years. Yet, my tumultuous upbringing, marked by an abusive stepfather and the scars of the Eureka Rebellion, fuels my resistance to oppressive authority."

There's a fleeting moment where shared empathy flows between them. Master Crawley momentarily diverts his gaze, nodding to the shadows of his past abuse. When his eyes meet Levi's again, they carry an unwavering encouragement.

"Levi, heed my advice: Never surrender. Never falter. Hold onto the faith I discern within you," Master Crawley asserts. His hand lands gently on Levi's shoulder, a gesture loaded with guidance and mentorship. "Believe in yourself, and let that belief be your anchor. It's a faith that can rekindle your latent potential." The air hangs heavy with shared understanding, a thread woven through their mutual struggles and aspirations.

The narrative within weeks sweeps into a montage, a medley of scenes unveiling Levi's transformation within the academy's tapestry: *Levi and Jimmy, the camaraderie unbreakable, stand on the school's sprawling oval. Laughter intertwines with the whisper of the breeze as they engage in a carefree training session of ball exchanges. Their laughter weaves through the air like a testament to their renewed connection.*

Inside Master Crawley's classroom, Levi's presence is a beacon of assistance. Sitting beside a fellow student, heads bent over an assignment, Levi offers guidance and encouragement. Mr Crawley watches his smile, a silent testament to Levi's newfound spirit of helpfulness, a testament to his evolving self.

A commotion disrupts the tranquillity of the recess. Two boys embroiled in a heated altercation capture attention. The head boy, Lewis, springs into action, but the conflict defies resolution. And then, a calm amidst the storm—Levi steps forward, defusing tension with composed resolve. The storm abates, and Levi's retreating figure becomes an emblem of newfound strength and harmony.

The room holds a stillness born of night's embrace. Levi sits at his desk in his bedroom, bathed in the soft glow of candlelight. The nib of his pen dances purposefully on paper:

"To my Honourable trustee, Mr Lynn,

I write, as promised, to provide an update on my progress. Embracing new circumstances, I find joy in how deeply I've embedded myself in college life. While not the brightest star, my Master of Studies envisions untapped growth. I remain indebted to my patron, my gratitude reborn with each dawn. This opportunity is a treasure, and I am humbled." Levi pauses, thoughts crystallizing like stars in the night sky.

"Yet, frustration grips me. A concern, a call to action, demands recognition. It pertains not solely to my journey; I possess the means to confront adversity. My heart aches for fellow students, victims of relentless abuse inflicted by a tyrant—a principal in name alone." His inner voice takes on gravitas, an undertone of earnest determination.

"This educator, if I can bestow such a title, lacks the virtue demanded of a principal, especially one representing our institution. Merciless, his cane wields unchecked force, breaching the boundaries of just discipline. He thrives on oppression, finding satisfaction in pain." Levi's inner voice wavers, but his words forge forward, fueled by purpose.

"I invite scrutiny of my words. The individual, Principal Stuart Batie, rarely merits his designation. His reign undermines confidence, wields fear as control, and diminishes potential. His dominion evokes the likes of a collapse of a Eureka mineshaft." As the ink flows, Levi's

voice assumes a triumphant cadence, *"Yours with gratitude and obedience,* ***Levi Brody."***

A flourish, a signature—Levi's testament on paper. The candle's flame wavers, casting fleeting shadows that dance upon the room's stage. The chapter concludes the curtain falling on a message etched in ink and emotion—a message with the power to reshape Levi's trajectory within the revered halls of Melbourne Academy.

Chapter Seventy-Eight

The Academy's grand lobby reverberates with an amalgamation of commotion and euphoria. Graduating students linger in a realm where nostalgia mingles with excitement, their imminent separation from the cherished institution casting a vivid vibrancy over the space.

Jimmy's irrepressible enthusiasm within the throng propels him towards Levi, who embodies the essence of revelry with his infectious smile. Their friendship radiates through the scene as Jimmy extends his hand to Levi, a warm and heartfelt greeting passing between them.

"Levi, my friend, farewells are the potion of countless emotions. Can you believe it? From once being dubbed a blockhead, I now stand chosen by Principal Morrison to serve as the head boy and captain of the rugby team for the year ahead. This transformation is astounding. Your unwavering support forged an unparalleled trajectory for me!"

Levi's eyes shimmer with genuine elation, "Jimmy, that's nothing short of incredible! Your father will undoubtedly swell with pride. The unwavering diligence and dedication you've poured into this year have yielded remarkable results."

The air is charged with a palpable sense of elation and achievement. Jimmy, an embodiment of gratitude, beams sincerely, "Levi, thanks to you. Your eloquent letter ignited a revolution. Principal Batie, my age-old adversary, was promptly replaced by the remarkable Principal Morrison, a change that has brought fresh air to the institution."

Levi nods, the semblance of a knowing smile gracing his lips, "Based on the experiences that have unfolded over the past year, Principal Morrison's leadership is poised to propel the Academy to unprecedented heights. Moreover, his vision of establishing scholarships for underprivileged students has metamorphosed the Academy into something greater — renamed Scotch College."

As they converse, Lewis steps forward, a picture of warmth and camaraderie. His farewell handshake with Levi encapsulates the bond they've fostered over time.

"Levi, as our paths part, I bid you goodbye. The treasure of our friendship shall linger, and I shall keenly feel your absence. Now... What destinies unfurl before you?"

Levi's gaze holds both contemplation and resolve, "Thank you, Lewis. The journey that beckons me involves a town auction, where I shall employ the generous twenty-five pounds bestowed by my benefactor to procure a horse. Mounted upon this noble creature, I intend to journey back to Ballaarat. My legal mentor, Mr Lynn, has divulged that my benefactor envisions an apprenticeship under the guidance of a legal professional in Melbourne. However, before embarking on this scholarly voyage, I've sought solace and reprieve at home, emancipating myself from the relentless pursuit of knowledge for a short span."

Understanding graces Lewis's expression, his nod a testament to their shared dreams, "I, too, am embarking on a similar expedition. Guided by my father's vocation as a solicitor, I tread the apprenticeship path. And as for your stepfather, whose presence was enshrouded in tumultuous waters? How shall he receive your homecoming?"

Levi's gaze remains unwavering, "Your conjecture is accurate. His career ascent has led him to supervise the Clunes Police Station, tethering him to that location. He has procured a cottage in Ballaarat Central for my mother's comfort. His visits remain sporadic, typically confined to weekends and holidays."

As their exchange nears its conclusion, Levi shares heartfelt handshakes with Jimmy and Lewis, the backdrop of fellow departing students accentuating the sense of transition. A chorus of well-wishers envelops Levi, bidding their farewells and weaving the final threads of encouragement into his journey's tapestry.

The scene now transitions, and Levi stands triumphant amidst the aftermath of an auction, now the rightful possessor of a resplendent white gelded stallion. Adorned with a saddle and bridle, the horse emulates Levi's resourcefulness and unyielding determination.

"In this instant," Levi ruminates, *"I stand unshackled. Alongside this magnificent creature, provisions tucked away and a modicum of hidden currency within my boots, I bask in the warmth of spring's inaugural sunny day. As though liberated from captivity or escaped from the clutches of paternal discipline. The emotions akin to those that pervade Snake Gully, Little Bendigo as a wag lad."*

With the urban boundaries relinquished, the very fabric of the world seems to transform, and even the stallion senses the newfound emancipation. The horse propels forward, its gait transitioning seamlessly into an invigorating canter. The first twenty miles dissolve into a swift blur as carriages and carts amass in a stream towards Melbourne. However, the path leading to the goldfields grows sparser, populated primarily by swagmen carrying their worldly possessions in swag kits across their backs. Levi acknowledges their presence with a proud tilt of his hat.

The sun gracefully dips below the horizon, and Levi erects a makeshift camp beneath the sheltering embrace of a towering gum tree. The tranquil surroundings offer an ideal haven for respite. As the stars emerge, Levi kindles a fire, the flames casting a warm and inviting glow. A nourishing repast of canned beans, dried beef, and a comforting cup of tea takes shape, leaving Levi enveloped in the tranquil embrace of the Australian wilderness.

Chapter Seventy-Nine

Levi's attention wavers from the crackling fire, the remnants of his culinary endeavour now dimly aglow. The fragrant memory of his meal lingers as an olfactory invitation that drifts through the crisp night air. Unbeknownst to him, the aroma has not gone unnoticed.

A lone figure emerges from the rugged shadows, a silent observer of Levi's culinary efforts. Against the backdrop of nature's wild beauty, the stranger's cautious approach echoes the uncertainty of an intruder. Attired in a manner that speaks of rustic authenticity, the stranger dons an open, long, black frock coat that cascades over a short waistcoat. Below, light-coloured moleskin trousers evoke the essence of rural living.

A Colt revolver rests confidently in a belt that cinches his waist, while a wide-brimmed, black bush hat rests atop his head. Trails of dust cling to his clothing, and the rough lines etched onto his unshaven face bear testament to untamed days. His towering build exudes strength and vitality, a testament to a life shaped by vigorous pursuits.

Levi's focus fractures as he registers the presence of the stranger. Silence hangs between them, a pregnant pause brimming with unspoken inquiries and undiscovered narratives.

A deep, reassuring voice punctuates the stillness, dispelling the unease like morning mist. "Don't fret, lad. Continue with your preparations. I have no intention of disturbing a man immersed in the pursuit of a hearty meal," the stranger offers, his words laced with courtesy. "I thought it only proper to be respectful. Tell me, are you en route to the goldfields or journey from there?"

Levi's response, a blend of intrigue and caution, punctuates the air. "I'm bound for Ballaarat. May I inquire as to your interest?"

The stranger's motives unfurl, illuminating the threads that connect them to this land. "This expanse happens to fall within my sphere of trade and occupation. I ensure that I do not unwittingly encroach upon the territory of others and keep watch for potential clients seeking my services."

As the exchange deepens, their voices weave together like strands of fate's tapestry. Levi's quest for understanding continues. "And what services, precisely, do you provide?"

The stranger's response dances on the edges of shadow and substance, reflecting the enigma that shrouds him. "Protection from bushrangers — those renegade outlaws and gangs that haunt these woods, poised to strip individuals of life and valuables. They've christened me 'The Raven,' a moniker acknowledging my signature long black frock coat. Some attribute it to a raven's associations with ill omens and loss. Others posit that, like the prophetic bird, I possess insight and foresight. Yet, rest assured, my principles are rooted in honour. I respect life and claim only what I deem fair. And you, young sir, what are your thoughts on the matter?"

A subtle shift in posture betrays the tension simmering beneath the surface. The stranger's fingers brush the pistol grip, a gesture not lost on Levi. In response, Levi straightens, a step back driven by astonishment and vigilance.

Sensing the currents of their interaction, the stranger interjects with a reassuring tone. "Fear not, lad. Harm is far from my intentions as long as none resides within you. In truth, I am inclined to partake in your meal. A strapping young fellow like yourself deserves fare beyond dried beef and beans. Allow me to contribute provisions as a gesture of camaraderie. Stay put, exercise caution, and I shall return with these offerings. You do travel unarmed?"

Levi's reply is swift and unwavering. "Yes, Sir!"

A glimmer of a smile graces the stranger's lips, a fleeting connection forged. "Ed is my name. I shall return shortly.

Meanwhile, tend to that fire — it shall serve as the foundation for cooking steak and eggs, a fitting accompaniment to those beans."

Raven reemerges, two horses in tow, one a pack horse traversing the untamed landscape. The rhythmic cadence of hooves on earth marks a new chapter in the enigmatic encounter between Levi and the stranger. With practised ease, Raven delves into saddlebags, revealing a frypan and an array of ingredients. The fire, rekindled and nurtured, becomes the crucible for culinary alchemy conducted by Raven's deft hands.

Both men find their places by the fire's warm embrace, its dance illuminating the contours of their shared space. A shared meal takes shape, transcending mere sustenance. Amid the sizzle of steak and the unspoken language of firelight, an unspoken bridge forms.

Gradually, questions emerge like pebbles cast into still waters, their ripples carrying the weight of curiosity. "From whence do you hail, lad? What draws you to Ballaarat? Your bearing betrays a journey marked by multifaceted aspirations."

Levi's response emerges, words infused with the essence of self-discovery. "Ballaarat is my anchor, a nucleus that beckons as I venture into the realm of the goldfields. The corridors of education called me to Melbourne's Academy. Now, I return from Melbourne to visit my mother after the culmination of three years away from home."

As Raven ponders Levi's narrative, a glint of recognition kindles within his eyes. "A college education, you say? A privilege often reserved for those of means. Forgive my inquisitiveness, but might I inquire about your name? Your presence carries a familiar resonance, and I, too, have journeyed through your homeland."

Levi meets Raven's gaze with candour. "Levi Brody, at your service."

Unexpectedly, surprise punctuates the air. Raven coughs, a piece of steak propelled forth in astonishment. His response straddles intrigue and bemusement. "Levi Brody, by chance, are you kin to Bill Brody, the Sergeant presiding over Clune's Police Station?"

Levi's affirmation reverberates, echoing their shared lineage. "Indeed, he's my stepfather!

Chapter Eighty

Levi's stomach weaves a tapestry of satisfaction, threads of contentment woven through the hearty meal now resting within him. The Raven's contented smile harmonizes with his words, "Well, lad, that was a good hearty meal if I do say so myself as the cook." Levi remains attuned as the Raven's tone evolves into a blend of assurance and duty. "I'm at your service to ensure your safety tonight, but I must collect my toll. How much would a college lad riding a fine horse have in his possession... hmm?"

With a touch of resignation, Levi responds, "Not much! As you know, my Pa doesn't earn much, and I only attended college because an unknown patron sponsored me. I used any spare money on this horse and the tucker to get me home."

Amusement and gravity mingle in the Raven's eyes, a symphony of emotions in their depths. "Well, lad, you'll have to come with me until I figure out how you can repay your toll. I can't have word spreading that the Raven has gone soft on his victims — it would ruin my reputation. My hideaway is more comfortable for the night than this spot where you intend to sleep. Pack up your belongings, and we'll be on our way."

Frustration punctuates Levi's protest, a response to the unexpected twist of events. "Is this really necessary? I haven't money, and I don't need your help!"

The Raven's demeanour remains unwavering, a gentle reminder of the power dynamics. "A policeman's stepson is an insurance policy that requires further investigation. Remember, I'm the one with the gun."

As the Raven paves their path down Ballarat Road, a turn onto a trail leading away from the main track marks a pivotal moment. Levi's heart quickens as he grasps the futility of escape in the face of the Raven's armed presence. Amid the receding waves of anxiety, curiosity unfurls its wings within him, urging him to follow and bear witness to the unfolding tale.

Their journey meanders, Raven and Levi becoming one with the wilderness for over half an hour, veering and swerving like partners in a dance choreographed by nature herself. Only when Levi's gaze lands on a distant hut, its interior glow, a beacon of warmth, does their odyssey come to a deliberate pause. With each step, the sense of anticipation within Levi swells, an undercurrent of wonder bubbling beneath the surface.

The hut's door swings open, revealing a young woman around Levi's age. She emanates a striking presence, black curls framing her face, her attire seamlessly merging masculinity with elegance. A red twilled shirt complements moleskin trousers tucked into tall, dark riding boots. Her features are a testament to a lineage rich in diverse origins, her dark brown complexion and captivating countenance speaking to her aboriginal heritage. As Raven dismounts and entrusts his horse to her care, Levi instinctively follows suit.

A tender note colours Raven's voice as he introduces her, "Sweet Pol, grab a lantern and take care of the horses. Our journey was long, and a strong drink would be in order. Our guest tonight is a gentleman — Master Levi Brody."

Inside the hut, partitions of hessian create distinct spaces, each infused with the cozy embrace of firelight. Levi finds his place by the fireplace, a silent directive from Raven guiding his movements. As he eases into the chair, his gaze flits around the room, mapping its contours, soaking in the humble haven that will cradle them for the night.

The Raven's voice, a gentle current in the narrative, shapes the next phase of their journey. "Make yourself comfortable, lad. I'll assist Pol in gathering supplies and setting up our sleeping quarters. The night promises clarity, but the temperature may gift us with a frosty morning."

Levi acknowledges with a nod, a quiet understanding passing between them. His eyes track Raven's movements as he and Pol work in concert, their coordination a testament to their unspoken connection. Soon, they return, bearing saddlebags and sleeping rolls, their presence weaving a sense of security.

The trio settles by the fireside, each movement a brushstroke in the masterpiece of their shared experience. Raven extends a mug of brandy to Levi, an offering transcending its liquid contents.

"This brandy will warm you from within. Allow me to introduce my daughter, Polly Ryker. Her mother, the Love of my life, was lost to us a few years ago due to Diphtheria if you're curious. Polly, or Pol as we call her, possesses a strength that often eclipses that of men. So, if the notion of escape crosses your mind tonight, remember that the bush will swallow you whole, offering nothing but a feast for hungry dingoes."

Levi's gaze lingers within the mug's depths, blending warmth and introspection. Firelight and brandy intermingle, casting shadows that dance across his features, painting a portrait of a young man navigating the uncharted waters of camaraderie and circumstance. His voice carries the timbre of contemplation.

"The amount of liquor you've given me surpasses any consumption I've known. Yet, an unexpected sense of contentment settles in, quelling fear and unease. It's as if I've stepped among old acquaintances, embraced by a sense of family."

In response, Pol's gaze intermittently meets Levi's, a subtle interplay of curiosity and recognition in her eyes. Her gaze mirrors the fire's dance, enigmatic yet inviting, a silent bridge between their worlds.

Levi's eyelids flutter open as the first rays of dawn peek through the cracks in the hideaway's walls. The embrace of a restful night's sleep lingers, his senses slowly adjusting to the warmth of the sleeping quarters he shares with the enigmatic figure known as the Raven. He moves with practised discretion, conscious not to disturb the stillness around him. With a quiet determination, he dons his clothes and secures his belongings before venturing to join the Raven and Pol.

The air is filled with a savoury aroma, a testament to their morning meal. The trio gathers around a rough-hewn table, an unspoken understanding settling over them. The tantalizing scent of ham and eggs dances on the breeze, complementing the camaraderie that envelops them.

In this intimate tableau, the Raven extends a cup of steaming liquid toward Levi, a gesture that transcends words — an offering of alliance, perhaps even friendship. As the Raven's eyes remain fixed on Levi, the gentle clinking of utensils accompanies their meal. Pol is engrossed in her plate, the focus of a young woman with her own thoughts and a captivating air of mystery.

The Raven's voice, a blend of exasperation and affection, breaks the silence. "Levi, my dear lad, you've managed to surprise us. Our resourceful Pol discovered ten quid secreted away in your boots while intending to properly clean them. Trust is fragile, and your lack of it has consequences. Unsurprisingly, the toll has seen an increase. My Night of contemplation and sleep was lost over the weight of your value to me. Every opportunity I seize, whether a mail coach or a passing traveller, becomes part of my legacy."

A pause follows, during which the Raven retrieves his tobacco pouch and briar pipe, a ritualistic motion inviting Levi into the Raven's realm. Smoke curls lazily as the pipe's bowl ignites, Raven's gaze an enigmatic invitation to delve deeper into his story.

The Raven's voice resumes, carrying tales of intrigue. "With mail coaches, my vigilant eye scans every letter in search of cash, my dear Pol as my partner in this endeavour. Worthless cheques meet the flames, an act of mercy for those drawn upon them. Unless they hold the promise of cash. Sweet Pol, meanwhile, collects credit receipts for banked gold and negotiable banknotes. She takes them straight to our contacts in Bacchus Marsh or Ballarat, where they are transformed into a currency more to our liking."

Levi interjects concern, tainting his words. "But with my disappearance, my stepfather and every police trooper this side of Melbourne will be scouring the land."

The Raven's chuckle is a knowing echo, his pipe's ember casting a warm glow. "Fear not, for we have our network — a haven of ticket-of-leave convicts and Irish sympathizers. In exchange for a receipt or two, they provide refuge and intelligence and a way to launder for information."

Levi's desperation seeps into his following words. "My presence will only attract trouble for you. Release me, and you can continue as before. I'm oblivious to your hideout's exact location."

The Raven's eyes narrow, his contemplation palpable. "You might be more valuable than you realize. A potential trade, a bargaining chip... exchanged for a sentence reduction or even a pardon. Yet, my capture seems unlikely. Old Ed is astute, after all. Still, with a bounty of two hundred and fifty pounds on my head, the police are motivated, hoping to claim it for themselves. Dead or alive, it makes little difference to them."

Levi's eyes widen as he absorbs the gravity of the Raven's revelation — *an outlaw with a price on his head, a shadowy figure navigating the edge of legality.*

The Raven's smile is cryptic, hinting at irony in his words. "And now, a little insurance against disaster, for my dear Pol. A Police Sergeant's son in my custody, the irony is indeed sweet."

Curiosity fuels Levi's subsequent inquiry. "As an outlaw, the Raven, does that mean you've committed murder?"

The Raven's response echoes with sombre truth. "Yes, lad. Murder it is. An accident, much like the demise of Dan Farley... your paternal father. Circumstances have forced my hand, propelling me into a life of hold-ups to survive on the run. I carry out my deeds compassionately, avoiding those who seem more in need than me. Often, I split the spoils evenly when folks are forthcoming. I've no wish to cause financial ruin. And women being searched are off-limits in my pursuits. Word has spread, leading gentlemen to entrust their wives as carriers of their valuables when journeying through these lands."

Levi's thoughts whirl as the pieces of this intricate puzzle click into place. "Is that how you're acquainted with my stepfather, Bill Brody?"

The Raven's affirmative response hangs in the air, a prelude to a narrative that began years before, setting the stage for a journey of discovery, alliances, and secrets buried in the Australian wilderness. As the sun's warm embrace extends over the land, unveiling untold tales of the past and the present, the Raven's story unfolds, casting its spell on the young man whose fate is now inextricably linked with the outlaw's path.

Chapter Eighty-One

Three years Earlier:

The first light of dawn paints the horizon with shades of gold, the sun ascending like a blazing conqueror, igniting the world with its fiery embrace. Against this backdrop of bygone days, a solitary Wedgedtail Eagle soars, its wings slicing through the currents as it rides the thermals, a lone sentinel of the sky.

Nearby, a modest miner's hut stands as a humble outpost amidst the vast expanse of nature. Edward Ryker, a man with calloused hands and determined eyes, moves with the rhythmic cadence of chopping firewood. The axe's striking wood sounds like a heartbeat, a primal rhythm harmonizing with the earth's pulse.

Besides Ed, his daughter Polly, a fourteen-year-old with determination etched into her features, hangs freshly laundered clothes on a makeshift line. The garments sway in the gentle breeze, creating a tapestry of domesticity against the untamed backdrop.

Their routine shifts as a lone rider approaches, accompanied by a single-horse gig carriage. The clip-clop of hooves and the rattle of wheels draw their attention. A wordless signal from Ed prompts Polly to retreat into the shelter of their home. Ed places his axe aside, wiping his brow with a sweat-stained forearm before assuming an air of quiet anticipation.

The horse and carriage come to a halt, revealing their passengers. A Police Trooper, resplendent in uniform, occupies the saddle while a Government Official sits within the carriage. Warren Templeton, the official, introduces himself with an air of formality.

"Howdy, Mr Ryker. A fine day for a ride. I'm Warren Templeton, and accompanying me is Constable Burns from Clunes."

Ed acknowledges the greeting with politeness, his gaze lingering on the strangers before him. "Good morning. What brings you to my neck of the woods?"

Templeton's expression carries a gravity that contrasts with the morning's cheer. "Business, Mr Ryker. Regrettable business, but government orders necessitate it."

Curiosity mixed with concern, Ed inquires further, "And what precise orders might those be?"

With a sense of duty, Templeton lays out the purpose of their visit. "As the Talbot/Clunes appointed resident Aboriginal Protector, I am here to collect your daughter, fourteen-year-old Polly Ryker. She's considered a half-caste native and, according to our assessment, no longer under the maternal mother's protection within the family."

Ed's frustration simmers beneath the surface, his grip on the axe handle tightening. "Are you saying the government holds the authority to make such decisions? Even when my dear Pol has a white father who toils honestly and diligently?"

Templeton's composure remains unwavering, a bastion of bureaucratic resolve. "Indeed, these are my orders. I am tasked with conveying her to the Ballarat Orphanage this day."

A surge of anger courses through Ed's veins, his voice tinged with defiance. "I will not stand for it! My sweet Pol is the light of my life, a balm for the ache left by her mother's passing. I won't allow her to be torn away, subjected to the horrors of an orphanage. They'd exploit her, reduce her to mere labour, then pass her off to settlers who would abuse and enslave her, keeping her away from her flesh and blood. You'll take her from me over my lifeless body!"

Yet, Constable Burns, the enforcer of the law, intervenes with his own form of authority. He unholsters his Colt Revolver, his grip trembling with apprehension and resolve. Dismounting swiftly, he holds the weapon aloft as a stark warning, his intent clear — he's prepared to use force to maintain control.

"Best you temper your temper, Mister," the constable's voice quivers with fear and conviction. "Mind the law, or I'll be forced to use this weapon. Step aside and remain still until the Protectorate's task is done. Refuse, and you'll be in shackles, heading back with me."

Closing the distance, the constable takes a position behind Ed, his revolver's barrel pressing against Ed's back — a silent yet insistent reminder of the consequences of resistance.

Templeton steps closer, aligning himself with a constable's resolve. "Continue as instructed, Mr Templeton. I assure you, this one will adhere to the law."

Within the humble confines of the hut, Templeton's entrance sets off a muffled commotion, the clash of wills and the shifting of allegiances reverberating within the small space. Ed's frustration mounts, a caged fury waiting to be unleashed.

As Templeton emerges from the hut, a figure in tow, the air is tense. Polly, dragged forth by her hair, calls out to her father with a desperate plea that reverberates through the charged atmosphere. "No, Pa! Don't let them take me!"

In that moment, a spark of rebellion ignites within Ed. He whirls around with a sudden, fluid motion, his arm colliding with the constable's revolver. The unintended result is a shot that shatters the stillness, the sound of a gunshot ripping through the air. The constable staggers, a hand clutched to his wounded abdomen, pain and fear etched across his features. He crumples to the ground, the power dynamic upended by an accidental twist of fate. Ed stands in disbelief, a witness to the chain of events he has set in motion.

Templeton seizes the opportunity, releasing Polly from his grip before retreating to his carriage. The sound of horse hooves pounding against the earth echoes his hurried departure.

In the wake of chaos, Pol rushes into Ed's embrace, the emotional reunion a testament to the bond between father and daughter. Ed's urgency shifts, his focus now on the injured constable lying partially conscious on the ground.

"Quick, Pol, fetch a clean towel," Ed's voice resonates with a sense of urgency, the need for action propelling him forward.

Pol hurries into the hut, and Ed takes charge of the situation. He positions the wounded constable on his back, his hands pressing against the wound to staunch the bleeding. Pol returns with the towel, offering it to Ed, who uses it as a makeshift bandage, applying it to the constable's wound with measured precision.

With grim determination, Ed lifts the injured constable's weight, carrying him toward the hut — a refuge now transformed into a makeshift haven, a place where destiny has taken a sharp and unexpected turn, leaving Ed, Polly, and the constable entangled in a web of defiance, consequence, and the unforeseen ties that bind them.

Chapter Eighty-Two

Five mounted figures emerge on the dusty trail, their silhouettes etched against the horizon. As they draw closer, the distinct forms of riders materialize. Among them is Sergeant Bill Brody, a man with a stern countenance that mirrors his authoritative aura. Templeton rides beside him, flanked by two police troopers. The horses' rhythmic hoofbeats blend with the whisper of the wind, a solemn symphony that heralds their arrival.

Ed Ryker steps out from the shelter of his humble dwelling, a picture of surrender, his hands raised in a gesture of submission. His gaze remains steady, unyielding, even in the face of armed riders approaching him.

"Keep your hands up, Ryker! Where's the wounded constable?" Brody's voice resonates with authority, demanding compliance.

Though burdened with his circumstances, Ed's voice remains remarkably calm. "He's inside. I did my best, but he succumbed to his wound."

Brody's response is as cold as it is accusatory. "Then you've committed murder, Ryker, and you'll hang."

A fleeting mix of regret and desperation flickers in Ed's eyes as he counters, his words a measured plea. "It was an accident. Ask Templeton."

The figure of Templeton, with a demeanour as unyielding as Brody's, steps forward, his voice carrying an air of finality. "It's murder! You killed the constable while obstructing an officer carrying out his official duty."

Brody's attention turns to the two constables, his orders concise and unwavering. "Smith and Burke, saddle their horses and bring them here. Templeton, go and bring out the girl and her belongings. Where Ryker is going, they'll provide his needs."

Inside the confinements of Ballaarat Prison, life buzzes within the exercise yard. Prisoners move with measured steps, their faces reflecting the burden of incarceration. Amid this orchestrated scene, Ed Ryker engages in hushed dialogue with Jack, a fellow inmate known for his resilience. High above, a prison guard stationed atop the bluestone wall surveils the prisoners, a silent observer of their interactions.

"Jack, this is it, my friend," Ed's voice holds a potent mixture of determination and urgency. "We should be able to push those two bluestone blocks all the way out. A final touch-up, and I'll be on my way!"

A gleam of admiration lights up Jack's eyes as he responds, his words carrying the weight of respect. "Ed, you're a true genius. Who would've thought a sharpened spoon handle could aid in a daring escape?"

Ed's voice carries a touch of practicality as he explains. "If the builder hadn't scrimped on the lime for the mortar, this chance wouldn't be mine. Get a few of the lads by the southeast corner. I'll finish the cuts, and we'll need their muscle to force the blocks out."

Jack's smile exudes camaraderie as he speaks. "Consider that side taken care of, Ed. A couple of us are with you. You don't deserve fifteen years for an accident. And remember, don't forget to write!"

In covert corners of the exercise yard, prisoners gather discreetly, nodding in silent unity. A game of "Two-Up" unfolds, cigarettes changing hands as stakes amid the orchestrated diversion. Amidst the chaos, Ed seizes his moment, his form slipping away as he retrieves a makeshift tool: a short-handled stick with a metal spoon handle affixed to it. His movements are deliberate, scraping away at the mortar that binds two bluestone blocks, the path to freedom inching closer.

A sudden staged quarrel erupts between Jack and another prisoner, Doyle, a well-coordinated distraction that draws attention. Amidst the uproar, Ed takes his chance. His boots vanish through a hole in the prison wall, a fleeting glimpse of liberty seized through ingenuity and the collective determination of fellow inmates. The exercise yard remains a scene of orchestrated chaos, a canvas upon which the promise of escape is subtly painted.

Dressed in prison drab, Ed Ryker navigates his newfound terrain with urgency. He careens down an embankment by the prison's southern wall, tumbling into a gully. Emerging from the ravine onto Grant Street, he's met by the rhythmic trot of a two-horse wagon. Swift and soundless, he positions himself behind the wagon, becoming one with its cargo of provisions concealed beneath a canvas shroud.

The discordant clang of a bell's toll reverberates through the air, a piercing announcement of an escape. The main gate of Ballaarat Prison creaks open, unleashing a flurry of armed guards along the prison's south and west walls.

Time passes, and the wagon, unaware of its precious cargo, carries Ed along Black Hill Road. A sign directs to the Black Hill Gold Mine, and as the wagon veers onto the trail, Ed emerges from his covert haven, vigilant.

Liberated from the wagon's confines, Ed bolts across Black Hill Road, immersing himself in the dense bush. Desperation propels his pace, every stride a declaration of his yearning for distance from his pursuers.

Exhausted but driven, Ed finds solace in the embrace of the Little Bendigo District (Nerrina) of Ballaarat. White tendrils of smoke spiral above the canopy of trees, an unexpected beacon of respite. Following this signal, he arrives at a rustic miner's cottage nestled in a woodland clearing. A vigilant Collie breed dog, tethered by a chain, greets his presence with frenzied barking.

Swift as a shadow, Ed positions himself behind a towering gum tree. The canine's uproar summons an elderly woman, a settler dressed in attire that speaks of resilience and years of toil. Her voice carries command as she admonishes the barking dog. "Jessie! Settle down; it's just another possum! I'm tired of your yelping. Your Pa will give you a good whack when he's back!"

Intrigued by this exchange, Ed steps forward, his posture nonthreatening, his hands raised in a gesture of peace. The woman, taken aback, retreats a step, her hand instinctively finding its place over her heart.

"Steady, ma'am," Ed reassures, his voice a soothing balm. "I mean you no harm. It was me your dog was barking at."

The woman's initial alarm gradually wanes as she scrutinizes the weary figure before her. "Lord almighty!" Her exclamation blends surprise and exasperation. "You should be more careful sneaking up on an old woman. You could've given me a heart attack. Ya have the looks of an escaped prisoner by your clothes? I haven't heard about one."

Ed acknowledges the truth with a compelling blend of sincerity and urgency. "I am, ma'am, but a trustworthy one. I was wrongly accused and headed home to ensure my child is properly cared for. I just need a change of clothes and to borrow that horse I see corralled over there. I promise you, everything will be returned."

The woman's scepticism begins to soften, eroded by the force of Ed's conviction. "I don't know if refusing you will make any difference, so I'd rather give you permission if it means there's some truth to your words."

Ed responds with profound gratitude, his voice echoing with sincerity. "Thank you, ma'am. God bless you! By the way, what name should I use when returning your borrowed items?"

The woman's gaze reflects a mixture of caution and compassion. "Huckley... Mrs Huckley."

The woman's decision becomes apparent with a touch of wariness yet willingness to extend aid. She turns towards the cottage, her steps determined, a glimmer of hope dancing in Ed's eyes. The promise of transformation, the echo of a second chance, beckons him as he stands in the clearing, a solitary figure on the precipice of change.

Chapter Eighty-Three

Perched upon the elderly woman's weathered grey mare, Ed Ryker ventures deep into the intricate labyrinth of animal trails that crisscrossed the bush. Each twist and turn carries him with a purpose, an unwavering determination to reach the enigmatic Gordon District to the east. The rhythmic cadence of the horse's hooves orchestrates a silent symphony, its beats harmonizing with the earth beneath, forging an unspoken partnership between rider and landscape. Every stride is a testament to his unyielding will, etching a portrait of resolve onto his features.

As the landscape unfurls before him, a sight of significance comes into view – a small, forgotten miner's humpy stands as a relic of time's passage. Its raw timber frame, hewed from the land's embrace, is a testament to an era long past. Time's fingerprints mar its surface, etching stories of endurance and toil. The walls, fashioned from split timber, witness years of sweat and labour. Above, a barked roof, though bearing the weight of age and wear, embodies the spirit of unyielding tenacity.

Stepping down from the mare, Ed secures her reins to a nearby hurdle, a makeshift anchor in this temporal dance. His gaze sweeps across the scene, absorbing its essence – a symphony of history and possibility. He deliberately peels off his twill shirt, exposing the well-worn undershirt beneath. Methodically, he rolls up his sleeves, revealing arms that bear the imprints of trials endured and hardships overcome. His resolve, resolute and unflinching, finds reflection in his actions as he begins to clear away the fallen timbers that bar the humpy's entrance. Each movement is a testament to purpose, a choreography that entwines with the remnants of the past, conjuring visions of a future within these rugged walls.

"Sweet Pol, I have found us a new home," his tender murmur voice carries a weight of promise that reaches far beyond the present. *"Not*

much to behold in its current state, but through my efforts, it will transform into a sanctuary. I assure you, my girl, I shall come for you – have no fear."

The narrative shifts, illuminating a new stage – the Dowling Forest Racecourse bathed in the warm, inviting late afternoon glow. Amidst the orchestrated chaos of preparations for the forthcoming Ballaarat race day, Ed Ryker assumes the role of a shadow, a spectre lingering at the edge of visibility. From this vantage point, he becomes an invisible spectator, observing the intricate ballet of stable hands tending to the horses with a keen eye. Their movements, choreographed with care and devotion, compose a symphony of dedication and artistry.

Within this bustling tapestry, Ed recognizes his moment. With the confidence born of unwavering purpose, he emerges from his concealment, leading the elderly woman's grey mare into the heart of the stable's bustling activity. Amidst the choreography of hooves and voices, Ed selects a majestic brown thoroughbred racing mare. His touch is gentle as he opens the stall door, an unspoken understanding passing between them. With a precision born of practice, he guides the mare out, his every motion calibrated to avoid drawing undue attention. It is a dance of subtlety, a performance of grace amid orchestrated turmoil.

In a gesture of trust and intent, Ed releases his horse into the vacant stall, a silent promise of restitution and gratitude. His thoughts remain unvoiced but reverberate with determination. *"The owner of this exquisite creature will be astonished as his horse is summoned to the track. The note I've left with Ma Huckley's horse will elucidate the situation and guarantee the return of the elderly mare."*

Unfazed by the stage's bustling setting, Ed guides the thoroughbred away from the hubbub of activity. His demeanour strikes a delicate equilibrium between confidence and anonymity, a dance of purposeful detachment. As he weaves among the stable hands, nods and fleeting glances acknowledge his presence, seamlessly integrating him into the tapestry of daily routines. And when the weight of scrutiny lifts, he spurs the thoroughbred into a gallop, a testament to its prowess and a reflection of his determination.

The journey leads him to the outskirts of the Ballaarat Orphanage, where the sun descends toward the horizon, casting the world in the warm embrace of gold and amber. Amidst the meticulously nurtured garden, a figure captures his attention – Pol, immersed in her labour, a portrait of resilience and fortitude.

Sheltered by the haven of a tree, Ed's fingers find a pebble, a silent messenger of connection. The pebble's trajectory is guided by intent, striking Pol's arm and setting events into motion.

With a startled movement, Pol turns, her gaze tracing the trajectory of the unassuming pebble. Recognition washes over her, her eyes locking onto the figure before her – her father. A word forms on her lips, barely audible yet brimming with incredulous joy – "Pa!"

In a heartbeat, the chasm of separation dissolves as Pol rushes toward Ed, their embrace a fusion of emotions long held at bay. The bush seems to sway in harmony with their shared exuberance as they reunite, two souls rekindling a bond that defies time and distance.

As the scene transitions, they are perched atop the waiting mare, a symbol of unity forged in the crucible of adversity. Together, they ride away from the orphanage, their figures etched as silhouettes against the canvas of twilight. Their journey to freedom commences, propelled by the shared trust of father and daughter and the unwavering rhythm of the horse's hooves that echo their determination.

Chapter Eighty-Four

Three days have trickled by since Levi arrived at Raven's secluded hut. Escape seems but a distant dream within the confines of his temporary captivity. Yet, the passage of time ushers in a subtle transformation woven into the fabric of this enigmatic tale. Once veiled in reticence, Pol unfurls her reserve, allowing the warmth of familiarity to kindle between her and Levi.

Beneath the outstretched boughs of a gum tree, Levi finds respite just outside the hut. The front clearing is a sanctuary where he seeks solace, embraced by the tree's shade. Across from him, Raven sits upon a rugged log, a figure of intrigue lost in the labyrinth of his own contemplation. The tendrils of smoke spiral upward from his briar pipe, a silent echo of his musings.

Levi's soft and almost ethereal voice carries his thoughts to the winds. *"The notion of escaping holds me captive in hesitation. The bush, a labyrinth of thorns and treacherous abysses, can confound even the most intrepid souls. To be lost in this wilderness is to embrace the fate of the countless gold prospectors before me – nameless skeletons strewn across the unforgiving land."*

From the hut's entrance emerges a figure – Pol. Her steps, once timid, now bear the grace of newfound confidence. She approaches her father, a partnership of understanding, uniting them on the log seat.

A sigh, almost inaudible, escapes Levi as he contemplates his situation. His gaze lingers on Pol, captivated by her natural allure. *"Ma's heart must be a cacophony of worry,"* his thoughts murmur, *"I might express my concern to Pol in hopes that she becomes the bridge to the Raven's understanding."*

Levi focuses on Pol, her beauty amplified by nature's embrace. *"Pol's allure is one of a kind,"* he observes, *"Her mixed lineage bequeaths her a charm that outshines the finest cosmetics. The deep hues of her skin, the cascade of ebony curls, and the delicacy of her features resonate with the exotic echoes of a distant Polynesian ancestry. Even in attire designed for practicality, her inherent grace prevails."*

Pol's presence embodies the epithet the Raven has bestowed upon her – sweetness itself. Levi voices his concerns to Pol as she approaches him, "Pol, My mother will sorely miss me and be concerned for my safety."

A voice, gentle and soothing, responds to Levi's spoken worries. "Fear not; in a matter of time, Pa will dispatch me to Ballaarat to carry out some banking errands. If, by any chance, you remain here, I'll ensure a note reaches your Ma through the Post Office."

The exchange continues, Levi's voice threading through the fabric of their interaction. "Addressing your Pa as 'Ed' is a challenge," he admits, "Given my predicament, I often steer conversations through questions or offer the necessary responses."

Understanding resonates in Pol's reply, her words carrying the weight of empathy. "I comprehend your sentiment. He was a good man before our lives took this tumultuous turn. And even now, he remains true to his essence despite the perilous path he's chosen for our survival."

Levi's gaze shifts towards Raven, a contemplative spark igniting his eyes. He voices his introspections aloud. "Your Pa exudes a watchful air as if anticipating uninvited intrusions. Yet, there are moments when he seems adrift in his thoughts, marked by a tinge of melancholy. His life, I dare say, is no enviable one. Bound to the shadows, a fugitive existence with the ever-looming spectre of reckoning."

Pol's response unfolds as silence, a vessel for the unspoken complexities of her emotions. Levi perceives a glistening tear taking form in her eyes, a testament to the profound feelings that words fail to capture. Swiftly, Pol rises from her seat and returns to her father's side, offering solace in the sanctuary of her embrace.

The morning sun paints the world in soft hues as Levi rests beneath the sprawling arms of a gum tree. Anticipation threads through the atmosphere as the Raven emerges from his abode, an enigmatic figure swathed in his black frock coat and bush hat. Dual saddlebags drape his form, accompanied by a lever-action Henry Rifle and Colt revolvers snug in his belt. Purpose carries him forward, a deliberate stride aimed at Levi.

Levi acknowledges the Raven's presence with a nod, curiosity brimming. "A hunting expedition, perhaps?" he suggests with a tinge of enthusiasm, "Anything is better than languishing in idleness." Questions sprout from Levi's curiosity. "And when might I be granted my freedom?"

The Raven's response is tinged with uncertainty. "That rests upon your ability to heed instructions and earn trust anew. Your recent actions have cast a shadow on your reliability, especially considering the concealed money. Today brings an opportunity for redemption. Abide by the expected conduct, speaking only when spoken to. Do you comprehend?"

Levi's agreement manifests in a nod, his demeanour assuming an air of compliance. Rising from his seat, he follows the Raven, his thoughts providing a murmured narrative. *"The Raven wears a sombre mantle today, a veil woven of intentions shrouded in mystery. Questions remain dormant within me – today, I embrace the enigma."*

The two figures progress towards the corralled horses – Levi's stallion, a gleaming coat of white, and the Raven's brown steed. The task of saddling up is executed with a quiet purpose. Side by side, they embark on the trail, Raven forging the way.

Single file, they tread the narrow pathways blazed by indigenous fauna. Levi observes his surroundings with a mix of unease and intrigue. *"The animal trails crisscross like a labyrinth, the bush unforgiving in its uniformity. An escape route devoid of distinctive markers."*

Time dances onward until their path converges with a thoroughfare, a well-trodden route to Ballaarat and Bacchus Marsh. Wagon ruts and hoof prints intersect the wilderness, leaving their mark. Raven reaches into the hollow heart of a towering gum tree, retrieving a note. His gaze shifts to Levi, anticipation twinkling in his eyes.

Words follow, tinged with a hint of triumph. "Favorable news, lad. Today, we shall see a mail coach passing; no troopers are in sight. Your role is straightforward – present yourself as injured, halt the coach, and smooth the way for my next move."

Levi's inner turmoil surges forth. "So, this is what you meant by hunting. But this will mark me as part of your gang. I'll become a wanted man myself."

The Raven's voice carries seasoned wisdom. "That is the intent – to meld you into the backdrop of the gang. Reflect before you act rashly. I shall shoulder the burden if they apprehend me. Or else, your Pa, the astute Sergeant Trooper, will find a way to absolve your involvement." A crimson bandana is tossed towards Levi. "Veil your visage, mute your words, and anonymity shall be your shield."

Levi's inner monologue regains its voice, thoughts racing. *"What a quandary. Attempt escape, and I'd be ensnared before I take a score of strides. Unarmed and outnumbered, I can only wish for a seamless execution. After witnessing the tumult of the Eureka Stockade and the tapestry of my brief life, Raven's hold-up might pale in comparison – provided no harm befalls anyone involved."*

Chapter Eighty-Five

The designated moment arrives, an intersection of paths guided by Raven's calculating hand. Levi positions himself on the ground, leaning against the sturdy trunk of a tree. His loyal white stallion stands nearby, a silent sentinel to the impending drama. Raven's gaze, unwavering and resolute, fixates on Levi.

"Levi," Raven's voice resonates with determination, the air heavy with purpose, "Your role is to appear unwell, beckoning as the coach draws near. When it halts, raise your mask and await my instructions. Do you comprehend?"

A silent nod from Levi conveys his understanding. Concealed within the undergrowth on the opposite side of the track, Raven retreats into the shadows.

Then, the symphony of rattling wheels and rhythmic hooves emerges, gradually crescendoing into a melody of movement. Around the bend, a one-horse buggy materializes, its occupants nestled within. The woman in the front seat is the first to spot Levi, prompting a subtle tap on her companion's arm, urging him to slow their progress. With cautious restraint, the buggy glides alongside Levi.

In an instant, the scene transforms as Raven emerges from obscurity, his face unmasked, rifle levelled at the couple. Fear and confusion flicker in their eyes, oscillating between Raven and Levi, their tremors evident.

"Hands up!" Raven's command slices through the air, authoritative and undeniable, "This is a stick-up. Remain still, and no harm will come to you. I am armed, and my aim is steady. Lad, help the lady disembark. Sir, keep your hands visible and remain composed."

Levi raises his mask, moving gracefully to assist the elderly woman's descent. The old gentleman follows suit, his movements obedient to Raven's directives. Raven supports him, his unwavering gaze sweeping the surroundings. Gesturing the couple into the cover of the thicket, Raven signals Levi to follow. Turning to Levi, Raven's following instructions, "Lad, take their buggy and conceal it in this clearing. Afterwards, inquire about their destination."

The old gentleman clings to his wife's arm as she struggles to maintain equilibrium. "Please, sir," his voice quivers, "Treat her gently. Our possessions hold little value. My pocket watch and my wife's two banknotes constitute our entire fortune. We are bound for Bacchus Marsh for errands at the post office and Grant's Store."

As Levi arranges the buggy, Raven tosses his rifle to him. He opens his coat, revealing the Colt revolvers nestled in his belt, and assesses the couple. "Two pounds wouldn't buy much," Raven remarks, studying the elderly pair's worn clothing.

"Those two pounds are a down payment," the old gentleman explains, "The remaining sum will be taken on credit. If you doubt our words, feel free to search our belongings."

Raven examines a covered wicker basket retrieved from the buggy. Levi's heart swells with sympathy and relief as he witnesses Raven's gentle demeanour. "What treasures lie within?" Raven lifts the cloth, unveiling a feast of roasted chicken, boiled eggs, and plain cupcakes. He turns to Levi, a glint of unexpected camaraderie lighting his eyes,

"It seems we have a luncheon to share with these good folks, lad. A considerable improvement over my dry rations. Fate appears to favour us. Fear not, sir, you are under my protection. I do not intend to exploit honest settlers unless they are prosperous squatters. Yet, our venture necessitates a pause. We await the imminent arrival of the mail coach. Setting you forth to Bacchus Marsh prematurely would be imprudent."

With grace, Levi assists the elderly couple back into their buggy, uncoupling their horses and tethering their reins to a sturdy tree branch. Raven divides the basket's contents among them, and they find shade beneath a towering gum tree. Their eyes remain alert, scanning both ends of the track, the anticipation palpable. Raven's grin widens as his gaze falls upon the rifle resting next to Levi.

"Keep that rifle within reach, lad," Raven advises, his tone a blend of amusement and guidance, "But don't entertain any notions – it's unloaded, unlike my reliable Colt Revolvers."

In the distance, the echo of wheels and the thud of hooves grows louder, evolving into a cacophony. A nudge from Raven propels Levi into position. The six-horse mail coach barrels around the bend, the driver's firm grip on the reins and the companion's vigilant stance signalling their awareness. The coach screeches to a halt, the dust raised by its abrupt stop settling around it like a shroud.

Heads emerge from coach windows, hungry for a glimpse. Levi averts his gaze, obscuring his identity, while the driver and companion assess the situation from the coach's footboard. The companion's authoritative command rings out. "All passengers, remain seated. I'll investigate – safety first!"

Just as the companion disembarks, Raven materializes into view on his mount. His presence solidifies with a commanding declaration. **"Bail up!"**

Levi raises his mask, moving forward with cautious determination. Raven dismounts, his relaxed posture belying the potency of the Colt revolvers he holds.

"Keep your focus on the coach, lad," Raven's instructions resonate loudly, "Open the door, and if anyone acts suspiciously or resists, be prepared to take action."

Guided by Raven's directives, Levi opens the coach door, relief washing over him as five passengers disembark – three men and two women. Levi extends his hand, assisting the ladies.

While Raven maintains his watchful gaze over the coachmen, the remaining passengers huddle in uncertainty. Under instructions,

Levi retrieves a rope from Raven's saddlebags, securing the coachmen to a tree. The two women, alongside the other passengers, navigate the process of relinquishing their valuables.

The scene morphs into an enigmatic tableau as Levi surveys his surroundings. Amid the passengers, a middle-aged woman dressed in solemn black attire exudes an aura of poise and elegance. Beside her stands a refined young woman adorned in a pristine white crinoline skirt. Linked arms convey a bond forged through the tempest of events.

Three gentlemen, each distinguished by their hat choice, complete the assembly. A straw boater, a bowler derby, and a fur hat with an upturned brim set them apart. Yet, the man sporting the fur hat captures Levi's attention.

Recognition surges through Levi, a jolt of realization coursing through his veins. An involuntary flinch betrays his emotions, and he hastily raises his mask a tad higher, averting his gaze. Upon mustering the courage to look up, Levi's eyes lock onto those of the man in the fur hat. A stern, penetrating gaze met him, with a subtle quiver of the nose revealing a suspicion that cut to his core. It is none other than Levi's Ballaarat solicitor, Mr Lynn.

Chapter Eighty-Six

The atmosphere hangs heavy with tension, a palpable unease enveloping the scene. The Raven seizes the opportunity to explore the coach's interior within this charged stillness. He navigates through handbags and carpet bags, deftly tossing them down from their overhead perches. With the agility of a seasoned intruder, he produces a key procured from a coachman's pocket, granting him access to the coveted box seat. With a practised twist, the compartment beneath the bench is unlocked, and from its concealed depths, the Raven hurls down two mailbags and a square metal box before making his descent.

In adherence to the Raven's authoritative instructions, the hostages have willingly surrendered their prized possessions, leaving them scattered like offerings on the ground.

"Collect your bags and form a single file for inspection. Place your valuables in front," the Raven commands, his voice cutting through the tension.

With an unwavering gaze, the passengers align themselves accordingly. The Raven embarks on his meticulous assessment, traversing the line methodically. Standing side by side, arms entwined, the mother and daughter quiver slightly, a shared apprehension evident in their demeanour.

Raven's stern countenance softens as he directs his attention to the two women, his voice carrying a touch of gentleness, "And what names do you lovely ladies carry, madam?"

The mother responds, her voice quivering with a mix of trepidation and resolve, "I am Mrs Redmond Barry, wife of Judge Sir Redmond Barry of the Supreme Court of Victoria. We were en route to Melbourne after visiting my sister in Ballaarat. Allow me to warn you, you rogue, that you've ventured into dangerous territory.

If any harm befalls us, my husband will unleash the full might of the Victoria Police Force upon you."

Raven's demeanour shifts, a touch of surprise colouring his expression, "Argh! The very wife of the hanging judge himself. Did you hear that, lad? The same judge sitting before the 'Eureka Boys' of the Stockade Rebellion when freed from the gallows when their fate seemed sealed. Perhaps fortune will smile on us as well. I reckon your concealed bags hold some delicacies not meant for gentlemen's eyes... And what's this? Quite a charming sight – ten pounds and a selection of jewellery at your feet. Gather them, lad, place them in my saddle bag, and bring the bags to me."

Turning his scrutiny to the young man adorned with a straw boater hat, Raven's inspection continues, "Let's uncover the contents of your possessions. It's an intriguing assortment, indeed. A handful of silver coins, a pocket watch with cracked glass and a silver chain, a well-worn pocket knife, a white clay pipe, and a tobacco pouch. There is little to gain from a young man who appears as substantial as Buckley and Nunn's department store. Best stow those away before I reconsider."

Progressing along the line, Raven's focus lands on the owner of the bowler hat, his tone a blend of amusement and scrutiny, "Ah, a man of refinement, it seems. Are you a banker, a real estate salesman, or might it be a gambler?"

The bowler hat's owner vehemently denies the accusations, "Neither, sir! I am a stockbroker specializing in gold mining shares."

Raven's gaze sharpens as he inspects the contents at the man's feet, "Ah, just as I suspected – a gambler of a different sort then! Let's examine your treasures more closely."

He carefully lifts the gentleman's watch with two other gold-plated items and a pocket wallet for further scrutiny, "This watch, an 18ct gold-cased Patek Philippe, Calibre 89, bedecked inside with more jewels than a jeweller's shop could offer. Quite the spectacle! Golden cufflinks and a gold snuffbox. It seems to be a treasure trove of gold, more than I will likely find in the coach's security box. Coupled with twenty pounds in notes. Your plans for indulgence in Melbourne are evident, sir."

The gentleman's scowl betrays his displeasure at this detailed assessment. Raven shifts his focus to the next person in line, his tone now inquisitive, "And who do we have here? An elderly gentleman emanating an air of dignity beneath his fedora. Pray, enlighten us – what occupation suits a gentleman of your stature?"

Undaunted, the elderly man asserts, "I am Adam Lynn, a solicitor from Ballaarat. I've encountered men more ruthless than you in my time, sir!"

Raven's curiosity piques at this declaration, "Is that so, Mr Lynn? And what brings a solicitor of your calibre onto this coach and into my realm?"

Mr Lynn's response is unwavering, "Financial matters and the enigma surrounding the disappearance of a young lad – matters that have sparked the curiosity of certain interested parties."

Raven's intrigue deepens, "And who might this lad be?"

Mr Lynn, with a surreptitious glance in Levi's direction, replies, his voice measured, "A young lad named Levi Brody. He traversed this path before vanishing."

Raven's attention sharpens, "I'll certainly be vigilant for this lad. Should our paths cross, might there be a reward for his safe return to your custody, sir?"

Mr Lynn responds with conviction, "Indeed, a reward can be discreetly negotiated."

Acknowledging this with a nod, Raven concludes, "I'll bear that in mind, whether fate brings me across his trail or I catch wind of him through the 'bush telegraph.' Now, my comrade will gather these modest treasures and ensure their safekeeping, preventing any other cunning rogue from attempting a misappropriation.

Chapter Eighty-Seven

Raven's gaze shifts toward the bound driver hostages, his eyes assessing their situation for a fleeting moment. With a commanding tone that brooks no argument, he calls upon Levi, the young man who has become a pivotal part of their daring escapade. The authority in Raven's voice is undeniable.

"Lad, untie the coachmen and ensure the others board the coach to continue their journey to Melbourne," Raven instructs, his words a directive that Levi is swift to heed.

Levi's fingers move deftly, untying the ropes that had previously bound the coachmen to their captive state. As the tyes fall away, the coachmen rise with a palpable sense of relief, a mix of gratitude and awe directed at the imposing figure of the Raven. Their steps are guided by their newfound freedom and Raven's compelling presence, and they move toward the waiting coach with purposeful haste. The Raven's vigilant eyes follow their progress, his two colt revolvers serving as a silent reminder of his authority.

Simultaneously, the passengers respond to the unfolding scene. With a sense of urgency, they scramble to board the coach, a mix of anxiety and anticipation spurring them onward. The coach driver, a man well-versed in the rhythm of the road, adds his voice to the commotion, his shout slicing through the air as he cracks the reins against the horses' backs.

"GET ALONG, MAPLE! CHARLIE! - PULL HARD!" The coach driver's command resonates, and a call to action propels the coach forward. The vehicle lurches into motion, wheels clattering against the ground, a cloud of dust trailing in its wake.

As the coach departs, the scene shifts to focus on Levi. He takes on the role of a collector, swiftly gathering the saddlebags laden with their ill-gotten gains. Meanwhile, the Raven shoulders a different burden – two mailbags and a secure metal box containing their secrets. Together, Raven and Levi move purposefully toward the clearing at the rear, where the buggy of an elderly couple remains.

The sound of their approach startles the elderly couple seated in the buggy. Levi's efficiency shines as he attends to their horses, securing them in place for their impending departure. However, the Raven steps forward, a small parcel in hand. This simple offering holds a more profound significance, a gesture that speaks volumes about the man beneath the enigmatic exterior.

"A kind stranger, moved by your plight, has offered this compensation of two guineas," Raven's voice carries a blend of solemnity and warmth, reflecting his intricate character. "That's two pounds and two shillings. Now, spread the word in Bacchus Marsh that the Raven conveys his regards to the Law Makers and the good folk there."

The old gentleman's gratitude is sincere, his words heartfelt. "Thank you, Mr Raven. And if you should happen to encounter that same kind soul, please convey my deep appreciation for his generosity."

The Raven's response is genuine, his chuckle a testament to their shared understanding. A light slap on the horse's rump sends the elderly couple to Bacchus Marsh, rekindled with a renewed sense of hope.

As the elderly couple's presence fades into the distance, the Raven's focus shifts back to the task at hand. Swiftly and efficiently, he unlocks the coach's security box, revealing its contents. Among the ten ounces of gold gleaming within are also several worthless certificates, an ironic twist to their daring heist. Raven's frustration is evident as he flings the valueless papers to the wind, a symbolic act that mirrors his disdain for the inconsequential.

With the mailbags carefully tethered together, he takes charge, slinging them over the front of Levi's saddle. The secure metal box, once a coveted prize, remains in Raven's possession, a testament to his resourcefulness and adaptability.

With the preparations complete, the two men set off on their horses, venturing back toward their hidden sanctuary nestled within the ranges. As they ride, the weight of the day's events hangs in the air, casting a thoughtful shadow over Levi's mind. *"I'm relieved to see that the Raven didn't resort to violence during the robbery, but the ordeal surely took a toll on those older victims,"* Levi's introspective voice punctuates the journey, his thoughts a testament to his evolving perspective on the Raven's chosen path.

Their horses carry them closer to their refuge, and another presence emerges as they approach the hut. Pol steps outside, her transformation arresting the Raven and Levi's attention. Her light, sleeveless dress has changed from her previous, more masculine attire, revealing a newfound allure. Her long hair, once a wild cascade, is now neatly bound in a bun. Pol's beauty is undeniable, and Levi's gaze lingers, captivated by her presence.

The Raven, always astute, doesn't miss this interaction. His words carry a teasing familiarity as he playfully addresses Pol, a glint of mischief in his eye.

"Now, Pol, you didn't have to doll up just for my sake, especially on your day off. You remind me so much of your dear departed mother when you're all dressed up. You've caught young Levi's eye — he nearly toppled off his horse!"

The blush that tinges Pol's cheeks is mirrored by Levi's own embarrassment. Pol's retreat into the hut carries a hint of self-consciousness, her departure acknowledging the unspoken dynamics at play.

With their horses now settled, Raven and Levi dismount. Their actions are practised, a testament to the routines that have become second nature. Within the cozy confines of the cabin, the Raven deposits the saddlebags and mailbags onto the table, their contents ready for inspection.

Amidst the mailbag's contents, several currency notes are found, and one detail catches Pol's attention. A playful revelation spills from Raven's lips, uncovering Pol's penchant for the romantic letters that see their way into her hands. Levi watches with curiosity and amusement, intrigued by this unexpected glimpse into Pol's private indulgence.

"Pol has a soft spot for reading love letters she comes across. She finds them rather amusing and has a collection of them. She dips into it whenever boredom strikes," the Raven discloses, a note of camaraderie in his voice, a shared secret that binds them further.

Pol's response is swift, her exit from the table swift and accompanied by a blush. The Raven's candid revelation leaves her momentarily flustered, a reminder of the intricacies that make up their unique dynamic.

Chapter Eighty-Eight

Levi seeks refuge beneath the sprawling canopy of a gum tree, its leaves rustling above him like a chorus of murmurs. The sun's gentle warmth filters through the intricate network of branches, casting a mosaic of dappled shadows upon the ground beneath.

In the hush of nature's symphony, Levi's voice, soft as a sigh, breaks the stillness. "To myself," he whispers, his words carried away by the breeze. *"My feelings for Pol have grown with every passing day. Her story is a tapestry woven with uniqueness, threads of Jaadwa aboriginal heritage entwined with her bush upbringing. The letters she reads are a portal to a realm of romantic narratives, igniting a spark of yearning deep within her."*

A burst of vitality emerges from the hut as Pol steps into the daylight, her presence akin to a breath of fresh air. She makes her way to where Levi sits, a romantic letter held gently in her hand. As the words flowed from her lips, laughter danced among the leaves, blending with the soft rustling of a harmonious melody. The shared mirth paints an image of camaraderie, vivid and alive.

"That's just one of many letters that captivate me," Pol shares, a playful curve touching her lips. Her eyes gleam with a mischievous light, and she continues, "Penned by lovers with souls of poets. Some are odes to nature's beauty, others brim with fervent expressions of love, and a daring few tread into the realm of the sensual. Yet, it's those that blossom from separation and solitude that truly resonate with me."

Levi's expression shifts, a sombre overtone clouding his features. Concern etches lines upon his brow as he asks, "But where does this fascination lead you, Pol? How do these letters find their place amid this unforgiving bush?"

Pol's gaze remains unwavering, her determination a rock in the face of uncertainty. "This won't be our forever, Levi. Pa has pledged that we'll bid farewell to this place and journey north when the coffers are filled. There, a life free from the clutches of the Law awaits us."

Levi's nod conveys understanding, the weight of their reality resonating between them. "May that dream unfold as your reality, Pol. A harsh world out here threatens both your father and you."

Silence slips between them, a pregnant pause where thoughts ebb and flow like ripples in a tranquil pond. The horizon holds the promise of an uncertain future, a canvas yet to be painted.

As time weaves its threads, the bond between Pol and Levi grows, their connection deepening like the roots of an ancient tree. Stolen glances speak volumes, shared secrets forge invisible ties, and subtle touches become their language. Amidst the whispers of the wind, when they believe no one is watching, their hands find each other, a silent affirmation of their unity.

Unspoken emotions bubble to the surface, finding expression in stolen kisses that hold the sweet tang of innocence and the poignant flavour of longing. As desire flares within Levi, his hands dare to wander, fingers tracing intimate pathways, a testament to his yearning. Pol's response is swift and playful, a gentle slap that speaks of unspoken boundaries.

Their interactions take on the air of playful camaraderie, a dance of laughter and joy that echoes through the air. In bouts of tickling and light wrestling, they revel in the connection they share, finding solace amidst the challenges of their reality. Amid this burgeoning connection, a silent observer senses the need for intervention, an unseen presence attuned to the subtleties of their hearts.

As the scene shifts, a new day dawns upon their sanctuary. Pol and Levi, seated upon logs, become the focus of the sun's tender caress. The light paints them in hues of warmth and reflection, creating a tableau ripe for conversation.

Breaking the silence, Raven's voice cuts through the stillness, measured and thoughtful. "Levi, it's time we speak of your future. My original plan was to keep you here temporarily, safeguarding Pol's well-being until I could secure a fresh start in a distant territory beyond the law's grasp. Yet, circumstances have evolved, and your connection with Pol poses a new risk." Levi's attention is rapt, his gaze fixed upon Raven. "I presume your religious teachings did not delve into matters of marriage?"

A faint uncertainty flickers in Levi's eyes as he shakes his head. "No, such matters weren't part of the curriculum."

Raven leans closer, his expression a blend of seriousness and understanding. "Pol, you venture inside the hut and allow me to illuminate this for Levi. The passion you feel for Pol, lad, is a potent force, nature's means of perpetuating our kind. It guides the union of man and woman in the bonds of marriage."

A question lingers in Levi's gaze, prompting Raven to continue. "However, given Pol's circumstances and her limited choices, I advise against entertaining thoughts of sensual engagements."

Levi's surprise is palpable, understanding dawning in real-time. Raven's voice takes on a strategic tone, the weight of experience underscoring his words. "To ensure Pol's future, I've decided to negotiate with Mr Lynn, the solicitor in Ballaarat. The funds he offers for your return will secure Pol's path to a life far from this wilderness. Do you grasp the gravity of my proposal?"

Levi's nod is a mix of understanding and relief, his gaze unwavering as he absorbs the implications of Raven's words. As the Raven departs, Levi is left with his thoughts, contemplating the magnitude of their conversation. Levi's inner voice emerges, a chorus of emotions harmonizing, *"I comprehend, even if it diverges from Pol's hopes. Our innocent intimacy has taken on new meaning. Yet, my devotion to my mother and the need to return to her eclipses any romantic yearnings. Pol is a cherished friend, and our connection shall remain anchored in that truth."*

A similar conversation unfolds between Raven and Pol. She returns to her less feminine attire, and their interactions turn distant, a facade of indifference carefully maintained. Pol playfully tests the boundaries, her flirtatious glances a gentle challenge. But Levi stands firm, resolute in his commitment.

Levi's voice reverberates in his thoughts, a tempest of feelings swirling within. *"Resisting the call of my heart is a formidable task. The longing to draw close, to hold her in my embrace, is a constant ache. Nevertheless, I must stand steadfast."*

As the sun dips below the horizon, casting hues of amber and gold across the land, Levi watches Pol from a distance. Frustration finds release in the kick of his foot against the dirt. Seeking solace, he seeks refuge beneath the tree that has witnessed their journey, a silent observer of the intricacies of their intertwined hearts. The winds whisper their unspoken desires, a destiny entwined with the threads of sacrifice and devotion.

Chapter Eighty-Nine

The hut's interior becomes a sanctuary of contemplation as Raven and Levi engage in a conversation fraught with monumental decisions. Levi's voice quivers with anticipation. "When will you initiate negotiations with Mr Lynn for my release?"

Raven's response is measured, his tone unwavering. "Today marks the day, lad. Pol stands on the precipice of departing for Ballaarat. She wields mastery over covert operations, including the intricate dance of exchanging stolen gold through the intermediary known as Mr Wilderman."

Levi's attention is unwavering, his mind absorbing each nuance of the unfolding plan. "And who, precisely, is this Mr Wilderman?"

Raven leans in, his gaze locked onto Levi's. "Wilderman is a seasoned practitioner in the realm of trafficking stolen goods. He serves as our conduit to intelligence regarding mail coach schedules and the elusive choreography of police movements. As part of our arrangement, Pol will deliver a letter to Mr Lynn, a missive concealed within the confines of the post office."

Levi's thoughts whirl like a tempest, colliding with the imminent strategy. "Could Pol, in addition, bear a message to my mother? I long for her to know of my unscathed state and the imminent reunion that beckons."

The Raven's affirmation is swift, a testament to their solidarity. "Certainly, lad. Such arrangements can be orchestrated. Furthermore, it shall fall upon Pol to guide your horse into Ballaarat. My racing steed is far too conspicuous and would inevitably draw the scrutinizing gaze of the watchful authorities."

Levi's shoulders relax, relief escaping as pent-up tension dissipates. He walks to a side table, his steps measured, and collects a charcoal pencil and a sheet of paper. With a determined spark in his eyes, he sets about weaving heartfelt sentiments into a message for his mother, his emotions converging in the pencilled words on the page.

Within the confines of Mr Lynn's office, an atmosphere of palpable tension hangs heavy, a fusion of concern and unwavering resolve enveloping Sergeant Brody and Mr Lynn. Seated figures, their expressions mirror the shared apprehension of the moment.

Sergeant Brody's voice reverberates with unyielding conviction. "Rest assured, my efforts have cast an exhaustive net along Melbourne Road, extending its reach to Bacchus Marsh. Alerts have been disseminated to every stable, inn, coach exchange station, and outpost. They stand poised, vigilant for the sight of a seventeen-year-old boy astride a white stallion. The directive remains unequivocal: immediate notification of the Ballaarat Police upon any sighting."

Mr Lynn conveys acknowledgment and gratitude weaving through his words. "Your dedication merits commendation, Sergeant. Nevertheless, the patronage of the lad lacks faith in the capabilities of the Ballaarat Police. This scepticism has prompted the engagement of a private investigator, tasked with expanding inquiries from Melbourne's vantage point."

Sergeant Brody's restrained frustration simmers beneath his demeanour. "The notion that my son could be ensnared in association with a bushranger during a hold-up eludes my understanding. Our endeavours to nurture him, to forge a promising path, have been a ceaseless labour."

Mr Lynn's gaze melds empathy with unshakable determination. "As previously conveyed, I bore witness to the hold-up of a young man seemingly burdened by duress and shame. His gaze evaded mine, averted by the weight of guilt. Drawing from the wealth of experience accrued defending countless accused souls, my stance is rooted in a presumption of innocence unless evidence dictates otherwise. We must locate him, affording him the opportunity for redemption."

A knock on the door interrupts the exchange, casting a new trajectory on the unfolding narrative. "Mr Lynn, a certain Mr John McCormack from Craig's Livery Stables awaits. He seeks an audience with Sergeant Brody concerning a white stallion."

Mr Lynn responds with a sense of urgency, his words brisk. "Waste no time. Bring him in."

John McCormack, a stable hand, enters his demeanour a mosaic of apprehension and anticipation.

Sergeant Brody addresses him directly. "What tidings do you bear?"

John's hold on his cabbage-tree hat betrays his unease, his gaze toggling between Brody and Mr Lynn. "Excuse me, Sergeant. A white gelding aligning with your description has just been delivered to Craig's Livery Stables. It was ridden by a native girl who directed her course toward Wilderman's establishment."

Renewed vigour pulses through the room, an unspoken understanding exchanged between Sergeant Brody and Mr Lynn. Sergeant Brody's voice carries a note of invigoration. "Exemplary work, John. If her path leads to Wilderman's, it alludes to a nexus with the horse we endeavour to trace. I implore you to return and extract the right hind shoe from the horse. It will serve as a breadcrumb trail to her origin."

McCormack acknowledges the directive with a nod, swiftly departing the room. Mr Lynn's eyes gleam with steely determination. "Fortune extends its hand to us, Brody. We cannot afford to squander this providential juncture."

Sergeant Brody's resoluteness emanates from his being. "I shall enlist the expertise of a proficient black tracker from the ranks of the Ballaarat Police. I and the tracker will assume an inconspicuous post at Craig's Livery Stables. Together, we will retrace the trail to its inception. Kindly relay to Mrs Alice Brody that my scheduled visit to her newly acquired dwelling on Doveton Street North must regrettably be deferred. My responsibilities demand otherwise. Farewell, Mr Lynn."

Mr Lynn's gaze is a blend of encouragement and anticipation. "Farewell, Sergeant. May fortune grace your endeavours."

Chapter Ninety

Bath Lane, usually a thoroughfare of openness, stands in stark contrast today as Wilderman's shop door remains shut. Pol's keen eyes take in the unusual scene. Testing the handle, she finds it unlocked. With cautious determination, she steps into the dim interior cloaked in shadows. Her voice pierces the darkness. "Mr Wilderman... Are you there?"

Guided by the faint flicker of a candle at the back, she advances. Yet, as the room illuminated by the feeble light comes into view, an involuntary scream escapes her lips. Wilderman's lifeless body is suspended from a rafter—his eyes empty, face bloodied, and features etched in agony.

Shocked and recoiling, Pol readies herself to flee. Yet, her escape is thwarted by the sudden appearance of a dark figure blocking the exit. She struggles against her captor's grip, but his strength is unyielding. More figures emerge from the shadows, their presence suffocating. Among them, Curly snatches the sack Pol carries.

"Now, lassie, settle down," Curly's voice drips with menace and authority. "We don't wish to harm you. I gather you're on an errand for the Raven—bearing his newly acquired treasures."

The sack is opened, revealing the gleam of gold and loot. The intruders close in on Pol, their intentions clear. Curly, their leader, stout and bald, exudes anger and power. The lanky figure beside him, dressed as a station hand, contrasts with his sardonic grin. The third figure, burly and imposing, clutches Pol in his grasp, dressed in the attire of a digger.

Despite her struggles, Pol's defiance remains steadfast. Curly steps forward, "Enough resistance," Curly's voice is ferocious. "Bull, won't hesitate to snap your neck. We propose an alliance with your master—that four heads united can be formidable. Lead us to the Raven, and we'll all thrive."

Pol's voice trembles, but her determination stands strong. "He's not my master. He's my Pa, and he wants no part in any gang. He's a lone operator, especially not with the likes of you—vile animals!"

Laughter tinged with malevolence fills the room. "Feisty, isn't she? Hold your tongue if you want to return unharmed and see your Pa again. Stir up trouble, and you'll be found outside the police barracks, gagged and labelled. Understand?"

Pol's captor tightens his grip, a stark reminder of her vulnerability. Pol acquiesces, her compliance forced, her thoughts racing, and her hope pinned on her father's wisdom. The intruders exit the shop, their departure surprisingly seamless. They proceed to Craig's Livery Stables, mount their horses, settle their fees, and set off. Unbeknownst to them, Sergeant Brody and his black tracker are on their trail, having witnessed their departure with the unmistakable white stallion.

As the sun sets, painting the horizon in hues of amber and crimson, the stage is set for the convergence of fates—a complex tapestry of intrigue and deception poised to unravel.

Raven's hut's interior is tense, the weight of uncertainty hanging heavy. Raven's measured footsteps echo off the walls as he paces, his mind a whirlwind of unsettling thoughts. Equally perceptive, Levi watches with a furrowed brow, mirroring the unease that lingers in the air.

Raven's voice is a mere whisper carrying a heavy burden; Raven mutters, *"Something's not right. This feeling of impending doom won't release its grip. I must ensure Pol's safe return."*

Levi, attuned to Raven's disquiet, approaches cautiously, his words a gentle inquiry, "Is everything as it should be? What troubles your thoughts?"

Raven turns to face Levi, his eyes a piercing gaze that reveals the depth of his concerns. "It's just a nagging instinct, lad. I must make my way to the crossroads and await Pol's arrival. With her absence, you might be tempted to make hasty choices. To ensure your safety, I must bind you until I return."

Levi's understanding is etched in his solemn nod. "I have faith in your judgment. If it means Pol's safe return, I will comply."

As Levi settles onto his swag, offering his limbs to be bound, Raven's touch is gentle yet purposeful as he secures the restraints. Armed with Colt revolvers and a mind that leaves no detail unchecked, Raven's preparations are methodical, a testament to his commitment.

With a brief touch of gratitude, Raven's hand rests on Levi's shoulder. "Thank you, lad. I won't be long. Stay steadfast until my return."

Driven by a steadfast determination, Raven steps out of the hut, the echoes of his horse's galloping gradually fading into the distance, leaving a lingering sense of uncertainty that casts its shadows over the place.

Chapter Ninety-One

In the afternoon's sweltering heat, Raven positions himself in a concealed spot near a junction. His senses are heightened, every nerve attuned to Pol's approach. The thoroughfare sees a parade of buggies, riders, and gigs, yet he remains motionless, unwavering in his commitment to protect Pol. Finally, the rhythmic rhythm of approaching hooves reaches his ears, and his focus narrows. Gently, he strokes his horse's mane, an image of controlled readiness.

"Why are we stopping here, lass?" Curly's irritation cuts through the air. "How much farther?"

Raven's voice, laced with authority, pierces the scene. "BAIL UP! Make a move for your weapons; death will be your companion!"

Emerging into view, Raven commands, a Colt revolver gripped in each hand. The sudden appearance disrupts the outlaws, their horses rearing and spinning, their composure shattered. Fear courses through them, freezing them in place as they confront the sight of Raven's weapons.

"Pol, my dear," Raven's tone brooks no disobedience. "Step aside. These rascals have explanations to give."

Pol's desperation is palpable as she interjects urgently. "Pa, they're murderers! They killed Wilderman and seized his loot, your loot too! Don't trust them, no matter what they say!"

Raven's gaze, unyielding, meets Pol's. "Stay clear, Pol. I'll deal with this. Curly, you're familiar. One of Jack Riley's underlings, correct? Are Riley's funds running low? Or have you taken the path of independence?"

Curly's voice wavers, recognition dawning in his eyes. "A bit of both, Ed. Jack wants answers—those missing bills of exchange have him fuming. He won't rest until you're six feet under, regardless of the time or resources he invests."

Sardonic laughter spills from Raven's lips. "Jack's a distant memory for me, Curly. I've fended for myself."

Curly's gaze sharpens, revealing more. "But there's more, Ed. Wilderman spilled about Lynn's reward for a missing lad, attributed to you. We suggest an alliance—the 'Raven and Curly gang.' Mutual benefit—protection from the law and Jack Riley, combining our strengths."

Pol's plea rings in Raven's ears. "Pa, don't listen to them. They're deceitful. We don't need their help."

Raven's eyes narrow, contemplative. The offer's weight presses on him, its implications vast as he keeps a vigilant eye on Pol. Their future pivots on this precipice, and his decision will chart their course.

Pol's desperate cry reverberates through the air, a piercing sound that catches the attention of two newcomers racing toward the scene. Swift and determined, Sergeant Brody and the black tracker round the bend, their horses skidding to a halt as they confront the unfolding chaos. Before them stands the Curly Gang, their faces contorted with surprise at the unexpected sight of police uniforms. Instinct takes over, propelling the gang into a galloping chase.

With unflinching resolve, Sergeant Brody and the Black Tracker waste no time, their horses pivoting sharply as they commence a rapid retreat.

The Raven, his astonishment palpable, doesn't hesitate to raise his voice, aiming to halt the fleeing gang in their tracks. "STOP!" his command resonates, authoritative and unyielding. "Hold your ground, or I shall open fire!"

Curly, caught off guard, risks a swift glance back. In that split second, his hand reacts, firing a shot that finds its mark in Raven's chest. The impact reverberates, sending a shockwave through Raven's body. He fights to retain his balance, clinging tenaciously to his horse's neck to prevent an untimely fall.

Amid the turmoil, Pol races to Raven's side. She dismounts with urgency, her fingers wrapping tightly around Raven's leg, desperation etched across her features. "Pa, No!" Pol's plea is raw with anguish. "Don't die on me, please! Don't!"

Raven gazes down at her, his face a mask of pallor, his pain evident in every grimace. "Pol, swiftly!" He manages to utter amidst the struggle. "Use your neck scarf as a makeshift bandage. Take my reins, guide me back, lass. The blood loss...it's too much. It's our only chance... Hurry!"

Raven crumples the scarf, pressing it forcefully against the wound beneath his vest, a desperate attempt to stem the flow of crimson. Pol takes the reins with a determined set to her features, her resolve unwavering, and steers them away from the tumultuous scene, riding at a steady canter.

The Curly Gang's pursuit remains relentless, their pace unyielding. As they draw nearer, gunshots punctuate the air, each discharge aimed at the retreating figures. The black tracker, a symbol of determination, becomes the first casualty, his life cut short as he collapses to the unforgiving ground. 'Bull,' unfeeling and ruthless, brings his horse to a halt, firing two more calculated shots into the motionless body of the fallen tracker.

Despite a wound to his back, Sergeant Brody clings to his saddle, driven by sheer willpower. His horse races onward, pushed to its very limits. A beacon of determination, Brody guides his mount relentlessly toward Ballaarat. His destination is clear: the Miner's Hospital, positioned at the junction of Sturt and Drummond Street.

The hospital's corridors are cloaked in sterile silence, a backdrop for the symphony of tension that reverberates within its walls. Doctor James Stewart stands with an unwavering focus in one of the private rooms. With meticulous precision, he wields his instruments, delicately extracting fragments of a bullet from the wounded body of Sergeant Bill Brody. Every movement is deliberate, every action etched with the gravity of a life teetering on the precipice of existence. The weight of this moment presses down on him, a constant reminder of the fragility of life.

Amid the controlled chaos of the operating room, a figure bursts through the entrance. Eyes wide with fear and anguish, Alice Brody, a woman usually composed, is now shattered by the sight that greets her. Her husband lies on the operating table, vulnerable and injured. The trauma etched on her trembling form and tear-streaked face is palpable.

A compassionate nurse steps forward, a beacon of reassurance in this whirlwind of emotions. With a gentle touch, she guides Alice away from the sterile battleground. Alice follows, her steps faltering, and she's led into a small waiting room—a space that offers little comfort in the face of the torment that envelops her.

Time slips by in a cascade of anxious moments, a torturous rhythm. Then, as if heralding a heavy revelation, the waiting room door creaks open again. Doctor Stewart emerges, his expression a canvas painted with sorrow that transcends his medical expertise. Alice's gaze flickers to him, a silent plea woven within her eyes. She braces herself for the words that hang in the air, heavy with an impending truth.

"Mrs Brody," his voice carries a weight of regret, "I'm deeply sorry to convey that the bullet's impact has caused extensive damage—a vital organ has been shattered and ruptured." He pauses, empathy reflected in his gaze. "I regret to inform you that Sergeant Brody hasn't survived. You're welcome to see him now."

Alice's heart feels like a lead weight, sinking into an abyss of sorrow. The words hang heavy in the air, each syllable a cruel reminder of the reality that has mercilessly unfolded before her. Her voice is a mere whisper, constricted by grief, as she nods in acknowledgement. She follows Dr Stewart's lead, navigating through the labyrinthine corridors until they arrive at Bill Brody's bedside.

She gazes upon his face, once animated by life's vibrancy, now stilled by death's cold embrace. His features retain a serene quality as if he's merely slumbering. Yet, the absence of his chest's rhythmic rise and fall is a brutal reminder of the finality of this moment. Grief crashes over Alice in a relentless wave, and she lowers her head onto his chest, seeking solace in the place that used to be his refuge. Her sobs are primal and unrestrained, filling the sterile room with the lament of a life severed too soon.

In the hushed corridors of the hospital, where life and death dance a solemn duet, a world fractures and shatters - within those clinical walls, an elegy for a love lost too soon reverberates—a melody of sorrow that echoes through the hearts of those left behind.

Chapter Ninety-Two

Pol's heart races, a frantic drumbeat echoing in her chest, as she carries the wounded Raven through the tangled wilderness back to their hidden refuge. A trail of crimson drops marks their desperate path, and each blood spot is a haunting breadcrumb leading the way for the relentless pursuit of the Curly Gang. Her determination is etched into every line of her face, a fierce defiance against the odds. Safety is only a step away inside the cabin, but the danger is far from over.

The door of the cabin swings open, revealing Levi bound and captive, his eyes widening in surprise at Pol's return. The urgency of the moment propels them into swift action. Pol's fingers work with practised haste, freeing Levi from his restraints. Together, they maneuver the weakened Raven into the cabin, his body a testament to his dire struggle. Every movement they make leaves a trembling echo, a path that the approaching danger would soon follow.

As they lay the Raven on his bed, a tableau of vulnerability and strength, the weight of the situation presses down upon them. Blood loss has stolen the colour from Raven's face, and his laboured breaths fill the room, a symphony of life-fighting to endure.

Breaking the silence, Levi's voice emerges, threaded with concern and a sombre truth. "Pol, I've seen this before, during the aftermath of the Eureka Stockade Battle. Your Pa's time is near. There's no use fighting it. We can't save him now."

Tears well up in Pol's eyes, a mixture of grief and desperation swirling within her. She kneels by her Pa's bedside, her heart heavy with the impending loss. Her voice trembled as she whispered to him, her words a balm for both of their souls.

"No, Pa... Please don't leave me. God, please, help him. He's all I have. Pa, I love you so much, and I always will."

The Raven manages a feeble response, his hand lifting slightly before falling back, limp and fragile. With a final exhale, he surrenders to the stillness that beckons, leaving behind a world forever altered by his absence.

Pol's cries of anguish pierce the air, a raw expression of her grief as it spills over. Her tears fall freely, a testament to the love she shared with the man who raised her, who shaped her world. Her body trembles as she collapses over him, her sobs a symphony of loss and longing, painting the room with the colours of sorrow.

Levi leaves the cabin, giving Pol the space she needs to navigate the labyrinth of her emotions in private. Unbeknownst to him, shadows stir at the edges of their existence. Three figures he glimpses, a foreboding trio, edge closer to the hideout with caution woven into their intent. Concealed by the embrace of trees, they inch forward, their purpose veiled in the darkness.

Levi's return to the cabin is swift, a silent understanding exchanged between him and Pol. Her eyes meet his, anxiety and urgency speaking a language only they understand. Levi's expression contorted with surprise, his voice revealing the tension in the air.

"Pol, there are three men outside... Who are they?"

Fear mingles with resolve in Pol's voice as she exposes the truth. "They're murderers, Levi. They shot Pa, and they're after you for the reward, or they'll kill us for what we know."

Urgency is a palpable presence as Pol tosses Levi the Henry rifle, a tool that may be their salvation. Levi's realization is swift, his voice edged with urgency. "This rifle's empty, Pol. Where are the bullets?"

A determined gleam dances in Pol's eyes, her conviction unyielding. "It's loaded, always has been. Can you use it?"

Levi's response is firm and resolute. "I can. Every Outback kid knows how. Pol, fire a few shots from your Pa's revolver through the front window while I slip out the back."

With practised agility, Levi navigates the window, a shadow melding with the night. He skirts the cabin's edges, moving silently toward cover, ready to engage their adversaries from an unexpected angle.

Pol's revolver breaks the silence, gunshots punctuating the air, defiantly responding to the encroaching danger. Curly's voice slices through the night, a command reverberating with a deadly promise.

"Give up, Polly! Your Pa's bleeding out. If he's not already dead, he will be. Come with your hands up, or we're coming in guns blazing."

The stage is set for a desperate dance of survival, shadows of uncertainty cast over Pol and Levi's fight for freedom. In response to Curly's chilling ultimatum, Pol's defiance ignites, translating into two resolute shots fired in their direction. The thunderous crack of gunfire reverberates through the air, a testament to her unyielding determination.

Meanwhile, Levi remains concealed in the depths of the wilderness, his vigilant gaze tracking the trio of villains with unwavering intensity. Among them, 'Bull' stands out, his hulking frame navigating the terrain with a calculated purpose. He maneuvers between the trees to secure a strategic position by the cabin. The other gang members remain cautious, a silent tableau of danger.

Bull reaches a side window of the cabin, his eyes scanning the interior. Levi prepares to issue a warning shot to alert Pol. However, the anticipated sound of a gunshot fills the air before Levi can react. Bull's agonized scream pierces the stillness, hands instinctively flying to his face. He stumbles backward, a whirlwind of pain and shock, before succumbing to the ground in a lifeless heap.

The remaining villains react with swift brutality. Shots pierce the air, aimed at the cabin, as they dash desperately for the front door. In that fleeting moment, Pol is absent from the window, leaving Levi to seize the opportunity. Emerging from his concealment, he aims at the taller of two adversaries, his finger steady on the trigger. Levi's proficiency acquired through hunting kangaroos serves him well in this dire moment. He squeezes the trigger precisely, the outcome a gruesome testament to his resolve. The villain's head erupts upon impact, a grotesque gore that paints the landscape crimson.

Levi inhales deeply, grappling with the weight of his actions. The realization of the life he has taken, even in the name of self-preservation, is a bitter pill to swallow.

Amid the chaos, Curly's advance falters, his bravado crumbling under confusion and fear. His eyes dart frantically between Levi, approaching with rifle raised, and Pol, poised in the cabin's doorway, her pistol aimed with unflinching determination. Pol's voice slices through the charged atmosphere in this moment of tense equilibrium.

"Drop your revolver, or I'll drop you!"

Curly's compliance is rigid, his movements a testament to the gravity of the situation. "Missy, I watched you both kill my mates. I won't take any chances with the pair of you!"

Levi and Pol, now united by purpose, close the distance between them and Curly, their intentions as clear as the moonlit night. Yet, Levi's surge of aggression cannot be contained, and it finds release in a swift kick to Curly's groin. A guttural cry escapes Curly's lips as he collapses to his knees, his strength yielding to the unexpected blow. Pol steps forward, the cold touch of her pistol's barrel pressed against Curly's temple.

Levi's intervention is gentle yet firm. "No, Pol, not that." He redirects Pol's weapon with a steadying hand, a silent message of restraint. In this perilous game, keeping Curly alive serves a strategic purpose — a pawn to be played in the tangled web of their circumstances.

Bound by shared necessity, Pol and Levi proceed to secure Curly with unyielding resolve. Ropes are wound tightly, immobilizing him without hesitation. Their actions are swift, a testament to their urgency. Pol's gaze shifts to Raven's lifeless form, a final gesture of respect and practicality. She wraps his body in a blanket, the weight of grief and responsibility etched in every movement. Levi assists in securing the bundled body onto the Raven's pack horse, ensuring its stability for the impending journey.

With their captive contained and meagre belongings collected, they stand before the cabin, which holds both bitter and sweet memories. Their attention turns to the fallen tall villain, an emblem of the chaos that has marked their lives. His lifeless form sprawls, starkly contrasting the vibrant landscape that stretches beyond.

Pol's voice resonates with a firm resolve as she addresses Levi, her words a vow to their circumstance. "Don't even think about it. They'll remain where they fell, nature's way for crows and dingos until the authorities retrieve their bodies."

The night breeze carries their shared burden as they prepare to depart, a tale of survival and sacrifice etched in the shadows they leave behind.

Chapter Ninety-Three

Under the cloak of night, Levi and Pol charge into the heart of Ballaarat, their horses driven by urgency but weariness etched into their every stride. Their steeds, breathless and lathered with foam, carry them through the dimly lit streets, the sound of hooves echoing against the silence. Their destination looms ahead — the police barracks, perched above a gully, a bastion of law in the darkness.

As they arrive, Pol remains outside with the horses, her presence a vigilant guardian over their exhausted companion. Levi, dishevelled and dust-covered, steps inside the barracks. His attire tells a tale of the chaos and danger he's faced, a narrative written in layers of sweat and grime. The foyer's lamplight casts shadows that play across his fatigued features. Weariness weighs heavily upon him as he walks, each step a testament to his trials.

The duty sergeant, a stalwart figure behind his desk, lifts his gaze from his work, surprise flickering as they settle on Levi. Levi approaches, a mixture of uncertainty and urgency driving him forward. The sergeant's voice, a blend of curiosity and concern, breaks the silence.

"What brings you here at this ungodly hour, lad? You seem like you've seen a ghost."

Meeting the sergeant's gaze, Levi's fatigue is palpable, his eyes reflecting the weariness of his journey. He takes a moment, collecting his thoughts before speaking.

"I'm Sergeant Brody's stepson, reported missing — Levi Brody."

The police sergeant interjects with an air of recognition, his tone a mix of surprise and familiarity. "Well, I'll be darned. I didn't expect you to pop out of thin air like this. I've got some sombre news for you, lad. Your stepfather, Sergeant Bill Brody, he passed away today.

Gunshot wound from some unknown assailants. And there was a black constable who met the same fate."

Levi's expression remains solemn; his determination is unyielding. "I've got the killer of the troopers and Wilderman out there, along with the body of the outlaw known as the Raven."

In a whirlwind of urgency, the sergeant's demeanour shifts. He springs to attention, his voice slicing through the air with speed. "Jones! Get out here, quick!"

A police constable rushes in from a backroom, hastily tugging on his boots as he emerges. The sergeant and the constable swiftly head outside, and Levi follows in their wake. The night unveils a tableau of revelation in the gentle glow of a torch lamp. A native girl, fierce and determined, sits atop a spirited thoroughbred, a Henry rifle clutched in her grasp. Nearby, bound rogue slumps wearily on a horse, his captivity evident. Tethered to a white stallion, a pack horse stands laden with a mysterious cargo concealed beneath a cover.

"Jones, escort the prisoner inside and lock him up," the sergeant commands, authority lacing his words. Then, he turns his gaze to Levi, his tone composed yet urgent. "Lad, lend me a hand with the body. We need to photograph it and send it to the coroner's office. You and the young lady here must provide statements to untangle this mess."

Time ripples, the scene morphing as hours pass. Inside the confines of the Ballaarat Police Station, Pol and Levi are seated in a dimly lit room. Across from them, the police sergeant's pen moves purposefully, transcribing their accounts meticulously. Pol's voice cuts through the silence, recounting the events, the tension of their recent experiences lingering in the air.

The sergeant's voice, a blend of seriousness and understanding, resonates. "Well, Miss, I can personally attest to the grim scene you've described. I was the one who discovered Wilderman's body. I've recorded your statements in full."

Levi and Pol nod, a sense of closure washing over them as their testimonies are documented. The sergeant's gaze softens, his demeanour touched with empathy. "For now, you're free to rest. But I must insist that both of you remain in Ballaarat until the Coroner's investigation concludes. Expect to be contacted for verification and further proceedings."

Levi offers gratitude tinged with exhaustion. "Thank you, Sergeant. As you suggested, we'll be staying at my mother's cottage. It's on Lydiard Street North."

Empathy lines the sergeant's expression. "That's the right path. Please extend my condolences to your mother. I'll do everything in my power to ensure her well-being."

As the interviews conclude, Levi and Pol rise from their seats. Leaving the police station's confines, they mount their horses again, riding toward Levi's mother's cottage. Amid a world of turmoil, they seek solace and shelter, the past hours etching their tale into the tapestry of Ballaarat's history.

. Chapter Ninety-Four

Levi crosses the threshold of his mother's cottage, weary from the trials that have befallen him. His gaze meets Alice, his mother, and he finds relief and emotion in her eyes. Without hesitation, she rushes towards him, arms outstretched, enfolding him tightly. Tears streamed down her cheeks, and he sensed the depth of her emotions in those tears. Her kisses rain upon him, and the warmth of her touch is a soothing balm.

"Levi, my dear boy," her voice trembles with joy and sorrow, "my heart is shattered with Bill's passing. I feared I might never see you again. Oh, my prayers have been answered... Thank you, Jesus. Thank you, God."

Emotions held in check, Levi finds solace in his mother's embrace. The weight of his recent experiences is temporarily lifted, and the comfort of his home surrounds him. But Pol, a witness to this poignant reunion, lingers on the periphery. Overwhelmed by the surging emotions in the room, she retreats to the next room, her own tears falling unbidden.

Pol's exit doesn't escape Levi's notice. As his mother continues to hold him, he excuses himself for a moment and follows Pol to the adjacent room. Alice, ever the maternal figure, trails behind, her heart guiding her to provide solace. Arms encircle them as they stand united, their shared sorrow flowing freely.

As the intensity of their emotions subsides, Levi takes a deep breath and introduces Pol to his mother. "Ma, this is a dear friend of mine who played a crucial role in rescuing me from the clutches of the gang responsible for Pa's death. Her name is Polly, but we call her Pol."

Alice's eyes softened with warmth as she extended a kind welcome. "Pol, my dear, you're most welcome here. Let's make our way to the kitchen. I'll prepare a hearty breakfast for both of you.

You look exhausted and hungry. While we eat, you can share your story with me."

Guided by Alice, they move to the kitchen, her arms still encircling them, offering a tangible embrace of support. Inside the cozy sanctuary of the cottage's kitchen, Levi and Pol take their seats at the table, weariness evident in their postures. The clinking of utensils and the aroma of food fill the air as Alice, the embodiment of maternal care, prepares breakfast for them.

Seated across from each other, Levi begins to recount the events that led to his capture and eventual rescue. Alice listens intently, her expressions shifting between sorrow and concern. "Now, Ma, you know the circumstances that compelled the Raven to become an outlaw after losing his wife and how he helped Pol evade the authorities and turned to bushranging for survival? I emerged from that ordeal unscathed, merely a tool for their future escape North and a fresh start. Mr Lynn informed the Raven about the reward.

Tinged with grief, Alice's eyes cloud with sadness as she responds, "Such a tragedy. Pol's father and Bill are both victims of the same gang. And now, justice has come to both you and Pol. It's an incredible tale, truly."

Levi's features darken as he shares another revelation. "Raven also revealed our family's history to me. I now know the identity of my birth father and how he met his end. I've learned about your own father, Jack Riley, and the torment he caused you. That very man, Jack Riley, sent those three thugs to Ballaarat. They're the ones responsible for Bill's death."

Alice's body tenses, her hands flying to her face in disbelief. She paces the room, her thoughts in turmoil. Levi steps forward, encircling her in a comforting embrace and leading her back to her seat. Alice's tears flow freely, a blend of sorrow and shock overwhelming her.

Levi and Pol exchange sympathetic glances, united in their shared history. As Alice releases her pent-up grief, a surge of determination courses through Levi. His gaze steadies, and a newfound resolve flickers in his eyes.

"Jack Riley," he murmurs, his voice a vow forged in iron. "This man has brought pain to you, Ma, and orchestrated Bill's death. His role in our family's suffering and crimes against humanity fuels my fury. The need for justice, to avenge our family's honour and cleanse the colony of this villain who has evaded consequences for far too long, is unwavering."

The room falls into a hushed silence, Levi's oath hanging like a solemn promise. As they confront the shadows of their past and the forces that have shaped their lives, a new chapter unfurls — one painted in shades of revenge and redemption forged by the unbreakable bonds of family and determination.

Chapter Ninety-Five

Levi sits in the tranquil confines of a solicitor's office, the weight that has long burdened his soul finally easing. Across from him, Mr Lynn, a man of legal knowledge and empathetic understanding, meets his gaze. The truth unveils itself, revealing a complex tapestry woven from shadows of despair and glimmers of redemption.

"Levi," Mr Lynn's voice resonates with a blend of gravity and relief, "the truth, in its entirety, comes to light. 'Curly,' also known as James Moran, the malevolent figure who cast a pall over your days, faces justice. Transported to Melbourne, he stood trial and was found guilty of three counts of murder. His destiny is sealed — the gallows of Her Majesty's Prison Pentridge await him."

Levi's eyes fixed on Mr Lynn, absorbing the weight of those words. The revelation marks a pivotal moment in their arduous journey. "Thank you, Mr Lynn," he responds, the terms carrying both gratitude and the fatigue that settled in his bones. "For your guidance, for your assistance, and for the aid of my benefactor."

A nod of understanding from Mr Lynn conveys the significance of the moment. "The circumstances dictate nothing less. But there's more. The police commissioner in Melbourne bestows upon your mother a pension, a tribute to the sacrifice your stepfather made in the line of duty. She receives one hundred pounds annually."

Levi's heart swells with pride for his mother's honour and relief at the assurance of her financial stability. Yet, his thoughts are drawn to another life claimed by duty. "And the Aboriginal tracker?" he inquires, his voice tinged with sorrow.

Regret clouds Mr Lynn's features, a flicker of sadness in his eyes. "Unfortunately, his family isn't entitled to the same pension, though they shall receive a stipend to cover the costs of a proper funeral. On a brighter note, the State Government acknowledges your role. It awards you the reward — two hundred and fifty pounds — for delivering the outlaw Raven's lifeless body, a sum to be yours whether he breathes or not."

Levi's steady and resolute gaze holds within it a determination that transcends their challenges. "Mr Lynn," he addresses, his voice unwavering, "about the tracker's family — could you, on my behalf, establish a trust fund? A yearly allocation divided from one hundred pounds of my reward. And for Pol's future, I'd like to establish another trust fund. Fifty pounds plus interest to be hers when she reaches twenty-one."

Approval and admiration gleam in Mr Lynn's eyes as he nods. "Your generosity knows no bounds, Levi. I shall draw up the necessary legal documents. Once the allocation is in place, you can place your signature upon them. Now, let's delve into the path outlined by your benefactor."

Levi's countenance shifts, his expression reflecting the depths of his contemplation. "Mr Lynn, I stand at a crossroads. The trials I've endured have left me adrift, a soul uncertain of where to direct its course. The turmoil has chiselled away at my character, and the idea of a predictable existence feels overwhelming. Restlessness plagues me, anxiety clouds my thoughts, and the future remains blurred. I sense the need for an adventure, a journey that may rekindle my sense of purpose."

A hint of concern underscores Mr Lynn's voice, a reminder of the responsibilities that await. "Levi, you must consider your mother, Pol, and the expectations of your benefactor."

Levi's gaze softens as he speaks of those who hold his heart. "My mother, dear as she is to me, deserves a life of contentment. Yet, my presence seems to deepen her own sorrow. As for Pol, our shared ordeal has forged a bond resembling that of siblings, built on mutual affection and understanding.

The conversation pivots, centring on Levi's benefactor. Mr Lynn poses a query of significance. "And what of your patron's hopes and aspirations? Consider the support he's extended."

Levi's response rings with resolute determination. "Should I regain the strength that once defined me, my benefactor's trust will be repaid. By retaining some of my reward — one hundred pounds — I release him from future financial obligations. My plan revolves around investing this sum in Melbourne in an enterprise of my own choosing. I aspire to evolve into a self-made man, a gentleman of honour who can proudly return to Ballaarat."

Mr Lynn's approval glimmers in his gaze, acknowledging the wisdom woven into Levi's choices. "Levi, if you seek guidance, I'd advise you to heed your instincts. Your intentions resonate with determination and an authentic desire for personal growth. I wish you the utmost success as you embark on this new path."

With a heartfelt nod, Levi conveys his appreciation for Mr Lynn's counsel. He has renewed purpose as he departs the solicitor's office. The journey ahead remains uncertain, yet his resolve blazes like a beacon, ready to shape his destiny anew.

Amidst the confines of Mr Crockett's tent business, Levi stands, enveloped by a sense of familiarity tinged with time. The interior bears witness to the ebb and flow of days since Levi's departure from his apprenticeship to attend the Melbourne Learning Academy. The once vibrant shop now mirrors the struggle of its owner, Mr Crockett, whose greying hair reflects the toll he faces.

"It's been a comfort to have you back, Levi," Mr Crockett's voice blends nostalgia and warmth, "even if it's been a fleeting visit since your return to Ballaarat. Opting for education over continuing your apprenticeship was undoubtedly the right choice. The tent business has weathered hardships since the alluvial gold's decline. Miners have shifted to cottages and huts, toiling in the vast underground mines."

Levi listens intently, absorbing the weight of Mr Crockett's words. "I'm truly grateful for the work you've offered me when I needed it most, Mr Crockett. Your kindness means the world to me."

A wistful note colours Mr Crockett's voice. "And having you here has been a joy. So, you're Melbourne-bound tomorrow, ready to leave your mark on the world. Best of luck to you! If only I were a few decades younger, I'd join you in seeking new horizons. Where do you plan to stay? The city has transformed beyond recognition."

Levi's eyes sparkle with enthusiasm as he shares his plans. "I've heard that the newly revamped Criterion Hotel on the southern end of Collins Street is the place to be. Constructed by Americans Samuel Moss and Charles Wedel in 1853, it boasts three stories, 28 bedrooms, bars, dining rooms, a billiard saloon, a bathhouse, a hairdresser, even a bowling saloon, and a vaudeville theatre at the rear. Rumour has it the bridal suite is adorned with amber satin sheets."

Amusement dances in Mr Crockett's eyes, tickled by the notion of extravagance. "Sounds quite posh and possibly a bit lavish. Then again, with that reward money you've got, it's no surprise the allure is strong."

Levi's smile holds a hint of playful mischief. "Indeed, it promises a haven for rest, a space to tend to my physical and mental well-being. After the recent trials, I need recovery from the exhaustion that's taken hold. A sanctuary where personal comfort takes precedence over constant hustle and social commitments."

Empathy softens Mr Crockett's expression. "No one, not even your mother, would begrudge you the chance for well-deserved respite following the tribulations you've faced. Take care of yourself, shape your path, and when next we meet, 'Sir' might be the fitting address."

Levi's laughter rings out, a testament to the bond they share. "Your unwavering faith and support mean much to me, Mr Crockett. I'll carry your words with me as I step into this new chapter of my life. Pol will now be under Ma's care and free of the Aboriginal Protectorate's clutches. "

Levi leaves the tent shop with gratitude, warming his heart. The threads that bind him to his past, those who have left an indelible mark on his journey, remain steadfast. As he readies himself for the city's embrace, his determination is fortified by the enduring friendship he carries forward.

Chapter Ninety-Six

Levi emerges from the rickety cab, greeted by the towering presence of the magnificent Criterion Hotel. The sheer grandeur of the building steals his breath, leaving him momentarily speechless. Levi's gaze ascends as the cab driver awaits payment, fixated on nine rectangular windows graced with delicate balconies on all the upper floors.

A knowing smile graces the cab driver's lips, a silent camaraderie between them. "Welcome to the Criterion Hotel, sir. A testament to the spirit and prosperity of the immigrant community. It encapsulates the essence of the city's vibrancy—a remarkable landmark in its own right."

Levi's nod expresses his gratitude, yet his gaze remains captivated by the architectural masterpiece before him. "Undoubtedly, it's a splendid building."

Tipping his hat, the cab driver imparts his well-wishes. "May you find joy in your stay, sir. Melbourne has much to offer."

Levi reciprocates the gesture, and his appreciation is evident. "Thank you, my good man."

With that, the cab departs, leaving Levi standing before the imposing entrance of the hotel. As he steps through the grand front portico, his fingers lightly brush the brim of his Fedora hat, acknowledging the magnificence surrounding him.

Within the embrace of the Criterion Hotel, Levi's days become a mosaic of experiences, each etched into his memory with vivid clarity: Levi immerses himself in the embrace of the luxurious bathhouse. The water cradles his form as he moves with fluid grace, his cares dissolving with each stroke. Lying on his back, he gazes at the mosaic ceiling, momentarily weightless—a respite from life's relentless demands.

Dressed in his finest attire, Levi stands amidst the vibrant buzz of the bustling bar. The clinking of glasses and jovial laughter envelop him. With a celebratory cheer, fellow patrons raise their glasses, encouraging him to partake. Levi's generous spirit has become a beacon for patrons at the bar, who cunningly encourage his drinking while savouring the fruits of his unwitting benevolence. Levi obliges with the cool touch of beer, a balm for his restless soul and recent addictions.

The billiards room resounds with the clack of balls as Levi engages in a strategic betting duel. Across the felt table, a formidable adversary awaits, each shot a calculated move. The tension builds, culminating in a decisive strike that sinks the winning shot. Levi acknowledges his opponent's victory with a gracious nod—another lesson within the losses of his developed gambling obsession.

Levi once again succumbs to the thrill of chance in the horse betting room. Amid the excitement of fellow bettors, he holds a ticket—a tangible connection to hope and uncertainty. The cashier's solemn expression shatters his hopes, delivering the verdict of defeat. In a gesture of frustration, Levi crumples the ticket, the weight of disappointment palpable in his hand.

Time marches forward six months, casting a shadow over the initial allure of the hotel, signalling a shift in Levi's journey. Once a picture of refinement, Levi slouches at the edge of the Criterion's bar. His appearance has faded, a reflection of the turmoil within. Dishevelled and weary, his once-impeccable attire mirrors the internal disarray.

The barman, a symbol of authority, attends to a spillage of Levi's making, their interaction a familiar dance. "It's time to call it a night, mate. You've had your share. It's time to head home."

Levi's response bears a note of bitterness, an echo of his inner struggles. "Don't presume to dictate my limits, you wretched scoundrel! I'll tear you apart like a rabid dog!"

Unfazed, the barman sets the boundaries. "Your tabs run dry at this establishment. From now on, it's cash only. If that doesn't suit you, the streets are your next stop. Clear?"

Levi's anger simmers, his restraint fraying. "You're all thieves, robbing me blind. I ought to summon the police to expose your worthless schemes!"

With a shaky motion, Levi pushes himself away from the bar, his equilibrium compromised. He stumbles onto Collins Street, his vision blurred by the fog of intoxication. A dim torch lamp illuminates an alleyway, casting an enticing aura. A sign above an entrance reads **'Riley's Palace.'** Fueled by intoxication and disillusionment, Levi stumbles forward.

Within the dimly lit sly grog premises, the air is thick with smoke, shrouding the scene in mystery. Curiosity and amusement dance in the eyes of the patrons as Levi enters. Two bar girls, their attire provocative, exchange a knowing glance as Levi crosses the threshold.

One of the bar girls greets him with a sultry smile. "Well, hello there, big boy. Care to buy a thirsty girl a drink?"

Levi's gaze, clouded by intoxication, lingers on the woman's revealing attire. His words emerge with a slurred cadence, guided by impulse and desire. "I don't recall seeing you here before. I'll buy you a drink only if you're generous with your time afterwards."

The bar girl's response carries a playful undercurrent laden with innuendo. "Generosity depends on your means, handsome one."

Levi produces a crumpled note from his pocket—a display of financial means presented with a flicker of arrogance. The scene unfolds, depicting Levi's descent into a realm where shadows thrive and temptation takes root.

Chapter Ninety-Seven

Levi's footsteps resonate through the narrow alleyway, each step a testament to his determination as he clutches a black bottle of whiskey concealed within his coat pocket. His path is purposeful as he pauses to collect several small wooden crates in the alley. Emerging from its shadows, he steps onto the dimly lit street, his intent clear.

The uneven pavement guides his shuffling steps, leading him to the entrance of a weathered boarding house. The moon's soft glow spills through a small window, casting a melancholic ambience over the interior. Levi ascends the creaky, narrow wooden staircase with resolute purpose, his presence almost ethereal as he leans against the bannister rail, allowing a rough-looking stranger to pass, followed closely by a woman of the night.

The faint moonlight pierces the darkness within his dim and frigid room, illuminating the modest furnishings. A small grated fireplace, a single bed, a humble bedside tea crate, and a worn wooden trunk holding his sparse possessions define the space's simplicity.

Levi's purpose remains unswayed as he breaks the wooden crates into fragments, meticulously arranging the pieces within the fireplace. With scraps of newspaper as kindling, he ignites a feeble fire. The room bathes in its soft, flickering light, accompanied by a faint warmth. Seating on the bed's edge, he takes deep swigs from the whiskey bottle before setting it aside. A shiver traverses his frame as he wraps his arms around himself, lying back on the bed, still fully clothed, even down to his boots. Drawing the solitary blanket up to his neck, he seeks refuge from the relentless cold.

The scene shifts, morning's gentle light filtering through the window, coaxing Levi from his slumber. He sits up, his head heavy from the remnants of a lingering hangover. His gaze falls upon a small medicinal bottle labelled "Laudanum – (tincture of Opium)," resting on the tea crate beside him. Raising the bottle to his lips, he takes a prolonged swig, the sound of his lips parting echoing in the room. He shakes his head, attempting to dispel the lingering effects of his indulgence. Advancing toward a small oval mirror suspended from a nail, he confronts his dishevelled reflection. Unkempt hair, scruffy, unshaven facial hair, and blemishes that mar his once-clear complexion stare back at him, starkly contrasting the image he once presented.

Speaking to his own reflection, his voice carries an undercurrent of introspection. *"I find myself ensnared within Jack Riley's vindictive web, entangled in the consequences that have cast a shadow upon my family. My vulnerabilities and the lack of restraint over my impulses weigh heavily upon my conscience. Months have drifted away, yet I remain melancholy, unable to discern a purpose or path toward change. Shame devours me, knowing I've disappointed those who once believed in me. My existence descends into degradation, bereft of immediate prospects for redemption. I dare not burden Ma or Mr Lynn with the weight of my sorrows, fearing their disappointment and the depths of my downfall, brought about by squandering my fortune to the precipice."*

Overwhelmed by emotion, Levi wrenches the mirror from its position, hurling it against the wall with a shattering sound that mirrors the tumultuous storm within. He stumbles back toward the bed, his head hanging in a mixture of weariness and turmoil.

Collapsing onto its edge, he shields his face with his hands, a portrait of a soul in a fierce struggle with its inner demons.

Caught within his addictions' relentless grip, Levi steps from the alleyway into a known opium den with an unrelenting need for relief. The space is dimly lit, permeated by the caustic scent of lye soap and steam that weaves a hazy atmosphere around its occupants.

He navigates past Chinese workers tending to their laundry tasks at the front of the shop, their curious gazes tracing his movements. Ignoring their glances, he continues toward the back of the establishment, where a sign bearing the words "AH LING CHINESE LAUNDRY" designates the ownership. Descending the stairs, Levi seeks solace in the embrace of the hidden opium den.

Within the basement's crowded expanse, Levi reclines on a divan, taking his place next to an elderly sailor in uniform. The basement is a tapestry of closely positioned couches, each occupied by various male patrons. Ah Ling, the overseer, moves amongst them, distributing long-stemmed wooden pipes adorned with brass cones.

Skillfully, Ah Ling fills the cones from his opium mixture, employing a thimble and a small horned spoon. Levi and the old sailor share an opium lamp, igniting the contents within a pipe and inhaling the intoxicating vapours with a shared purpose. Levi takes successive draws, the intoxicating smoke filling his lungs to capacity.

As the opium's effects take hold, Levi's senses are momentarily overwhelmed. A surge of euphoria cascades through his mind, rendering him momentarily breathless. The sedative properties of the drug offer a fleeting respite from his physical and emotional anguish. A tranquil smile graces his features as he surrenders to the drug's numbing embrace. Levi is fading into the darkness of an opium-induced dream sequence. He enters this realm, guided by the intoxicating influence of the drug. Soaring within an out-of-body experience, he is immersed in a tapestry of sweet dreams and memories of simpler times.

In this dreamscape, he perceives the presence of those he cherishes, their energy taking form as ethereal rays of sunlight that envelop him in a sense of serenity. His mother and Pol materialize before him, their gestures radiating love and forgiveness, beckoning him to return to the warmth of their embrace.

Within this enchanting realm, all transgressions are forgiven, and the burdens he has carried become inconsequential. Levi glides through this ethereal landscape, a smile of liberation gracing his lips, his worries dissolving in the wind. The dream sequence then fades to black, relinquishing its hold on Levi's consciousness.

As time grips his consciousness, Levi emerges from Ah Ling's laundry, his state of mind altered and his movements erratic. He navigates the laneway in haste, his steps faltering and unsteady. As Levi ascends the stairs of his boarding house, it becomes his refuge, his grasp on the bannister a lifeline. In his haste, he stumbles as if pursued by an unseen force, his fear tangible in his frantic glances over his shoulder.

Finally reaching his room, Levi fumbles to unlock the door. Anxiety courses him as he surveys the space, seeking signs of danger. He stumbles within, his body collapsing onto the bed. His mouth hangs agape, and his expression is vacant and stupefied. Gradually, his eyelids droop, succumbing to the overwhelming aftereffects of the opium.

Hours pass, and Levi gradually stirs from his drug-induced stupor. His body is drenched in sweat, trembling from the ordeal. A wave of panic washes over him as he sits up, his mind grappling with the stark reality of his situation.

Levi addresses himself hushedly, his words reflecting his inner turmoil. *"It feels as if I've been plunged into the depths of hell itself...*

consumed by feverish torment. The haze of opium lifts, revealing the agony and suffering I've inflicted upon myself. I stand as but a hollow shell, lost in the depths of self-loathing. Salvation appears unreachable, a fleeting mirage. The abyss of degradation I've descended seems unending, forgiveness and redemption mere illusions. I am left to confront my conceived fate, forever ensnared in the clutches of darkness – the very Devil himself!"

Levi paces the room, his movements becoming increasingly desperate. He tears at his clothes, discarding his coat and shirt until he stands exposed, his chest bared. An internal voice, sinister in its origin, tightens its grip on his thoughts, leading him further into the shadows of his own mind.

This internal voice becomes more pronounced as Levi's desperation deepens, urging him toward a precipice he dares not acknowledge. *"This darkness, this force that haunts my mind, beckons me to end my own life — to seek peace and, in doing so, to erase the memory and legacy of Jack Riley, the tormentor of my family. To cleanse the rot that has seeped into the heart of Melbourne Town. If I perish, let Jack Riley perish with me so that my death might bear a purpose beyond my own demise."*

Levi's mind teeters on the edge of a precipice, the weight of his struggles and temptations pulling him closer to the abyss of his darkest thoughts.

Chapter Ninety-Eight

The darkness of the night wraps around Levi like a shroud as he arrives at Swanston Street, a reluctant visitor to the realm of his demons. A chilling sense of purpose guides his steps, an inner darkness that seems to take the reins of his actions.

The grand stone mansion before him stands as a monument to his intentions, its imposing presence mirroring the weight of his mission. Yet, there's an additional weight carried within him, the heaviness of alcohol coursing through his veins, emboldening his resolve.

Concealed beneath his jacket, his fingers curl around the hilt of a hunting knife, its cold presence a reminder of the sinister task that awaits him. With steps unsteady, Levi navigates the sprawling driveway, his eyes drawn to the warm flicker of candlelight spilling from a window. Despite the haze of intoxication, he moves with a semblance of stealth, his determination fueled by a potent cocktail of anger and fear.

Through a window, curtains slightly parted, Levi's gaze lands on a figure that confirms his location. Jack Riley, a stout, older man, is absorbed in the pages of a manuscript. Levi's heart pounds, the moment charged with a gravity he can't ignore. He prowls along the mansion's perimeter, a predator sizing up its prey, searching for a chink in the armour. A creaking sound guides him to a back door, and his attention is drawn to an older woman with a candle moving toward an outdoor privy.

Levi seizes the fleeting opportunity, slipping into the mansion with calculated precision. The hallway is a corridor of shadows, and he maneuvers through it like a spectre. A guiding thread of dim light leads him to a closed door, its edges emanating a faint glow. With a surge of resolve, he thrusts the door open, stumbling into the room like a storm breaking through a barrier. Jack Riley startles, papers tumbling from his grip in a cascade of surprises.

The words escaping Levi's lips are a venomous echo, slurred but menacing. "Open that drawer... and you'll meet your end, Riley." The knife he brandishes dances in the air, a deadly waltz between them. But Riley's reaction is a puzzle, an enigmatic amusement that speaks of experience. His calm and measured response weaves a different thread into the narrative.

"Now, lad, what has prompted you to seek harm upon Old Jack Riley?" Riley's voice possesses the cadence of a seasoned negotiator, a maestro of conversation. "I'm open to hearing your grievances and finding a path to amends, like true gentlemen." The words hang in the air, suggesting there might be more beneath the surface than Levi's quest for vengeance.

Levi's voice is a torrent of emotion, fueled by a fire smouldering for years. "What you've done, you cur... it cannot be undone... because it includes murder! You're a bastard with blood on your hands!" The room trembles with the weight of his accusation, his voice a blade slicing through the tension.

Riley's demeanour remains inscrutable, his grin an enigma. "What murders are you accusing me of, lad? To lay such charges at the feet of Old Jack Riley!" His voice resonates with a quality that suggests a hidden truth, a revelation waiting to be unearthed.

Levi's voice trembles with fury and pain, a torrent of emotions he can no longer contain. "You know perfectly well the murders I speak of, you despicable, murderous scoundrel! The deaths of my father... and stepfather - Dan Farley... and Bill Brody." The room seems to close around him, a claustrophobic confinement where secrets and resentments collide.

The charged atmosphere shifts abruptly, shattered by a voice that pierces the tension like a blade. A hoarse voice from the open doorway, a harbinger of a reckoning. "PUT YOUR HANDS UP!

I'VE GOT A GUN — DROP THAT KNIFE!" Levi's instincts kick in, and the knife clatters to the floor, relinquishing power in the face of a new threat.

From the doorway, a male figure steps forward, scooping up the knife and positioning himself protectively before an older female figure who gazes at Levi with curiosity and concern. Riley's voice slices through the moment, a conductor restoring order to a chaotic symphony.

"Thank you, Bernie and Cloherty. You are both dismissed to return to your quarters. I will take charge of Master Levi Brody from here. Please close the door behind you."

The figures retreat behind the door, leaving Levi and Riley in a charged silence. The weight of Levi's impulsive actions settles like a leaden shroud around him. The room is a theatre of shadows, reflecting the murky truths brought to light.

As the door closed, Levi stood in that dim room, the gravity of the situation pressing down on him. The revelations from Riley's lips hang in the air, a tangled web of truths and lies that threaten to suffocate him. Riley's voice breaks the silence, a calm amidst the storm.

"I would offer you a port, Levi, but it seems you've already indulged," Riley's words are almost casual, a veneer of normalcy stretched thin over the circumstances. He pours a glass of port, the liquid's rich hue contrasting with the heavy air. "Now, where were we before we were rudely interrupted? Ah, yes, you were asking me why I did what I did."

Levi's gaze remains fixed on Riley, a maelstrom of emotions swirling beneath the surface. The room feels like a steaming boiler, the walls closing in around him as he grapples with the enormity of the situation.

Riley's voice is a thread in the silence, guiding the narrative forward. "Your father, Dan Farley, raped my only daughter of her innocence, the love of my life, my precious child," Riley's words are etched with bitterness, the scars of old wounds still vivid. "She became pregnant, and he coerced her into running away, promising marriage. But things didn't turn out quite as planned."

Levi's eyes narrowed as the pieces of a puzzle he never knew existed started to fall into place. "When I sent someone to inquire about her well-being, Dan Farley committed murder — they hanged him. Nothing to do with me," Riley's tone is matter-of-fact, a recitation of events that shaped their intertwined fates. "You've been misled or wouldn't be here accusing me. As for Sergeant Brody, he was killed by rogue employees of mine who have met their own demise."

Levi's voice trembles, a fragile whisper carrying disbelief and anger. "I know better." He lifts his gaze momentarily, locking eyes with Riley, a charged exchange that speaks volumes in the silence. Then, his head drops again, overwhelmed by a nauseating sensation that washes over him like a tide of uncertainty.

Riley's voice weaves through the heavy air, a blend of remorse and confidence. "Levi, my boy, I had high hopes for you. I've lost my only daughter's company to her own disgrace and my wife to a broken heart over her loss," Riley's words are imbued with a genuine sorrow that lingers in the room. "Don't you think that as a lonely old man with time on my hands, I don't suffer from the shame of what I've lost due to my pride? I come from the same roots as you. I clawed up from the gutter and fought against those who tried to hold me down.

Levi's voice trembles and slurs – "I don't give a damn!"

"Then, my lad, you came along, and I followed your journey. You showed me that you have the Riley blood in your veins. You didn't cower to anyone; you stood up for yourself with the Diggers at the Eureka Stockade. You were there to help them, just a lad behaving like a man. Oh, I was so proud of you, and I knew then that you had the potential to be something I never was. Unspoiled, fair in your dealings, with the intelligence for good without my stupidity and arrogance. Lad, I am your Sponsor – the Benefactor you dreamed about!"

Levi's voice cuts through the thick tension in the room, a blend of defiance and resentment lacing his words. "I don't care if you were my sponsor. I would never have accepted your offer if I knew where it came from. If I kill you, I'll do the town and our family a favour. Nobody will hang me except me, which I fully intend to do after taking care of you! Now I know why my life is tainted. My blood is stained by you, leading me to this wretched fate. I can never live a normal life. The world will be better off without the Two of Us!"

In response, Riley's words are measured, his tone hinting at detachment. "Is that so? Destiny has brought you to my door, lad, and it seems to have altered all my immediate plans. You can hang yourself after I'm finished with you, for all I care. I'll depart from this world with a clear conscience."

Chapter Ninety-Nine

The room closes in, its walls pressing on Levi from all sides. The heaviness in the air mirrors the weight of Riley's words, the revolver on the desk glistening ominously in the dim light, a potent reminder of the fateful crossroads that now confronts Levi. Riley's voice slices through the silence, unravelling the intricate threads of his audacious plan.

"I was contemplating suicide just before you entered after reading this latest mining report," Riley's words reverberate with a mixture of despondency and resignation, offering a fleeting glimpse into the depths of his despair. "It informs me that I've lost all my accumulated wealth in a gold mining venture at the East Ballaarat gravel pits. I invested every penny and convinced every nobleman and his dog in Melbourne to take shares in the venture. But it's all over, lad. The goldmine turned out to be a dud. All gone in a month producing just five bars of gold."

Riley's movements are precise, his actions deliberate as he retrieves a bag from the floor and sets it on the desk, unveiling the glint of five gold bars. Levi's eyes oscillate between the bars of gold and Riley's countenance, grappling with fathoming the enormity of the revelation.

"Yes, it's over. I may still have my criminal interests, but they're all dead too," Riley's voice carries an amalgam of bitterness and reluctant acceptance. "Dead like me. Shot to pieces without the safety net of protection I've worked hard to establish over twenty-five years."

Levi's heart drums in his chest, an unrelenting rhythm that echoes Riley's words, painting a grim tableau of a crumbling empire and the impending fall of a once-almighty figure.

"Supreme Court judges, lawyers, the police commissioner, government officials — they'll all be baying for my blood when they hear the news," Riley's voice assumes a resigned tone, each syllable laden with the weight of an impending reckoning. "Everything I've built now sinks into the depths like a stinking privy once the investors discover their losses in the morning."

Levi's inner turmoil momentarily takes a back seat as Riley's world unravels before him, the looming spectre of a reckoning casting its dark shadow.

"My strength came from my power, and without it, I am weak, reduced to nothing," Riley's words are imbued with a palpable desperation, the sound of a man grappling with the loss of his dominion. "To regain that power, I'll take away their control over me. I'll take my own life with my own hands and leave them empty-handed."

As Riley dabs his face with a handkerchief, Levi's thoughts whirl, a chaotic storm inside his mind. The room seems to tilt and spin around him, and he's abruptly yanked into sobriety by the sudden focus of Riley's words.

"Now that you are here, Levi, my plan has changed somewhat," Riley's voice is measured, his gaze piercing as it locks onto Levi. "The revelations I shared were meant to set things right before I departed. However, your presence signifies a departure from honour. You stand poised to take my life, devoid of gratitude for my past benevolence."

Levi's inner turmoil clashes with the bizarre proposition that Riley is lying before him. The man's words are surreal, like a game with deadly stakes.

"In this world of dog-eat-dog and hunters and gatherers — the Rileys were born to hunt to eat... or die trying, and we don't eat Dog but feed it to the Hungry!" Riley's words combine irony and madness, reflecting a mind pushed to the edge. "It's in our Blood. We are gambling men, Levi — *The Risk Takers In Life*."

Riley's gaze bores into Levi's, demanding his attention, his comprehension. "Now I'm offering you a Life Choice at the throw of a penny," Riley's voice is eerily calm, the offer bizarre in its audacity. "With the toss of this penny as Heads, I will walk to that door, call on my servant Bernie, and have him escort you to the front door."

Levi's mind races as he tries to grasp the gravity of Riley's proposition. The choices presented to him are beyond anything he could have anticipated.

"After you leave, I will depart this world by this gun, and you are free to go about your business or death as you please," Riley's words are chilling, the finality of his statement hanging in the air. "However, if that penny lands on Tails, I will lock that door, and you will exit via the office window with this bag of gold and a note with the address to a good friend named Fred Bailey."

Levi's mind reels, his heart pounding in his chest as he grapples with the implications of what Riley is proposing.

"Bailey, for a gold bar, will smuggle you onto a boat to wherever you choose," Riley's voice carries a note of urgency. "Once you have sufficient time to make a run from here, I will take my life as planned, and You, My Boy, become labelled my Executioner, and not only do I achieve the power over my fate in death but your future as well!

Levi's voice is a mixture of disbelief and incredulity as he responds, "You are Mad! Why would I attempt such a gamble and play your silly game?"

Riley's grip on the revolver tightens as he responds, his voice carrying a chilling resolve. "Because, my lad, you came here prepared to die, anyway, and take my life, which I will facilitate myself. I will shoot you down here and now if you don't oblige."

The room seems to close around Levi, the weight of the moment pressing down on him like a vice. The revolver barrel points directly at him, a stark reminder of the life-and-death gamble he is being forced to take.

"It will look like you took my life in a struggle as a murder-suicide with my servant Bernie, a witness to your desire," Riley's words hang in the air, the reality of the situation sinking in. "So, there are now three options on the table. One that means you die right here and now. To be clear and set your mind — Head you walk to the front door, a free man — Tails you leave by the window an accused murderer. What's it to be?"

Levi's mind races, his thoughts a whirlwind of fear, anger, and desperation. The choices before him are impossible, each with horror and consequences. As the room pulses with the weight of his decision, Levi realizes that the game before him is not just about life and death—it's a gamble with the essence of his existence.

Levi's mind stretches like a sombre expanse, more sober and transparent than it has been for days. The weight of his choices is an oppressive burden, leaving little room for contemplation or hesitation.

"I'll take that gamble," Levi's voice cuts through the heavy air, a fusion of determination and resignation echoing in the room.

Riley seizes a writing pad, pens a note, and slips it into the bag alongside the gold. His movements are deliberate and purposeful. Retrieving a penny from his desk, he rises from his seat. With a flick of his thumb, the penny takes flight, a slow-motion dance in the air. It bounces gracefully before finally settling — 'Tails Up'. Riley strides over to the door, locking it, still holding the revolver. He then stations himself by the window behind his desk, pushing it open to the night breeze.

"Levi, it's a pity that circumstances have unfolded in this manner for both of us," Riley's voice carries a hint of melancholy, the weight of their intertwined destinies palpable in the atmosphere. "We've played The Game of Life, taking our chances on the spin of a coin. And now, the time has come to reconcile our accounts and bid our farewells. May fortune favour your path, whatever it may lead."

A pause lingers, a moment of shared intensity as Riley's gaze pierces into Levi's eyes. A fleeting glimmer of emotion dances in Riley's irises before he smiles, a smile that seems to hold a lifetime of stories.

Without further words or wasted breath, Levi seizes the bag and hurls it out the window, his body following suit. Fueled by determination and alcohol, he hurtles himself down the driveway, the bag of gold clutched tightly in his hand. The world becomes a blur around him, a cascade of colours and sensations melding into a single, chaotic symphony.

As he reaches the midpoint of the driveway, he can't help but cast a backward glance at the illuminated window, which has played witness to the most crucial moments of his life. A flash of light pierces the night in a heartbeat, followed by the distant yet unmistakable sound of a gunshot. The scene blurs and fades, leaving the outcome in an uncertain void.

Chapter One-hundred

Levi stumbles away from Riley's imposing mansion, his steps unsteady and his mind a tempest of confusion. He follows the path back to the heart of his own dark realm, thoughts colliding within his head like a cacophony of clashing waves. The calico bag, now heavy with the weight of gold, becomes both a physical burden and a metaphor for the tangled mess he's found himself in.

As he enters the boarding house, the ascending occupants on the staircase eye him suspiciously, their intentions far from benign. The atmosphere is thick with malevolence as he ascends the dimly lit stairwell, each step a reminder of the treacherous journey he's embarked upon.

Inside his small, meagre room, Levi collapses onto his bed. Exhaustion and sorrow wash over him in relentless waves, each crashing into him with an unrelenting force. His mind reeling like the dark reveries of a daydream, *"The chance to end my suffering, to rid the world of that wretched Jack Riley by my own hand, has been cruelly snatched away by the whims of fate,"*

Levi's voice is a mere murmur, his words heavy with the bitterness of his circumstances. *"Now I bear the weight of a murderer's label, even though I know the town would see my actions as a strike for my family's honour, an attempt to cleanse Melbourne Town of its darkest stain. Survival is my sole path forward, fraught with moral complexities and the relentless pounding ache in my head. The outcome must be set right. Despite the false accusation, I must find a way to escape the clutches of the law. This gold, this tainted treasure, becomes my ticket to freedom."*

With a trembling hand, Levi reaches into the bag, withdrawing the note Riley had written for his associate, Fred Bailey. He reads the words silently, the ink etching a promise onto his consciousness:

"Dear Fred,

Should a letter arrive, penned by my hand from my grandson Levi Brody, I implore you, as my trusted business associate, to assist the lad in boarding a boat to his chosen destination without hesitation. In return, he will provide you with a pound-weighted bar of gold. Farewell, my old friend — ***Jack Riley***."

Levi's weariness wraps around him like a heavy shroud as he succumbs to the embrace of sleep on his bed, his consciousness slipping into oblivion. When he awakens, his body trembles and a disquieting sensation ripples. Without conscious thought, he scratches at his arms and chest, desperate to soothe the torment of his withdrawal from the unrelenting ache for liquor and opium.

"Nausea and withdrawal, my constant companions," Levi's voice is a mixture of self-loathing and despair, a whisper to the empty room. *"The price of my reliance on liquor and opium. A craving simmers within me, a yearning for a dose to quiet both body and mind. But time is a luxury I cannot indulge in. The hours I spent in slumber mean the city's constables are likely combing the streets in search of the presumed murderer of Jack Riley. It won't be long before their relentless pursuit leads them to my doorstep, to the sanctuary I call my own."*

Levi's reflection in a hand mirror reveals the turmoil he wrestles with — a visage gaunt, clothes dishevelled, burdened by the weight of the bag of gold he clutches. Urgency propels him as he abandons his room, descending the staircase with unsteady steps. His destination is the exit door, and he emerges into the daylight, squinting against the harsh brilliance of the rising sun.

Through winding shadows and dingy alleyways, Levi moves with caution, each footfall a testament to his unwavering determination. He follows the address penned in Riley's note, a path that guides him to a dilapidated house on Market Lane. This forgotten passageway links Bourke Street to the heart of Chinatown, its history etched into every brick. Amidst the decay, a solid red door with a lion-head knocker demands attention, a beacon against the backdrop of neglect. Levi's knock is forceful, reflecting his eagerness to pierce the veil of uncertainty.

A small opening materializes in the door, a fragment of light casting a shadow as a voice emerges from within — harsh, vigilant. "Who is it? State your purpose," the voice demands, scepticism woven into its tones.

"I come bearing the message of Jack Riley!" Levi's words tumble out breathlessly, urgency lacing every syllable. "I am in dire need of a conversation with Fred Bailey!"

"What matter compels this urgency?" The voice's scepticism remains wariness in its cadence.

"Murder... and the pursuit of an escape!" Levi's response crackles with the intensity of his purpose, his heart racing in synchrony with his words.

"Stay right where you are!" The command cuts through the air, and the aperture snaps shut. Time hangs suspended, the seconds stretched thin with anticipation. Finally, the door creaks open, welcoming Levi into a dimly lit expanse. Cold stone floors bear witness to the lingering scent of tobacco, a testament to years gone by. The room's colonial origins echo through raw-sawn planks and vintage charm.

An old man, his grey hair cascading like a waterfall of memories, acknowledges Levi's arrival with a fleeting glimpse of a wicked countenance. The man guides Levi through a dim passageway, and they step into a semi-lit parlour. Here, a smoking oil lamp casts a soft, eerie glow, dancing upon antique furniture that tells stories of epochs past. A gilded birdcage, home to a vibrant Corella, adds to the tapestry of oddities that fill the room.

Seated in an armchair, a man of Continental European heritage gazes at Levi with an air of quiet authority. His attire carries an undertone of sophistication that contrasts with the surroundings. His intense scrutiny feels like a probing touch, and a curved briar-smoking pipe rests between his teeth.

"Good day to you, Sir," Levi offers with respect.

The man's response is a mixture of sarcasm and calculation. "What goodness can this day claim? Especially considering your circumstances. Are you a fool or merely attempting to be cordial?"

Levi humbles himself, his voice laced with respect. "Cordial, Sir. I carry a note from Jack Riley and a gold bar, hoping to seek your assistance."

As Levi hands over the note, Bailey's fingers trace its contents, his muttered words enigmatic. Bailey's gaze shifts to Levi, dissecting him with an intensity that borders on invasive.

"How many hours have passed since your 'atrocity'?" Bailey's question is probing and assessing.

"Since last night, after midnight... before dawn," Levi responds urgently. "I've been framed. Riley's life ended by his hand, yet I'm unjustly branded as his executioner."

Bailey nods, processing the information. "Very well. Ten hours have slipped through the hourglass, giving the constabulary a considerable head start in broad daylight. Meanwhile, you roam the streets, a pawn in your own folly. Do you possess a plan, or is your mind equally barren?"

Levi's response carries a determined edge. "I have a destination — the Swan River Colony in Western Australia. A haven where the troopers' reach might falter, granting me the time to secure passage to England or, perhaps, India."

The stakes are high, and Levi's destiny hangs in the balance. A high-stakes game unfolds, where he must gamble with everything he holds dear, hoping the odds will finally be in his favour.

Chapter One-Hundred-One

Bailey's dismissive snort greets the notion of heading West. "Humph! Most 'Perishers' head North to the new colony of Queensland, where a man can truly vanish and meet his demise, both in name and body, if he's not careful. Heading West is a foolish game. While it may be isolated from the rest of civilization, you'll find yourself locked in a tight-knit and curious community with limited options until you secure passage on a westward-bound ship."

Levi's determination stands unwavering. "I don't care; I'll take my chances! My mind's made up!"

Bailey concedes, his expression resigned. "Very well then. Old Alby here will run an errand for you and find a shipmaster heading towards that direction, willing to turn a blind eye in exchange for another gold bar; I assume you carry one in that bag, judging by its weight."

Levi confirms his possession. "Yes, I've another one-pound bar, weighing fourteen troy ounces and worth over forty-two quid. With that, I could purchase a hut and some land!"

Bailey's words ground Levi in reality. "Not in this town, you can't. Unless you want to end up with a noose around your neck. It'll take another gold bar, and consider yourself fortunate that Riley had the foresight to send you to old Fred Bailey. I was once his business associate and clever enough Not to invest in his so-called 'Sure Thing' mining venture. As the only honourable man left in Melbourne Town without a grudge against him, I'll do right by you out of respect for our past association with Riley. You'll need to stay here until Alby has completed the arrangements."

The weight of the situation descends upon Levi, and though the price is steep, he nods in reluctant agreement. Bailey observes Levi's response with a piercing gaze. "I'll have Alby prepare a tub of hot water for you and find some decent clothes. We may not be fancy around here, but judging by your appearance and odour, you've been living under far worse conditions."

Levi stands at Bailey's doorstep, flanked by Bailey and old Alby. "Alby has secured a booking for you aboard the sleek passenger liner 'SS Great Britain,'" Bailey reveals, respect evident in his tone. "A three-mast auxiliary steamer with an iron hull and the power of steam when the wind proves stubborn. He's ensured your cabin is fully equipped and your meals served discreetly, safeguarding your anonymity. Onboard, you shall go by John (Johnny) Cartwright."

Levi expresses his gratitude, his voice sincere. "I am deeply grateful to both of you. Your assistance means a great deal to me."

Bailey's practicality remains unwavering. "Alby has also readied two carpetbags for you to bring along. They hold secondhand clothing of a humbler class sourced from a curiosity shop. This way, you won't draw needless attention parading in the latest fashion. Farewell, and may luck shine upon your endeavours."

With his destiny sealed and course set, Levi is escorted to the docks in a handsome cab; the driver behind him protects Levi's identity. Levi carries two carpetbags onto the shipping port, guided by old Alby's instructions. Approaching the Purser, stationed like a guardian on the gangplank, Levi's heart races with anticipation. Alby delivers a note and exchanges hushed words, veiling the specifics from Levi.

The Purser's keen scrutiny falls upon Levi, and a nod from Alby signifies approval. A young lad in a starched uniform is summoned by the Purser, entrusted with guiding Levi to his cabin. As Levi walks toward a raised hatchway, a broad white line on the wooden deck marks a boundary, accompanied by a sign: **"FIRST CLASS PASSENGERS ONLY BEYOND THIS LINE."**

Levi's gaze lingers on the narrow hatchway leading to his cabin. With each step, his heart races as if echoing the thud of the ship's massive engines below. With all its shadows and secrets, his past feels like an anchor dragging him back.

Just as he was about to cross the threshold, a sudden gust of wind swept across the deck. It carries with it a whisper, a haunting echo of voices from the past. Levi freezes, the world around him blurring into a surreal tableau.

The ship's crew, passengers and the bustling port fade into obscurity. In this suspended moment, Levi is transported back in time, standing on the precipice of that singular act that set the relentless cascade of events in motion.

The voices grow louder, accusing, pleading, and mourning. The faces of those affected by his actions materialize in the air, a spectral jury of judgment. They are the silent witnesses to his choices, the lives he has altered, and the bloodline he has forever changed.

With trembling hands, Levi clutches the edge of the threshold, torn between two worlds. The weight of his decisions bears upon him, threatening to engulf him in a tempest of regret and remorse.

Then, as suddenly as it began, the apparition vanishes. Levi stands alone on the deck, but the weight of his past remains. With a deep breath, he takes that final step, crossing the boundary that separates his old life from the uncertain future.

As he disappears into the corridor, the ship's horn bellows, a mournful cry reverberating through the port and out to sea. The world watches as "SS Great Britain " sets sail, carrying with it the echoes of one man's journey, a voyage across the ocean and through the depths of his soul.

Don't miss out!

Visit the website below and you can sign up to receive emails whenever Richard Moorman publishes a new book. There's no charge and no obligation.

https://books2read.com/r/B-A-PZQV-TLZPC

Connecting independent readers to independent writers.

Milton Keynes UK
Ingram Content Group UK Ltd.
UKHW011300221123
433051UK00008B/402